D1312733

sick friends

By the same author | NICKEL MISERIES

E. P. DUTTON & CO., INC. | NEW YORK | 1969

IVAN GOLD

a novel

sick friends

To Vera, who came later.
For *H.S.*, who was there.

Man is a creature who walks on two legs and is ungrateful.

DOSTOYEVSKY: *Notes from the Underground*

Now, you perfectly know that you are looking at things as they do not necessarily have to be looked at.

THOMAS MANN: *Tonio Kröger*

We were dealing with a very old, very deep blocking of the motion of physical self-gratification with the right hand.

WILHELM REICH: *Character Analysis*

part 1

CHRISTA ENTERED MY LIFE SEVEN MONTHS AGO, in late January of this year. Our man in Arizona, Dave Denby, was the contact. He had written as far back as November that his cousin was passing through New York after eighteen months abroad, and if I had any luck she would look me up, as he had asked her to do, on her way home to California. "Cousin" turned out to be a euphemism for I'm still not sure what. Orientalist, photographer, lover, father, Denby has no interest in baseball. But he will write, on occasion, a rich cryptic prose, and after I determined that she was not really his cousin I stopped wondering. She was not the first woman he had sent my way. The summer before, 1964, a fairly well-built young lady turned up and held my attention for a couple of evenings, but nothing came of that. However, he had not praised that one too highly. He said simply that she was a talented concert pianist, was coming to New York to in some manner further her career, did not often sleep with her husband, had just acquired a coil, and seemed eager to try it out. As it happened she did, with a shaggy minor poet I introduced her to, and then, so far as I know, went back home, that part of her mission accomplished.

But Christa seemed to be something else. "She is in many ways the best woman I know. She was good when I saw her last, and to judge by her letters, has explored herself and the world considerably since. She would like to marry me, and god knows were life made that way I would like to return the favor. But this does not prevent either of us from falling quite wonderfully in love-and-everything now and then. Well, I want you to know her. You might see what I see, if she gives you a chance . . ."

I do not remember taking this very seriously, or anything but skeptically, but I hoped she would call. My life at the time, as at most times, permitted, encouraged, needed new female faces, and as the days passed and she didn't phone I began to fear that she had been and gone. Not that there lacked other distractions. There was Leslie Dale, gray-eyed, seventeen, who I met on New Year's Eve through the thoughtful matchmaking of my literary agent, who was also the agent for her mother. (But by mid-January, Leslie was back at her New England boarding school.) I had an unusual, expedient relationship with my next-door neighbor, Sarah Shwartz. Jane Mason, who had left her husband and followed me east from Tucson, where I went to visit the Denbys in April of 1964, had not yet transferred all her broad affections from me to my friend Robert Kane, but she was out of town at the time, in

Philadelphia, where her father was dying. I had but recently
recovered from severe mishandling by Gillian, a blondly
beautiful, most acerbic British R.N., who I courted for three
weeks and mourned for nine; she was and remains the most
perfectly made woman I ever fucked, and one of the wittiest,
and the way I recovered was to meet accidentally at a party the
girl now woman who left me for dead in Provincetown in
1953, the summer between finishing college and being
drafted. Her name is Sandy, and I never touched her. But she
haunted my thoughts, this is the truth, for much of the next
nine years. I did not recognize her at the party, nor did her
name tell me anything, as she had recently married, but she
knew me. She had even read my book. Blonde, delicate, Epis-
copal bitch, she had ended up marrying the most Jewish man
in the world. It burned my ass. We went off and sat together.
After wooing her awhile from my position of small eminence,
from a stance which in effect said, "Despite how shabbily you
treated me, look how successful I've become," I got her to
agree to a luncheon date. She worked in an office on the West
Side. This accomplished, I should, as Pisacano says, have disappeared myself, but I spent the next several hours spooking
her, spooking her husband, then back to her again; finally she
said, "I can't even understand what you're saying, you're so
stoned, you've got your date, why don't you buzz off now,"
which was how she had dealt with me in the old days. I had
succeeded in reestablishing the footing of my twenty-first year.
The fiasco (since I was sure she would not now have lunch,
much less fall in with more ambitious plans) drove the blonde
British nurse—who, though slightly meatier, was modeled
on Sandy, anyway; what I had come to think of as my ideal
type—right out of my head and guts, right into the painless
past.

Women apart, of course, I had some things I was supposed
to do. From a publisher I had received an advance on a novel

large enough to make unnecessary any other type of employment for a couple of years, and this was just as well, as at thirty-
two I had come to be or to feel myself unemployable in any
nine-to-five nexus, both temperamentally and in terms of any
skills. I had barely—and possibly temporarily—escaped
being a casualty, total-disability, of a liberal arts education.
When Christa finally phoned, early one Wednesday afternoon, I was seated at my desk, having exhausted all other possibilities: been to the local greasy spoon, the bank, the A&P,
the launderette, walked around the apartment, played darts
with myself on a board acquired with plaid trading stamps,
and was typing up a dream, one carbon, in which my father
phones while Jane Mason is here, but then unexpectedly
turns up in his underwear. White, clean underwear. He's very
thin. He'll catch cold. We decide to treat him kindly. The carbon was for Frank Covington, my therapist, who I was
scheduled to see that afternoon. A sweet man, good on
dreams.

I may even have worked, or retyped a page or two, for when
the phone rang I remember being generally pleased with myself, in good form, deep-voiced, and suaver still when she iden-
tified herself. "Suave" is a word I would guess has never been
applied to me by anyone on earth—but it's all in how you
feel.

Her speech was oddly accented, low, halting, and I cut short
her introductory remarks which seemed to be causing her embarrassment.

"Dave told me you might call. How long are you staying in
New York?"

"I don't know."

"Well, why don't we have dinner?"

"All right."

"How about this evening?"

"That would be fine."

"Where are you staying?"
"I'm in Washington Heights."
"Oh, Jesus."
She chuckled. "Yes."
"You know the city? We could meet somewhere central
. . . listen, why don't you come down here? We could have a
drink, then go out for dinner, to the Village maybe."
"All right."
All right. Some days there is no improving on the bachelor
life. I exercised, showered, washed some dishes, then took the
bus up to see Frank. I produced the dream, lay on his couch,
and bent his ear about Sandy for the hour. I said she was the
archetype, she initiated the pattern for all subsequent disasters. And at that party I had blundered on the chance to redress old wrongs, and I blew it. There's something wrong with
me. "What do you think the dream means?" Frank said. I
mumbled some cooperative inanities, then drifted back to
Sandy. It was not the most productive hour. When I came out,
Robert Kane was in the waiting room. I had pep-talked him
onto Covington. We had been to college together. Huge-
faced, stick-thin, marijuana-worshipping mystic-manqué, an
identical twin, did he miss our Jane Mason, then off in Philly
observing her father's demise? He would never say. I chatted
with him briefly, then raced home to tidy up the web.

I occupied, still do, the first-floor rear garden apartment in
a three-storey building in the vague but pleasant section of the
city between Stuyvesant Town and Gramercy Park. The
apartment itself is small—two rooms and undersized kitchen
—but cozy. The opening gambit, the grand tour, is always
the same: the garden ("Yes, I planted a lot of it myself"), the
screened porch ("Very rare in New York," though I have no
way of knowing if this is true and though it is almost as useless
as it is quaint—broiling under its tin roof in summer, un-
heatable in winter), the study (once the bedroom), and the

chief, living room. The ceilings are very low. Near the turn of the year, in time for the child Leslie, too late for the nurse, Gillian (but it was always her cat-infested apartment we used), I gave Goodwill Industries my thirty-inch bed, moved my desk into the back room, shoved my beat-up sofa onto the porch, and acquired a trundle bed, plus something called a "joiner," a long piece of foam rubber which filled the crack between the single beds. It was an attractive, high-priced, persimmon piece of furniture, good as a couch, a quite comfortable double. And not long after, thanks to my neighbor, Sarah Shwartz, I came onto a rug sale at Bloomingdale's and bought a thick, teal, handwoven Portuguese rug, which added much color and tone. Sarah, in addition, had made me drapes out of wine-colored burlap. Several paintings by people I knew brightened the walls. The amenities were satisfactory. No yawning double bed to make a girl uneasy; yet she occupies it from the start. I sit, to begin, in the black basket (Macy's; stuffed plastic) chair across the room, but graduate at some point to the floor. Returning with a drink, I perch or flop on the couch, depending on how drunk I am, or the company is, or my assessment of the combination. And then, if the gods will, the slide from the couch to the blue, lush springy rug is natural enough, if not what you would call imperceptible, and later, maybe, the warm, cooperative venture of opening and making up the bed.

It had gone that route before.

Straightening the apartment took me to five in the afternoon. She was due down at six thirty. I phoned in a fifth of scotch and a quart of gin. Around six I went out and walked down to First Avenue. In the low twenties is a Chinese takeout place (a kitchen, not a restaurant) said to be the best of its kind in New York; who knows what to make of such superlatives. I had used it quite a bit before, in similar situations. I usually order the Cantonese lobster, exotic but reasonably priced, a couple of egg rolls, and while it's being prepared I stroll down to the liquor store on Twenty-third Street for a bottle of wine. But by January, I had already taken to buying my wine by the case, from a place in East Harlem, run by boyhood friends of Paul Pisacano's. A case consisted of four gallons of quite drinkable dry red California wine, priced at only eight dollars and change. Paul had been buying his wine (he drank nothing else) this way for years, and I found myself imitating him in this as I found myself aping him in other things. He was an architect, man-of-property, part-time painter, lover of ladies, noisy sage; he was my most recent friend and quite possibly the best, for which proximity was partly responsible. I had met him briefly in London in 1960, five years before, but did not get to know him until I moved into his New York neighborhood in 1963; in both cases Dino Gardella, my original Bronx Sicilian, who I hooked up with in Barcelona in 1959, brought us together. Paul and Dino had known each other since grade school. Gardella—plunged, back from Europe, into a disastrous two-year marriage—was the first of the two males I put onto my therapist, he was the man through whom I met the British nurse . . . to dangle these real-life involvements is artless, to try and knit them up may be absurd. However that may be. Dino, or some hyped-up fragment, was the central figure in the book I had just been paid the large sum of money by a shrewd but starry-eyed editor to write; or so I was in the habit of telling anyone who asked. I could describe it to the last detail. It dealt with our disjointed year in Europe together. The fact was I had been working on such a book almost from the day I met him (abandoning some other unwieldy project to do it), it had long since proved unworkable, I had given it up, returned to it, re-begun it, left it, and all the publishing largesse in the world was not going to make it a novel, or me a writer, which was the real fear I had come to nurse and nourish. And if I was not a "writer," at this stage of the game I was nothing at all.

In my junior year at college I enrolled in the course called

Colloquium, with its high-powered reading list—I was trying at the time to be an intellectual, although, measuring myself against my fellows, I knew the odds were long against. But
I played no sports, lacked a business head, was unpolitical,
and rarely got laid, so the choice of what to become seemed
limited. I wrote a paper for this course called "Christs Compared." It examined the figure of Jesus as variously depicted
in the gospels of Matthew, Luke, and John. I didn't think it
was too bad a job. One of the two instructors agreed it had
merit. The other, who also co-instructed the advanced creative writing course, was short, dark and dapper, a slick
Jamesian scholar of whom it was said that he had been a full-
time beachcomber before turning to teaching. Now he was an
associate professor. He stopped me in the hall one day. "Mr.
Sams"—he smiled—"I have just finished reading your
paper on Christ. It seems an inch or two away from real
thought. Why don't you continue writing those wonderful
short stories of yours?" The import was clear. There are those
who write fiction and those who think clearly. Or, if the skills
conjoined in some exceptional cases, I was not one. It came as
a painful relief. Given a little talent, muddle-headedness
could become, or be made, respectable. The attitude was
hardened in my senior year. I was having some trouble deciding whether to enroll in graduate school or let myself be
drafted. Neither much appealed to me. I was wandering
along Riverside Drive one spring afternoon trying to think it
through, enormously distracted by the lounging coeds, when I
spotted a genuine man of letters, whose course I was taking. I
had never spoken to him outside the classroom and volunteered few enough remarks inside, cowed as I was by my peers
and by the man of letters himself. All during college I was apt
to make remarks in classrooms more pertinent to the landscape in my head than to the matter being discussed. And I
had the misfortune to know this the moment the remark was

out. But I had heard second-hand that the professor admired a story I'd published in the college literary magazine, so I made bold to approach him. He dealt with me briefly and seriously and in a kindly manner. Afterwards I knew I would go into the army. Naturally he hadn't pushed the army, but he made it plain that Graduate English School was death to the creative spirit. At any rate, to my creative spirit. Not that he made that particular distinction, the way the beachcomber had. He cited his own case. When he was younger he had wanted to write fiction, and in fact published two novels and several stories which still hold up well, but the emphasis had gradually altered. Years of association with the Academy had sapped the time and energy needed to pursue his first love, and though he'd gone on to become a first-rate teacher and critic, and though the cultured world held in very high esteem his life and labors, he confessed himself a disappointed man.

So I went down to Whitehall Street at six in the morning to become a writer. The army wasn't bad. I wound up as a cryptographer on a forgotten base near Kyoto. There was not that much to code or decode. I managed to be off duty more often than on. I spent the greater portion of my free time in the small shack I rented up the road.

When I finally got back to New York, twenty-four years old, ex-GI, prematurely bald, seasoned traveler, somewhat worried by the lack of low-priced whorehouse-bars in my native city, but hoping to get by on memories, my mother sent me to graduate school. There is no other way to describe it. I'd returned to her orbit and her ken, she exercised an influence. What is less easy to fathom is how I managed, then as later, to live in the apartment, which was fairly small. I shared the bedroom with my sister, who was sixteen. Harry and Martha slept on the high-riser, in the foyer. One night I got back in the small hours from some truncated adventure. I locked both locks and prepared to tiptoe through the foyer. Martha slept on the outside bed. Her mouth was open. The lamp was on over her head. She was half reclining, head rolling to the side. She still wore her glasses. Her hands clutched a book. She woke briefly and mumbled something as I passed. I took off her glasses and shut the light. I was home. Now she could retire in earnest. Harry tossed and murmured, "Gee whiskers!" but remained asleep. You didn't hear that said much nowadays. I wondered what the etymology might be, plus what battle he was waging with it. I continued to the bedroom. Ann slept soundly. Her nightdress was up around her neck. Her thighs were round and plump, her bush was full. I looked away as if scalded. I forced myself to look back. If this was a test, I determined to pass it. One can't ever learn enough about life. One's sister's cunt is in the public domain. It was in large part bravado. Queasy, I went off to the toilet. I brushed my teeth. The sink, the old, familiar, rust-stained sink, rose and rebuked me. How many pounds of sperm, since my bar mitzvah, had I poured down that drain? Yet there I stood, before the same mirror that had watched my adolescent horror when I had finally to admit (I imply no connection) that the pimples would scar, since they already had; that had watched me slyly as I leaned against the door and jerked and tremored and delivered up my seed in cautious silence. Ah, but the mirror, the sink, meant nothing. How many of my drunken staggerings into the pockmarked Oriental night had been symbolic attempts to wipe out masturbation or practical ones to forfend it? I didn't feel like toting up. I'd had an odd evening. I'd been making it, standing, in her kitchen, with a genuine airlines stewardess, though not one of the best, when the key turned elaborately in the lock, which was her roommate being tactful. I'd had the moment's outrage, impulse to carry on, and let the roommate fuck herself, but of course we buttoned up instead. And tacked on sickly smiles. I raced home with almost eagerness. Something had been begun, something, soon,

would have to be completed. It was far from easy. Balls re-
tracted; cock remained perversely minuscule. There seemed
no real need, despite the rage and rationale. But I hung in,
racked my nonpictorial brain, and managed. The moment of
release was quite intense. After cleaning out the basin with
toilet paper, soap and water, removing some clots of hair from
the drain for which I was not really responsible, but which
might trap a telltale sign, I commenced as always to despise
myself. Although Ann had played as little part in the chiefly
tactile imagery as had the stewardess, which was none at all (a
rehash of some special moments with the slut I had lived with
for a couple of months in Japan), I passed a guilty and resentful night. A mere six inches between our beds. She was being
immodest-to-provocative. She could have worn bloomers
below. I had a few dollars in the bank. I resolved to look for an
apartment and a job first thing in the morning.

Instead I went to graduate school. Harry played a part in
this. Perhaps she enlisted his help, or he may have been acting
on his own. It was not always easy in those days to tell them
apart. Previously, when each was each, and the world was
young, they assaulted in me where they found them what they
took to be aspects of each other. This balled me up quite a bit,
as Covington could tell you. (And lately, where it no longer
matters, they've passed each other in the night, to where Harry
will use *Saturday Review* polysyllables more or less ineptly,
and Martha discourses with passion but no real wisdom on the
Market.) But then, in '57, he seemed as puzzled and upset as
she that I would want to live elsewhere, spending money, it
hardly mattered whose, when I had a perfectly good home
where I was. And, strange as it seems, I could find no short and
civil way to counteract the argument. That point made, he
switched to the other. We were sitting in the living room,
which had been more or less off limits through most of my
youth. I suppose I enjoyed these conversations, or sitting in

the room, for we talked there fairly often. Harry chewed on his cigar and fixed me with his deep blue eyes. He had once been very handsome, on the Gable model, and still looked strong and kind and wise at certain moments. "What do you want to do with your life, son?" Shocked by the size of the question, or its source, I reminded him that I planned to be a writer. He chewed and nodded, as if this were in fact a reasonable goal. "But what do you want to do to make a living, son? What will you have to fall back on?" He had me there. I couldn't imagine what to tell him. I tried saying that some writers made a living writing. But he was shrewder than I— or she—would give him credit for. He used my own superciliousness to disarm me. He said he knew a few himself: TV writers, sports writers; one even lived in the building; but that my sort of writing was of such a high order of seriousness that I would probably need a job in order to survive. And, "I don't want you working with your hands and breaking your back the way I had to do. That's why I sent you to college. To be something. But you have to think more of the practical side. Or else . . ." He shook his head. I saw his twin brother Abe in the gesture, and in the unspokens: Or else you'll wind up a bum.

He had a vision then of having to support me, to keep Martha happy, forever.

While she wanted me in green bondage, bankrupt, soul-mated childhood, forever.

So I went to alma mater with her two hundred dollars in my pocket. ("Leave your own money in the bank, Jason. Let me do this much for you.") She, at least, knew what she wanted. She wanted me to be a full professor. Then one day she'd come and take a seat in the first row in the course I'd made my own, the one they crossed continents to enroll for, *Love and Death in Dreiser, Aleichem, and The Wind in the Willows.* I must have wanted this a bit myself, for I went, paid the money, and enrolled. Wandering the campus, I found myself staring into young male faces, seeking my undergrad self, and the friends of that time, pounding on a door that had long since shut behind me. Near the library I ran into the man of letters, in the company of two colleagues, rushing off somewhere. He did not seem to have aged at all. I hardly expected him to know me after all these years, what with the stream of people racing through his life, students and others, and the fact that I had published nothing in that time, and my general penchant for invisibility, and the conceit that I had altered dramatically through hard living in the Far East, but he did. He waved, called, "How are you, Sams? Writing? Can't stop," and vanished. I was momentarily warmed. I wondered if he guessed what I had come for. Would he be disappointed, or would he want to recast his advice? I sat for a couple of days in a gigantic classroom behind a rococo brunette (no accident), while a pipe-smoking chap wrote names and drew diagrams on a blackboard which seemed to relate to Richardson's *Pamela*. I couldn't start the book, I couldn't imagine what diagrams would have to do with it in any case. I couldn't think of anything sufficiently winning or unclumsy to say to the brunette. Wispy strands of hair escaped her coiffure, rested damply on her neck. I stared at her columnar neck. I breathed on it. If she turned toward me, so much as a profile, I looked frozen-faced away. I was bound to perish of this fuguelike yearning. I dropped out of graduate school, on the last day possible to get one's money, or the better part of it, back. Immediately I felt better, almost light-hearted. Martha was upset, took the news like the personal affront it was. She suggested that I keep the money anyway, but I refused. Not long after, she recovered. She's used to betrayals of this sort, they're the warp and woof of her life. She is bouncy.

I grew ill. I had a fat cyst cut from my abdomen, above the navel, with a local anesthetic. I had a murkily caused recurrence of a mild but unspeakable disease I'd first contracted in Japan. They'd called it Non-Specific Urethritis (NSU), but this time around I suspected cancer. I consulted our family doctor on the sly, the one who had removed the cyst. He sent me to his GU man, who fingered my prostate, pronounced it "boggy," then squirted a red fluid with considerable force into the eye of my dick. I hope to experience nothing hereafter, certainly no "cure," which causes more 'raw pain. Nor could I piss for hours afterwards. On the brink of the sixth such session, I called a halt. I asked him if he enjoyed inflicting pain, or if he believed that undergoing it was useful to the sinner. I said that despite his Park Avenue address, and multitude of treatment rooms, his methods were out of the Dark Ages. More important still, they weren't working. My bargaining position was lousy, I saw, and I backed off and apologized. He said it was just as well I had, I'd been extremely rude, he'd been thinking of putting me out. I got him to write a prescription for Aureomycin, which had cured it in Japan. Now, too, the thing cleared up in days. My luck had turned. The Veterans' Administration approved my application to go off to London to study Japanese, though with cautionary words and no real good will, and I set off on another apprenticeship, my knapsack once more filled with borrowed time. I got the degree (B.A. Hons.), which I will never use. I met Esha from Kuala Lumpur. I met Britta from Malmö. I met Dino.

Five years later, 1962, I crossed the channel to Paris at my own expense to take the oral portion of the Foreign Service Exam. (I had passed the written part on the strength of an essay defending the values of American Culture against the hypothetical onslaughts of an unfriendly Pakistani.) I had not much use for the man of letters now. He'd robbed me of my youth; he'd cost me my career. Safely niched, bemoaning his lost fictional fortunes at a prestigious twenty-five G's a year, he'd sent me up the spout. (I was thinking fairly consistently in Anglicisms by then. I'd tried living in Spain, I'd tried living in Sweden, but I always limped back to a relative sense of adulthood, to the pubs and the language.) I was thirty years old, with no money, with skills atrophied at best, with terrible dreams. I drank more than was actually healthy. But courtesy the U.S. Government, again, here was a final chance to contract in, leap off the treadmill, shed all superannuated dreams of glory. Later, maybe, stamping visas in Istanbul, I'd do some Writing on the Side, produce something jeweled and modest, some minor classic, and fuck the rugged heights I'd once believed I had a shot at and strangers with nothing to lose had encouraged me to scale; but I would not have sacrificed my life for an (at best) posterior glory, nor courted poverty and discontent in the sick belief that worldly deprivation was a condition of achievement.

So have me, gentlemen, I am selling out.

I flunked the oral; will spare us all the weary, witty, why and how.

Britta had come up at my invitation from Pamplona, where she was working at the time. She met me after the ordeal at a café near the embassy. I tried to explain that my dismay at failing was not untempered by relief. God knows how much she understood, of that or anything. She was Swedish, nine tenths mask. We strolled around the tawdry, jaded city. She window-shopped, which was the pleasure she missed most living in Pamplona. They tried to pad our bill, exorbitant anyway, when we left the hotel. We checked our baggage at the station and walked some more, ate sandwiches, drank wine, stepped around *clochards,* and wound up at the zoo, where she spent some time admiring, as was her habit, a masturbating chimpanzee. I left her that April evening at Gare d'Austerlitz, on the train to the border, and went back to London. Two months later I was back in New York, and two months after that she was married. I received a letter (we remain in touch) not long ago. Her English is as good as ever. She confided sadly that she believed now she'd wed too soon. She hardly knew the man (an "erection engineer"), they have no common interests. All that engages him is their infant son and soccer on the TV. At least, she writes nostalgically, forgetting the worst of it with me, if he were interested in sex . . . but not even that. Take heart, lilla vän, I wrote back; things are bound to improve. I didn't mention that I thought I understood just where the trouble lay. Hers was a formidable machine, nor can mother-hood have much improved it. It had large and overlapping lips, and sometimes, it seemed, a face to go with them. So pretty a girl, so monstrous below. If such a snatch is not spar-ingly employed, it can turn you off forever.

What is a "writer"? A writer is one who writes, and though my book of critically successful, commercially damned short stories had come out in April of 1963 and led to all sorts of indirect bounty on which I would now be able to survive until 1967, that book had in a real sense caught up with me and bailed me out: its contents spanned nine working years, the most recent item had been completed in 1960, I had been tight as Esha since, hanging on in Europe after exhausting the GI Bill and waiting (as my old man put it, along with one of his checks) for my ship to come in, becoming enraged by book re-views, nauseated in bookstores, feeling each panicked morn-ing that life—the ship of life!—had passed me by, then limping finally back to the U.S. in crisis in the summer of 1962 to a psychiatric clinic by the fall, a part-time job in the post office, a marriage to liquor and anxiety, then the book, good reviews, a round of fellowships, a large piece of money, the ca-reer which to the exclusion of all others I had been driving for since age ten, and thought at thirty I had blundered past, and now seemed stuck with. But I had just been given the time to find out for sure, and, as I said, I already had the wine, three gallons of it, so I sat around Sun Luck's and waited for the lobster. (As it turned out, Christa and I never got to drink any wine, not that night.) The Chinese there are young, handsome people, if a little on the snotty side—but I never get on well with waiters, bartenders and the like. I gave them money, they gave me food, I got home around twenty past six, poured a double scotch, and sat on the couch to wait. The apartment was too warm; I opened the window a bit facing on the garden. The door chimes sounded promptly on the half hour.

I buzzed back and quickly opened the door to the apartment, so I could watch her walk the twenty-five feet toward me. Christa. I do not think I even knew her name at that point. Denby may have used it once or twice (instead of "cousin") but it hadn't stuck, and I had not got it straight on the phone that afternoon, certainly not her surname. We exchanged hellos and I let her past me, in. She was wearing a black leather coat she had picked up in Europe somewhere, under it a bulky black sweater and a black skirt. I hung her coat away in the only closet, in the former bedroom. She sat on the couch, and in due course, because of the heat, most of which came from unadjustable pipes, she took off her sweater. She wore a white long-sleeved blouse beneath. She seemed generally a little broader than I thought I liked them. Her legs were not really heavy, the calves were there, but they lacked the well-turned ankle we have come to cherish. Her skin was pale. Her hair was dark reddish-brown, thick-textured, piled high, not too high, and her eyes were as near black as eyes can be. Her nose taught me the meaning of the word *aquiline,* which popped into my head, and was exactly right, but I had to look it up later to define it; and her mouth . . . I can't quite picture her mouth. No matter. I rated her B — off the opening ten minutes, she reminded me (though I can hardly understand it now) of another big-boned girl I used to date, a classmate of my sister's (Hunter College, '61), a girl I had not seen for more than a year and of whom my memories were pleasant and bland (though it had ended tempestuously and badly). She did not knock me out—not doll-like, not blonde. But I was in my lair, relaxed as I ever get, there was booze, there was food, the complex self to refurbish and communicate, she was new game, she was feminine enough. (And if the world's dullest dog but a guest in my house, I would, elaborately gallant, have made the best of it; bestowed selected pieces of myself; and with liquor she would have improved.)

She accepted a drink, scotch, ice, a little water. I fixed her a double, and poured myself a second. We had Europe and Denby to kick us off. She had met Dave in Berkeley in sixty-one or two, sometime before he married Keiko, but well after that lovely lady had come to the U.S. Dave met his wife in Japan; I had known them both there as well. After he went back to the States, I took charge of her for the few more months that I remained—she was one of the few Japanese girls I ever had to do with on a non-carnal basis. Her brilliance and youth aside, her respectability aside, I suppose—in making no move—I was respecting his rights. He enrolled at Berkeley for an M.A. in Japanese, and about a year and a half later Keiko found a sponsor in the Bay Area (having missed out on a Fulbright, as Denby tells it, because her hair was too long) and came over to join him. It had been a long and thorny road, ending in their marriage in 1962. Somewhere in here he had known Christa, like him a native of those parts, like him a student at Berkeley.

Whatever had passed between the pair—just looking at Christa left small doubt that it had been enough—she could never know him as I did, if only because she had never known his wife. Dave had been badgering me to come to Tucson ever since I returned to New York in the summer of '62, and finally I did, in April of the following year. We had not seen each other since I passed through Berkeley en route back from Yokohama, almost seven years before. And there in the desert, basking in their garden, drinking tequila, taking the slightly pregnant Keiko to watch the Cleveland Indians in spring training (while Denby taught), playing chess with Dave, nipping (the three of us) as far into Mexico as Hermosillo, I relaxed and grew lucky. So the next year, around the same time, I went out again. Things were not so simple then. They had a small child. I was armed with Jane Mason's address, thanks to Robert Kane. Bob Kane had grown up with and spent some time in Mexico with the man she married, a wispy, moony painter of great sensibility and no way to live in the world. The couple survived for a time on Jane's pittance of a fellowship on her way to an M.A. in English lit, while Roger, the husband, wandered the transfigured campus stoned on LSD, or laid bare the essence of saguaro, or compliant nudes. A friendship blossomed between him and Denby after Jane split for New York on my heels. It had begun to take shape while I was there. Dave—his snobbery justified, from all I could tell of the climate—did not have many friends in Tucson. He was in the habit of inviting old buddies to visit for a week or two, or for as long as Keiko could bear it. All were from the West, apart from myself. Yet he took to Roger almost as soon as they met. Their early conversations were fantastic: Denby guttural and garbling, making private jokes of enormous sophistication, Roger stroking his sparse red beard and laboring to share his psychedelic wisdom, eons elapsing between phrases, and finishing up, if an interruption did not spare him, with some crippled coda, nothing of any weight. Or that I could measure. But I was most often busy empathizing with Keiko, recently become a mother, without friends of either sex, intellectually starved and undervalued (a student of philosophy in her college days), sitting around among the deep thinkers waiting for a conversational bone or a tactful command from the master, dreaming, in Sonora, of Kyoto smells and stones. Alone, she would complain to me of how he drained her, picked her brains for his dull classwork and scholarly tracts, siphoned off the energy she needed to try her hand at writing or at the potter's wheel; and now, at thirty-two, had come this new urgent mouth, this new impossibility to be herself, to be more than a source of supply. Yet how she glowed in Dave's presence, when he got back from teaching, how she shone when she handled the child. Which of us can ever read them? Her complaints were genuine, so was her joy. If I felt strangely betrayed by her inconsistency, this was my problem. So I left Denby with a local friend, in '64, and the friend without a wife.

Christa, holding forth now from the couch, knew none of this history, which was an advantage I could live with. And suddenly, listening to her, I found another: Orientalist, photographer, lover, father (no lack of energy), Denby was also a nocturnal writer of fiction, had sent me a long story not many months before, which began with a letter to a girl traveling in Europe ("Dear Baba . . .") and then moved into events which the letter merely sketched—a tale of an anguished, brief affair with a young lady pregnant by another, told in disorganized, treacly fashion yet with the power of its pain; I didn't try to place it for him, as he'd requested, though I criticized it gently, at some length, through the mail. And now I was abruptly certain that I had "Baba" here before me, that Dave's letter to her had been a real one, and that she did not know the story existed, much less that I had read it. Feeling both guilty and godlike, I tuned back in to her surface detail.

She had, she said, a master's degree in Fine Arts, which like my own second degree—the manifold uses of the GI Bill— from London University in Japanese, she did not seem to have put to any obvious use. Before she left for Europe she had been working part time in Berkeley as a data processer. She said that she was twenty-six. Europe, of course, was very fresh,

particularly the island of Mykonos, where she had spent the
last three months of her eighteen, except for the final few days
in Luxembourg, waiting for the flight back via Icelandic Airlines. She painted a good, grim picture of those last three days,
constant rain, pre-return depression, aimless waiting, alcoholic middle-aged American occupying the next room,
eyeglass-glinting Czech (she thought) who yearned toward her
always over the top of a newspaper, always from a facing table,
where she ate alone in the cavernous, chanderliered dining
room, but never approached her, never spoke.

She had a second drink, then a third. I was very loose, drinking more than she but holding it as well as usual, calculating
the impression I was making and finding it good. It was a Dale
Carnegie special. All the world loves a listener. It was not my
usual role, but I could manage it, and though she was
anecdotal, and though the ghosts of boredom and distraction
hovered, as they always will, she was seldom really dull. She
had a painterly eye, unlike most painters I knew she was
articulate, and her portraits of places and people conjured
up a vivid Europe, a new, exciting Europe, over and above the
fact that every American's always seems a bit or a great deal
better than one's own. She had a funny little self-conscious
shrug, a clumsy yet appealing gesture which she seemed to use
when a story or a point did not come off quite as she would
have liked, or when she felt obliged to suppress the information which would have made it do so. When she smiled she
unveiled a double set of the deepest dimples I had ever seen.
She told me of the cat that had adopted her on the island, and
about that time my own alley-colored, tough on the outside
but jelly below neurotic creature came back from wandering
and wanted in, face dirty and a little scratched from his tentative (mostly yowls) pugnacity, regarded her briefly on the way
to his plate, and I had scored a few more points, for cat-lovers,
do they not, affect to understand each other.

"You know, I don't even know your last name."

"Sarkissian. S-a-r, kiss, i-a-n."

"Armenian?"

"Yes."

"You're my first female Armenian."

"Oh?"

"I once knew a drunken Armenian writer, in fact a pair of them . . ."

And so the subject switched to literature. I modestly mentioned my own additions to the form, gestured to the book where it sat in the bookcase behind me, and then sprang my Chinese surprise. She accepted the trickery smoothly enough. I reheated the lobster and egg rolls and we sat down to eat. We brought our scotches with us, worked on them instead of wine. I lit candles, doused most of the lights, and we ate Cantonese lobster off a low round table, seated on cushions on the floor. I hadn't lived in Japan all that time and learned nothing. I felt marvelous. She also seemed to be enjoying herself. She grew more animated, shrugged more, introduced an open-handed gesture, equally ungainly, equally endearing, and went on talking. She talked as if she hadn't talked in all the time she was abroad. Possibly she hadn't. Finally, rudely, I called her on the European bits, for it seemed to me a certain dutiful quality had crept in, as if she felt she had to account to the stateside crowd for her travels, or else prove that her particular journey, in these highly mobile days, was in any special way worthwhile. So I told her I had lived in Europe for five years, and before that—broken up by nine months back in New York—for two and a half years in Japan (I, like Denby, having been discharged from the army there, to begin to become—the official version—a Japanese scholar; he meaning it and making it, I not), and that my main impression of my time in Europe or abroad generally was one of extreme disorientation, a feeling of vagueness and outsideness and unreality which seriously threatened my shaky (at the best of times) identity, and when I saw I'd struck some chord in her, though maybe not the one I wanted, I pulled back a little ("Well . . . I wasn't in the best of shape, I was locked up inside my skull; most people, you certainly seem to, probably get more out of travel than I did"), and then we ate and drank, silently for a time, and looked each other over.

She was staying with an elderly Armenian couple in Washington Heights, friends or relatives of her father's. She had been born in New York, but the family moved West when she was three. She had some dim, childhood memories of the city. Not as a separate skein but interwoven with her European tales were stories of her family—father dead two years, mother living now in a posh San Francisco suburb, beautiful but square eldest sister, Jane, married to a broker, three children, also somewhere in northern California. She, Christa, was the youngest of three daughters, born two years apart. Her parents had married late and had the children later. The middle daughter, Marcia, had married a Swedish physicist and was living now in Stockholm. Christa felt closest to her—for a time, in Berkeley, the pair of them had lived together—and had visited her on this trip. At some point during Christa's year and a half abroad her mother had flown over and joined her for a week in Italy, then gone on to Stockholm. Her father, a weak, ambitious, boisterous man, had become violent and paranoid in the few months before he died. She made her ties seem suffocatingly close and odd, her speech becoming the while more careful, more precise, not an accent, I realized, but rather fighting some accent; I was afflicted with the urge to jot this observation down. I started to pull out my notebook, thought better of it, excused myself and went to the toilet. I wrote standing up. When I got back I cleared the table. I was both pleased and annoyed that she made no offer, token or other, to do the dishes. She returned to the couch, and I sprawled on a cushion on the floor. We switched back to

Denby, that tall, pink-smooth anomaly in Tucson, she mentioning him now in such a way as to leave no doubt they had
been lovers, though she never did more than imply it, and
though I had of course assumed it from the start, and now the
name "Tim" began to come up, took on a fuzzy identity, a man
she had known a long time in California, who had accompanied or pursued her to Europe, and with whom her life
there, as before she went, was elaborately intertwined.

So . . . there could be no doubt she had been fucked before. This never ceases to amaze me. That they can lie on their
backs and open their thighs and permit a foreign object or a
succession of same to be introduced into their bodies . . . a
staggering idea. They're sick, the whole bunch of them. As
sick as their sisters on the other end of the spectrum, the
leaders-on, cockteasers, color-them-blue. I kept my legs
crossed where they stretched toward her, across the wavy teal.
Her legs were also crossed. I could glimpse, nonetheless, a
patch of thigh above the sheer brown stockings. It was close to
midnight. We were both fairly stoned. We had spent an intense five hours, much real information had been exchanged
—I imparted a good deal more than I have let on here—she
had expressed dissatisfaction with the Washington Heights
arrangements, was generally at loose ends, fair game, much
more attractive, earthy, disheveled, than when she came in, we
had broken bread by candlelight, she had announced herself
available by several signs, and so I moved. (And if I was wrong
about this last, or in some manner blew it, at that alcoholic
point there would be no real harm—to the ego—done. Or
not until I woke alone and rehearsed my errors in the
morning.)

I came, with a new drink, and sat on the far end of the
couch. I reached out an arm—one of us was talking—and
touched her hair. It was less wiry than it looked. I dropped my
fingers to her neck. She looked at me squarely then. I couldn't

read the dark-eyed gaze, and didn't try. I made a little sound and closed the gap between us. I leaned to kiss her, gentle and tentative even when I saw she wouldn't resist, then harder, parting her lips; her mouth opened, I pressed her breast, and the preliminaries were over. Which is not to say we did not toy and clutch and mingle spit for quite a while, but this was in the game, in the joy of delay, for when the moment came I made no perfunctory passes at the mystery of her brassiere but ran my hand up under her skirt, directly to her crotch, caressed, groped her there, and we graduated to Bloomingdale's, the sweating, weaving toil of countless underprivileged Portuguese. I took off her shoes. I unhooked her stockings and ran them part way down her legs. It was awkward work, so I stopped, stared at her with myopic meaning (glasses swept off, carefully disposed of, when the necking began), and started unbuttoning my shirt. Her fingers went to the buttons of her blouse. We undressed ourselves, down to our underwear, pausing once or twice to kiss and caress, then I undid her brassiere. She had large, flowing breasts, fine brown nipples; I nuzzled them on the way down. I grappled off her underpants and shed my own. And she was a neat, dark-haired bonanza below. I played with her briefly, she seemed to discourage my fingers, she was wet enough, the first time you owe them nothing, and I climbed on.

There was some trouble. Trying, seven months later, to recapture a drunken sequence which can seem as remote as a past life even from the next morning is no easy matter, it is tempting to invent, and I may be confusing our first groin-to-groin encounter with what did transpire the following morning, but I believe there was trouble—her face contorted when I fumbled, it looked like pain, and I think I backed off a little and poised on the threshold, or just over, working in my patient cock like a safecracker, listening, but when it was in it was in, and I felt I could fuck her forever. I had had Leslie just a few days before, but Christa had been for some time what we agreed later to call "inactive," or so she said, and her body was hell-bent on enjoyment. She moved. She moaned. Less drunk, just watching in the mind a full-blown, brand-new lady pump and pant like that, with or without myself astride her, might, with a touch or two, have set me off, but I was all in control of my responses, the quintessential stud, no tricks, no hands, just prick-length constant driving of such duration and so much mutual pleasure that the idea of frigidity and impotence anywhere in the world became obscene, an anachronistic construct from a benighted time, and when she finally went shuddering past her ending I turned off the talent and came galloping after, and we lay on the floor covered with balls of blue fluff in absolutely perfect eyeball-to-eyeball afterglow, filled with self-love and wonder, and I said, "You'll spend the night," and of course she said yes. I trundled out the second bed, raised it, inserted the joiner, and together we secured two sheets and a wool blanket and the afghan my mother had made (a labor of love), and we climbed in. She let down the masses of her hair. She kissed my eyes, I nibbled her breast, and Christa Sarkissian and Jason Sams, for the first time since the world began, went to bed together.

I woke much too early, around six, the effects of the scotch, very sleepy, but not hung over, not feeling bad. I gulped some milk straight from the container, then took a long quiet leak around the perimeter of the bowl. When I came back to bed her eyes were on me in dark, sleepy neutrality, her chestnut hair draped over the pillow. She was on the inside of the bed, near the wall. I wasn't sure she was really awake, until she smiled a little and reached out her hand. I took it and wriggled in. When I was younger I could never mount them from the left, having to vault over and begin again if I found myself so positioned; but I had overcome this odd handicap without even realizing it, God knows when or why. I moved to

her under the blankets and kissed her, a little wary of my
morning mouth, but she raised no objection and tasted, herself, as sweet as could be. I squeezed her hard brown nipples.
She made a small yes noise and meshed her fingers in the hair
between navel and crotch. She bit my arm. I ran my hand
down her flank and with the back of my hand I stroked her
bush, which was darker than her hair, more the color of her
eyes, flanked by fine, blonde downy hairs on either thigh, the
triangle itself perfectly that, a most esthetic machine, as her
entire person seemed reasonably pleasing the dangerous
morning after. Once, in Japan, I woke next to a girl of sixty
with an eye missing and skin like parched leaves . . . but
these are the risks you run in foreign lands. This home-grown
Armenian lady was no daintier than she'd seemed the night
before, her hands were large, her feet were large, she had pronounced dark bags beneath her eyes, an ambitious bone on
her right foot, under the great toe, protruded in what might
be thought (as it turned out she thought it) unsightly fashion,
but she aroused my non-compulsive AM interest, which is not
always the way it is; I flipped my hand over and probed her
excellent box, and she flinched, she blanched, she put my
fingers away.

"What's the matter?"

"The muscle is damaged there."

"How did that happen?"

"I had an . . . operation a few months ago. The doctor was
clumsy . . ."

"Jesus." I leaned down and kissed her belly. "Wait here."

I came back with a small jar of vaseline. I had a large one, a
huge, unopened, pop art one, but there was enough left in
the small jar. "We'll use this lovely stuff." I unscrewed the lid,
swept two fingers in, and put the jelly everywhere. On and in
her parts (gently; staring in her face the while), over the head
and down the length of my attentive cock, topside and under-

side, took that organ in my hand and played outside her for a
second, then slid right in, right up to its base, right up under
her nose, and we were at it again, slow, slow, quick-quick slow,
an anticipatory face of discomfort she made turning into
something which did not seem so different, so that I asked her,
really uncertain, "Are you in pain?" and she shook her head
no. The nagging worry, when I came back from the john and
kissed her, the first time, that, faced cold sober with this much
woman, this much newness, I would go off on entry if not
sooner, as in the bad old European days with (in our early
stages) Britta, let alone with Esha (a nightmare throughout)
—this worry faded and was gone. At first I had been annoyed
when she announced her damaged muscle, that unlooked-for
obstacle turned me off, and then I was suddenly pleased,
malely, vindictively pleased, at my way around it. A spot of
sadism, who will deny it, does wonders for the sense of performance. And the mission helps, too—to rid the world of one
more ounce of female bullshit. So again I fucked her well.
Even with her juices on, and grease everywhere, she had a
marvelous cunt, I knew its every tremor; I kissed hard into
her moans, I moved my hands from face to breasts to under the
cheeks of her large but shapely ass, pulled her to me, let her
pump awhile, then held her tight, but it was much too good to
last forever, it was almost too good to bear, and for all the right
and wrong reasons I wanted her with me—I said into her ear,
"Sweet thing, are you close?" the remark itself retarding things
a bit, at least for me, for she nodded her head, face beautifully
contorted, shook loose from my restraining hands, heaved us
onto our sides and she was over, and I came right after,
emptying into her long and glorious, the second time we ever
made love.

The third time was several hours later. We slept, or she did,
while I lay in a twilight zone, drained, yet far from content, for
I had killed a morning (if I ever worked at all, it was in the

morning) and I did not know if Sandy would see me for lunch
that afternoon. It was the appointed day. Since the party,
about three weeks before, I had not been able to bring myself
to call her and confirm it. Even now I considered just turning
up outside her office building, waylaying her at one; but I
thought better of it. As a romantic, disarming device, the Appearance seemed to work for some—but it had failed me
often in the past. Too risky, too petitioning—you laid yourself open to their nastiness. Better to chance the put-down on
the phone; I got out of bed to call. I went into the study, which
has a wall extension, and shut the door. On the opposite wall
in what was once the bedroom is a mirror, about four feet high
by nine feet long. Some lady, I truly forget which, some Henry
Miller fan, had me fuck her from behind in front of the mirror, commenting the while, but it struck me as a dull, cerebral
thing to do, or maybe the dullness and cerebralness belonged
to the lady, and I did not repeat it. Now, rehearsing a few lines
for Sandy, rehearsing an attitude (how to be contrite and gutsy
at the same time?) with which to woo the real love of my life, I
regarded myself in the mirror, God's naked gift to returning
travelers, and I could see, almost, what they saw. I was just under six feet tall, neatly russet-bearded (a few gray strands),
cleverly balding, ornamentally muscled, fairly hairy, the kind
of good lean body that would go to fat or pot without regular
exercise and with as much liquor as I consumed, but at the
time I was well into the Canadian Air Force Exercises, con-
scientiously, almost daily, plus fiddling with an isometric bar,
and I was harder and flatter than I had been in ten years. I had
long, shapely legs and was adequately equipped between
them, despite all dreams and fantasies. My nose was large and
fleshy, I had a self-indulgent lower lip and a concealed upper,
my eyes were deep-set and (more than one unkind or disen-
chanted lady had described them) fishy-blue, all surrounded
by the fake toughness of acne's aftermath. A suspicious, pre-

maturely patriarchal face, a Middle European Jewish face (though I was technically third-generation: both parents born here, their parents shortly off the boat), the tight caution bred in, perhaps, if not merely learned from the cradle. My posture was lousy. Observing myself, trimming the hairs in my nose, I tried to work into the frame of mind where if she canceled out it would be her loss. I thought I was having success. Yet while I dialed the number my crotch, empty as it was, shriveled with apprehension. My voice, when she came on the phone, was phlegmy—gone the fine baritone Sarkissian had collided with—and I had work to do to keep it from trembling.

The ultimate conceit of our self-made anxieties—not to labor it, she upbraided me mildly for not phoning sooner (and, since I brought it up, for drinking to excess the night of the party), but she had programed me in, she was quite agreeable to being bought lunch at one. I felt as good and cocky, when I hung up, as the moment before I felt fearful. Christa was fully awake, hands behind her head, flattening and lengthening her excellent breasts, one knee up, thighs slightly apart. Women not half as endowed will look good posed that way. She was occupying my half of the bed, so I sat cross-legged by her, on the floor. She came up on an elbow, rested her face on her hand and looked me over. We were, by this time, rather intimate with one another—less, I think, result of the sexual congress than the use of the vaseline. She focused between my thighs. Suddenly she smiled—she had a very merry smile—and lit up the room.

"You have a Greek penis."

"I have a what?"

"I think you heard me."

"What the devil is a Greek penis?"

But I knew. Or didn't give a damn. Who would probe and spoil an obvious compliment to his privates in repose? I decided, as she didn't reply, that she meant the way the member

is represented in classical statues of the gods. I was absurdly
pleased, like a very apprentice cocksmith praised for the
length of his stream, and to cover my embarrassment I turned
the talk back to her problems.

"What's the trouble you were having there?"

"A muscle at the entrance . . . it's become spastic. I had an
abortion . . . fairly recently."

"In Europe?"

"In Tangier. The doctor was very old . . . it was horrible . . ."

"Christ. That must have been painful. I mean psychologi-
cally as well."

"Yes."

"What have we . . . last night, this morning . . ."

"I take pills."

"Uh huh."

I got up and went to the study for my cigarettes. I had
smoked three while laying siege to Sandy. They were on the
dresser, next to the isometric bar, which gleamed hopefully,
but I was taking the day off. I had delivered that line above
("Christ . . ."), lame as it looks, with real compassion, yet
mingled even then with wariness. I was no more involved in
the girl or in her past than if I had been reading about them
both, I absorbed details with a simple human and complex
professional curiosity, fairly detached in both cases; and yet
abortions in Tangier performed by old and clumsy doctors
upon ladies I allowed to spend the night . . . I felt vaguely
implicated. Abortions. They were the central experience of
our time. Had I known any girls in the past ten years who had
escaped one? A couple. They had the babies. Eve Harris, lean
Irish barmaid who was crazy about Salinger, for one. She succumbed on a beach at nineteen, lost her cherry and conceived
a child. It can really happen. She bore it. By the time I met her
in a north London pub, she had a seven-year-old son living

with her parents in Cork, the real joy of her life, and she had a jerky English suitor in London of five years' standing who she had never slept with. She never even told me when I knocked her up. She got hold of some pills. They shook loose the fetus, nearly killed her, and all her hair fell out. The first clue I had to my no-longer-impending fatherhood was the summer night I dropped into the pub after a two-week absence and found her wearing a kerchief. It was too warm for a kerchief. Eventually she had to tell me why, and then the rest came out. Her hair grew back, and her affection for me was strangely undimmed. We still occasionally correspond.

I had never been caught. Or never been tapped. There was a married woman (and I place her now as the Lady Before the Mirror) who laid it, price and all, on the head of her husband, there had been one or two with too much pride or genuine uncertainty; there are those who need to be cut into every so often, and need to go it alone, through some repudiation of their function, confirming their notion that the world we live in is no place for the fair . . . forgive such slight psychologizing. It's no more, perhaps, than a healthy, sexless, self-destructive drive, femaleness the means rather than the cause. In Sarkissian's time, I had never been caught, although I had been made uneasy, in the sense that her own revelations made me so. I suppose it has to do with other men. If you have aborted you have conceived, if you have conceived you have almost certainly been laid; and such is the only proof there is. Hymens, doses, testimonials . . . all inconclusive. Only abortions and babies are relatively foolproof. And if you have a past, ladies, statistics indicate that you will have a future. And possibly become *enceinte* at inconvenient times. And have to submit to perhaps barbarous proceedings and emerge with horror tales bound if not actually calculated to shake Our equanimity. Gillian had a son when she was twenty, which she gave up for adoption, and two abortions since.

(These, she said, despite a diaphragm. When I knew her, she had finally settled on a coil.) She liked to discuss them in detail (I possibly encouraged it), particularly how the doctor packed her cervix the second time, despite her professional advice, and she almost lost her life. Jane Mason, my Tucson poet, had been nailed at seventeen. It was a sad and breathy story as she told it—her father, now mercifully dead, took the hard line, drove her into the snow on the heels of opinions which led her, thereafter, to seriously question her value, and this was connected with her wild yea-saying since. And many more. I looked over at my desk, violently shook my head, and drove the sickness from my mind.

I came back puffing a Pall Mall. I offered her a Marlboro, one of her own, from the pack on the bedside table. She refused it. She was flat on her back again. I sat beside her, ran my finger down the thin blonde line from belly button to mound. The cigarette was a hazard, and tasted lousy. I snuffed it out, climbed over her, and lay on my stomach on the inside of the bed. I kissed and licked and blew into her ear, and it turned out to be, as it is said to be, a truly erogenous zone. She scrunched up her shoulders, giggled, moved down to bite me under the armpit, down my side, with a skin-marking fervor I did not find pleasant, although my cock rose to the occasion, but she was also stroking the underside of my scrotum, well under, with a gentleness exact for that most tender and interested place. She went on down and ran her tongue along the insides of my thighs. She looked up and smiled. If this was teasing, I was for it. I pulled her back up, length to length, hugged her hard, ran my hands down her broad back, and slowly, making use of the omnipresent vaseline, I worked my index finger into her ass. I pulled my face away and looked at hers. Her eyes were shut tight, her mouth was open, she was making a humming, moaning, equivocal sound, not objecting, but I eased the finger out anyway, short of the middle joint, and went into her properly as we lay on our sides. Old sperm and petroleum jelly took me past the drugged, wounded guardian at the entrance, the Tangier legacy, then I pushed over on top of her and thrust for dear life. I began to sweat, there was work to it now, the slightest failure in vigor and concentration would cost us our shot at three in under twelve hours, which was more than we had done to others or had done to us since the fleshpots of the East, when five times a night was *de rigueur* since we were younger then and paying for it . . . this brief, nostalgic excursion cost me the edge, and I petered out for the time.

"Let's take a break."

"Yes. I have to go to the bathroom."

While she was gone I put some water up to boil. The stove was no more than three feet from her head, thin, unlockable wooden door between us. I put the water on full blast and rattled the pot onto the stove, hoping noisiness would somehow compensate the lack of privacy. That, anyway, roles reversed, was how I would have liked it. Certain functions are absolutely private. Acoustically as well. On this I feel strongly. Yet one must steer a course between outright projection and blind conviction that one's habits, problems, are unique. I climbed back into bed. Perhaps, when she came out, she would want to get dressed. If we were done, then we were done, but the taste of more had left me wanting more. Something had been begun, something, at some point, would have to be completed. For the psychic economy's sake. It worried me a bit. The toilet flushed. She came back, sat on the edge of the bed and lit a cigarette. I looked her over inch by inch; I'd earned the right; I'd used her body well.

"The trouble with us is"—my mouth on her belly—"we don't make love often enough."

It was her turn to squash the superfluous butt. She glanced at my dormancy. "You're not really up to it." She bent over my

prick and took it in her mouth, held it while it swelled, a moment longer, and then she was on me, stuffing me in her, her
hair flowing in my face until she straightened, strained for the
ceiling and rode me like a goddess, great nippled globes
swinging together, belly round and heaving, smooth-thighed,
cunt sucking at me with a sweet popping noise so that I had to
turn off, to endure, these visual and auditory joys. I grabbed
her hips and held her still. She bent to me, dimpled, and we
kissed, to call it that; we attempted to swallow each other.
Then she came down and she turned over. Or else I turned
her over—I do not truthfully recall—but, as the primate
people say, she presented. She was not up on her knees but her
fine sloping buttocks were raised, she had managed that, and
I ran the head of my Greek penis down her crack, but only to
reprise the probing finger, only to announce we had a future,
and I entered her from the rear. And she moved. Even on her
face, she moved. This threw me off, I flopped out once or
twice, but reentered smoothly, we found our rhythm, she gave
me a good pale profile on the pillow, tongue between her teeth
and eyes shut, spattering of moles on left cheek, we went this
way awhile, and then I pinned her. I flattened her out,
scissored her legs, and had my way with her, hard short tender
thrusts which would have put me over, but she also had notions, and large, strong lady that she was she somehow moved
us, flipped us over so smoothly that she never lost me, shoulders to my chest, backside to my balls, but Christa on top, my
aching cock deep enough inside her. I would not have thought
it possible. I couldn't move, but it was lovely all the same. She
squirmed on me gently, I cupped her breasts, then she rolled
off, I mounted, and we drove in all earnestness into the sunset,
once more a textbook special, answer to answer, or quite close
enough.

  "You're so very good," she said.

  "I'd never done that before."

"Done what?"

I came off her, rolled away, and took her hand.

"The . . . how shall I say . . . reverse flip?"

"Oh. Did you like it?"

"It was priceless."

"One can't move very much."

"This is true. You like to move?"

"Yes."

"I'd noticed."

"You find it unpleasant?"

"No, babe, not unpleasant. A little overexciting, maybe."

"The water is boiling away."

"So it is. You want some coffee?"

"I don't drink coffee."

"Tea?"

"That would be nice."

"I've got some bags. We'll both have tea."

I climbed over her and went to prepare it.

"You have any plans today?"

"I suppose I'll go back to Washington Heights."

"You want to take a shower?"

"Yes. After tea."

"I've got an appointment uptown, on the West Side. We can take the same subway. You doing anything later on?"

"I thought I might go to the museum."

"Which?"

"Modern Art."

"What's on?"

"I don't know."

"I'll meet you there."

"All right."

"About four?"

"Yes."

"Good."

While she was showering I unmade the bed, slid it away, and wiped out all signs of the debauch. As a double, the bed took up most of the room. When she came out I showered, shit hastily, dressed, fed the cat, checked the locks on both back doors, and strolled with my prize into a clear New York January morning. The Grosses—too apt a name to change, despite the risks—were standing there waiting for the garbage truck. In the midst of their kingdom. They were the superintendents for about six other houses on the block as well as mine. I greeted them; Mrs. Gross greeted back. I told Christa who they were. The Empire State Building gleamed and glistened and poked its aerial skyward. If I owned a camera, and knew how to use it, I would treat that building the way Monet did Rouen, nailing it from all angles, in all situations and seasons, at dawn, in rain, from under its great bulk, capturing its needle-thinness riding in from Kennedy . . . every man should have a hobby. I put my arm across her shoulder, she slipped an arm around my waist, and we walked, at lovers' pace, toward the Twenty-third Street crosstown bus.

"Did you buy that coat in Hamburg?"

"No, in Florence. Why?"

"It looks like a Hamburg coat."

"You mean it looks like a prostitute's coat."

Was that what I had meant? "Not exactly . . . more specialized. Whips, spiked heels, three-hundred-pound ladies . . . anyway, it's very attractive, looks very warm."

It turned out she had been to Hamburg. On the bus she told a tale of walking up the Reeperbahn at ten in the morning, chaperoning a nineteen-year-old American boy she'd met somewhere, digging the houses and the glass-enclosed merchandise (even then a working hour). She became engrossed in her account, seemed inordinately interested in whoring as career or pastime. But many women are. The adolescent boy for companion was a nice touch. Her store of European anecdotes, I realized, was probably inexhaustible. We held hands on the bus. We didn't try to talk much over the roaring of the subway. People looked us over. The sallow, sullen New York faces seemed to brighten when they lit on Christa. She gave off heat, she took up space in a totally splendid way. Or so I imagined. Or I may have imagined it later. Her black eyes returned the gazes. Her hair was neatly up again, nose sweet and sharp, big legs modestly crossed. She was mine.¹ I might never see her again. If so, I would survive it. Lunch was the main issue. I left her at Fifty-ninth, trying to look tough and tender, saying I'd see her at four. She nodded. I left the train, not looking back. Tired as I was, nagged as I was by the idea of wasted time, I felt fairly beautiful myself. Or worked on it, climbing into daylight.

I was early. I went into a bar not far from where Sandy worked, a block from the Coliseum, and ordered a bottle of Schlitz. I love bars, the beery stink of them on entering, then sitting in the dark getting quietly, insightfully stoned, or laboring under that impression; the way even the neighboring prattle is enhanced (let alone one's thoughts) as the ale goes down. I take a lot of notes in bars, the majority legible. But I have to keep changing locales. I radiate an orneriness (it predates the beard), and after half a dozen times it is no longer tolerable to have to pretend not to know the bartender, just as he chooses not to recognize me. I suppose as a child I hankered after, or believed I possessed, invisibility. Now adult, my considered view is fuck it. It's part of what I am; it used to bother me; in places like bars it does so no longer. I'll cross the street on the way to the supermarket to avoid people and shopkeepers I've seen around too long and too often to begin now to say hello to; if I chance ever to look at them, at this far-gone point, they'll look away; I live with that too. Yet in my heart of hearts I know, as I knew I was suave, that I am charming; very nearly sweet; that this gruff, surly exterior conceals

. . . a machine for the manufacture of self-serving bullshit. But this is harsh. And harshness toward oneself, Frank tells me, spills into the world. If Sarkissian (no shopkeeper) had found in my poor person something to her liking, as it appeared she had, she would not be the first to do so and not, with God's help, the last.

I had a draught beer before I left. The best I can say for it is that it was superfluous. The bottle, on an empty stomach, struck and settled well, I flushed with feelings of usefulness and manhood; the glass had added queasiness. But it would pass. I went to pick up Sandy.

I waited in the lobby of her office building. She stepped out of the elevator a few minutes late, part of a crowd, and cocked her head at me slightly—"Follow me, boy . . ."—and went outside. I came after.

I mimicked the gesture. "What's this shit?"

She looked up at me, from the luminous, ironic green eyes I am likely always to remember. "I can't afford to be seen with a beatnik. Someone from the office might take you for my husband."

"You can't afford to be seen with a what?"

"I see you've fortified yourself."

That pulled me up. The true bitch disarms you verbally, at once, with a frontal assault; the ball-breaking deviousness comes later. You can rarely say you weren't warned. I breathed elaborately into my hands.

"I had a beer. What do you mean 'fortified myself'? You don't scare me, Sandy."

"I didn't say I scared you."

That was true, she hadn't; trapped into self-revelation by a cliché. Down several points in the first few seconds. But perhaps no one was counting. I hulked along beside her. She was a silvery blonde (not the sun-color of twelve years before), she had a thin white line of hair above the thin patrician lips, was long-nosed, sharp-chinned, generally horsey-faced; a few months older than me (and doomed to age more rapidly), housewife, secretary, owner of Siamese cats; I tried to fathom the pain she had caused me. The facts of the matter yielded little. I had picked her up on the beach one sunny day. She was reading a magazine whose next issue would contain my first published story, so I had what you could call an opening. She was curt, then skeptical, then suitably impressed. She had such lovely downy thighs and arms. Her voice was downy too, though with a cutting edge. She was the high-cheekboned shiksa-doll every hairy tribesman will pant after, the luckier ones from afar. At the time, although twenty-one years of age, I had laid only two girls in my life; neither experience, need I say, came anywhere near my expectations. I had a rich inner life and a well-developed wrist. I had never picked up a girl in my life, except at dances, to which I rarely went, until that moment. Sandy, therefore, was my first intimation of the sexual uses of the literary life. Sexual only in the broadest sense. I don't think I was alone with her more than once after that first day. Although I pursued her everywhere. She worked as a waitress in one of the coffee shops—espresso came out of my ears. As I became more hangdog, she became more brittle. Walking the dark roads one night with a male friend, watching a red light swing and blink on top of a girdered tower in the middle distance, I contemplated killing myself. I was crippled with yearning. In this frame of mind, I entered the army. My chief recollection of basic training is waiting for Sundays, which I spent writing her letters, drafting them several times. Finally she relented, empathized, showed compassion through the mails. She said that all the while I was desiring her in Provincetown she was going through the same thing for a wraithlike painter who was in turn occupied pursuing someone else. So she well knew the depth and nature of my suffering. But this letter only enflamed me more. On my last furlough before being shipped to the Far East, I took a bus from New York to Boston, where she was working as a live-in maid. This was the "Appearance" I mentioned. I appeared, she let me in, the family she worked for was out, but she had a male companion. The three of us chatted for an hour. There were many silences. I drank her in, I pleaded silently, I smoked a dozen cigarettes. Her friend didn't leave, nor did she give any sign that she expected him to. I mentioned that I was on my way to Korea (which was possible), where I would probably be killed, although the truce was already in effect. It made no great impression. Eventually I departed, so I had her alone in the vestibule for about sixty seconds. There was nothing to say. There lacked even the context for a goodbye kiss. I got back on the bus and rode all night and had breakfast at Hector's Cafeteria on Forty-fourth Street. Three days later I was in Pittsburg, California, awaiting shipment overseas.

The first crippling waves in Provincetown and after . . . rebirthed by that maniacal Boston journey . . . then months of dull anguish. In Japan I fucked my brains out, I jerry-built an identity radiating from my crotch, and seemed to forget her. But when I got back to New York in 1957 I tried to find her. It wasn't difficult, she was in the N.Y. phone directory, but I kept putting it off, rehearsing, and when I finally called, a roommate said she had left for Europe the day before. I tried again in 1962, when I returned from Europe, not so cathected then, or not with her, but balled-up enough; she was in the book then too, but her phone was disconnected, and she wasn't home on any of my pilgrimages. I left a note, but she never replied. And then, Christmas of 1964, I met her with her brand-new and first husband, singing (my Sandy!) the praises of lox and blintzes, certain restaurants on Second Avenue.

So much for unrequited love. The self-poisoning pursuit of that which puts you down. Building it in the tinker-toy mind into the ideal mothering world. Now I was wiser; my

perineum ached from my Armenian travels; I would never be
twenty-one again. But I knew no more about my bondage
than that it was over. And that it felt delightful to be free, and
buying my ex-jailer lunch, with an afternoon of culture up
ahead. When I was at my worst (with Gillian), this was how
Pisacano cheered me, through the daylight hours, and himself
as well: by pointing to the jug of wine, the hour, and out beyond his windows to the poor bastards (our brothers) who
worked at pointless jobs not of their choosing, from nine to
five, regardless of mood, regardless of personal chaos. We—
artistic, solvent men of leisure—had the freedom to goof, the
freedom to be free. This thought colored my ruminations too,
I had an excellent sixty seconds as we drew near Tenth
Avenue.

I asked her where she wanted to eat.

"Didn't you have any place in mind?"

I had, in fact, researched the neighborhood. My agent, a
knowledgeable lady, tipped me to a couple of good French
restaurants nearby. We went to one of those. It was almost
empty, there were no waiters in sight, and I started for one of
the booths.

"They show you to a table."

"Oh. They do?" I stepped back and hovered awkwardly by
the entrance. Finally a waitress wandered by, gestured for us
to sit anywhere. Without comment, I ushered my superior
bitch before me. We ordered martinis, followed by frog's legs
for me, sautéed brains for Sandy. She passed on the wine, so I
drank a couple of beers. We did a fair job of summary on our
respective methods of survival in the decade just gone. She
had taught Art (when I met her, age twenty-two, she was describing herself as a sculptress), lived in Europe, lived for a
time in Greenwich Village with the painter she had lusted
after in Provincetown, until she dumped him for her husband, a more settled type, to whom the painter had himself in-

troduced her . . . here I felt some jealousy, some deeper
pang, for she had got, if only to discard, what she had thought
way back then she wanted. I asked if she enjoyed married life.
She said she did. She extracted much *nachas* (her word) from
her Siamese cats. She had no plans for children. How many
times a week did she fuck? I thought also of asking, but refrained. She mentioned some unmarried girl friends and I
expressed polite interest—as her contemporaries, and
mine, they would be too used, too clobbered by the steam
hammer of urban courting life. I told her a few selected facts
about myself. She seemed most impressed to learn that I was
teaching Creative Writing one night a week at a reputable
university, and she threatened to sit in. I encouraged it. I was
having a good time, she was still quite decorative, had become
a *mensch* once past the opening bullshit, her attempt from
habit or atavistic memory to maintain the upper hand, and it
was Sandy who noticed that it had got to be five minutes past
three. I walked her part way back, told her I was on my way to
the museum.

"A good place for pickups, they say. Is that why you go?"

Reverting, out of doors, to her old sweet self.

"So pretty," I said, "and such a cliché-ridden bitch. Beard
equals beatnik, bachelor equals stud. Whereas what I am in
fact is a frustrated family man with traditional literary goals
and a weak chin and a date with a lady with a profound interest in the visual arts."

"All right, Jason. Thank you for lunch."

"Thank *you,* my dear." I shook her hand warmly, and ran
for the crosstown.

I was about twenty minutes early. I paid my dollar, walked
in, and wandered. She was right, the place was filled with
snatch, sweet and young. Too young, on the whole. Somewhere between sixteen and thirty-five must be the ideal age for
a single gentleman of almost thirty-three, but I hadn't found it

yet. Some, like Gillian, had lived far too long, others, like Leslie, not nearly long enough. I looked at legs and faces, then I tried looking at paintings, and thinking proper thoughts, but without real success. I felt self-conscious and fraudulent. I rarely go to museums alone, although painting is the one non-literary art I give a damn about. I buy them from my friends. I hang them carefully, and look at them from time to time. Perhaps someday I'll join the Print-of-the-Month Club and pore over the works of the masters in the comfort and privacy of my own home, reproductions hopefully of fine quality, although I couldn't tell the difference. This seems sensible. But public consumption, consumption in public, no. Baseball apart, I hate what goes on in the arena. I've never been to an opera, to a ballet once, to concerts rarely. The high points of theatre-going have always been the intermission and the exit. Shakespeare, for example, is much more gripping on the page, where oneself sets the scene and plays every part, undistracted by ambitious set designers or actors' "interpretations" or the coughing presence of three hundred other culture-seeking bodies. Any good play is better on paper—a poor one can at times be helped by staging. Whatever value art has, it had better have in private. At best, or worst, lying in bed, consuming it hand on the crotch of your mate. This is the real virtue, or (given the fare) the real possibility, of television. Fiction, therefore, is the highest form, since it *demands* solo response and intensity. No filters, no scrims. The best fiction cannot be read, is foolish to hear read, aloud.

Thank you. Nor is aesthetics my especial field of competence. Museums in the company of a loved or merely knowledgeable one is something else again. Some profit may ensue. At worst it gets you through an afternoon. And you're bound to absorb data, if not enlightenment. I have gone the museum route with Jane Mason, once before Christa's time and once during, so I am no longer sure what this particular exhibition

was. I could check it, but what does it matter. It was Beck-
mann or Bonnard. I didn't see her come in. I spotted her looking out the glass wall into the garden, at or past Lachaise's
mammoth lady. She was leaning slightly on the glass, in three-
quarter profile, looking very private, very fetching; I came up
behind her, touched the shoulder of her Hamburg coat, and
we were reunited.

"Hello."

"Hello."

"How was Washington Heights?"

"Not very stimulating."

"Have you looked around yet?"

"No. I was waiting for you."

"Shall we . . ."

I padded along behind her, happy, deferential, letting her
go her way, occasionally going mine. I dropped an aside or
two on content, color, line, intending to impress with the
innate sensitivity which underlay my willful ignorance. She
was a most intelligent consumer, she'd had enough after an
hour, and we departed. It was already dark, cold and raining. I
suggested a movie, she agreed, and we taxied back downtown,
to the Gramercy Theatre. Movies are fun with a lady—
watching their prim kneecaps, touching their faces in the
shadowy dark. She put on glasses, which I'd not seen her wear
before. For some reason this endeared her to me more: sweet
proofs of vanity, vulnerability, humanness. The film was an
anti-war epic as conceived by Chayevsky, shmaltzy, earnest,
but not really bad, not the way underground kitsch is bad, or
Frenchified fakery. I've forgotten the name of it. Afterwards
we went across the street for a hamburger, and started back for
the apartment. I took her hand and grew an erection, or half of
one, and felt a little bad about it. Perhaps I owed her—friend
of Denby's, passing through—more than myself, something
in the way of social life. Maybe I was lonely for a different

brand of company, or, less noble still, wanted to show her off. But I led her past Pisacano's loft and his light was on. I asked if she had any objection to visiting an architect-artist-entrepreneur, friend of mine, she said no, and I rang his bell. I usually telephoned first, his social calendar was unbelievable, but there was no booth nearby, and if he was busy he didn't have to let us in.

The buzzer rang, and I sent her up the three flights before me—for the view of her, of course, and to spare us both the one I fancied I presented. Since the time I went bald in Japan at age twenty-three, in minutes, as I like to recall it (and hair loss is minimal since), I have not liked the thought of my women walking behind me. Whereas the view from the front, if I hold my head high, presents no sign. A harmless vanity. Probably also a pointless one. Some women like bald men. Some genuinely admire males with bay windows. In the history of the race, men with tiny dicks have surely been adored. But I sent her up ahead, and as we started the last flight, Paul opened the door to his loft and came onto the landing.

I could not see him standing there without feeling the bizarre hope that the Gillian thing was not yet over, that if *he* allowed me ingress, so must she; lovely, intelligent British girl, how could she make so final a judgment on so complex a human in three lousy weeks? But of course it was not Paul who had linked us but Dino, Gardella it was who brought her to my house, sat her on my couch, and, after that night, never called her again. But it had taken me almost half a year to clear the decks, to ring her up one lonely November Saturday night, and she had been quite agreeable to my stopping right by, though I had had in mind some future time. So we commenced. In mid-December we ended. She had not met Paul, he had never, to my knowledge, seen us together, although I'd had trouble enough making peace with Dino's having had her once or twice, in a manner of speaking, despite the fact that had this not occurred I'd never have met her at all. Balling Gardella early on (they'd had only three dates in all) was one of the things I'd been into her about that final night. I had become fed up, as it seemed to me then, by the totality of her preoccupation, by how monochromic her cleverness was. (Once, over dinner, I had speculated on the inventor of the candle. She replied, Eve. Once we passed the house of a doctor she knew, whom she described as collecting intellectuals. Does he mount them? I asked. Gillian: He would like to. *Bright Sayings* for the *Sexual Digest*. I was delighted by them at the time.) We'd been to the theatre that night to see *A Severed Head*. When we got back to her place she mentioned, again, that she was a writer, which is to say, had written things. She'd taken a writing course in New York, at some rival institution, where the instructor had thought highly of her work. He also thought well of her personally. She still saw him socially— she had seen him, she said, the night before—though it was entirely platonic. I knew who the instructor was, I knew something of her habits, and a non-carnal tie seemed unlikely. I poured another scotch and asked to see something she had written. She went to the dresser in the bedroom, and produced a piece entitled *My Three Pussys*. I pointed out that she only had two. Read on, she said. I read on. All three were soft and furry warm. But one was different. It needed special care and handling. It was drawn chiefly to men, who invariably failed to treat it properly. The piece continued thus for several pages. I lack the heart and memory to summarize it further. It was typed, but covered with red comments and corrections made by the man who gave the course, still one of our better cocksmen, once one of our better writers. I flew into an eloquent, puritan rage. I more than implied that her brains were in her box. I asked why she didn't take up some hobby. Sub-

scribe to the *Manchester Guardian*. Specialize in cold showers.
I asked how she could have brought herself to sleep with
Gardella, of all the impotent Sicilians, the first night he ever
took her out. She sank into her rocking chair. Tears split her
rosy cheeks. She looked still lovelier, and very vulnerable. She
said she had been lonely. That it hadn't worked out anyway.
(This I knew, from Dino: that he had pooped out at the stick-
ing point, in line with his general troubles.) That, upon re-
flection, she wasn't sure it was really any of my business. I became contrite, almost gentle. I said her essay showed a fine
command of language. I allowed that my remarks were out of
line, certainly jaundiced if not actually sick. She said bitterly
that she had been faithful to me through all of our twenty-one
days. I took her to bed in her baby-blue half-slip and screwed
her mightily, too drunk to ejaculate. And early the next morning she evicted me tersely ("Go home." "What?" "Go home"),
leaving her bed to hunt up the missing sock I'd been on the
point of going off without. She wanted no traces. They don't,
it would appear, have to abide such judgmental rudeness from
whomever they're enjoying at the moment. Whatever their
habits. I wonder if I have really learned that yet. (Frank was
interested to know why I always seemed to get mixed up with
promiscuous women. It was not an easy question, and I asked
him to define his terms.)

After she heaved me calmly out that Sunday morning, I
found it difficult to live without her, which is to say with
myself, and spent most afternoons with Pisacano, drinking
his wine and eating the specialty of the house, hamburger
and onion drowned in a sauce he made from Campbell's
cheddar cheese soup and the red wine. Some days we varied
this with an Italian spread, prosciutto, salami, Fantina, fresh
bread, bought in a saluméria on Twenty-sixth Street, more
Bronx paisanos from out his childhood, but also the street
on which Gillian, born and raised in Brighton, England,

lived. Now, initially, I did not assume he knew her or had ever even seen her simply because he bought his supplies on the street. He'd shopped there for years. And I was far from ungrateful for his nursing care. Apart from those long lunches, I hardly ate. The thought of fixing a meal, or eating alone in a restaurant, would give me the dry heaves. This throat-tearing phenomenon occurred as well at other times. After a stormy, dreamy, blondish night repairing things, reshaping, retracting things, howling and thrashing at my blunders, I'd retch at the prospect of getting out of bed, then be wracked further on rising, though it was better, all told, to be moving around than not. I lacked the self-love and the will to exercise, began the day often with an ale or two, and grew a little paunchy. Writing was out of the question. I understood then clearly, as clearly as I knew that I would never make it, what had decided me at so tender an age to be a writer in the first place. Because I knew that I would have no life. Was doomed to endure and had better try redeeming the solitary pastimes. And so it had fallen out. I screwed up constantly in the world. I said the wrong thing. I was blind to my guts, even after two years plus on the couch. And if your own makeup is a mystery, if you lack all but the foggiest grasp of who and what you are, how in the world presume to know, convey, anything of value or illumination on the fates of others? Clearly not possible. Nor could I come to terms with wanting less: an "entertainer," whatever that might mean, I'd never be. Thus it presented itself, losers both ways: the impulse, the goal itself, born of worldly failure; but purblind to the world, since to myself, no hope in hell of bringing it to pass. There went December. No cunt, no career, but I had Pisacano. He cooked, fed, listened, consoled, guyed, advised, and generally enjoyed himself. I tried not to begrudge him that. Whose motives are unmixed? He was two years older than I was, taller, heavier. He had survived a five-

year marriage which could still bring him days of bitterness
five years after it was over, and during those second five he
had accumulated, first-hand, a large store of wisdom or opinion on the care and handling of the weaker sex. His hi-fi
blared while he straightened out my life. Sometimes I'd get up
and turn it down. When I'd eaten and drunk and talked
enough I'd walk home and crap out on the blue rug, except on
Tuesdays and Thursdays, when I'd take the bus uptown and
repeat my sad story to Frank. On those days I would try to stay
fairly sober. This sequence, these lunches, went on for several
weeks, and appeared therapeutic. But as distress lessened self-
disgust increased, at the verbiage, my overdetailed cries of
pain, and this was followed by twinges of distaste toward those
to whom I had revealed myself. (Pisacano was not the only
one. Jane Mason got an earful. And neighbor Sarah Shwartz.
And my literary agent. I was an Ancient Mariner, without the
sense and courtesy to stick to strangers.) And, finally, something else accrued: the suspicion, then certainty, that I had
surely piqued Paul's interest in singing her praises (for that
British R.N. had grown fantastic, close to perfect in my mind),
that he had acquired her phone number from Gardella (since
I had taken care never to mention her last name), whose
loyalty to him was greater, older, than it was to me . . . that
he had called, seen, possessed her at least as quickly off the
mark as I had, and that they now shared a large laugh at my
expense as I sat there moaning at his table, complimenting his
cooking, trying to keep myself alive. I put this to Dino, who
denied giving Paul the number, or being asked for it, and
swore not to if he was. That, also, was to be expected. Now I
had good reason to dislike Dino as well, for being put in the
position (if he was not simply lying) to do me this odd, large
favor. Label me no labels. I knew of Pisacano's interest in and
talent for laying the wives and ex-wives and nonwives of his
close male friends. And then, if possible, feeding the friends. I

had met, months back, one ignorant cuckold who dined there often. I had even met his wife, on a separate occasion. Whenever I ran into him at Pisacano's I could barely meet his gaze, in embarrassment for him and contempt. And now, through my own conniving, my turn had come. The graphicness with which the idea presented itself lent it strength and credence. I do not usually think in pictures. His fat—as I fleshed it— Sicilian lob thrust past her outer and inner lips, rived that tight blonde place over which I had, for three wild weeks, so delicately labored, and she, hard-breathing, loving every moment . . . such pictures drove me wild. I was obliged to drink them into fuzziness. Then one afternoon, sitting around with Paul, I became absolutely certain that what I had chiefly suspected (and chided myself for suspecting) had in fact happened. I'd telephoned Gillian nervously, uselessly, a few days before, and she had put me off by saying she was in the midst of being sold a Britannica by a door-to-door salesman, was on the point of purchase, and couldn't talk to me then. I suggested she hold off and look at the Columbia Encyclopedia, which was cheaper and handier, and hung up. My first thought was that she would spread her unbelievably firm and silken thighs for the book salesman; the situation seemed tailor-made. I trust I've made it clear she dearly loved to fuck ("I could die happy now . . ."—her odd, flattering remark one morning when I brought her milky body out of torpor into a deep, endless orgasm I amuse myself she will remember), and, appetites apart, she would have the salesman as profound insult to me, the most painful way to write *finis,* for she knew that once she screwed someone, anyone, else (though I would never know for sure), I would accept that my tenure was over. Yet I was still aware, after this call, and the involuted thoughts which followed, barely hinted at above, that I was flirting with madness, or magic, just as surely as I knew the reverse a few days later drinking wine with Pisacano in my with-

ered garden, a very warm afternoon in December. He was on.
He is very verbal by nature. He was sick to death of the pro-
longed listener role. He was telling me about women. His
contempt for them is large. It was a conversation we have had a
hundred times before and since, sometimes reversing roles.
Basically he attacks them in their intelligence. By nature or
conditioning, he's unconcerned with cause, they grow up
stupider than men. If ever he found a chick who could carry
his glove cerebrally, he'd give her an edge. But they all demand, and all they demand, is pussy points, a premium for
having a snatch. A chick who can think is a contradiction in
terms.

"Like a dumb Jew."

"What?"

"I knew a guy in London, an American, who called 'dumb
Jew' a contradiction in terms."

"Okay, father. We all have our ethnic bag. But believe me,
baby, they don't think! We fill in the balloons over their
heads!"

"Yeah."

"Fuck it, let's talk about real things. You get your big
money yet?"

"The first week in January."

"How goes the book?"

"I can't write, the way I feel."

"Shit, it's what you always feel, right? You're a hard-nosed
sufferer! Do work, do writing things! You're using up your
boy-wonder time!"

"Maybe I ought to try using this."

"Using what?"

I gestured vaguely toward my life. "Nurses, attitudes . . ."

"No! no! no one wants to know about you and your hang-
ups, baby. Go write a real book."

"Have some wine."

"I got it."

"I could phone her now, I guess. She's probably just waking up. She's working nights . . ."

"Ah, Christ, you come on like a lovesick beard. No wonder they split, you must be terrifying to women. Listen, I'll do you a favor, I'll rip out your phone."

"She was the best thing I ever had."

"In absentia. You'll get another one. Maybe next time you'll pitch your own ball game. I know some nurses. Those white stockings turn me off. Nurses are a creepy breed."

"How do you mean?"

"Ah, they spend their time surrounded by disease and death. And not doing anything to ameliorate it, like a doctor does. They're propping up pillows. If they're not screwed up to begin with when they pick the gig, they have to get that way."

"Maybe."

"No maybe."

She was night nurse then for a young, recently vigorous millionaire (whom she referred to as her "case"), thrown from a horse, who suddenly found himself facing life paralyzed from the neck down. She told me how bravely he bore it. She told me of bedpans, physical therapy, the trouble she had turning his inert bulk, the pathos, fascination, the rapport between them, her popularity with his family, so that she had hopes of a large gratuity when it was over. (And did, I discovered later, receive one.) Jesus, I came to feel keenly for that once vital millionaire. I thanked my stars I couldn't ride a horse, or even, any longer, drive a car. But there were other ways of being wasted. Plane crashes. Mysterious retributions of the body. I put myself unwisely in the rich man's shoes; he couldn't even commit suicide. He was sustained in his trials, Gillian said, by some faith or other; I would have no such solace. And probably, as I lay there useless, grateful to her for small favors, for pillow-propping, some stoop-shouldered, bearded, ambulatory shmuck describing himself as a writer would be fucking my night nurse to death. Such items passed through my head, such guilty, dangerous identifying. But toward what seemed her shallowness, her callousness, I took a charitable view. It was put on. It was the toughness she needed to cope with the horrors of her profession. Yet now, following Paul's lead, I wondered what turn of'mind had led her to choose it in the first place. Charity? Love? They seemed to not explain enough.

And then my cat, my survivor, appeared from a neighboring yard and walked along the fence, close to where we sat, and made his presence felt. He had just recently come by the talent. There is nothing that smells quite like that spermy stew, and as we moved our chairs Paul talked of pussycats, of a woman he knew who had a pair, spayed females, docile, sweet, no trouble at all.

"Lady cats are better, father."

"I had one, but she died."

"I'm hip. You got no luck, with ladies or pussycats."

As I tried for a quizzical expression, he rose, went inside, came back with my transistor radio. He could not sit anywhere too long without music. His favorite jazz station, WLIB, had just gone on the air. I knew I'd never mentioned—though perhaps I had revealed everything else—that Gillian had two spayed female cats. I tried to put my brain in order. I scrabbled for sense, for a line.

"Dig into the sounds, Sams! Live! Forget dumb broads!"

"That's where we started. All broads are dumb broads in your universe. This one happened to be bright."

"Bright? What do you mean by bright? She belongs to the Book-of-the-Month Club and dips into the Encyclopædia Britannica to find out what she was reading about? Forget it, baby! They don't think like we do!"

My guts turned over. I received new insight into human perfidy. Not only had the worst transpired, but he needed— my asshole buddy—to concoct this cerebral meringue, drop exquisite hints on nurses, cats, encyclopedias, from behind his devious mask of innocence and helpfulness . . . I said nothing then. I maintained a grip. But after he left I kept drinking. I fell asleep. I woke up. I drank some more. Then I phoned. I put it to him. He denied with laughter, denied with vehemence, claimed to be flattered, claimed I was crazy, and extracted just this token for his patience: "Sure, daddy, I'd dig balling the chick who balled the famous blocked author, Jason Sams, she must have this and that going for her, but I never even laid my fucken eyes on her!" I chose, in a while, to believe him. I believe him now. But I may still have been proving it, six weeks later, when I brought my new bed-ridden lady up to the loft on only our second night together.

Paul appeared groggy. It turned out he had been dozing. He was wearing white Levis, an undershirt and no shoes. He took up his screening stance, arms folded and legs wide apart, but it must have been automatic since there was no one there, no one to conceal. Modern jazz blasted from his two large speakers, the "hip din," he called it, in which he was always immersed. He beamed a warm, sleepy smile when I got to the top of the stairs. He hadn't even looked at Christa.

"Father! Come have some wine."

"Paul, this is Christa."

"Hello. Come drink wine."

We followed him in, sprawled on cushions on the floor. Apart from three low cast-iron stools and the swivel chair, there was nowhere else to sit. His loft went right through the building. At the rear of it, close to where we entered, were the kitchen and dining areas; three murky windows overlooked back yards and other windows; off to the front and left, where two more windows faced the street, he had his desk and drafting table. Also at that end was the bedroom, a curtained-off alcove, filled almost entirely by dresser and double bed. After Gillian, a sick joke passed between us: "Pisacano, you got Twenty-sixth Street in there?"

"No, father, she just left."

I was apologizing this way, yet not without nausea. At times I'd carry it jokingly past the joking point and peer, for my heart's ease, past the curtain into the bedroom. But there was no need for this tonight. Paul fetched a half-full gallon jug, three glasses, and joined us on the floor. I got up and hunted down the only ashtray. Pisacano doesn't smoke. He leaned back on his elbows, knees up and thighs wide, an expanse of white, seamed denim pulled tight across his pudenda. Positioned for childbirth, very male. I sprawl like that myself, at times, and watch their eyes. With Paul I think it was less conscious, or less calculating. In this he was fairly democratic. Gents and ladies were subject to the same onslaughts, the same vistas. His bare feet were odorless, likewise his crotch from that remove, but he gave off maleness like a smell, and his accent, that night, was all Bronx, the most literate corner tough to ever make it out of Pelham Parkway. And he was not putting the rhythms on; he simply enjoyed making no effort to avoid them. The kind of effort I rarely any longer had to make myself, so thick the neutral overlay. I had never met a New York Sicilian before 1959, articulate or otherwise, and now I owned a pair of them. I tried to use Paul in my life as I had tried, with less success, to use Dino in my novel. He was especially loud that night; volume went with the particular style, and there was the usual need to shout over the phonograph. Christa sat to my left about a foot behind me, her legs tucked under, her hand lightly on my back. Occasionally, secretly, she'd squeeze my side, to make certain I was there, I thought, as well as to remind me of her own delicate, assaultable presence. That was how strongly he was coming on. Yet he talked almost entirely at me, including her rarely, with a glance, when he deemed some remark simple or gaudy enough to elicit her appreciation. How we got onto politics and war I do not know—probably I mentioned the film we had seen—but we stayed there. Lyndon Johnson had just offered the North Vietnamese a billion dollars to build and tidy up their country, which, if they failed to accept, he'd cut their fucking hearts out. This was officially described as "policy," and proof of American generosity. The press dubbed it "the carrot and the stick," but did not seem to draw much moral from the phrase. (More recently has come and gone another assault on the senses and the language, a "peace offensive." An olive branch, a kick in the nuts. Which I adduce in the main to show how far and slowly we have traveled—March of 1966—to reach this point in our travail.) The sire of those two Texas misses, those blue ribbon kine, had gone on the radio. In the pukey, pious, patronizing style which made Eisenhower seem kin to Demosthenes he had explained the ins and outs of the red peril to the kindergarten which was his nation. Gunboat diplomacy, Pisacano said. Napalm. Where the nineteenth century meets the twentieth. Gook equals nigger. Munitions industry. Cesspool of a nation. He was on nonstop, drinking wine, happy, and I didn't interrupt, as he was difficult to interrupt and he was not saying anything I couldn't agree with. It was one of the few times he outdrank me, though I was downing my usual portion. Christa, when I turned to look, had barely sipped her wine. I winked at her, something I rarely do; she smiled slightly and clung to me more. I wasn't able to decide whether or not she was enjoying herself. I gave it up and turned to Paul.

"Bug out then, stop pissing and moaning, if you don't like it here."

"I will. I can't. Got things to do."

Sarkissian stood abruptly and began to tour the loft. She paused to examine the huge, somber abstracts which covered the brick walls. The conversation, the monologue, halted. Perhaps he needed her in the audience after all. But he made an approving face at me, for her sense, her taste, in leaving the theatre for the museum. For the paintings were his. He got up and went to the toilet. I got up and turned down the phonograph. When he came out he called to her, "What do you think?"

She shrugged, smiled. "Some aren't bad."

"You a painter?"

She mumbled something.

"What?"

"I'm trying to be."

"Yeah! I can tell by how you look at them. Those are from an early period. I'm getting better, going to do great things!"

He sat and poured us both some wine. In a few moments she wandered back to her cushion. Paul didn't push the art line, nor look at her again. He even rode over some remarks, demurrers, she tried, overcoming shyness, to insert into the now desultory but still somewhat political conversation, barely acknowledging, let alone troubling to refute, them. I became indignant on her behalf, suddenly stoned, sufficiently entertained, impresario needs likewise sated, stood, said farewell, and we departed. "Ciao, bubele," he said, seeming as pleased by the prospect of solitude as by company. Halfway down the stairs, I heard the volume being turned back up to normal.

I was weaving, walking badly, on the short journey back. I took her arm.

"What did you think?"

"About what?"

"My friend Pisacano."

"He . . . paints on a large scale."

"Is he any good?"

"I don't know. I can't really tell."

"He's a forceful type."

"Yes."

"He's not always that overpowering."

"Oh."

"Did you have a good time?"

"All right."

Her pauses, her yesses, her all rights . . . they were weighty with footnotes, gnostic, crabbed, implosive glosses whose mystery was their charm. I made them convey that she had his number—noisy, showboating wop, genuine New Yorker—but that uncouth, scary, eldritch as she may have found him, he yet redounded to my credit, pointed up, beside our Aryan Californian, our scholarly, dignified comrade now in the Southwest, my eclectic taste in friends. All this I read in or into her sweet grunts and groans. My own New Yorkness, as I said, was cloaked by Ivy League cadence and an ear bent by foreign travel, though I would still lapse into Lower East Side diction and dicta in the company of the clan (father's side); strive, rather than lapse, with those *bulyoks* of the blood, for a bogus, tough equality. As well as on given nonfamilial occasions. Even Pisacano could bring it out at times. I sit on a manhole cover, a fumey personality which may yet put me into orbit. But we arrived safely home. I fed a very hungry cat, raised the second bed, and went to wash. She hung her coat and came back with the bedclothes, which I kept hidden, Japanese style, in the closet. She had begun to make the bed when I came out of the toilet. The rubber joiner was in place, the bottom sheet was spread. I helped her finish it. It was one forty-five. I set the alarm for nine. I would leap from bed and attack the machine, compose prose while my lady slept. Such was the plan. I more than suspected I would not effect it, but intentions can be soothing. I doused the lights except for the lamp on the table at the head of the bed, stripped to my underwear and climbed in. She returned from the back room in black panties and black brassiere, possibly the same set she'd worn the night before. I didn't inquire. Instead of climbing me she stepped over the bedstead (arm of the couch) on her side, the inside, and wriggled beneath the covers. "Good night," she said sweetly. "Good night, baby," I said, and even drifted off, and roused myself, and thought it over for about ten seconds before I closed the gap between us.

"You sleepy?"

"Yes."

"Me too."

I kissed her eyes. Her mouth. Her dainty moles. The hollow of her neck.

"The light's in my eyes."

So it was. I reached back and clicked off the lamp. Creating novelty. We had not yet lain with each other in darkness. Yet even then I considered letting it go. The groin sent up its A-OK, want, grow, enter, do, but how much more vigorous, I thought, we would all be in the morning. If she had exhibited, maintained, a degree of reluctance I might have refrained. Mildly amused, perhaps, at how swiftly we had run the course, from passion to domesticity. Or feeling victimized. Or pleasantly relieved. But you blew your cool, my love. Breathed now rapidly, kissed back, her hands began to wander, and I dropped mine as well to the tight silky tuft and stroked her outside. She moistened through the cloth, under my palm. We'd done our work during the past twenty-four hours with a minimum of foreplay, we'd confounded the texts, but there's as much for John as Jane at times in diddling that dark mystery, a fact played down by the primers, since the ladies have been short-changed for so long, and there ought be no reward for duty. I insinuated a finger into the thicket. In my time I have fumbled with the worst, and come up empty-handed, but Christa's was a good hard appendage, as proud and unblushing as it was decorous in size, and before long it became important to lower her pants and (more carefully, over the brow of that throbbing cyclops) mine, and throw the covers back, and take her in by moonlight. There was no hurry still. I kissed her armpits, I bearded her nipples with care. I had schemes. I yearned toward every orifice. Nor was Sarkissian idle. She bounced, she bit my shoulders (I was fairly well anesthetized), and with both hands she found me, and a blunted nail strayed into my ass. And out again quick enough, so it was hard to read intentionality, but I was not so wine-soaked as to miss any cues, real or accidental, and I instituted the bowling ball approach, thumb in snatch and middle or index finger in anus, the grip entire, the world in your hand. With my other hand I cupped her breast. This held her steady for a while. She gasped, moaned, but lay fairly still. Then I withdrew the thumb, substituted the member, and we fucked for a good several minutes with my finger up her ass, lying, perforce, on our sides. Delight and labor stretched ahead. With each downstroke I dug the finger into barely yielding flesh; she made her impassioned neutral noises, no nearer epiphany than I was, nor even directed that way, yet heart in the work, if I could judge, at least as much as mine. By all indications more. Well . . . the wise ones come to love the journey, the being done to, since it's so often what they have to settle for; yet that being said, and granted, I felt some envy all the same. That they never lose. They learn never to lose. Not for this reason I slackened, stopped; kissed her, retreated fore and aft. I arranged her backside toward me. I ran a thumbnail down her back, she shuddered accommodatingly, I borrowed some wetness from up front and with the side of my hand I applied it.

"Let's try it here."

Not a trace of ambiguity. Nor was I sober enough for embarrassment, though not so drunk that I did not appreciate being this way liberated. She replied "Mmmm," a noise of quiet assent that certain women make, usually in some less physical context, as if you had just put your finger on a universal truth (as perhaps you have) and they know enough to love you for it, from that part of their nature which is wide-eyed, childlike, which knows the man is master. And wants it no other way. It turns me on, that "Mmmm"; it crowns them queen. I kneaded her cheeks, I began the ascent. She said, "You'll need the vaseline," which seemed likely, and had in fact occurred to me, but I wasn't going to risk departure; now I hastened through the dark and fetched it. We had shifted sides in our endeavors. She lay on her belly, on the outside. Yielding to impulse, a passing gallantry, I knelt beside the bed and bussed her ass. Then I propelled myself over, opened the giant jar and lubed the pair of us, in and around her, down the scimitar's length, and, even then a prince of patience, I sought her with my thumb, the digit slipping in as nice as pie. In and not quite out I moved it, between those edible hemispheres, Sarkissian contributing not a word. Then out. Scouts returned intact, I mustered the legions.

But why assault that citadel? What need? God alone may know. Covington may know. Even Sams has an idea, or a better one now than I did then. When I was seven years old in Coney Island I jabbed a Good Humor stick into my female cousin's rectum and found it rewarding. She suggested a different game, a frontal game, but I was simply not interested. I was definitely on the receiving end of mother-administered enemas through childhood, though I cannot recall the emotional tone. When I was twelve I was fiddling with my next-door neighbor, a red-haired contemporary, standing behind her while she affected to gaze out the window, when to my amazement and horror my finger disappeared inside her, which was my first confrontation with the fact that little girls were not merely smooth little boys. (And pissed through their behinds.) Needless to say, I never went near her again. Does this explain enough? Points up, at least, how late the cunt came in my life. I suppose I was busy with schoolwork.

Christa. Her body stench all around, in the air, on my fingers, liberated by their intrusion, mingled with the viscous odor of the vaseline, and my own funky smells. It was all pleasant enough. I spread her cheeks, with an index finger once more teased the target, and introduced the curving thing, or just the head, which did not strike me as much greater in circumference than the greased thumb, but this seemed not to be the case, resistance was encountered, and she yelped beneath me, a highly unattractive sound, and when I pushed, nonetheless, infinitesimally further, trying for a purchase, she yelled, "No, stop, please!" more command than plea, so I stopped, and said, "We'll go easy."

"It hurts. It's bad."

"Is it bad? We'll go slow."

But what is "slow"? The slightest movement broke new ground. As I hung there, I thought it over. The sad fact was I'd never known much success in this area, however one defines success: never sunk it to the hilt, come only once (rubicund Jane Mason), and could never divorce plumbing that well, or wanting to, from unwholesome satisfactions. The most agreeable, the most interested, all evinced signs of pain which seemed much separate from pleasure. (And from passion as well—which involves, morphologically, a little agony.) They shook loose, or asked me to desist, and like a shmuck I always did. Like a shmuck, I say, because I always regretted it, and impugned their honesty, later. And even if their complaints were genuine, how do you define compassion, having come that far? Don't you drive onward for their own sweet sakes into cherry or not-even assholes? Taking your pleasure, getting it done, the surgeon's rationale, cruel to be kind, although risking criminations and abrupt departures during the next quarter of an hour? I remain in the dark. My experience is limited. Including the more conventional. I had never—saving Sarah Shwartz, and disregarding still the nightmare of Esha— fucked a virgin, so I had no clear idea what their resistance quotient was. In mind or in flesh. I suspected that pain was a part; and that virgin or no, in their lives as in their fantasies, rapee was a role they lusted after. For sex is, is it not, at least early in a girl's career, the perpetration on her person of unspeakable acts she is traditionally obliged to delay and resist while she knows she was made for them (and yearns for them) to happen? While the halfbacking male's move, the *comme il faut,* is to feint or thunder past the lips that say no no to the yes yes in their eyes? A tenable position. The area is far from over-explored. I'll be thirty-four in seven weeks, and I'm still learning. But my views to the moment: they will fake you out and they will put you off. And if you take their demurrers at face value, back down from misplaced charity, wait for ripeness, they'll go out and have somebody else who doesn't hear too good—a body less squeamish, less weighted down with sensibility. What they're after all the time. So why not be somebody? Here is the true saint. From largeness of heart he hangs in, permits them to "succumb." And if he learns soon enough that succumbed they are triumphant, that they lose to win, hold now a lien on his real and symbolic pecker . . . there is the test and measure of his sainthood.

Where were we? Poised, still, over Sarkissian's rear. Dipped inside her, to a point. Causing, if we deem her truthful, disconcerting pain. And suddenly in trouble. Because, thinking, I began to lose hard interest, I'd soon be unequipped to disregard her plaints and bugger her despite them even if I were willing to give so much away; and somewhat panicked by this impending loss of choice I thrust substantially, maybe a tenth of an inch, and milady screamed, but I held fast, she screamed

more loudly, shattering the cat's repose, the peace of the garden apartment, she squirmed, twisted violently, and so I gra-
ciously withdrew. She flipped over in haste. I doubted she was
inclined toward conversation, but I knew well I wasn't, so
took her face between my hands and kissed her hard, full of
many things, and fucked her hard, snorting into her subtly
colored hair, into the pillow, dropped an indifferent load in
passing and sped right by it, until she started to flex and rise
beneath me, and I had the thought (to speak of cruelty) that I
could dissolve her possibilities, pull out and leave her thrashing, but each man's ego is unique, mine own demanding less
rarefied satisfactions, and I hung in without suffering, would
like to say I came a second time but no, but had it genuinely
up and brought her on. Following, I rolled over onto my side
of the bed and passed out, because, to tell the truth, I had
drunk too much wine.

In the morning, around eight thirty, preceding the alarm,
in ample time to shut it off, Christa and I—to spare you
tedium—made love. Afterwards I popped some aspirin,
milk, she drank some water, and we slept again. It was several
hours before I was able to stir. I got up and put some water on.
I fixed our respective beverages and brought them to the bed.
We spent the next couple of hours in bed. Lying, sitting, sipping, smoking, exploring, toying, talking. Talking. I had,
clearly, given myself the morning off, and all the mornings off,
without guilt or fuss, until such time as the muse demanded
my attention. I knew, if I left it to her, it would be never, but
I was determined to enjoy myself, enjoy Christa, not blame or
stone either of us for my neglected labors, since I had been
goofing off for years with nothing like so lovely an excuse.
Once more I have the impression that I chiefly listened. She
had only one string fitted to her instrument, like a minor
writer, and like a good one she plucked it to yield a certain
complexity, a variety which one would have doubted, from

the dust jacket summary, could be there. Later she would claim I had a quality which drew her out, a mock-avuncular veneer, and I have heard the same from other places, so there may be something to it, but doubtless it was also in large part our nakedness, the great wet togetherness we had created and passed through in the brief time since we'd met which gave the context, and no doubt she is not the first female to regale her lover, the father-fucker of the moment, with tales of past defeat and glory, nor I the first incumbent to want to believe he was able to enjoy them. Anyway, her saga grew rounded; she filled in some of the gaps she'd shrugged past on opening night, but not all; never all.

"For something like six weeks I was living with a man in Madrid, an American, and, well, one day I woke up pregnant."

"Who was he? How did you meet him?"

"I . . . can I begin a bit further back?"

"Be my guest."

"I had to leave Paris, for various reasons, and decided to go to Madrid. On the train I met a young man from Ohio, or else he only taught art history at some university there, and we sort of hit it off. He asked me to break the journey with him near Aix-la-Chapelle, to see if we could meet Chagall, a special interest of his. I thought why not, it seemed a better idea than jolting on the train all night."

"You had no *couchette?*"

"No, I was trying to economize. We got there around dusk and found a sweet little hotel near the station, and we took a double room with twin beds, still economizing. It . . . well"—she smiled her total smile, remembering—"sometime toward dawn, I suppose it was, I heard his bed creaking, and then the lamp went on. I could see him reaching for his glasses, then deciding against, and he lumbered over—he was rather heavyset—and he . . . how shall I put it . . ."

"He made the obligatory try at your virtue."

"Yes, something like that. It was endearing, in a way, that he felt he had to."

I contributed a chuckle at how endearing this was.

"Anyway, it was no problem, and we stayed friends. After breakfast we asked directions to Chagall's house and found it without any trouble. But it was locked and guarded by an old man in a blue uniform, and he went into a very rapid tourist spiel the moment he saw us, so we went back to the hotel and caught the next train to Madrid. And when we got there . . . I didn't know anyone in Madrid."

"What made you go there?"

"I'd never been."

"Mmm. What happened?"

"The art historian—I really can't remember his name— he had friends there, one of whom was expecting him, a man who'd been living in the city for some time, teaching English. I agreed to tag along. And that was how I met George."

Well, if the art historian had not much appealed to her, this second *hombre* did; she never got round to leaving his apartment. He was about thirty, she said, taking courses in Spanish besides teaching to live, planned to go to Italy at some point to repeat the process, with the goal of returning eventually to the U.S. to teach romance languages. I had known one or two like that myself, aspirant linguists, during my GI-Bill-backed sojourn at the University of Barcelona. I had even pretended to be one. On certain bitter-cold days in the winter of 1959, if Britta was out, and I could get the furnace to work, and there was Fundador, you could find me in our dirt-cheap six-room apartment on the Calle Londres, translating parts of *Don Quixote* into Japanese. Although in point of fact I knew neither language. But it was easier than trying to write fiction. So I suspected my compatriots as well, on or off the Bill, of being poets at heart. And in fact several were.

"Was George writing, or maybe meditating, a novel-on-the-side?"

"Not so far as I ever knew. He drank, though, as if he was. He drank more than anyone I'd ever known."

"An all too human failing."

"When he was gone during the day I walked around the city, or went to the Prado, or just stayed home and worked. I got more work done while I was living there than anywhere else in Europe. In fact, it was the only place I did any serious painting . . . George never quite adjusted. He always seemed a little shocked to see me there when he came into the apartment."

"I think I know the feeling."

"He took a week off at one point and we drove down to Granada . . .", did the caves, got rooked by the gypsies, and George clobbered someone in a bar, or was himself clobbered. Up to here she did her recollecting fondly, with the same gusto as the day before. But when she discovered she was knocked up, the idyll ended. How did George accept the news? Did he propose marriage? Offer an abortion? Invite her to leave? Here I draw a blank. Perhaps she didn't say. But my impression is she never told him. She just disappeared. Her man Tim, her Berkeley man, who she fleshed out now as her deflowerer, five years before, when she was twenty-one, materialized in Madrid as he was to do throughout Europe where she was, sometimes with, often without, her encouragement; he made the contact in Tangier, and he accompanied her down.

I was listening. I was a long way from being bored. I asked intelligent, leading questions. And yet, and yet, I had a sound theoretical grasp of the dangers of the pastime. I knew that it was infinitely better to pretend they were born when you met, sprang full-blown from your head or loins, and to do what you could to insure that they maintained the fiction. I knew this

full well. Yet I indulged her, or us both—for I felt I was safe
at the moment. I was not that fond of her, one. And two, I had
not really mastered her cast of characters, not been drawn into
the pantheon, had no real feeling for these names, these disembodied pricks, those which had been inside her and those
(more endearing) which had not; I was her total present, but
more even than that—she reduced them in the telling, they
came out props and dummies, bit players at best, detours
down her destiny road . . . we all do it, I suppose. But she
was artful. Committing no libel, maligning not a soul. A
shrug, a smile, a wry, well-turned phrase, and there they were,
in all their robotized frailties, with all their lacks and gaps,
viewed by us both through the wrong end of a telescope, and
that, at the time, was all right by me, they were midgets indeed
for all I cared to know, the way she limned it was exactly the
way it was.

Tangier. In the company of one's first love or lover, pregnant by another man. Picture the train ride down. Picture the
crossing from Algeciras. Have you been to Tangier? Myself,
never. Fill in the sights and smells. Throw in street cries, a
handful of Sandy's beatniks. Fly a flag from the Tangier Hil-
ton, if such there be. The doctor was a doddering Frenchman,
close to eighty. A burly woman thirty years younger, possibly
his wife, helped out, screeched, berated, Christa was not sure
for what, but surmised it was about his penchant for fiddling
with the clients, above and beyond. Tim stayed with her as
long as he was able. He held her hand. Finally he left. Then
the ancient was inside her, brutal or bungling, clumsy or mad,
no anesthetic or numbing pill or shot, and she screamed (I
knew the scream) in horrid pain, and Tim heard her from the
street and tore back up. He tried to get in, but the woman
blocked his path. And it was already over. They tried to send
her off at once, but she was too shocked or too weak or too
stubborn to leave. They found her a soiled couch in a back

room and she lay there awhile. Tim stayed until she sent him
away, came back in an hour, and took her to their hotel. Picture a bleak, cheap hotel. "It was the one"—a deprecating
shrug, a smile—"where William Burroughs used to stay. Or
so they said." And this, in itself meaningless brushstroke,
jolted me into her tale. Nothing else really had. She had told it
in her odd warm voice without self-pity, with an eerily remote
third-person detachment I was content, also, to be sheltered
by; injecting the literary figure, the real-life ex-junkie, who
even as she spoke—give or take a day or two—was holding
cultural court for the greater glory of Grove Press at the
nearby Chelsea Hotel, this somehow shattered the façade; or
mine; it made me feel her pain. Or, at the very least, the size of
the indignity visited on her person; the price a woman could
be made to pay, for that poor reason, for taking her simple
pleasures.

   "How did you meet Dave?"

   Because, really, I had had enough. I was grateful for the
flash, it was duly filed, perhaps someday I would use it, but
clap or worse, occupational hazards of the male, could be said
to balance things out. I had escaped them both, the clap and
worse, yet could adduce nonetheless, along related lines, a
fearful string of personal anecdote. By and large, I saved such
stories for the page. Maybe I resented her artfulness without
art, her fluency, the easy impermanence of the spoken word.
Then too, when she reached me, with her Burroughs throwaway, I became aware of other, aforementioned dangers. Yet
the area I moved to, our loaded common ground, was hardly
designed to forfend them.

   Denby was still courting Keiko, who had begun to grow res-
tive, though not yet to the point of issuing the ultimatum
which finally got them married, and Christa was "with," expecting to marry, Tim. They met—she and Dave—through
Devereaux, a friend of Denby's who had been courting

Marcia, the middle Sarkissian sister, but thought to switch off
when he laid eyes on Christa. No one will fault him for that,
but I have met Devereaux since, in Tucson, and neither can I
blame my wench for being barely interested. When Dave told
her (almost at once, that dungpile of integrity) that his plans
seemed to include early marriage to a Japanese girl, Christa
began to cry. Thus was the air cleared; thus they began.

"He had his fiancée and I had mine. We were something
very special for each other. I'll always be grateful to him. He
. . . didn't let me fall in love with him."

"How did he go about preventing it?"

"He . . . by not letting me achieve orgasm."

"You're not serious."

"It's true."

"But Jesus, how could he prevent that?"

Which I thought I answered as I asked it—trying to dodge
the accompanying shaft of satisfaction—the poor bastard, my
epicene buddy, highly skilled in other areas, went off too fast.

"He would withdraw when he saw I was close."

"But my god, that's uncivilized! That's inhuman!"

"Yes."

"Didn't it make you hate him?"

"No . . . I loved him . . . I don't know. I was getting the
other thing with Tim. Dave and I had something else."

I was able, although barely, to believe it. My faithful correspondent, my procurer in the Southwest, father of one, husband to a winner, scholarly in the ways of the East, with a
phlegmy, guttural way of talking which cost you until you adjusted (and even after) up to half of what he said, a useful device for commanding attention in a room . . . some kind of
sexual monster. Did you ever get to know people? Not unless
you fucked them, for openers, and not so often then.

I found this tangent even less rewarding than the subject we
had left. Yet I did not rise and dress, I did not switch us to the

weather. She was turning me on. I felt an erection somewhere in me against all the odds, like a bulb must feel its
flower. I was the mortal enemy of all such squandering.

"What happened after Tangier? Did you go back to
Madrid?"

"Yes."

"With Tim? Or did you go back to what's his name,
George?"

"I stayed with Tim for a few days, and then we . . . he
left. I didn't want to see George. I ran into a friend of Marcia's, a doctor, from Berkeley . . ."

. . . now married, but badly, with a child or two, someone
her sister had been torrid about before meeting up with her
Swede. Christa, newly aborted, had him now. In Madrid. The
sex was terrible, the sex was very bad. I didn't press her for
details. The sex always seemed to be bad, one way or the other.
If they weren't knocking her up they were pulling out on the
point of her climax . . . I took special pains to let it go. I
took a healthy view: that her robustness so far had been un-
typical, that despite appearances her threshold was as high as
her luck was bad, that it was Sams—HIMSELF!—all modest, magic seven inches, his mark, his various bumps and skills,
who'd brought the miracle to pass. I glimpsed us pure and iso-
late from the ongoing sexual stream. Perhaps we had something unique. Perhaps we would also turn out—with orgasms, yet—to be "something special." Because I knew,
despite the desperate ruminations of the night before, that
she'd freed me from my usual bind: feeling victimized and
cheated if they failed to make it, feeling used and cheated
if they too readily did. Eunuch or dildo: no middle way.
But Christa had a cunt and other parts that damaged my
neurosis, which I died to explore, would not soon exhaust,
doubted I'd tire of. However. She had not stopped talking.
She would not stop talking. She described now a second round

with the same man, the doctor, in some Scandinavian country, and now the sex was good, so very good I could not possibly want to hear about it, my incipient harden vanished, I felt all sexed out for that morning, verbally and in the flesh, and I excused myself, went to the toilet and showered a long hot while, soaping the pubes with care, restoring my body to myself. When I came out she had disposed of the bedclothes, trundled away the bed, and was sitting naked in the basket chair, looking through my book. I was pleased by this, but when I told her to wait for the movie, she put it down quickly enough, smiled and went to shower. While she was showering and dressing I fixed us breakfast, bacon and eggs, large glasses of Sacramento tomato juice, and some brown bread no longer fresh (I did not use bread much). She came out of the back room fully dressed, in the black skirt, white blouse, brown stockings of our opening encounter and the fleet hours since. She was delectable. They look so good enrobed, preceding or just after. I experienced a shooting tremor through my dormant dick, some arcane message of appreciation. I had become enamored of her nose. I was enraptured also by her ankles, their very thickness, which I had marked as debit (that "B —" shit) right after she walked into the room. Now I could see that their heaviness, the odd bone in her foot, the bags beneath her eyes, all other signs of grossness or fleshly imperfection, had helped to arouse me, and keep me that way. Clearly it was time to go over my sexual holdings, my *Vogue / Playboy / Sunday Times Magazine* pastiche, buy this, sell that, and come up with a new portfolio where the shape around the crotch was concerned. I felt potentially huge. I felt like screwing after coffee, or in half an hour, but (preferably) not Christa: some new untried body-type, some shy wild unfamiliar lovely who might be strolling just then, unsuspecting, by my door. "The antidote is feet!" the European Gardella used to say. (He had no minor fetishes.) "When I get too bugged by it all I keep my sanity by reminding myself that all cunt has feet!" Ah but, Dino, all cunt has cunt as well. Fucking, it would seem, begat the appetite, deprivation cum abstinence begat . . . muddy waters. Meat-beating, perhaps. Early in our association Covington practiced therapy by anecdote. I would dwell at length on my compulsion and distress. I was then thirty-one years old, I had been making New Year's resolutions for fifteen years to halt this self-abuse (for that was what it had become, since I reacted so badly). Where would it end? "You remind me," chuckled Frank, "of the man who approached Chief Justice Hughes on the occasion of his eighty-fifth birthday, and asked him, 'Judge, at what age does a man stop masturbating?' And Hughes said, 'My good man, you'll have to address that question to someone more mature than I.' " It was a pleasant story, but did not much alter my habits.

But all that was many moons before. In some other life. Sarkissian, Christa, was leaning over the table mopping up my A&P eggs with stale pumpernickel, there was a fleck of yellow on her cheek, and I was digging her to death. I had not the slightest doubt that it was mutual.

"You have some egg on your cheek."

"Oh? Which?"

"That one."

"I'm somewhat sloppy."

"Welcome to the club."

"You seem neat enough."

"I've been told, in my time, that I eat like Henry the Eighth."

"They're probably wondering what's become of me."

"Who?"

"The people in Washington Heights."

"Why don't you call them?"

"I think I'd rather not."

"Well, you're a big girl."

"They're old friends of my father's . . . it's not the ideal place to be."

"Too far from the action?"

She smiled back. "That, yes, and it's . . . restrictive. They're fairly old, and set in their ways. The man is out all day, the woman is very kind, but . . ."

I hesitated but a moment. She came, as far as I could tell, with a built-in departure, although she had talked vaguely of looking for work in New York, somewhat less so of visiting friends in Baltimore, and, still in a way Abroad, was generally and genuinely uncertain what to do with herself. But there seemed little doubt that she was California bound. The idea of playing house with her had enormous, immediate appeal. It would, right off, keep me from the others, the flawed ones I knew and the mind-perfect lovelies I would break my back to meet in the fruitless, time-eating battle against loneliness; it would keep me at my desk. If she had cost me any time at all so far (and the verdict was unproven) she'd done so because she was new. Having her around would be a different matter. I'd be an unbrave (which was all I had ever aspired to) Hemingway: do the work, fuck the special chick, and last. Except for a few days with Jane Mason, when she arrived breathy from Tucson (and found me sitting here with Sarah Shwartz), before she got her own apartment, and we flopped together on the thirty-inch bed which was what I had at the time until I took to sleeping on the sofa, and then putting her on the sofa, and she reacted with the gush of tears she was then and may still be given to; except for those few days in July of '64 I had not lived with anyone since Britta, our final six months (following eight in Barcelona) in Sweden, leading up to and briefly away from the day we didn't get married.

"Sarkissian!"

"Yes."

"It occurs to me I have an extra set of keys. Why don't you

move in until things come clear for you? Passable food, talk on
a high level, use of the subzero back yard . . ."

"Mmmm."

"Mmmm?"

"You'd let me stay here?"

"I'm *inviting* you, I'm *asking* you to stay here."

"Well . . . I would like to."

"We would love to have you."

For the cat had taken a shine to her as well (sniffed around
her ankles as we spoke); whereas once he'd perch upon my
chest at night and lick the moisture from my beard (if I had
taken pains to wet it), and burrow under the blanket as soon as
I stirred in the morning, he now divided his attentions; did
not abandon me outright, kept a paw in, but tried to have it
both ways. And I was nothing but pleased at his response to
the guest or to the situation: by his ambivalence, tact, poor
discrimination, greed, whichever it was. Apart from this, he
steered clear when we made love, which was no small thing;
once in late '63 I dated a brick shithouse from El Paso who
owned an untutored beagle who crapped in the bathtub at the
best of times, and if you have never risen and fallen on a southern belle with a beagle named Hank licking your ass, the smell
of his new turds wafting from the toilet, then you're poorly
equipped to appreciate a cat who practices discretion. He was
quite conventionally marked, grays and whites, gray masking
one of his yellow eyes. He was what was left of the pair of
eight-week-olds I had begun with. The female had not survived the pregnancy I arranged with a handsome passing tom
just short of her first year. She had come into season much
sooner than the male of the house was equipped or inclined to
do anything about it. Her noise and gyrations were driving
me crazy, so I put her outside when the black tom smelled her
out. He grabbed her by the neck and took her out of sight. I
watched them through the fence. It seemed to make her
happy. She, my female, striped tabby, was much funnier,

much wilier than the other, less neurotic (he hadn't even been housebroken, rare for a cat, when I got him), I dug her more, but when she bought it under the vet's knife (after I finally got her there), unable to deliver the kittens I had let die inside her, under the impression that that clicking sound she made, and her refusal to eat, were natural parts of labor, I became deeply enmeshed with my survivor. Even when he came into his own and started to stink up the house with spray, I would not have him altered. That little quirk confirmed our bachelorhood. The beard-licking ritual, the earnestness with which he went about it, sent me sometimes into wild laughter. We had a working relationship. But I somewhat suspected it was not conducive to mental health, his or mine.

Now we would have company.

"I'd better take my pill."

"Pill?"

"The . . . pregnancy one."

"Oh. Yeah."

When she had downed the pill she made us more coffee, and more tea, and we decided that she would move in that same evening. It was then about half-past two. She would go up-town and pack, wait around for the old man to come home from his rug store (if that is what he had) so she could take a formal farewell, and taxi down around six. She would tell them that she was moving in with a married couple she knew, who lived not far from me, a little way up Third Avenue, and she would also give this couple my address so that they might forward any mail which came down from Washington Heights. (Though she expected to get most of her mail at American Express.) Simple complications. And, except that she left there around five (phoning me first to say she was en route), and never got to see her host that final time, this was the way it happened.

part 2

I GOT THROUGH THAT AFTERNOON BY REREAD-
ing parts of my novel, *Gino Travels,* which was more fun and
considerably easier than adding to it. I had a thousand fragments. I had enough notes (Gardella's own problem) for a lifetime. I'd tried to make the book's disintegration (which had
commenced early on) an integral part of the book, which was
hopeless. I copped out on basic matters, like my life with
Britta. And yet . . . I liked the prose. The more I drank
(wine) that afternoon, the less laborious it came to seem, the
more I liked the prose. I found myself wondering—with
what a high-octane mixture of modesty and arrogance!—if I

would ever write that well again. I decided probably yes, but not this day.

I had told Christa she would have no trouble in phoning a cab, but she had ended up in an unmetered vehicle which set her back considerably more than the two-fifty or three dollars I had guessed at (she would not say how much more), as well as on the butt end of a ten-mile conversation, which mildly impertinent to begin ("What's a nice girl like you doing running around by herself on a rainy, windy night like this?"), moved rapidly to intimations that she was not as nice as she should be, and then to suggestions that they take advantage of this and alter the course of the journey. She described the driver as white, Italian, thirty or thirty-five. I did not know what her financial resources were but assumed they were scanty, and apologized for the misleading information. I offered to pay all or part, but she declined. On the other matter, I more than shared her low-grade indignation. Every third psychotic cocksucker in the city seemed to drive a hack. I had my share of taxi stories. I had been spit at a few days before by a sullen young Negro with a hipster's goatee who dealt with my ten-dollar bill as if he thought it was a one. He knew bloody well it was no one. There was more to this cab ride than is useful to go into. The confrontation was not clearly black and white. It may have had to do with our different taste in beards. But briefly, fuck negritude and overcoming and brotherhood and guilt, baby. I mean to pay now and hereafter what the meter reads only. The situation deteriorated rapidly and he loosed an oyster when I stood outside his cab. Missed. Fortunately roared away. So how much worse it must be on the distaff side. As Molly X, the only black girl I ever laid with regularity, used to say, "It's a hard life for a girl," and she meant more than the insides of taxicabs. Prey to the prong of the stranger (let alone

their friends). The more attractive they may be, the less freedom they possess. Not walk the late-night streets alone. Or sit
on a park bench. Or down a thoughtful, solitary shot at the
local. All they have gained is the vote, all they have shed is the
veil. And worse still in foreign parts, particularly for the
American girl, accustomed to (however little) more maneu-
verability. I have heard certain tales. Lorn, long-haired Susan,
the sick, statuesque puss who sculpted the six-foot plaster
phallus which stood for a while for a lark (in a more recent
time) in my garden, claimed she was stoned, thrown at, on the
isle of Crete, fair-sized pebbles, from some unseen source. For
no immediately apparent reason. She was strolling. She read it
as profound assault on her muliebrity, her very cuntliness,
and I'm inclined to agree. A photographer I know in her middle twenties was followed for seven hours through some
Sicilian town (is it worse, perchance, on islands?) by a pint-
sized putz who redoubled his attentions, dying with laughter,
when she turned to confront him with threats of the police.
(She had finally to retreat to her hotel.) Let alone true horror
tales. Dispatched and dismembered on the autobahn. Those
who drop from sight to end their days in a North African
whorehouse. They're game over there, our wandering beau-
ties, to begin. So that things worse than or similar to this
recent misadventure had likely befallen Christa, in her eighteen months abroad. Yet she was right, were that the burden of
her complaint, to expect more civilized handling in her native
land. Well, well, I'd try to make it up. I took her large, battered suitcase, assorted packages and paper bags into the back
room. I had cleared one large dresser drawer and one small,
and made some room for her in the closet. She didn't unpack
at once. We sat on the couch and had a celebratory scotch. We
talked little. I scratched the back of her neck and held her
hand. I scrunched down into the sofa, beard on my chest, and
contemplated my shoes. My mind was briefly empty. She

covered my hand with both of hers and brought it slowly to her mouth.

"Your hands are . . . sweet."

And so I learned I could live with that compliment. I have been told (before and since) with admiration, sometimes with awe, that my balls are large; I have heard how many miles a certain red-haired lass would walk for the chance to be lanced by my silken sword (lyricism hers); my knees, of all things, have been called sexy, but I was sure no girl I'd known until that moment could have gotten away with this one, by which I mean given me pleasure. For I had not thought I wanted my hands to be "sweet." I wanted them to pack a Dempsey punch. I wanted them to build a bridge, rip open a mountain. I reclaimed the limb and looked it over. Nail-bitten, small, definitely on the tender side. She liked it. She had kissed it. I looked into her face. In her deep black eyes, in the smile she bestowed at that moment, I saw myself a giant.

The hit songs don't lie.

I said, "They barely make an octave."

"You play the piano?"

"No."

"Oh."

"You?"

"No."

"My sister got all the lessons. I was culturally deprived."

"You have many siblings?"

"Just the one sister, nine years younger. I thought I'd mentioned that."

"Perhaps you did."

"That may be why I'm indifferent to classical music. Or high culture generally."

"I don't think I could live without classical music."

"Oh? Let's pick some up on FM. Maybe I'm educable."

"I wouldn't want the responsibility."

"Some jazz, then."

But I settled, down the dial, on the wasteland between—
"When I Lost My Baby I Almost Lost My Mind." Similar
soothing sounds. We continued our gentle, refracted conversation. We necked a little. She put her head in my lap and I
stroked her hair. In a little while I cooked the steak I had defrosted in the afternoon, plus some frozen asparagus, while
she looked through her dogeared paperback copy of *The
Waves*. That, and an omnibus called *Mysticism East and West
Through the Ages,* or something like, had been left behind
by the last occupant of the room she lived in on Mykonos.
And then we ate, once more by candlelight, and this time
drank the California wine.

She had offered to set the table, but there was little enough
space in the kitchen for one body at a time, even if she had
known where things were kept. The set of plastic delft dishes
(Triple S Blue Stamps; housewarming gift from my mother),
utensils, glasses, were in small cabinets set right above the sink
and stove, right over my head, as I seasoned, broiled and labored. I told her to relax. She was still my guest, I said. An old
bachelor doesn't grant the table-setting privilege lightly. And
afterwards, putting her to dishwashing in the altered circumstances struck me as too calculating, cheapening my hospital-
ity by seeming to exact a return. So I cleared the table and set
about the scullery chores. I was anxious to avoid the kind of
pileup I'd had to face that afternoon. There are times (the
afternoon was one) when washing up engages me completely,
seems a creative rite, rendering clean and new what had been
soiled and used before; but I rushed through this batch. She
finished unpacking and was seated on the couch when I joined
her, looking through a large sketchbook with a green cover. I
sat a distance away, beside her.

"What's that?"

"Oh . . . nothing. Some sketches. Mostly of Greece."

"Can I see?"

"They're not very good. But if you wish."

I sidled over. She leafed through the book, exhibiting some, flipping past others. Along with the ink drawings was a quantity of prose, haphazardly interspersed, paragraphs in a thin looping hand which she seemed to be screening and from which I looked elaborately away, since₁I felt tempted to read them. The sketches were mostly of the Greek islands—a few portraits, a few fishermen, but the greater part vistas: lakes, mountains, village squares. She threw in a few self-deprecating words with each. Her line was spare, thin and spidery, like the writing, and she was marvelous on texture. I don't know how she did it—mere pen and ink, little round squiggles—but her stone walls looked like stone. She was a witch with stone. I said as much, not even undercutting the praise by announcing how poorly qualified I was to judge. She shook it off, she said they weren't much. But the fact is she blushed with pleasure. It took some effort not to kiss her, but I managed; one had to keep one's plastic judgments separate from sentiment; wage a constant war against such sloppiness.

Except for Jane Mason's party, which I went to the following night, we were together almost constantly through the next eight days, which brought us to the ten-day point since we had met. I'd rise as a rule about eight, go into the back room, shut the door, and thump through the Royal Canadian Air Force Exercise Plan for Physical Fitness, a pretty damn-fool way to start the day when you think about it (particularly as they became more arduous), some carry-over from my weight-lifting days, boyhood notion of the body beautiful, or lovable, and disturbing my roomie slumbering lightly on the other side of the wall (the running-in-place did that), but I'd emerge eleven minutes later triceps bulging, belly rippling, covered in sweat and virtue, get under the shower, and come out of that cleansed inside and out and feeling nearly beauti-

ful. She'd be awake all right, though not always out of bed;
sometimes I would rejoin her. But usually not: dress, prepare
breakfast, in some manner start the day. Or she would undertake the breakfast chore; she knew her way around the tiny
kitchen now. A couple of those mornings she went out immediately after eating, to American Express to pick up her mail,
and from there to wherever her affairs or impulse took her.
And I, I did some work, or groundwork—mostly typed a
monologue, Sams to Sams on Sams, hoping thus to claw and
blunder through to the definitive conception, magic way to
bind together what I had, and brilliantly effect what was
to come (sections I had already brilliantly effected—and
was mortally sick of—too often in my mind). And as the dense,
coded, single-spaced pages piled up, pages which would lose
all meaning for me in a week's time, if I were foolish enough to
throw good time after bad and even try to reread them, I was
able to square the day with myself; convince myself it wasn't
wasted. I wasn't ready. You couldn't force this kind of thing.
When the moment came the muse would visit, nudge me
roughly or tenderly, however she wished, and I'd come crash-
ing through. So I was waiting. For her key to turn in the lock.
I got a terrific charge when that happened. I kept the chain
always on the door (I lived in mild, insistent terror), and especially loved that last moment, getting up and taking off the
chain, letting her into home and hearth all over again.
Whenever I went out—psychiatrist, lunch with agent,
launderette—I'd tell Christa to put it on as well. Sometimes she would forget. Then I would remind her that New
York—no Mykonos, no Berkeley—was far from the world's
sweetest town. Although I had no statistics. All I knew was I
had been robbed twice in one week in my first apartment
after coming back from Europe, a five-floor walk-up at
Charles and Hudson streets. It was a sublet, a ten-by-ten hole,
in keeping with my salary, fifty dollars a week for part-time

duties at the post office. The room and kitchen were top-floor rear, with a fire escape leading to the roof. The roof door could not be locked. Neither could the one on the twin, adjoining building. Nor the front entrance to either tenement. The downstairs bells didn't work. Odd people came and went, often knocking on my door, on unlikely errands. The door lacked a peephole and a chain. There were sounds throughout the house, at all hours, of scurrying and violence. All this apart, I was not, then, in the best of shape. I doubted the good will, I doubted the neutrality even, of people I passed in the streets. Drinking calmed me, but I moved toward a five-dollar-a-day habit, which was well beyond my income. Yet through it all there must have been serene, productive moments, until they got a fix on my post office shift. I worked Monday through Friday, seven to eleven P.M. It's cause for wonder, now, how I held out so long. Weeks before I'd drunk myself to bed on a Saturday night, but woke before midnight to noises on the fire escape. The opulent double bed, with its purple counterpane, was right under the pair of windows. (It consumed half the tiny room; I'd sublet from a pudgy fairy, ad in *The Village Voice,* who'd gone to do something theatrical in the Southwest.) I peered groggily out. I could see only legs. I knocked on the windowpane. He vanished up the fire escape. I fell back into sleep, feeling the weight of it the following morning. I took to sleeping with a hammer and a bread knife under the bed. It seemed to help to have a choice of weapons. When they finally came they smashed the windowpanes. They made off, the first time, with my Olympia portable and a cheap transistor radio (AM only). I'd bought the typewriter in London; it had a £ instead of $ sign. While living in Barcelona, I'd had the Swedish letters *ä, å* and *ö* affixed for Britta's sake. So it was serviceable in at least two languages, and seemed to summarize my European experience. I was naturally attached to it. That night, around midnight, half blind from sorting mail,

I arrived home to find my door thrown open. Empty soda bottles lay and stood in the hall outside. Every light was on. Wind whooshed through the broken pane. Shoeprints stood outlined on the unmade bed. More even than fear I felt violated, fucked and drained by a malevolent giant. I phoned the police. They came in jig time, calling me Jason from the moment they arrived. I was too humbled to object. I could even see their point. If you lived in a burglarized shithole, if you earned fifty a week, the Law was obliged to *tutoyer* you. They were a detective and a pair of cops. They made fairly light of my loss. I gave them the Olympia's serial number, which they jotted down, but held out small hope for its recovery. I wondered if I was supposed to tip them to look harder. They milled about, filling the apartment. I was not eager to have them leave, but they did, and again I got through the night. It smashed me the next day, as had the trousers on the fire escape. I saw Covington that afternoon. In his sweet, gray voice he suggested the YMCA. It seemed a good idea. I slept for two nights at the Y on Thirty-fourth Street, not far from where I worked. A sailor a few rooms down was robbed of his wallet on the very first night. I maintained my cool. I felt fairly well protected by the law of averages. On the third afternoon, refreshed, I returned to my apartment. I shook off apprehension as I neared the top of the stairs. Only the bottom lock was locked (I almost always locked both). I turned the key and walked in. The piece of laundry cardboard I'd stuck into the shattered pane was intact. Shards from another pane, the other window, glittered on the bed. Books lay scattered on the floor. They had rightly surmised I kept some money in a book— ten dollars at the time—but had not discovered it. My clothes were stacked fairly neatly on the bed. The pockets had been turned inside out, but every garment was accounted for. Nothing at all had been taken. There had been nothing to take, clothing apart. I felt a little offended. The Harris tweed jackets weren't bad. But I'd received the message, shaking in the sunlight. I couldn't live there any more. I returned Greenwich Village to the junkies, the faggots, the brave girls from Minnesota. I picked up the phone and called my father. He was not working at the time. He asked no questions. He was there, climbing the five flights, in half an hour. I was packed and ready. He grabbed the two heaviest cases. My mother was waiting in the car. I wished he hadn't brought her with him. She always looked lost and strange to me outside her own apartment. I was afraid to look into her face—of the pity I might find there, or the secret glee. I got in wordlessly and we drove off, myself and the authors of my flesh, back to the house I grew up in, after a brief attempt to make it on the outside. I was thirty years old. I had lived close to five years on the Continent, not a few in the Far East, these credentials would emblazon my dust jacket, but I couldn't live alone in New York. *Merde;* I'd as soon not go into it. This ten-minute journey from the West Side to the East Side took place in March of 1963. After a month of drinking Harry's booze and licking myself into shape I quit the post office for reasons of health and took the Greyhound to Arizona. While I was there my book came out. (I had known that it would.) A foundation gave me a grant. (I had suspected they might.) I came home by jet. Some five days later, when Harry woke me at seven thirty in the morning to autograph a copy of my book for presentation to his twin brother, I got off my laurels and found an apartment. For a while, in the new place, I slept with a length of lead pipe beside the bed. Ground-floor rear with garden seemed at least as open to access as top-floor rear with fire escape. I triple-bolted the wooden door which led from house to porch, and kept checking the lock on the thin metal door which led from porch to garden. On the porch, there were storm windows backing up the screens. The lead pipe was still around in Christa's time, tucked in a corner of the study. I did not know if I could ever use it. But I contained enough free-floating rage, and violent curiosity, to almost look forward to the sanctioned chance, defending one's property and privacy being so sacred a charge.

So I impressed on her the need to keep the back doors locked when she was out and the front chain on when she was in alone. But most of the time we came and went together. To my favorite restaurants. For walks. To the movies. Once, even, to the theatre. To visit friends (mine). Explored the A&P together. Sang love's refrain together. Played games.

"Sarkissian"—one post-prandial, planless night—"you play chess?"

"Yes, a little."

"NO SHIT! You're beautiful! Let's play chess."

"I'm not very good."

"Me neither."

So while the snow fell, the cat twitched in dreams, steam banged through the pipes with an irregular, homey noise, we curled on the blue rug within easy reach of the jug of Zinfandel and played six or eight games over a couple of nights, and though I had not lied to her about the nature of my talent, I was bad in some other, some Class C league, while she made busher blunders; I let her (made her) take certain moves back, but it didn't really help; and though I was good at it, and suggested it, and would have relished it, she would not let me have the instructional role. So we switched briefly to darts, British style. I taught her the rules, she had a certain flair. But my endless bouts of solitaire on top of my old-world training had left me unbeatable, and that game too went by the boards. "It's pointless to go on playing with this great difference in skills," she said; fuck *le sport*, she wanted to win, and sadly, yet secretly seconding the view, I agreed to a halt. We had a few visitors. My young editor and his younger wife dropped over one evening. It turned out that the wife and I (life's endless, impossible fictions) had grown up in the same apartment house, but with the eight-year age difference I'd never noticed she was there. Pisacano came by briefly one afternoon to try to entice us for a ride to his New Jersey holdings, failed, but stayed awhile; but mostly we were alone. She did some sketching, she wrote a number of letters, using the typewriter when it was free, which was most of the time: to her mother in California, her sister in Stockholm, to Denby in Tucson (I owed him one myself but couldn't find the mood; besides, I'd be risking duplication in the circumstances), to a man in Berkeley, Donald Something, a name she hadn't mentioned. (I offered to mail a pile for her one evening, knowing she knew I'd check the addressees, and she let me have them.) And we went on with our dialogue. Or I decided, for a number of reasons, it was time it became one—that I open more, contribute more. The matter of the psychotherapist exercised me most. After twenty-eight months of it, I was barely convinced that I had one. I'd begun at the clinic in September of 1962, once a week, then twice a week, then switched to his office seven months later when foundation monies left me too rich for total charity. Frank Covington. He was, I have already said, a nice man. I never did learn much about his private life. He was in his late forties, appearing younger, although wholly gray. Weakly handsome, my own height, body nondescript and trim. Head slightly large for his body. He was well-read, loved to quote hopefully apposite lines of poetry. He was nondirective (short on life advice). What you would call eclectic in approach. He thought on his feet—uhh, uhh—weighing each remark. He was tacting himself to find out how I felt. I had no way of measuring how much he had done for me. I knew I didn't love him, but he confirmed my opinion that I didn't have to. Whatever we had between us, he suggested, was per se a transference. Hopefully beneficial. For $12.50 an hour, I wouldn't argue. Sometimes I lay down,

sometimes sat up. He had to suck back yawns in the latter instance. Despite backslidings such as Gillian, and withholding
credit for my sudden swollen income, I thought I had made
progress, taken inner soundings, since my Charles Street days.
I could stroll in the streets now without fear or favor. I drank a
wee bit less. I ran my writing course with something like
aplomb. Yet could I ever be sure I would not have made such
small, shaky strides on my own? It was best to assume I would
not. Else I risked perpetuating my snotnosed, snide ingrati-
tude, life-style, defenses, my problem. Plus have to face whatever rage would be attendant on the thought of so many twelve
fifties wasted. Better all around to imagine (however modest)
inroads. Two and a half years is not long; Sams is a tough nut
to crack. From time to time I toted up the rewards. I knew now,
roughly, what I looked like. (Once, in London, years after it
sprouted, I shaved off the beard. The face below was not one I
knew or cherished, was not my original face ((though it remained the one I gave myself in dreams)). Letting the beard
come back, then, helped not at all. At last, three years later,
under Covington's tutelage, I'd learned to operate behind
that prickly, Pentateuch façade.) I knew what (working at one
tenth of capacity) I had managed to accomplish, and that my
scheme of writing my way into heaven—present, lengthening paralysis, nightmares of failure, to the contrary—were as
reasonable as my fears of winding up behind the European
edition of the *Herald Tribune* and fourteen empty cognac
glasses with a great, inchoate novel in my head like thirty
thousand other egos who expected any moment to begin to
Write, Get It Down, so their lives should not seem total zero,
had not been reasonable. ("You're a poor custodian of your
talent," a nice, bitchy girl I never laid although she blew me
once once said to me; it rankles still. "You're the Great Stone-
face," said Mrs. Chambers in the seventh grade when one of
her rare witticisms surprised and failed to amuse me; that hurt

as well; I'd always taken it for granted that behind the moun-
tainous bosom and the steely gaze she specially loved me for
my intellect.) I knew, better than ever before, how I came on.
With my tough, compassionate exterior, litworld *succès
d'estime,* I wowed them in the early stages, duck soup to seem
what they had always wanted, and I did not like to tarnish the
image early or late by admitting freely I was crazy. Or worse
yet, weak. Or worst, a me-too hobbyist, a mid-sixties chaser of
the fashion. (Though it had been different early on. For the
first half-year with the man I would take pains—with women
—to put it on record: "I'm not half so sturdy as I seem, I'm a
deeply bugged human, I see a therapist, love me anyway."
((Or maybe because.)) I felt I was transparent, that the bright
ones would pick it up at once or soon enough, so better to confess. Then too, if I repeated it enough I might come myself to
believe it. Somewhere this changed, probably following the
first trip to Arizona.) For while I knew what small, continual
deaths, widening ripples of despair, heartbreaking sameness
of trouble, had led me to the couch and kept me there, believ-
ing in it or not, I knew as well how skilled I had become or
thought I had become over the years in hiding the rot from
all but the practised eye, and even from the eye on brief
exposure. And perhaps this was all that the Good Life en-
tailed—keeping the rot concealed; lonely, tight-lipped, constant caulking of the vessel which contained it. Glue and
spit. Will power. Emerson. Vale of tears. Everybody suffers.
Life the Great Therapist. Only the weak caterwaul and/or go
under. I could not quite shake these transcendental notions.
If there was anything to them, then I was, indeed, open to the
existential charges of fraud and cowardice. I needed no outside assistance, I could level them against myself. Some of my
best friends, Denby, Pisacano, no more fucked-up than the
world is, had spent no time on the whore's couch (the way
Frank straightened and dusted, like short-time London ladies,

before I was halfway out the door); they suffered and bumbled through. And there were those times, frequent since Christa, when feeling very rare, sometimes without the bottle, if more often with, say laying her gently back upon the blue rug of a wet, dismal afternoon, or less than gently, taking her right through her clothing, pushing aside those black silk drawers, or going down to guide her toward submissive frenzy, tongue and tenderness, or putting in time at the machine, and bugger the result . . . there were those times when I'd watch all the reservations and resistances come rushing back, which had kept my brains my own during the growing-up years. Then I had cunningly come to regard the blackness I lived in as the price of my calling, a moiling Dostoyevskian shit's creek was the necessary ambience, and if anyone had suggested (as no one did) that I Needed Help, I would have wondered with all ill will if I was not being offered a permanent cure for myself. (Dino, one London two A.M., our separate single beds in the room we shared in Wiley Mews: "No, Jason! You got it wrong! I don't *have* problems! I *am* my problem! I AM my problem!") It was not, quite, the tired idea that the Artist is on the face of it Neurotic; simply that, if he happened to be, maybe you shouldn't mess around with the balance. And then, running all this through, I would remind myself that I had not had a single thing to lose: that by the time I turned myself over to the fixers (which was while still abroad, in England, almost a year before Covington), I had already not written in several years; there was scarcely a trace of an artist to be compromised. Nor was there much of one yet. To call my constipated straining with *Gino Travels* "writing" was to stretch the definition. More doubts. More dangers. With my newly subsidized leisure, I'd follow them down. Wherever this was at, these larger, current questions, I decided to tell Christa where I disappeared to two afternoons a week. She had a right to know. The old idea kicked back (my transparency, her insight) that she already knew. Her eyes were wise. She had shown herself intuitive in many ways.

"Sarkissian, I have a confession to make."

"Oh?"

"I'm married."

"I see."

"No, that's not true. I am not now and have never been married. But I see a psychiatrist twice a week."

"Do you need it?"

"Need it? Sure. I don't know. Yeah."

"My sister goes to one as well."

"Which sister?"

"Both, in fact. But I was thinking of Marcia."

"She sees a Swedish psychiatrist?"

"Yes."

"Which language do they use?"

"English, I expect."

"Have you had any experience with it?"

"No."

"Oh. Well, that's where I go to, anyway, Tuesdays and Thursdays, from two to three. And Monday nights I teach at the U, from six to nine. Now you can plot my movements at all times."

"Why are you in it?"

"In therapy?"

"Yes."

"Uh . . . writer's block."

"Has it helped?"

"You see me typing up a storm."

"Mmmm."

"Listen, why do you keep your cigarettes in the refrigerator?"

"Do I?"

"There's a pack of Marlboro in there."

"They're . . . not precisely cigarettes."

"What are they precisely?"

"Two cubes of sugar."

"Cubes of sugar?"

"That's right."

"LSD?"

"That's right."

"Where did you get it?"

"From Dick."

"Who's Dick?"

"The . . . painter friend who lives nearby. I stayed with them a few days before I went to Washington Heights, but his wife didn't care for the arrangement."

"That's where you got the LSD?"

"Yes."

"Have you tried it?"

"Not yet."

"How do you know Dick?"

"From Berkeley. And I saw him the last time I was in New York."

"I didn't know you were here before. I mean since you were a child."

"No, you didn't . . . It was early in 1962, right after my father died. I quit my job and stayed here a few months."

"I was still in Europe, then"—in the English countryside, in something called a Short-Term Rehabilitation Center, receiving weekly injections of magic, therapeutic lysergic acid 25, six shots in all, in alternate cheeks of my ass—"Have you ever had any LSD?"

"No. I smoked a bit of hash in Europe. I . . . have some with me. But I haven't used any for some time."

"Hash? Is that marijuana?"

"No. It's hashish."

"You brought it with you from Europe?"

"Yes."

"Jesus. You're a live one. I didn't realize. You're in the vanguard of hip."

"That isn't so."

"Well, when you're ready to take any LSD, let me know and I'll hold your hand."

"Is that necessary?"

"It's wise, Sarkissian. It's definitely advisable."

"Shall I call you Sams?"

"Why?"

"Why do you call me Sarkissian?"

"Because it fills the mouth, it's a pleasure to say. Sams lacks character."

"Hmmm."

Which was light years from "Mmmm"; this one an evaluative noise, followed by silence, while my glib explanation hung there and, one could see—a petulant shrug, a downturned lip—was found wanting. What an entirely sexual mouth she had. I am still hard put to describe it. I let the silence hang. She took her lighter from the table and toyed with it. It was a weighty, primitive machine, a long rope in a cylinder that was sparked by a wheel and somehow set to smoldering. You put your cigarette to the glowing end of the rope. A Greek fisherman had given it to her. It was totally convenient. No fluid, no flint, only the rope to replace at some dim, distant time.

"You know, we really ought to get a U.S. patent on that thing. We could make a fortune."

"How do you go about it?"

"I don't know. I'll ask Paul. He's got a business head."

All that I'd meant by this remark—my accidental superiority to the world of commerce, good sense in keeping a hand in (through friends) all the same—was lost on her, I suspected, yet she had picked up something to agree with, glanced at me, nodded vigorously, looked away; I could not help wondering then whether (and how badly) I'd erred by bringing her up to the loft that night, whether all I'd done was to set up another dull, honky-tonk disaster in the frantic attempt to prove (to whom?) that I was cured of the need . . . and did she know what was passing through my mind, was that what her glance had conveyed? I got up and strolled away from the abyss. I couldn't live as if my brain was open to the world, even if it was. And I had to grant her the same freedom of thought and action I reserved for myself.

My "freedom of action" had taken me to Jane Mason's party the day after Christa moved in. I'd been invited weeks before. Her apartment was on the Lower East Side, right around the corner from where I lived from ages nine to twenty-one, and retreated to periodically after. Through some hip gerrymandering the whole neighborhood had come to be known in some quarters as the East Village. Forty years later the same tottering tenements housed potheads and PRs and poets, instead of Italians and Jews. Given my heritage, then given my beard and aspirations, I should have felt at home down there, one way or the other. Instead I hung between worlds—the insular, bigoted, dollar-mad one I spent my young manhood cagily repudiating, at cost to myself, and the disaffiliated, half-ass, artsy-craftsy one it had become. To walk those streets, past ageing Mendy's vegetable stand, behind some long-tressed, brainless twat you had to yearn for, became a morbid, jangling pilgrimage. Although living less than a mile away, I was safe in my amorphous neighborhood, porch and garden. And there Jane Mason had been safe with me for a while. The first time I visited her place I was appalled. It was a four-floor walk-up, a lousy railroad flat in Junkyland East, top floor rear. I feared she would get herself killed, and it would be my doing for luring her (without intent) from however bad a marriage, however barren a Southwest life, on my second trip to Tucson in

1964. And so I acted, in her house, not so differently from how
my mother had when she huffed up five flights the first and last
time to visit me on Charles Street, took a slow look around,
said, Why did you do it, Jason? You know we would have
helped you out financially. To think of my son living in a
place like this. It's worse than the places I lived in as a girl. I
was furious, unmanned, I would have loved to kick her out.
And now I caught myself behaving similarly with Jane. I tried
to control it. I contented myself with suggesting that she put
locks on all her windows. But her radar is good, nor was I as
subtle and secretive as I wanted to believe. Impressionable as
a rule, absurdly open to the views of others, she here drew the
line, persisted in liking her place, seemed almost strengthened
by my lack of approbation. (Fixed it up quite pleasantly, and
in the two years she lived there, was never robbed.) So I went
to her party, six months after she moved in. I knew what she
was up to. She meant to call attention to certain changes in her
life. (I give this kind of ritual, periodic bash myself.) She'd just
gotten a new and better job, at an art gallery. Bob Kane, my
friend and co-analysand, would be officially installed as para-
mour. She wished to be surrounded by her lovers, past, present and future. I dug her enough to let her use me this way.
Letting her do so would help square certain injustices I fancied I'd committed. Also, what the hell, I liked parties. They
helped fill my pocket notebook (for later transcription of
legible entries to the larger one). Sparked by drink and close
quarters, insights abounded, flying glimpses of the way it is,
basic chemistry. For whatever you want to do, there is a
writerly excuse. For goofing off. Getting high. Giving pain.
For rising in the morning.

"Christa, I'd ask you along, but it isn't really that kind of
party."

"I didn't ask to be asked along."

"Right, you didn't. Would you like a drink?"

"Perhaps a little wine."

"Me too. Some wine. I'd better pace myself."

I tipped the jug, poured uneven amounts into two tall glasses, handed the short one over. I had some fantasy of turning her into an alcoholic, or whatever it is I was. How boorish to inflict your hang-ups on strangers who pass through your life. But how rude not to offer, or arrogant to assume she couldn't refuse. Despite her sometimes awkward, more often charming girlish gestures, as if she were still trying on, trying out, the female role, she was a woman of twenty-six, she knew her limitations or she should have, she had been around. I was mothering her in my head, then feeling bad about it, as later in the evening, with the same result, I would try to father Kane. My mind tumbled on. She received the glass in both hands and carried it to the hassock. I sprawled on the couch. I doubt it was the day's first drink, or mine. I forget what we did on our first full afternoon, alone or together—where, if anywhere, we went, what, if anything, I had accomplished. I remember being weary. I turned one of the bolsters sideways and half reclined. I still had an hour to kill. I regarded her regarding me. She sipped her wine. I entertained an odd, unbidden image: that I looked like (but how would Christa know?) my mother's father, Isaac, lying just this way at a Passover seder; I hadn't been to one in seventeen years, which was the year he died. They were joyous affairs (which was not how I recalled them on my father's side; but that bearded martinet died when I was five), crowded, melodic, alive, and there had always been a special bond between us. I was his first grandchild, I'd been named after Jacob, his father. I can still get a whiff of him at times, his private brew of Turkish cigarettes and schnapps and sweat. So he passed briefly, as I lay there, through my head and body. And did I give off—or were the emanations, to begin with, hers—the waves and aura of this private history? For she was speaking of her clan. She inter-

rupted herself at once—"This might not interest you . . ."
but it did. She knew in all detail her own conjunction with
that grisly heritage. Who had escaped the Turks and who had
not, in what manner each blood relative expired. Until that
moment I had known literally nothing about Turks and mas-
sacres. Of rape. Drownings. Slaughter by gun. Two million
dead. Diaspora. Lebanon, Iraq, Australia, four hundred thousand here. All I knew of until Christa 'was Saroyan—he had
once meant a lot to me, gave me my earliest sense of the craft
and the role—and the two lightweight sots, writers, already
mentioned, I met at an art colony the previous autumn. If I
had absorbed anything about Armenian history and troubles
from reading Saroyan, it had long since vanished. Christa re-
paired much of that. She framed herself against that backdrop
of genocide and carnage. She brought it up to date. Her parents had married in Turkish Armenia and effected separate
exits, rejoined in New York and lived there long enough to
produce all three daughters, and for her father to commence
his record of failure. An unprofitable upstate farm (her earliest memories), some real estate disasters in the city. Then they
moved to California, where he barely squeezed out a living as
an insurance salesman. (This dismal emphasis was hers.) She
still had a scattering of relatives and family friends in New
York, including the ones she had briefly stayed with. Then, I
believe, she went into her early years in California. I can't be
certain. I had drifted off. The wine, or her careful, overartic-
ulated tone, or both, had lulled me. I felt it coming and I
mumbled, warned, "I'm going to nap awhile." She was still
seated on the hassock when I woke. She had replenished her
wine. She was reading. I bolted up and squeezed my temples.
She was reading my book. Book? Could so unfeeling a clod—
outstripping my own worst fears—as I had just revealed myself to be ever write a *book?* I was genuinely shamed; I was
inordinately pleased. I had not been able to nap, unless drunk

out of mind, in several years. I thought that I had left the talent back in childhood. Had I suddenly regained it? If so, like Churchill, I now had the means to carry on forever.

"How long was I asleep?"

She was wearing her glasses. She read on for a line or two before looking up. She shrugged. "Fifteen or twenty minutes."

"Jesus. I haven't dropped off like that since I was a baby."

"Mmmm."

"I feel marvelous. An odd time to fall asleep, though, in the middle of your story. Let's say it means I trust you."

"All right."

She flashed a moderately dimpled smile. She showed no distress at my gaffe. I already suspected she would not turn out to be the simplest human being in the world to understand, but it was possible also she felt no distress. As I'd learned to do from Frank, I tacted myself—who else is ever there?—and concluded that if *she* had crapped out in the midst of any account of mine dealing with the six million, I'd be similarly disinclined to take it personally, or feel that the six million had in any way been slighted. But this was hypothetical. It was more than unlikely I would ever give one. No one nearer than a third cousin or great aunt had died in that war, nor had I come to know any of the kin who had escaped to this country. In any larger way, short of the largest, I felt no involving urge, no outraged identity. Doubtless the loss is mine: clues to my physiognomy and soul lie in there somewhere, back in some *shtetl* or some oven, and someday I will look into it further, for just such private reasons, but my opinion at that moment was, Jew me no Jews, six million me no six million. Don't disturb me with alarums of the Third Reich resurgent, nor clog my mailbox with Hebrew calendars from the Haifa School for the Blind. My lady, now, was closer to the maelstrom, she existed because a pair of people slipped away from a pogrom, and even so there was something of rote to her account, she spun it like some dutiful or Apollonian bard, free of warmth and ragings . . . but this, I'd come to see, was her general anecdotal style. Anyway, I'd slept; woke, brushed my teeth, put on a coat, requested, after a moment's thought, that she do me the favor of answering the phone, and went off to the party.

I arrived early, already fairly oiled, hopeful of good talk and charming company. Two hours later the pickings remained lean. Jane was a woman—their name is legion—who accumulate through life (or invite to their parties) only those female acquaintances less handsome than themselves. She'd gone to college in the East, so she knew any number of plain girls living in the city. I thought, in the circumstances, to zero in on Jane herself, discuss old times, but she was manic, very much the bustling, nervous hostess, attempting to give equal time. I went out to the kitchen and joined up with Kane, who leaned against the refrigerator sipping a gin, aloof or shy. He would have loved to roll a joint and suck it in congenial company, himself and Jane, but was prudent and parsimonious in a crowd. Yet he seemed content enough without it—teased me about this and that with barbed, disconcerting irony. He was living in the world. She'd done that much for him in their few months together, and would do more in the time ahead. She was the first girl he'd gone to bed with in several years, possibly the first in his life who had ever pursued him. She must have mentioned four times a day that she loved him. She oohed and cooed in bed. Her morning breath had never been the best (no longer my problem), but this could be adjusted to. That subsequently, when he was truly opened, peering wide-eyed from his catatonic shell, earnestly considering giving up his mad unwritten opus (Hindu-Christian-Buddhist-Pagan-Anthropological-Mythical-Mystical-Social Treatise on the World from Its Magical Inceptions to the Uptight Present Times) and doing some art reviews, which he hoped to sell, she dropped him and turned her attention to some other hopeless case, having just returned from her quickie divorce down South, where (she charmingly confessed to me later) she lowered her pants several times for disparate types in the course of a week in various parts of La Ciudad, not without real peril to her person, well, this is another story, nor one about which I can too easily moralize. And no real harm done anyway. Kane was open to Covington at last; the fifty-minute silences became rare, he remembered dreams, leapt forward, came part way back to us, and if Frank took the credit due Jane, no real harm done there either.

Has there been a first-rate novel about twins? I haven't looked to see. It seems a precious lode. It interests me, at any rate. I was sired by one, which did not simplify my life. Bob Kane's being born one did little to ease his. In our college days he came to the house several times and Harry took a liking to him. He offered him cigars, and clapped him on the shoulder. Once, I remember, both of them were there, Bob and his twin brother Dick, and Harry, might I say, was nearly beside himself. (Today, whenever I see my father, he runs through my friends of that era in a time-stopping litany, do I still see this one, what do I hear from that one, with special affection for the Kanes.) There was a time, as recently as five years ago, when it was no simple matter to tell Bob and Dick Kane apart. They were the only children of a toy executive, who mostly traveled, and a woman of high culture. They were raised together, played high school football together, dated together, held virtually all other interests and possessions in common. But they attended different colleges, trying to attain separate lives. I met Bob Kane in 1951, in our sophomore year. We were both nineteen. I envied the breadth of his talents: he wrote poetry, acted, painted, projected a play about Nijinsky, read widely in Eastern philosophy and religion a decade before they would become coffee-house chatter masquerading as the zeitgeist. Dick, who I got to know later, plodded toward a B.A. in sociology a few hundred miles up the coast. They seemed to have found their different places. But they were drafted together on graduation, in 1953, and stationed together for two years, in Fort Benning, Georgia. When that ended, Bob went to Mexico City to paint and Dick went to graduate school, throwing over sociology for a master's degree in Fine Arts. And in the years that followed, he built a life. He taught at a Long Island prep school, began to sculpt (specializing finally in Chinese boxlike structures with complex mirror systems, after a long apprenticeship during which he produced, exclusively, life masks of his face), and married a girl from Texas, elder sister to the mistress of the incontinent beagle, an unbright, devious girl with simian features but a nice cowy build, deep painterly ambition, some real drafting skills, and an unerring nose for the fashion: when the hour was ripe to be abstract-expressionist, she was; when pop art was in, or beginning the downswing, pop she feverishly produced; struggling at this instant, or when last I looked, to discover her voice, or whether she has one, and I wish her all success. Sculpting made difficult—they shared a studio—by his wife's small notoriety, her knack of installing herself in time for a one-man show in some toppling giant's shadow, Dick began to write. He had, he discovered, a stiff, erudite style, well suited to the long view. He became the chronicler, esthetician-advocate of fairyland, where boundaries fade, history merges with art, paint becomes theatre, theatre is noise, spontaneity is enshrined, inventiveness, however limp, is loved, shmuckdom on a given day is genius; he strove to render fresh and even daring areas and approaches whose possibilities for moving or useful statement had been exhausted forty years before; ultimately an apology for his wife's work, or substitute for his own, but a genuine book, a fact-filled book; I treasure my inscribed copy, and I'm pleased to report that it enjoyed a de-cent sale. By this time as well he had learned to live with a five-year backache and a headache of slightly shorter duration, infirmities which dated from the time he began to believe that his wife was sleeping around, and which thereafter, since they really laid him out, sort of obliged her to do so. (Desexed, narcissistic twin, frantic high-clitted bitch, pelvis like a blunted spear, I doubt they fucked with real intelligence, ever.) But they hang together, after eight long years, from fear of the unknown, or some deeper thing, which a man with a couch could elucidate, did either employ one, sucking sustenance from other people's still more baleful disasters, a life of its kind for our times . . . while Bob Kane went down. I still have his letters, from 1956, while I was living in Kyoto, which begin to describe it. Amphetamines and mescal and maryjane and tequila and groovy visions * shading to full-blown psychotic episodes, the whole freaked-out mystico-Mexico life, talents unused and expiring, a police bust, jail, expulsion, pad in the East Village, or Lower East Side (right up the street, in fact, from where Abe Sams, a *doppel* on his own, held hand on gun protecting the patrimony from bums, thieving mainliners, Puerto Ricans, and the like, the junkyard from which he'd eased out my father years before; the dominant ((though five minutes younger)) twin by birth, my Uncle Abe, and with

* ". . . And all the visions are not on pot or peyote. Maybe the best are, or you get a feeling of them, of their location, and can turn them on (if you don't try) like seeing in a bus: Mexico more real because I was not, I was a story, literature, which would tell itself despite all I might do to interfere, and outside was just the world (manifested now in the shapes of Mexico). And this was just the reverse of the situation of—was it a week ago or two?—turning on in my room here and having everything outside disappear, dissolve in the same brilliant light that streamed into the darkness through the thin cracks in the double doors, disappear and become *Literature;* the Spanish voices from downstairs turning to characters from Lorca, the light a Lorca-light, burning plains, adobe, etc.; eventually becoming inhabited by names, symboled beings in the shape of words, Goethe, Nietzsche, Proust, Sartre, etc., etc., etc. *All Literature*—All of it—and only inside the room was real. (Though it later took on the nature of a stage.)"

the foresight to produce a dynasty, two sons, *bulvans,* my cous-
ins, who followed him into the trade; let me be clearer, since I
mean to drop it now, the animus is no longer between them, if
ever it was; it lives in my own guilt, my mother's short-
changed rage; these sixty-year-old twins, poor sundered
lovers, still phone each other three times a day), living on
drugs, once-fine brain addling, commencing his so-called
book while his so-called friends robbed him blind; then pulling out abruptly, briefly, when his father died. His father died
at dawn, alone, in a suite of rooms in the Tokyo Imperial
Hotel, a set of toy trains running on the floor the while—or
this is the official version. And Bob went to live with his
mother. He was then twenty-nine. They drank a lot together
and discussed the theatre section of the Sunday *Times.* He
dabbled with paint. She was respectful when he sat watching
the ball game, protecting his privacy, even from his friends.
She ignored the hemp he was trying to grow in the garden. In
due course he broke, one weekend, during a visit from brother
Dick—whose features and body had coarsened, while Bob
grew still more pasty and lean; only strangers would confuse
them now—and wife, accusing Dick of having always despised him and feared him, yet having at the same time in
some horrible way dispossessed, become him; claimed to be
fearful of incursions still to come, physical and spiritual, and
offered violence. He was tranquilized, hospitalized, released
in six weeks, and went back to live with Mrs. Kane. He
couldn't apply for a job; he feared returning to the city. Once,
when he did come in to visit, and we were well into a jug of
wine, I said that the scene he was playing, Life with Mother,
seemed *gothic* to me; the soul of tact, I didn't pursue it in the
face of his hurt. But the next time I saw him he let me sell him
Covington.

    And I'm delighted that it's him, my familiar, no threaten-
ing, well-hung stranger, replacing me in Jane Mason's life.

(Or I assume this reasonable posture when the shock wears off.) We kept it in the family. I passed the torch. I'd been trying to drop her ever since she arrived in New York the previous summer, so she simplified matters by dumping me. This makes the best of it, of course; rejection is always a drag, whatever one's own plans. (Of Jane I still think fondly, my "rubicund librarian," as I called her, bespectacled blondeness, too-large belly, quaint-hip poetry she wrote, conical African tits.) In the kitchen, his whey, oval face smiling down, Bob Kane teased me hard. Along the lines of my recent worldly success —grants, sizeable advances—and how little I had really done to earn it. He seemed so sure that he was being good-natured, and so clearly wasn't, that I flushed with a warmth close to love and clapped him on the shoulder. He seemed a little stunned by this, and I know I was myself. Rotarianism, drunk or no, is not my style. I have what may still be called a "touch problem," shrink from being clapped and grabbed (as from clapping and grabbing), particularly by males. Bob being similarly afflicted, perhaps a little worse, what made me come on that way? I'd known the man for fifteen years, and never, it was abruptly clear, had I been easy in his company. I'd never found the proper mask, never felt, with Bob, the way I thought I wanted to feel. I'm certain it was mutual. Yet we were friends.

"Well, buddy," he says, "digging the party?"

"I can't say it really grabs me, no."

"How come? Too many intellectuals?"

"Yeah, that must be it. Also a nagging sense of responsibility. I left a lonely lady back in my apartment."

"Your little teenager?"

"Little teenager? Oh, I told you about Leslie. No, she's gone, she's back at school. This one is something else, a California girl just back from Europe. My Japanese scholar friend in Tucson put her onto me when she came through . . ."

A thin-lipped grin. Real distress colors his irony. "You know, I'd settle for a fourth of your supply. Teenies, girls from California by way of Europe via Tucson . . . how do you do it, man?"

He has Miss Mason, but I don't think he really trusts it, yet: doesn't know if he can hold it, or even whether he wants to. And it's true that I'm breaking his balls. He's right to counter-attack; I only wish he were better at it. And I know what I'm doing, what uneasy role has claimed me. I'm playing Pisacano to his Jason Sams, wise-ass worldling to his lonesome poet, while denying fortissimo that my money, my wenching, my crassness in any way subverts my sensibility. But no one has said that it has. If I wanted to drive a cross-country trailer for a living, singing madrigals from coast to coast, with a one-legged whore in the cab, no one was likely to object, least of all Bob Kane. My father, perhaps, or at one time—mocked, with some reason, my automotive skills, been genuinely mortified by the music; but those formative days were far behind.

"I . . . was thinking I'd go to Baltimore sometime soon. Perhaps the day after tomorrow."

"How long will you be gone?"

"I don't know. A few days, a week . . ."

"That long?"

"Probably not. I can't be sure."

"Well . . . okay."

She had warned me of this journey. She had a classmate named Daisy living there, now married, with a young child. I had hoped, pretty nearly expected—for when things are going well, life can seem a series of such ripe contingencies—that she would make the trip in the middle of February, when Leslie Dale would be in town for a few between-semester days.

I wanted to see Leslie Dale. I acknowledged her claim.
Though she knew we were star-crossed, affected amazement at
her luck, tried to stay cool in her letters, she let slip nonetheless that I was one of her two favorite adults, the other being
her besotted Medusa of a widowed writer mother. At seventeen Leslie was unformed, a little on the chubby side, an indifferent lay, but I did not shrink from my responsibilities. I'd
once more take her to my bosom, indulge my guru and Pyg-
malion drives. This involved putting her up a night or two,
guilding her sensibilities, and fucking her a couple of times.
With Christa in residence, it was not going to be easy.

"Would you rather I went some other time?"

Would I rather it didn't appear she read minds?

"No, dear, go when you please. Come when you please.
You're a free agent."

She left a couple of days later, on a Sunday, informing her
friends with a collect call the night before. We lay around till
noon, then she threw some things in the plaid case I'd borrowed from Sarah Shwartz. I'd phoned Sarah at work and
asked for it on Friday afternoon. I had the keys to her one-
room apartment as she had a set to mine. I had not seen her
since Christa moved in, though I could hear her pottering at
the sink, singing along with her Streisand, through the
kitchen vent. She hardly ever went out, except to her job.
When I had anything going for me (let alone a boarder), I'd
lock her out of my life. When I'd landed in the shit, or felt
bored or lonely, I'd.drop in, or ask her in, spill my guts in
depth, we'd both get stoned, and I'd likely spend some time
between those porky thighs. The exchange of keys was useful.
When I was out of town, or late of an evening getting back,
she'd feed and love the cat. If she wanted a piece of meat defrosted during the day for her solitudinous evening meal,
she'd phone from her office and I'd go next door and yank it
out, though not always with good grace. She was twenty-six

years old. She was Jewish, Brooklyn-born, and hung up on her mother, obvious manifestations of any of which incensed me. Her grocer father was long gone (I hardly knew a girl at that time whose father still lived). She could hear my women come and go, and sometimes, she said, through that same vent, could hear them performing. I suppose she alternately liked me, raged alone, or wrote me off as a nut. Paul, noisily contemptuous, labeled her my "sexual insurance." There was little enough drama to our first drunken coupling, or any that I recall, but she claimed to have been a virgin. I suppose it was technically so. It was helpful to believe it. Every man should do everything once, even late in life. Deflower a virgin. Raise a cat. (Suck a cock? Kill a man?) Cultivate a garden.

I wished, however, in category one, that I had done better than Sarah Shwartz.

One thing she did which was nice was describe her first orgasm, if such it was, as "blue."

Christa showed no curiosity about her benefactress, though she seemed pleased enough with the bag. We went for brunch to Arthur's Corner, a newly opened restaurant on Twentieth and Second Avenue. It was little more in its appointments than a fancy luncheonette, but it had a broad, exotic menu. They were featuring a squab luncheon for $2.35. I felt suddenly festive. I thought of my tiny apartment, which had proved in a pinch it could live two, if not in commodious fashion—I would have it returned to me now. I would have *myself* returned to me for the space she was gone. Not that her presence had much impinged on my movement; but I'd brought to bear a certain nervy solicitousness, a gratuitous hotelier's concern, and it would be good, whatever its source, to be able to shed it for a while.

I would have *myself* returned to me; which did not preclude a sense of loss impending, a nudge of regret. Trying, as always, to have it both ways. Endangering either. As we studied the menu in the window, I squeezed her waist, then turned and kissed her ear, the dainty fraction showing through her hair.

"Listen, let's have some squab."

"I'm not that hungry . . . it's expensive, isn't it?"

"Expensive?"

"It says two dollars and thirty-five cents."

"Christa, you have no real conception of my income. All right, you dine on Ry Krisp. I'm for the squab."

She ordered it too. We sat in a booth to the rear of the restaurant. While we waited I phoned Penn Station to check on trains to Baltimore. She hadn't bothered. She assumed they ran often enough. There was a convenient train at two, an hour and a half away. The meal was marvelous. Everything was tasty—spinach, stuffing, wild rice, salad, rolls, right down to the ornamental crab apple. We stuffed ourselves in silence. Finally I broke it.

"You know, you're the world's luckiest lady."

"Why do you say that?"

"Friends to visit down the Eastern Seaboard, a hearth to return to . . ."

She did some impatient, shrugging thing, accompanied by a hot dark glance which did not (since I could not tell what it aimed at) disturb my equanimity, though I was fairly certain it was so intended. My remark was innocent, affectionate, daubed at worst with a diffusive irony, but this is how some of us talk. Or lead our lives. But the silence closed down again, bringing home, if nothing else, that we were strangers.

Finally, over coffee, she said, "Am I making you uncomfortable?"

"Is that your intention?"

"No."

"Why should I be uncomfortable?"

"We're . . . not saying much."

"We were gorging ourselves."

"Mmmhmm."

"You'd better let me have your address in Baltimore."

"I have no pen."

I handed her my pen. She scrawled Daisy's name, address and phone number on a paper napkin in the back-slant, loopy hand I'd learned to recognize.

"You may be the only Californian left-handed female painter in the neighborhood, you know?"

"I suppose it's possible."

"Is anyone else in your family left-handed?"

"Marcia is. My father was."

"They say it screws you up a bit."

"Do they?"

"But they're in no great shape themselves." I pocketed the napkin. "Thank you."

"Why did you want it?"

"For emergencies, I guess. Maybe your old lady will call. Maybe just so I'll know where you are."

"Oh."

She'd phoned her mother once, collect, while I was there, and given her my phone number and address, but she continued to receive her mail at American Express. On some of her out-mail, however, she had written my address as a return, so it was a matter of time before they would be arriving Sarkissian c/o Sams. As innkeeper, this would present me with a minor problem. A number of locksmiths on earlier occasions had pronounced my mailbox key unduplicatable, and so I had no spare. I would always be *au courant* with what she got. I decided we could learn to live with that. We caught a north-bound cab on Third Avenue. Penn Station was a ravaged cathedral, in the midst of being destroyed or rebuilt or replaced, it was impossible to tell. Networks of naked girders, broken vaults, garbling loudspeakers, wandering crowds, called up all the mysterious, oddly homogeneous European terminals in which so many of my dramas had been played, what a tear-jerking wealth, over five years, of arrivals and departures: St. Pancras, Gare d'Austerlitz, Victoria, Estación de Fráncia, Malmö, Esha, Britta, Jason, Dino, en route, hello, again goodbye . . . and it occurred to me that Christa, so newly back, so mobile in her time abroad, must have had her share of them too. We located the ticket booth after some trouble, she brought her round-trip ticket, and we still had time to wander. We paused before the mock-up of the mammoth indoor sports-arena-plus-station they were erecting on the site. After careful study we could find no provision for entrances or exits, and shared a laugh at some poor architect's expense. Then without warning I was delivering a lecture on priorities, the morality of building multimillion-dollar sports arenas while half the city lived like pigs—what was wrong with the Madison Square Garden we had, in which I'd spent so many rousing adolescent hours? what was the trouble with the Penn Station they were ripping down, with its inspiring Greek façade?—and from here it seemed a short journey to the illness of our Times, by way of the White House and the shrewd, sick, gross, ignorant man it had seemed at the time we had no option but to put there, who conferred with his bloody lieutenants and talked to us of peace, then spread unspeakable destruction . . . I thought I was railing, to an audience of none, and broke off to peck her dark, Armenian cheek in the everlasting present. Dark . . . the girl had a way of being pale and dark-complected at the same time. She said, "We had just come to Barcelona when I heard that Kennedy had been killed. It was in the lobby of a hotel we were trying to get into but it was full up, some feria or other. We wound up in the attic. It was so chaotic . . . my Spanish wasn't very good, the whole episode was unreal. It was a day or two before I could believe it." Well. It was a day or two before we could believe it in the King's own, in our own wild, familiar land. I wondered who her "we" was, almost a reflex, without real curiosity. Then some terrible Martian message came crackling over the P.A., which seemed to relate to her train. The departure board was not functioning. We strolled toward gate 5. The queue began to move just as we got there. It was fairly long, moving slowly, and I decided not to wait, not strain at small talk. The welling sadness I chalked up to habit, the nature of stations; there was no other way at that point I cared to explain it. I'd known her less than two weeks, barely time to grow attached; besides which she was returning in two or three days' time. I kissed her near the nose, handed over Sarah's bag, which I'd been carrying.

"No maudlin farewells, puss. Enjoy yourself. I'll see you later."

"Yes."

I took her hand, carried it to arm's length, dropped it slowly and departed. Seconds later I glanced back, but she was already part of the moving throng.

And I was lonely. I walked south along Seventh Avenue and east down empty side streets, through the grim Sunday pall which lay on that part of the city. It was cloudy and cold. At Twenty-third and Fifth I went into a pay booth and rang Paul, but he wasn't home, or wasn't answering. I assumed it was the latter. He was a genius at letting the phone rattle on when he was occupied. Scoring points with whomever he was with, avoiding complications. On my part, I could not resist the lure of that machine, its open-ended promise, and I've picked it up at times, in positions, I'm reluctant to describe. I tried to think of someone else I might want to spend time with, but no one came to mind. I walked by Paul's loft. The windows were shuttered, no light came through. So he was away after all, probably in Jersey, scrabbling after that first million. He'd been on the verge of seven figures ever since I'd

known him. According to Dino it was nine parts bullshit, and
I could never follow the fiscal maneuverings when Paul attempted to describe them (though I was flattered that he tried,
and he let me find some virtue in my ignorance), but for all I
knew, or cared, his fortune was assured. Whereas Dino was less
charitable. But they were always backbiting each other. It was
one more variety of friendship.

I was suddenly glad of the solitude. I remembered the bottle of Johnnie Walker Black. She'd bought it tax-free at
Luxembourg Airport, but not sprung it on me until the night
before: "I'll leave this for the house," she said. "The house
thanks you," I said, and guaranteed to leave a dram for her return. I'd go back and court that waiting fifth—introduce
myself, leave my card, move in at a sensible hour. In Sweden,
with Britta, almost always in the bag by the time she returned
from office work at five, I'd patiently explain that no, little
friend, I hadn't been drinking alone, I never drank alone, I
was partying with the troupe in my head, the soon-to-be-born,
my characters. She was too kind or dim to say that downing
aquavit with them from nine to five was no way to bring them
to the light. But by then, 1961, we were close to the end of our
time. I walked more rapidly. Thoughts of the phone, as well as
the scotch, moved me now. It might bring adventure on my
head, maybe even riches, if I were only there to pick it up. And
I thought also of my Underwood-Olivetti, which I'd be able
now, if not obliged, to face in earnest. I'd seen a cartoon a few
days before in which a man lolls besotted on a couch, tie
askew, idiotic smile, bottle dangling from his hand, while at
the typewriter close by the winged muse pounds fiercely. It
had wrung forth a laugh. It was as funny as a blow to the kid-
neys.

The cat was seated by the door when I sprang open the second lock. He greeted me in his fashion, which was to turn his
back the moment my face appeared. I don't know who he

was ever expecting, but it didn't seem to be me. He wanted
out; I unbolted the doors and let him into the garden. Soon he
was high into the overgrown, tree-high privet planted in a
neighboring yard but with its limbs extending into mine,
leaping and picking his way through the winter branches.
They buzzed him near the top, one of the four pair of bluejays
who lived there all year round, making squawking passes
inches from his head, fearless. These brazen, gaudy birds
seemed more so where my pussy was concerned. It took, I
thought, more of his energy and concentration to keep his
footing in the branches than other passing felines seemed to
expend. But he was a late starter. He'd caught no bird of any
description in our fifteen months together, which was all
right with me. And even now, to malign him no further, he
kept his head, concentrated on footwork, ignored their scold-
ing swipes. He was playing in their ball park, there was some
bravery in that. He leapt the final yard onto the fence,
meowed, and strutted along the fence toward the house, cocky
as if returning from some triumph.

I was home. Alone. It felt fine. I sniffed for her presence. No
heavy scent fogged the rooms. Whatever I thought I had detected in her Hamburg remarks, she did not confuse the idea
of femininity with the idea of the whorehouse. Her worldly
goods were for the most part tucked away, in her suitcase, in
the closet, in her bureau drawers. A few pens and brushes, jars
of paint and ink, sat neatly on the drop-leaf table. She would sit
on the hassock when she drew, hunched over that table. It did
not look very comfortable, but I had no better arrangement to
suggest. I was most often in the back room when she worked
(or my going there would trigger her attempts), but popped
out from time to time to check on the silence. She appeared
uneasy only if I peered over her shoulder, so I soon stopped
doing that. Otherwise, not looking up, she drew and penciled
on. I looked into the closet. She hadn't had much clothing to

begin with, and had taken some of it to Baltimore. A gray wool
dress, a pair of skirts, the white blouse, were bunched neatly on
the left. Natural enough when she was there, they seemed
alien to me now. Her suitcase was pushed under the old, de-
crepit sofa; with her help I'd carted that sofa in from the porch
some days before and moved it to the back room. A portfolio
of drawings leaned against the wall in the closet, beneath her
clothes. I handled it, without moving it, leafing through. I was
looking for the green sketchbook she'd already shown me, but
it wasn't there. Perhaps it was in her suitcase, or in one of her
drawers, or she had taken it with her. The drawings, I noticed,
were signed "Sarkissian," and they were dated, as far back as
1962; I was pleased to see she had a practical side, had taken
samples of her work abroad. With mingled fear and virtue I
left the folio as I'd found it. But when I stood, my eye landed
on the dresser, and amid the jumble of things, the chessboard,
chess pieces, isometric bar, matches, magazines, what cosmet-
ics she used, I saw the manilla folder crammed with her mail.
I'd noticed it before, but could easily ignore it while she was
around. Now I knew, if it had ever really been in doubt, that I
would do no work that afternoon.

I rolled in a piece of paper all the same, stared a bit, then
dated the page. I spun round in the swivel chair (on long-term
loan from Pisacano) and went to the kitchen for the Johnnie
Walker Black. I poured a healthy shot, threw in a couple of
cubes, returned to the desk and lit a cigarette. The date
seemed to commit me to my journal, which I'd been neglect-
ing of late, at least since Christa arrived—it contained, for
example, not one entry relating to her presence. On the other
hand, my novel was not writing itself, to my occasional surprise; it would be wiser to plunge into *Gino Travels,* the part
I'd been circling for weeks, the Paris/dirty postcards scene.
Debating, I sipped at the scotch. Bells sounded in my head,
intimations of chemical changes. I remembered that the

brand was as special as the circumstances in which I had received it, and resolved to make a connosieur's effort to note
the difference. I sipped again. It tasted thin, ordinary. Perhaps my palate was at fault, perhaps they faked you out in
Luxembourg (just as "Colgate" toothpaste has a different taste
from land to land); you only bought the label when you
bought at tax-free ports. Why couldn't I relax, joyously pretend, at least, that I was living well? The telephone rang, blasting through the house. I'd turned both phones to "loud" when
I came in. It rang a second time, a third; I was letting it ripen,
trying to shape the adventure. Only Gillian came to mind,
halting, British-voiced, abject, pleading to be allowed to drop
around, to be shriven, forgiven, and in her white stockings,
which I loved, ceremoniously fucked in the ass. In all likelihood I would permit it. I had the time to smile widely in the
wall-length mirror, condoning my transparency, playpen
vindictiveness. I picked it up on the fourth ring. It was Gardella. A flush of disappointment; though he was, I thought
wryly, Gillian-connected. It did not seem portentous or risky
that my hero, so to speak, should phone in the midst of my
struggle to get him down. Any time he called, these days, I
could say that the battle was in progress. And I'd lived
through this kind of hopeless magic long before. After he
left our London room that morning, retreating penniless
with no prospects back to the U.S., and after I'd spent the
next few days in bed in the dark recovering from him and
from the first attack of what would become a chronic iritis, I
woke one morning to my ending, Gino had traveled, finis, and
wrote my heart out for the next couple of months until I got a
letter from a new address, not the Bronx, and damn if that joc-
ular candidate for bedlam had not gone and gotten *married,*
to a girl he'd met two weeks before. The letter went on to describe their new West Village apartment, the furniture they
were acquiring, and how she was Jewish, beautiful and a

buyer. Again I took to my bed, this time with Beckett's trilogy, which is nonparagraphed, so there was no real way to stop, and when I rose again, depleted, and sneaked back to the novel, there seemed no choice but to start it over. Similar dislocations, open-ended vistas, had plagued me in the years since. This was the main trouble with working from life—your people didn't lie down. But by now, I fancied, I'd hacked my way out of that jungle.

Until this call, I hadn't heard from or tried to reach Gardella in quite a while. This was the way it had been ever since I got back from Europe in the summer of '62 and met him accidentally on Sixth Avenue (we had stopped corresponding months before) and he took me up to meet his spouse: a couple of contacts close in time, then a long spell with none. These had grown longer before, during and after his murderous divorce. He had married a girl of whom Pisacano might say, perhaps he did, that she was sent up by central casting, an arid foul-mouthed garment-center bitch with intellectual pretensions, perennial taker of New School philosophy courses and poetry workshops and noisy second-guesser of where the prof went wrong, the perfect girl to marry if you wanted your balls sewn into your head, or to merely spend the better part of every day in bickering and anguish. She would burst into his room at the end of her working day to see how many pages he had written. (He was substitute-teaching at the time.) Dino professed himself flattered by some of this, accepting of the rest, for a year and a half. Then he had almost broken a blood vessel in his neck trying not to kill her. Now, under Covington's tender tutelage, he had just started dating again, and this was how he'd come to phone. (And apropos of Frank, I affected to be amused that the gray man slipped on several occasions and called me Dino, as he had also apparently once called Dino Jason . . . but I was closer to enraged. And uneasy with that reaction, too. A terrible ambivalence! But how could I really complain? Wasn't Covington's precisely the sort of confusion my book was trying to be about?) He had dropped off a girl somewhere in my neighborhood—it was wholly in keeping with my idea of Dino that his dates should end on a late Sunday afternoon—and thought he would stop by. I suspected I was second choice, that he had rung up Pisacano first, but I had still better reasons to refuse. I would love to see him, I said, even on such short notice, but I was well into something and couldn't break off now. He was very understanding. He'd go home, he thought, and do some work himself. I said I'd call him later in the week. I hung up, glad of my will power, dismayed by my fraudulence.

I wondered what Sarkissian was doing: reading me, per- haps, at this very moment. She'd taken the book along. Now, why should I be disadvantaged in the world, more naked than my friends, because I'd thrust a volume into the public do- main? People had already analyzed it to death, and me as well, and they weren't always wrong. Her art work was fair game by this reckoning, although I knew it was the letters I was after. (As for that treasure chest, why—usually so circumspect— had she left the goddamned thing around?) I looked to see that the door was locked, the chain in place. I went to the closet. Gingerly I carried the portfolio back to the desk, pushed the typewriter out of the way, and began leafing through.

Europe was largely a bust, as she had said: a couple of har- bor views, some fishermen emptying their nets, and that was all. Whatever else she'd done during the past eighteen months must have been contained in the green book, unless she'd sent some of it home to California. The earlier work was not re- markable. A pen-and-ink standing nude, '63 (which I have good reason to remember), with a pronounced art-class flavor, a young bearded man seated on a patio staring sensitively off toward mountains. Others which I moved quickly through, hurrying to what she'd done while she was here. There were perhaps a dozen dated Jan/Feb 1965. At least, I thought, one of us was working, and experienced a rush of midwifely joys. And I liked them, too, after studying awhile. They were in crayon, chiefly oranges and blacks, thick, chaotic swirls and swatches from which figures seemed almost to emerge, hints of limbs and torsos and featureless faces struggling toward birth, toward Bethlehem; my response was more verbal than visceral, but it seemed to fit her style. I hoped she made the scene one day, à la the young Mrs. Kane, so I could do a piece about her for the *Art News*. Broadening my own career horizons as well. I gulped some scotch. I was having a fine time. I turned reluctantly to the last drawing in the folder. It was different from the rest. It was in pencil. It was of me . . . of her . . . it was of Christa being fucked, is the way to describe it. The beard was trimmer than in life, eyes a little wilder, hairy buttocks leaner, but indubitably myself, astride an ample female whose hair fanned over an invisible pillow, her arms and legs protruding from beneath my covering weight, the face turned on camera but features merely suggested by brief wavy lines, which yet could not conceal that it was Christa, and that the drawing belonged to her. I fell into it just that way. I knew exactly how it looked, felt, smelled, to be fucked by Jason Sams. That leering satyr had her pinned, chest to bosom, leg over leg, ass raised slightly for the downthrust, pounding it home, in all his naked shame and glory. She'd rendered every inch of violence, lad tearing into lass, which is a way of looking at the act of love. I got up and walked around. I splashed some water on my face. It didn't help. I had perceived what I had perceived: that I existed for her in ways I did not exist for myself. *Madre*. A little dull home truth, quirkily presented, can shock you near to madness. That others do not see us as we see ourselves.

I was living now with a much more formidable woman than

the one I had seen off a few hours before. A wise man would
have learned from this, cut his losses, stayed out of her mail. In
my case, there was not the slightest chance I would not be into
it now. She lived in my house, she impinged on my fortunes. I
was virtually obliged to probe past the teasing glimpses she'd
allowed me in her unsolicited and highly edited accounts,
which created curiosity much more than they assuaged it. In
particular I'd get a better line on Denby, see what he had put
into her head regarding me, whether (or how) his epistolary
manner to the pair of us differed, and maybe also learn how a
man of such exquisite taste and timing as to withdraw his
penis when the lady teetered on the verge could yet manage to
hold her esteem, as he so clearly did. But I knew I would not
stop (nor even begin) with Denby, once into the pile.

I became wonderfully cautious. It seemed imperative that
each letter be replaced exactly as and where I found it, more to
prove my competence, no doubt, than for practical reasons.
For who has memorized the exact shape and order of his mail?
Perhaps someone has. A broad fidelity, at least, a samesideup-
ness, ought to be maintained. I opened the portfolio. It contained an impressive quantity of letters. Rubber bands kept
some in small, tight piles, but a great many were loose. Not all
were in envelopes. Some faced one way, some another. I went
off to the kitchen, washed down two Vitamin B-complex pills,
and wished that I had drunk a little less. I was going to have
trouble remembering what went where, and if I kept drinking, I knew, I would stop caring. I took the top letter (disturbing nothing) from the pile. It was airmailed from London. I
give it here in its entirety.

Jan 16

Darling C

Got your wild, wild letter today. By God you are a menace!
Even through the letter I felt the vibrations. I got hard just read-

ing. I wonder that the hotel didn't catch fire. It's only thanks to the general blindness of men that a line wasn't formed at your door. Are you lucky they are blind or not? I look forward to your "virginal vulva" with unconcealed lust and excitement. But if you are so "brimming" as you call it, can you save it? If no exceptional people: masturbate! I've decided that's much less destructive. Whatever, please be careful of infection. I want my Christa so hungrily and by then so ravenously, it would be hell to have you sick.

Yes, I'll buy Doridene. I asked on the way home and they have "Doridine" is it the same? Sedative? I'll try it and see if it's good.

Write me here. I have reservations for Feb 10, but can go 13th or 17th. Best I suppose is you see Daisy in Baltimore and I can come there and make you in Daisy's warm house. Or if some hitch, tell me where and of course I'll agree.

You must make good your promises. An aggressive Christa to carry out lustful designs on me. That provides me with material enough to keep me warm for a lot of lonely nights.

And more later. Keep warm.

All of it.

T.

All of it. Straight off the mark, I had this neatly and completely fucked myself—bulled my way into her wild and woolly past and found it waiting in her future. There was a sense of justice in it all. What I hadn't known had done me no harm. *T* was her Tim, of course, purloiner of her cherry, holder of her hand when she gave up some other man's fetus in Tangier. Such acts, in tandem, add up to love. One could not compete with love. It had not occurred to me until then that I'd wanted to. Our entire brief association, as deeply as I'd bothered to explore it, had been based on her being in transit, elsewhere committed in mind and body, as unlikely to make any claims as to want to be claimed. That, at least, was the way it had started. Proximity had wreaked some changes, ending in the desolate way I had felt at the station. Or I upgraded that

feeling now, deciding at the same time that I hadn't a hope in
hell of holding her as more than a lark on the face of this
glimpse into her mail. Nor would any sane man want to. What
kind of letter was it to write to a girl? What torrid epistle,
rather, was this one so clearly in response to, lifting and quot-
ing back its spiciest phrases? I had known she was interested in
sex, but this was ridiculous. The safest approach was to regard
her as a colleague, partner in intrigue, worthy of my own
machinations and concerns. In fact, my current problem, how
to work in Leslie Dale, paled beside her own. The letter was
dated two days before we met, she had gone right out (before
she could have received it) and met an exceptional person,
there was absolutely no need, my brother, to destructively or
otherwise masturbate; of what substance was he made, this
priapic, saintly male?

She had just gone to Baltimore. To Daisy's warm house.
She'd worked it out, the clever bitch. I poured myself a drink.
I toasted her success. I sought new pregnant meanings in our
over-the-squab exchange. Then I realized the dates were
wrong: that (unless he'd changed his plans, and so informed
her at American Express) he'd not be arriving for another
week at least. So she had gone, in fact, to visit with her girl
friend, spouse and child. The crisis, if there was to be one, lay
ahead. My heart began to race, striving to bring it near. I
jerked myself back to the job at hand. I barely cared now what
went where. I rippled through, ignoring a rubber-banded
packet from her mother, letters which spanned the eighteen
months, addressed to Mykonos, Stockholm, Paris, Rome,
Madrid. I fished out a long, lone one from her sister. It was on
airmail paper, toilet-thin, two pages of single-spaced type-
script, both sides of the page. It was difficult to read unless you
kept it from the light. Specialized voyeur that I'd become, I
struggled through. It was an unparseable mixture of her own
anguish with advice to her younger sister on how to live her

life. The distinction between herself and Christa did not seem
so clear in her head. Even so, much of the instructional stuff
seemed solicited, a shrill response to specific dilemmas and
complaints. I remembered Marcia's story, as Christa had outlined it early on: how she'd met her husband-to-be in Berkeley, had an affair, dropped him, met him years later in Paris
entirely by accident, followed him North, and married him in
Sweden. By this letter she had left him, or his hearth, was living alone in Stockholm, seeing a psychiatrist once a week,
about to look for a job, and trying to think things through,
large and small—the meaning of marriage, the meaning of
her own, her place in the cosmos, why Måns, her husband, was
so adamant about refusing to join her in treatment (which refusal had triggered her departure); an intricate stew of brainy
insight and emotional confusion and that too-easy identification with Christa which spelled Danger. ("It's what always happens when they try to think, bubby," says Dr. Pisacano.) My
heart went out to that Swedish physicist, a (no doubt) serious
and simple type, who had taken to wife so deadly a sample, so
egregiously female a screwed-up American miss, whose quest
for authentic feminine selfhood in a world of crumbling values plus suchlike horseshit—I cannot quote exactly here—
had robbed him of peace, led to pain and disorder in his
world. Or would have in mine. He might have been cut from
tougher cloth. I applauded his decision, whatever the reasons,
to not come skulking into therapy behind her. And I had
some indignation left to spare on Christa's behalf (though I
couldn't really quarrel with some of the judgments: "Why
must you still cling to Tim? Why can't you let him go?"), in
the consanguine clutches of this smart, strident bitch, this
willful, baleful influence. I'd had enough of Marcia for the
time. I refolded the letter, returned it to the envelope, the envelope to the portfolio. I was ready for Denby now. There
were seven or eight in his pile, return-addressed, of course, to

the university, so as to keep Keiko in the dark. They went back
as far as July. I didn't plan to read them all. I was most interested in what he'd told her about me, and I took out the most
recent, sent to Mykonos, dated mid-December. It began,
"Dear Baba." I skimmed through, and found what I wanted.
"You might want to look up Jason Sams, if you pass through
New York . . . a good person, writer (beware the beard), secretly in love with my wife, thinks I don't know, just fell in or
is about to a great pile of publishing money and claims to be
thinking of turning in his psychiatrist for an accountant or a
lawyer . . ." (I claimed, of course, no such thing. But clearly
the lady had already known, if she paid attention to her mail,
that I was seeing the Man, long before I'd agonized over
whether or not to tell her, and she kept her counsel when finally I did. My admiration grew.) I was suddenly put in mind
of a section from one of his to me, which had been too difficult,
too remote, to puzzle over at the time. I dug it out, that February evening, and do so now.

> . . . My cousin sent a letter which arrived yesterday. She is one
> fucking shrewd bitch; acknowledging the well-put invitation to
> look you up in NY, she fires back with a cutting, Go have your-
> self, DD, you can't tuck your conscience (or something) away
> with my skirts, even with the best of intentions. The exact words
> were: ". . . as much as you'd like to settle that little question be
> it there or back when it wasn't so much which way I'd fall as on
> whom. The point being I don't fall on but up. You protesting
> too much notwithstanding. It's not satisfaction you'd rock back
> into but relief." So, I say, if she does happen to ring your bell we
> may both consider ourselves blessed. I have begun a novel . . .

"Dear Baba . . ." They all began that way, as had the letter
which prefaced his "story." But the world goes barreling on:
"Baba" was living in my house (all thanks to Dave), complicat-
ing my life to no small degree, and I was deep into their mail.

Like the rest—if without the lover's poverty of invention, the sister's convolutions—Denby would respond more than innovate, counterpunch, pick up her leads. She'd taken some drug or other in her travels, methedrine, god knows what—Dave was not completely clear—and had tried to describe its effects. Obliquely, one gathered. He praised her courage, confessed his curiosity and envy, and begged her to take detailed notes the next time, for his sake, her sake, the world's: "Teach us, Baba, tell me what you felt, tell me how it was . . ." There were, as well, dollops of personal detail, comments on his scholarly pursuits, how marvelous Keiko's pottery was, how boring was his job, his ambivalence toward fatherhood, or the vistas it presented, a trip he was thinking of making (had made by now) to the coast, alone, to see about possible publication of a book of his photographs (text by himself) centering on the desert . . . the yield was shrinking, or my interest was. I folded Denby back in place. There was a fat, recent letter from a man in Berkeley—I remembered the name, I'd carried her answer to the mailbox—which I started to reach for, then let it go. *Bastante,* for one session. I closed the portfolio. It looked pristine enough, unless she had planted some secret sign. Knock off, why don't you, such paranoid shit. She'd forgotten the letters were there, or trusted me not to explore them, or didn't give a damn if I did. To compound the complexities I'd let loose by merely opening that Pandora's box was to go wholly out of my mind.

An idea came to me. Rather a title did. (It was always a sign that things were going cerebrally and badly when a title for a story preceded its inception.) I'd write something called *The Reader.* There is this curious fellow, see, whose life was smooth enough until he pried into his lady's papers and effects. I jotted it down, title and quick summary, into my notebook, glad to be entering something after all this time. My stomach sent an urgent, noisy message; I boiled some water,

threw in two knockwursts and two eggs, went back to her portfolio. I opened it, removed the letter from Tim, took it to the
typewriter, and copied it entire.

And then I wolfed my lonely dinner. I thought of many
things. Like what had become of the cat. What must I look
like with mustard in my beard. (Went to the mirror to check it
out: not very bad, in fact, rich yellow daubs smeared across the
red.) How eager I was for Christa to return so I could write
her a letter with my cock, hand-deliver it to her virginal vulva,
a mash note from the throbbing present. I made some effort to
relax. I'd lost as good or better through insane jealousy, and
not that long before. Such jealousy *was* insanity, directed at
the unalterable tangle of their pasts. Why must a clever fellow
like myself live through such madness? I couldn't say, mopping up knockwurst and eggs as the sky darkened. I concluded
merely that to fuck them nicely, in particular as they enjoyed
it, did not seem the best way to hold them. Consider Christa,
consider her Tim. She ran to him for the finale, when Denby
yanked his prick from out her warming fires. Indeed, that
busy scholar might have had the answer—keep them hanging,
tactically discontent, so they come dashing back for more. Except, not Christa. Resourceful wench, she would have it both
ways. I pictured her racing or hopping (cradling her appetite)
from one end of Berkeley to the other. She shouldn't have, it
wasn't nice. A lady shouldn't offer her soft, sweet wares to two
buyers at a time, whatever her excuses, however timely or
basic her confusions about Sex and Love. Covington had
framed a doubtful piece of wisdom, once, which (still em-
broiled with Gillian) I'd labored to accept. On the strength of
countless therapeutic hours with wives whose husbands would
not screw them well, or often, or at all, he could assure me
that they went for many moons without redress, against the
day when the situation with the man of their choice would
improve. Uh, uh, Jason, women are different from us. They

channel their prurient itch, which in any case is more diffuse, they do not drop their drawers at the first onset of desire. (He's speaking to me on my own level.) And perhaps, in his experience, it was so. Yet the cases he cited were in wedlock, which, changing times or no, alters many things, and Frank— though he turned out to have affinities I dared not suspect at the time—had not met all the women in the world.

I piled the dishes in the sink and cut up some liver for the cat, who was yelling at the back door, then I lay on the rug beneath the afghan and switched on the transistor, meaning to be lulled by world news, but never heard it. The radio was whispering, battery nearly dead, when I woke at half-past nine. I sprang up, bulled around, washed my face and went into the garden. It was windy and cold. I came back in and made up the bed, the outside, single, for the first time in a while. This didn't help my mood. I poured a glass of wine. I drank off half and lit a second cigarette before I dialed.

That goddamned miracle. In seconds I was in Baltimore. I spoke briefly to the husband of the house. He put her on.

"Sarkissian!"

"Yes."

"It's me!"

She laughed. "I know."

"Did you get there okay?"

"Yes. It's only Baltimore."

"That's true, that's really all it is. Are you having a good time?"

"It's a little early to tell. Their baby is fairly new . . . it's a very domestic atmosphere."

"When are you coming home?"

She laughed again. She sounded very pleased and gay. "I don't know. In a few days. I just arrived."

"Sarkissian."

"What?"

"I'm going to bed. I miss you. Come home soon, babe."

"I'll telephone, the day I'm due."

"Good, I'll probably be in. Unless I'm spreadeagled on Frank's couch, or at the A&P. Jesus, why didn't I give you the spare set of keys? Anyway, I'll be here. Good night, love."

"Yes, good night."

I polished off the wine. It was only ten o'clock. I felt like going out, though not far. A block down First Avenue was a local, one of those places, plush and rough, which feel hoodlum-run and maybe are. The broads who use them, grey-hound or zoftik platinum-blondes, painted to the eyes, stir up a pile of adolescent fantasies. Or mine. I made sure I had my pocket notebook and a ballpoint pen. I'd sit at the bar, drink a beer, and jot down whatever came. I'd been there a few times before but knew no one, as was my custom. It was fairly crowded. I strolled along the bar. A young, short, pimply snot stroked his chin and cheeks and prodded a friend as I went by. I am a man of peace—fearful, civilized, what you will. Flight over fight is the motto. Knives and guns apart, these days, who knows what unprepossessing pimp is a karate black belt, anyway. In Spain, I rose above all sorts of feeble-minded sallies (*"Mira la barba! Es Castro, verdad?"*), and in Sweden as well. Most people are shmucks, you learn to live with that. But unfamiliar things were rumbling in me now. I had turned around and was staring down into his stupid eyes.

"You see something funny in having a beard?"

"No, man."

"Then what was this about?"

"I was scratching my chin."

The feebleness of this enflamed me more. Who knows what would have ensued; scorn and irony, most likely, nothing more; but I was made aware just then that he was not alone. Not merely for the friend whom he had nudged, who was even frailer, less minatory than he, but for the group of five or six which closed around us. I could see that for the moment they were moved mostly by curiosity. I sensed as well that they were all together.

"Lincoln," I said, "had a beard."

"Moses had one too, didn't he?" one of the newcomers helped out, a wise bastard.

"You're fucken ey," I said, and removed myself from danger. At the end of the bar, by the jukebox, was an empty stool. I squeezed in. The bartender arrived directly and I ordered a Schlitz. I eased out my notebook—the spirals had caught on the pocket—and doodled two three-dimensional boxes, a trick I'd learned in the third grade. In one I wrote FEAR, in the other RAGE. Let some man of science work it out from there, build on my shoulders. I drank some beer. I willed my heart quiet; it was breaking sideways from my chest. The bartender came back.

"The kid down the other end wants to buy you a drink. What'll you have?"

I glanced painfully over. Past a couple of the flashy dames I'd gone there to appreciate. My enemy raised his glass. I smiled or scowled; neither of us knew which. I think I would have accepted, had I known the protocol. But what was it? Was I supposed to join them, and struggle to live at their level? Or drink my free drink surlily, or with a bemused smile, and consider all forgiven? What did I have to forgive? If anything at all, could it be obtained so cheaply? Why wasn't I simpler in my mind, or able to let them be? None of this agonizing, I believed, showed in my face. I turned back to the bartender.

"I already have a drink."

I gulped from the glass, left the rest, and used the exit just behind me.

This high excitement did some salutary thing (or else it was the liquor, or the call), for I fell straight into bed, glad to have it for myself, and slept right through to morning.

I phoned her again two nights later, Tuesday, at half-past six in the evening. Again the man of the house answered, pointed out that it was dinnertime, suggested brusquely I call back in an hour. I said it was a long-distance call, and he put her on. She was very sweet and warm. She'd had about enough, she said. She'd be back the next evening, about this time. I said I would be there.

I had forgotten what she looked like! The features, one by one, I could recall, but no more reassemble than I could my mother's, five seconds after that good lady walked out the door. And what I did recall I did not trust; probing her letters and drawings had added a dimension, made her dimmer and larger than life. But when she rang the bell, toting Sarah's bag, she was the same full, dark-eyed, basically unpretty girl I'd seen off (minus maudlin farewells) at Penn Station, brimmings and vulvas and methedrine in the Greek isles had changed her no whit in the flesh. There in the vestibule I kissed her on the mouth, held her hand, which was cold as out of doors, all the way to the couch, sat her down, plopped down beside her, and asked her how it was.

She said that it was not so nice.

"I went to the museum one afternoon, which was pleasant . . . the baby seemed a problem, but they weren't getting on terribly well, in any case. Daisy wants to go back and live in Berkeley, but he's got another year of school. He won't let her go off for a visit, either. He spends nearly all day in the library while she's home caring for the baby . . ."

"What's wrong with that?"

She shrugged. "Something is. I was witness to a dish-throwing scene . . . I don't think it would have happened if they hadn't had the ready-made audience."

"Your friend—Daisy—threw dishes?"

"No, he did."

"Sounds like a wild man."

"She had it coming, in a way. She was at him all the time."

"How do you mean?"

"Oh, so many little ways she has of attacking his masculinity
. . . some rather subtle, some not so."

"Such as?"

"Must I really go into it?"

"No, I guess not." I couldn't say I cared much for her com-
placent, almost gay assumption of our vulnerability. "Sounds
like you had a great time."

She laughed. "Yes." She took my hand and held it in her lap.
The outlook improved. All she'd meant to do by invoking it
was to shut out that shaky world, that crumbling tie, to exalt
and protect our (hers and mine) sweat-free, perpetual honeymoon. Sure. Bad-mouthing others was bound to save us from
their troubles. Yet with what grave consistency she practised the
pastime. I could think of no one, in any context, to whom
she'd given a good press. Her sugar-cube friend, as an example, up the road: smiling, warm-voiced, she had described the
wife as thin, provincial, dry, but it was not just the wife's
discontent with the arrangement which ended her stay there
after a couple of days but some ideological dispute with the
host himself—he'd been a serious painter, once, believed in
himself and his art, given it top priority, but had become ob-
scurely corrupted by wedlock, his talent or impulse twisted or
lessened . . . she'd tried to show him how he'd changed since
last they met, he did not take it kindly . . . something of this
sort. My memory, as so often, fails me. Yet her manner did
conspire in this—her fuzzy, sweet, exasperating way of rendering her inner states and ties. A wealth of charm, reasonableness, what seemed even logic suffused her most negative
accounts, so that—especially if her pauses, omissions were
also working well—her judgments would at times seem wise,
almost inspired. Yet they were will-o'-the-wisp, impoverished by
paraphrase, beggaring recall. Which judgment of my own was

still in the making at the time. I switched off *chez* Daisy, or the cogitation it produced, and asked after my own slim volume. Had she had time to read the stories? Two of them, yes. Had she liked them?

"They were . . . all right."

"All right?"

"Well written. You're very competent."

"Thank you. Did you receive any other impressions?"

"I can't really discuss it now, Jason. I'm not feeling very verbal."

"Okay, babe." I regretted, quashed, the rush of irritation. I accepted her rebuke (the weight of it borne in my name). No reason in the world for her to love my prose, nor for me to require it. Let alone on such short notice. "You want a drink?"

"Sure."

"Have you had dinner?"

"I don't feel terribly hungry."

"Nor I. There's some cheese we can nibble on."

I'd picked up a pint of Johnnie Walker Black that afternoon and poured it into her Luxembourg fifth. I fixed two drinks, sliced up some cheddar, and brought the repast to the couch. She had let down the tumble of her hair, removed her shoes, tucked her legs in their brown casings beneath her, made some small adjustment to her breasts, and fell to the scotch and cheese. She was home. I desired her. Without the vengeful undercurrents of three nights before. I was naturally better than my worst self, a soothing thing to know. It was time to put some feelings on record, or define them in the attempt.

"Sarkissian," I said softly.

"Yes?"

"I don't know what your long-range plans are, or even if you have any . . . but you're welcome to stay on here awhile."

She nodded. I saw no way to press for a less equivocal re-

sponse. I wasn't even sure I wanted one. Let the remark sink
in, send out its ripples for a while. She leaned over and picked
up the WBAI monthly program guide. She'd gone through it
about a week before, marking off things to listen to, but had
got around to very few of them, a circumstance I'd already
teased her about. Now there was a Sean O'Casey play in progress, duly circled in red, and she switched it on. Whichever
one it was, we listened to the end. In Ireland and out, the man
reminded us, life can be a thorny road, "a r-rough and tawny
road."

And later that night, when we went to bed, it turned out a
little so. I'd written some letters to selected friends abroad,
she had listened to music and read, and we retired about ten
thirty. She made up the bed herself. I entered it first. She was
wearing bra and panties when she came, which I took as a neutral sign. And to kissing, and general mood-building, she was
responsive enough. But when I slid my hand from knee to
crotch, but had hardly touched her there, she flinched, shuddered, as so many of her gestures were large.

"Jason, I don't know if we can. I've been having some
trouble . . ."

I said, "We solved that, dear puss. We opened up the pass,"
smiling through the sense of *déjas vu,* still gentle.

"This isn't that. This is some other thing."

"Some other thing? Ah, dear Chris. Dear baby." For I
wanted her badly. I do not think I disbelieved her, but whatever she had, or had conjured, was not going to withstand my
lust and tenderness. And she knew it, too. I fixed her black
eyes with my filmy blues, to make a virtue of the very thing
she'd pilloried in her drawing, the hard-nosed male, his ur-
appetite, and came up above her resting on my elbows. This
way is SOP, they say, or in certain cultures, heaven knows why,
precluding as it does all but basic contact, I almost never use
it, but it was useful now to look down into her face. She'd shut

her eyes, compressed her lips, and was working her pants down over her thighs. I helped them off, overlooking how dutiful she seemed. She was no Victorian lady suffering connubial duties, this much I knew. I opened her legs, looked at her cunt, kissed the high ground, worked the length outside her, insinuated, parted flesh, and eased deliciously inside. Ahhhhh. Four long days had passed. Lust and tenderness I vouch for, even a hint of sacrament in that soft entering, but something more. For I had lived to love again, after rendering a pair of pajamas ready for the laundry well before their time, a modest marathon, twice the night she left and once more in the morning, nursey blondes and fleshy ingenues in starring roles, and might have gone for four had not the prostate shrieked its warning. And here I had survived, again, made it to the ritual dip and cleansing. I could have hardly spent the night beside her unfucked in such a frame of mind. So most or all of the importunateness came from here; I had at least to grant the possibility. But not dwell on it. I worked in slowly, gyrating from the hips, the way Britta had loved it, gauged the way she yielded, then dug straight and hard a moment before she was ready . . . her eyes sprang wide, mouth shaped an O, and she thrust up to join me. I had my hands now where I liked them, surrounding those lovely cheeks, face buried in her neck, settling for the job ahead. I hovered on the lip, stroked deep, and held. A few times more. Soon, something else. I planned a leisurely meander through the repertoire. But it was not to happen. With scarcely a warning sign she blasted off, moaning, clawing, writhing, biting deep into my shoulders—there was barely time to check my choices. I would have liked to see her face (the light was on), but was positioned badly and not really eager to change it. The deeps of her nostrils was all I could manage. Tales of multiple orgasms to infinity, perpetual readiness, their legendary appetites shot through my head. But also real chapters from my life, in which some of them evinced disinterest right after coming analogous to the man's. I didn't care to risk this second possibility, nor did I feel, any longer, especially eager for the first, the lengthy virtuoso scene, and rode in with her on the final wave, scrambled up the shore alone a yard or two, shot forth an endless load, dropped some saliva on the pillow, and groaned out my pleasure.

Beached whales, we lay that way awhile. The first thing I saw, looking up, was her water glass, on the night table. She never retired without it. I decided I had missed that too. I sipped from it.

"Want some water?"

"No." She sounded faint and far.

"Christa"—her name felt strange and clumsy in my mouth —"you're beautiful. You're the best there is."

When this brought forth no response, I twisted to see her. She was staring straight at the ceiling. Gently I disengaged— is this not said to be, for them, a moment of great loss and emptiness?—but she seemed not to know. I lay beside her, looking down. She shook her head violently, covered her face with her hands.

Alarmed, I reached out and touched her hair. "What's wrong?"

"I'm leaving."

"What?"

"I'm going away . . . taking leave of my senses . . . oh!"

"Chris, what is it? What can I do?"

"Nothing. Please. Wait. It feels like I'm going crazy . . ."

Her distress was as real and frightening as it was ill-timed. She was as entitled as the next to a spot of madness, but must it follow hard on what was almost a declaration of love? As my helplessness began to build, and sour, I saw that it was over. She had uncovered her face, which shone with sweat, and was staring once more at the ceiling.

"Are you all right?"

"I think so. Yes."

"Do you want the light on or off?"

"It doesn't matter. You can turn it off."

I went to the toilet. I switched off the lamp on the way back. We lay a moment in silence. I reached for her hand. "Will you be okay?"

"Yes."

"It's weird, isn't it? Has this happened to you before?"

"A few times, yes. But it goes away quickly. Good night."

"Oh . . . good night."

Dismissed, concerned, relieved, I rolled over and was asleep in a moment.

I bolted up around seven thirty, slipped on a robe, and began typing in the back room. I didn't even put the coffee water on. It was a newly minted dream which had propelled me. I wasn't due to see Frank that day, and preferred as a rule to produce them fresh, turds still steaming from the night before, but this one seemed too good to lose. Samuel Beckett was a woman, we were courting. We were seated on a couch. I planned to propose. But I moved in for a premarital taste, we embraced, and the scene faded on the brink, dirtily suggestive, Hollywood style. When the lights came up again we were well married, well into the domestic give-and-take. It had worked out as well as those things can, but Beckett was blocked, had not written a word in several years. I felt to some degree responsible, and tried to apologize. But Sam said morosely not to sweat it, baby, it's the price of love.

I made the customary carbon, which I folded into my wallet, and stuck the original into my looseleaf notebook. I put the water on to boil and came back to bed. She was curled to the wall, but I knew she was awake.

"The typing disturbed you?"

"Yes. It's all right."

"Sorry, love. I was recapturing a dream."

"Oh. A dream."

"You thought maybe it was the great American novel?"

"I didn't think anything, Jason."

Which was almost certainly true. I was trying to turn her into gadfly and comrade, pussified Socrates—who could fault her for turning down the job? (And, in the days which followed, I took to setting up a "dream corner," pencil and index cards on the floor at bedside, so I could jot the mothers down without disturbing either one of us, without involving the creative noise and tools.) I started breakfast—bacon, eggs, Sacramento tomato juice, which is the best there is—and we ate out on the porch, facing the dormant garden, for the February morning was behaving like June. Afterwards she washed up, the breakfast dishes and the load left in the sink, and went off to check her mail and buy some art supplies. I asked her to drop a pile of wash, mostly mine, at the launderette. I pushed some papers, then really worked an hour or two. I was playing darts and drinking coffee when the telephone rang. It was my agent. She had just sold my book of stories to a publisher in Sweden. I'd had some thought of returning to the typewriter after lunch, but this buoying news ended the working day. I went out to pick up the laundry. The runty man there knows me, or the pillowcase I use as laundry bag, which has a flowery border. We rarely exchanged more than the necessary syllables, but this time he smiled and complimented me on my wife. He said I had a very lovely wife. I took as much pleasure in his praise of her as in informing him I was not married. Feeling very high, I rang up Paul when I got back and invited myself for lunch. We used a quart of wine, at least, to wash down the Pisacano special. Of Christa he said, "She's a winner, man. She's really in your corner. She's the best I ever saw you with." To which I replied that he had never laid eyes on Twenty-sixth Street. Or not, I amended, so far as I knew. He took real pleasure in my afterthought, rocked back with wild guffaws, and repeated his opinion of how screwed up I was.

I staggered home and slept, making sure to leave the chain unhooked. I heard her come in, but couldn't stir for twenty minutes more. Then I showered, shaved around the beard, and she cooked up some lamb ragout she'd come back with the ingredients for. It tasted fine. While I dozed she had emptied the laundry bag and put my unmentionables in their proper drawers, which pleased and unnerved me more. My editor phoned after dinner, from somewhere in the Village, and I invited him by. He came with his wife. We talked and drank into the night. Christa had met them before, but had been rather shy. Now she loosened up, chatted freely with the wife, mostly about California. Allan phoned me in the morning, on some other matter, and said what a good woman she was. When I hung up I turned to the bed.

"That was Allan."

"Who?" she said sleepily.

"Seeman. My editor."

"Oh."

"He was extravagant in his praise."

"Of what?"

"You, babe. My laundryman, my editor, my neighborhood buddy, they all think you're the greatest thing that ever happened. What do you do to them?"

She yawned, shrugged, seemed displeased, then produced her big, sudden smile. "I probably charmed them."

"Wow. Yes. You really did."

And minutes later, chances are, I did a thing I loved, which was watch her move through the world of my rooms in her underwear. Those rounded hips, narrow sloping shoulders, full boobs and thighs—Jesus, she was fair. To come up behind her while she gazed half-naked in the mirror was to have it all. I made the error once of saying so. She disputed, told me how much thinner, trimmer she'd been in olden times, like two years before. In her own opinion now her ass was much too large, overall physique unique and odd, dated at best (she called it "pear-shaped"), one breast slightly larger than its mate (and what mother's son with an imbalanced scrotum even gave a shit if this was true?), feet ugly, dimples due to missing muscles, nose unmentionable. A wreck, overall.

"You make a strong case, Sarkissian. But to me you look in your prime. Or one of your primes. They say around thirty-five is the best."

"That's when you begin to chase seventeen-year-old boys."

"Yeah, I suppose it is."

And one evening, as she sketched, out of my own deep perversity, I asked her why she didn't draw me. If I had a drink in hand, I said, I'd sit for her forever.

"I have drawn you."

"You have?" There was no need to feign surprise, for I hadn't thought she would admit it. "When? Can I see it?"

"No, not yet. It's . . . part of a series. I'll show it to you when it's completed."

She was so much more skilled a dissembler than myself. I had the feeling she knew I'd been into her things; she'd looked long (if in passing) at her portfolio of letters the night she came back; but I could have been wrong. About everything. Perhaps she was really doing a series? I hoped not. Indian temple sculpture would pale beside.

"And you don't need me to sit for you?"

She did not. There were times, she said, when she preferred to work from memory.

Indeed there were. Most often in bed, or else late at night, on the rug, lubricated by the wine, she went on gleaning. Possibly I would have discouraged it if I had thought of an easy way. But probably not. I cut down my questioning, I even tried to turn it now and then if she went on too long or fondly about Tim, but I didn't begrudge her, on the whole, a serious, listening air. I was the girl friend, the brother she had never had. And should this seem to reek of virtue, as it does to me, the approach gave me still one more way to possess her. By weighing, reassembling all she volunteered with what she repressed, when I knew what that was, I'd finally be able to surround . . . what? her basic mystery? anything I really needed?

I learned during this time that the abortion she'd already described had been her second. Compared to the tale she told now, the Tangier trip was an African holiday. She'd come by the first right after her MFA, while supporting herself with some part-time job. Tim was not in town. Denby was, but his peculiar habits made it possible for her to pinpoint the man as one she worked with, a mere one-night stand (I clucked and shook my head in disbelief and sympathy). His subsequent desires, as with George in Madrid, she did not make clear. Tim returned in ample time to undertake his shuttling chores. They drove to Tijuana, armed with a doctor's name and address. The trouble began right over the border, when they stopped to ask directions. They felt they were being tailed, decided that this was unlikely, and went on to the address. The doctor himself let them in. They chatted, wary but amiable, got to the point, money changed hands, she had just gone off to undress when the police burst in. They roughed up the doctor, insulted her, threatened Tim with jail. They confiscated most of the money, for some reason not all. They escorted them back to the border.

They drove all night to San Francisco. In the morning she boarded a plane, alone, for Seattle. She had the operation there. She was airborne again within the hour, not even feeling bad, or much of anything at all, groggy from the anesthetic, in mild shock.

I found myself wondering who footed the bill for all these escapades.

She drifted again to her recent travels, concentrating on Italy, a young man she'd known there, somewhat younger than herself, inordinately handsome, not especially bright, who squired her to places she would not otherwise have seen. That he'd screwed her as well I automatically assumed, though she had the goodness not to spell it out. I'd come to doubt that she had spent twenty minutes alone with any adult male in all her nubile life without fucking him, too. I had worked up by then substantial fellow-feeling for Tim, who was hooked on a most extraordinary lady, a life-force run wild, and something more insidious than fellow-feeling: I'd begun to see how he could do it. One must take great pains not to follow in those footsteps. Drunk, in the saddle, one did not believe there was much danger. One even tried to be sporting. Let her have her dashing Antonio, young Italian stud; that, after all, was what so many of them went to Europe for. With her buddy down the block, however, quarrel or no, I must have handled it less well; the real proximity could have bothered me, and I ventured too close to home.

"If you're asking whether I ever slept with him, Jason, the answer is yes." Looking and sounding very put upon.

"I wasn't asking that . . . when was it, since you volunteer?"

Two safe years before, her aimless, pre-Europe, father-mourning journey to New York.

Her mother, from whom letters now came regularly, she described as fat, complicated, wise. (Her most gentle portrayal so far.) I countered with tales of mine, less flattering. Once, when Martha phoned me, I held the receiver a distance from my ear so Christa could share my dismay at the nervous, strident tones.

Then one Thursday morning, our fourth week plus a day,

Leslie phoned long distance, collect, from her Cape Cod boarding school. Instinctively I went to take it in the back room, and I kicked shut the door.

"Jason, it's Leslie."

"Hello, little one."

"Are you alone?"

"Yup."

"Are you sure?"

"Sure I'm sure. You think someone sleeps here every night? You think I'm running a hotel?"

"I don't know. I'll be in tomorrow for a whole week. I really want to see you."

Delivered on a childish, nice, peremptory note, as if she thought she had a right. I decided she did. Minor literary figures in their thirties should not seduce however eager seventeens unless they're prepared to bear some extralegal risks. And that eager she had not been anyway. It was on our second date. I took her home around two, chatted with the pair until her mother liquefied herself to bed, then we nestled in on the couch. I was her first author, her very first beard, she was ready for some heavy, hairy necking, but she drew the line at her pants. Since I knew she was no virgin, I became judiciously outraged. I took it very personally. I promised to withdraw from her life until such time as she grew up. She could drop me a line when she thought that had happened. I put on my jacket and my coat. She followed me to the door. We taxied back to my place.

Such the heavy-handed origin.

"I want to see you too, Les. Call me when you get in."

I asked Frank that afternoon what he thought I ought to do.

"What do you want to do?"

"See her, lay her, I don't know. Keep her on the fire, really, for some other time. I can't have her over the house, and I don't want to spend the night away, even if we could get her goddamn mother out. Don't be such a nondirective bastard. Give me a little advice."

"Uh . . . tell her your sister and brother-in-law are in town and staying in your apartment."

"My sister . . . ? Hey, that's great. Then even if she phones when I'm out and Christa answers, I'm covered. From Leslie's end, anyway. And I wouldn't have to see her at all, or only for lunch. Frank, you're a master."

So on paper it was solved. I'd probably screw it up, I was an indifferent strategist, or felt one then, but maybe I could pull it off. From Covington's office I went to a tavern, had several draft beers, looked through the evening paper, and ceased to worry. I got home around six. We'd left the house together that afternoon, stopped at the shoemaker's, then ridden the First Avenue bus uptown. She wasn't back yet. I opened a quart of Ballantine Ale, switched on WLIB, jazz, the Billy Taylor show, fed the cat, cleaned his box, and turned to Murray Kempton's column, which I had saved for last. It shaped up as a civilized evening. The steak I had removed before we left was defrosted; she could cook it, when she got back, or, should there be some festivity in the air, we would go out for dinner and the steak would keep. When she wasn't in by seven, and I'd polished off the quart, I broiled the steak, heated the frozen asparagus, sprinkled them with Parmesan, and fed myself. She arrived while I was mopping up. She hung her coat in the back room, came and sat on the couch. I joined her there. She looked weary and unhappy.

"Where've you been, my love?"

"Out, around, picking up my mail."

"How'd you make out?"

"Not very well. Just one letter from my brother-in-law . . . Jason, I've got to leave for California."

"What? Why? When?" Whence—shocked as I truly was— this odd desire to smile?

"Tomorrow. My sister Jane is having a nervous thing, a

breakdown, if they still call it that. They want me to be there."

"The sister in California? The one you said was a square?"

"Yes. What does that have to do with it?"

"Nothing. They flip out too, I guess. But what can you do for her?"

"Not much . . . they want me there, I have to go."

"What are you doing for money?"

"My relatives are meeting me at the terminal. They've bought the ticket."

"What time must you go?"

"The plane leaves at nine thirty in the morning."

"Christa, I have to adjust to this. You *must leave?*"

"Yes."

"Right. Okay. It's too bad, dear. We were just getting acquainted."

"Yes, that's true."

"Christa."

"What?"

"Will you be coming back?"

"Yes."

"How long will you be away?"

"I've no way of knowing, yet. I'll call you when I know."

"Right. Anyway, you have to come back. We just brought those boots in to be reheeled."

Not even sexy, low, worn, European things, for which she claimed a special fondness, and not enough money to replace them. The shoemaker had shaken his head, that afternoon, but promised us his best.

"The boots don't matter," she said.

"Sure the boots matter."

"Oh, all right, they matter."

Soon after she went to pack. When I followed her a bit later to inspect, grieve at the portents of departure, I noticed she had left a thing or two—a blouse, a dress—hanging in the closet. Sign or oversight, I let it sustain me.

Ah what prodigies of love we made on the eve of our parting. Perhaps. Love we made, I know, but can't dredge up the
mood or quality. In the morning, not. I woke first (she had
turned out to be, if left alone, a fairly late riser), around
seven, before the alarm. I remembered to shut it, put up coffee, and took a shower before I roused her. I wanted a leisurely
departure. I was rueful, angry, unsure at what, and feeling, all
in all, fairly good to feel this bad. I followed her around while
she dressed, came up behind while she stood at the mirror,
watched myself kiss her neck, surround her box, nuzzle her
hair. She bore it awhile.

"Jason, I'll be late."

"No fear, love. It's only half-past seven." But I went and
dressed.

Coffee and tea was all we had.

"Goddamn it, Sarkissian, back to washing dishes all by myself."

"An old bachelor like you must be used to it."

"I'm not that old. Anyway, I adapted quickly to the new re-
gime."

And then there was nothing left to do. I carried her heavy
valise into a crisp, blue February morning. We walked toward
First Avenue. The old Italian cobbler, early at his last, waved
as we went by. Christa waved back. I've been down that street a
thousand times before and since, but that remains our only
contact. But my shoes seldom seem to need repair. The East
Side Air Terminal on Thirty-eighth Street was our destination. I tried for a cab on the corner, without success. It was
drawing near the morning rush hour, and New York cabbies,
as we know, go off-duty en masse during the rush hour. At best
they play the pointing game, point imperiously where they're
going, toward their beds, and if you find that direction congenial you'll nod and point in turn and they may let you join
them. Some expecting gratitude, others not—they're men of
several temperaments. The pointing problem, anyway, we did

not have, since First Avenue ran only north. The off-duty signs kept winking by. I led her toward the bus stop. There was ample time to take a bus, but I wanted her alone these final moments, just as I was not really eager to prolong them. I placed her on the queue and stepped back into the gutter. An empty cab stood across Twenty-third Street, waiting for the light. I signaled him, did so again when the light turned green, and he came sliding up. I opened the door and beckoned to Christa. She arrived just as did a tall well-dressed man who tore up from the corner. He was wearing a hat. It was reason enough to despise him.

"What the hell do you think you're doing? That's my cab. I hailed him at the corner."

"Get in," I said to her. I half pushed her into the cab.

"Get out," he said. She didn't move. He stuck his head in the front window. "You saw me at the corner, didn't you?" The little Puerto Rican barely shrugged, stared ahead.

"Man, get another one," I said. "We have to catch a plane."

"Get the hell out of my cab."

I thought he was going to put his hands on her. I slammed the rear door shut, inches from his nose. This was a signal to the cabbie, who sped away. He stopped at the next traffic light, though for a moment it did not seem he was going to. The light was green. That would have been an exit—Sarkissian speeding up First Avenue, her suitcase, which we'd both forgotten, waiting on the queue, himself pugilistically engaged with some prick of a company lawyer to whom he gave away six inches and forty pounds. Not that his size was an issue just then. Midget or giant I would have laid him out, or tried to, had he touched her. It was an unusual feeling. I started toward the cab, but some people on the queue called me back for the valise. A bus pulled in just then, cutting me off. I raced around the front of it and picked up her bag. Time enough for that irate son of a bitch, true spawn of the city, to cover the distance, yank her to the pavement by her auburn hair, wing off in the chariot . . . but he had faded. I lurched up and climbed in. The driver moved off. A red light stopped us a few streets up. "I don't know," the hackie said. "Not his cab. I stop for you."

Well, fuck you too, amigo. Speak when it matters or hold your tongue. I mumbled some remarks at Christa, apologies for or putdowns of my countrymen, but couldn't look at her. I was being ripped in half. A pair of buzzsaws worked toward each other through the center of my body. This eased a little by the time we drove up the ramp. She fumbled genuinely in her purse, but I wouldn't let her pay. She exited on the left, the curb side, and I came dragging the suitcase after. She was already cloaked in distance, fearfully remote; I surmised she was as eager as I to have it ended here. If I ran into her relatives she would have to explain me away. Nor did I really care to meet them. I dropped the bag at the foot of the escalator, gripped her shoulders and kissed her.

"Have a good journey, love. I can't think what else to say. Too bad you're leaving. It's not my idea." I began to feel teary.

"Goodbye," she said. We stared another second. When the helplessness began to build, and take over my face, I turned and left her.

I walked the mile back, along Second Avenue. I slowed past Gillian's block, peering also the other way, toward the river, in case she was just coming off night duty at the hospital. Near the end of it, when I was no longer privileged to see them, she told me she had painted her privates gentian, administering to herself for the monilia she more than implied I had myself induced, and maybe it was so. But bear in mind she was the type who thinks she has contracted ringworm from her cats. Locked out, then, how I longed for a glimpse of that purple pussy, to kiss and make it well! I chuckled at the memory as I walked by her street. I strained to put a wry face on my confusion. Scheming my guts out to fit Leslie in, or put her inventively off—it was no problem now. She'd probably phone today. I'd see her, no question. At Twenty-third I went into a sandwich bar, suddenly ravenous for an ethnic sandwich, as Jane Mason has it (*lantzman* on her mother's side), cream cheese with lox on rye. I skipped the coffee. I was full of coffee. Then I went home.

I had left open the door which led to the porch. I'd never forgotten to shut it and bolt it before. But no one had robbed me in the hour I was gone. The puss tried to join me in the john, but I edged him out. I looked keenly forward to the first wholly private session since late in January, and even a friendly cat would mar it. I'd not mastered ease in all the time she lived there (and drunk and consequently diarrhetic the few days she was in Baltimore), nor very often, in shared quarters, in my life; a fair argument, itself, for bachelorhood. It's the acoustics which bother me. Everyone shits, to be sure, but why advertise? I see my mother's prissy hand in this, for what succor that brings. And I was moving very well indeed, body restored to and relishing its rhythms, beginning, middle, and waiting for the final drop, when the telephone rang. It was ten minutes past nine. No one ever called me this early. I imagined the worst. Would my sister get the bulk of the estate? It would be only just. Though I hadn't wished so irreversible a fate on them for many years. I'd have (to make the best of it) a funeral to observe and file away. I'd been to only one in my life up until then, my mother's father's, seventeen years before, and needed refreshing for the set piece I might one day be called upon to do. The phone rang a third time. Already cheated of perfection by the summons, I decided to answer. With a shorts-hampered shuffle, paper crammed between my cheeks, I got there on the fifth ring.

"Hello?"

"Hello."

"Ah, sweet puss. Where are you?"

"At the airport."

"Christa, it's so *lonely* here. The apartment is so empty
. . ."

"I know," she said. Then, incredibly tender: "It's only for a
while."

"Listen, call me when you get there. I mean in a day or two.
What's today, Friday? I'll be away over the weekend . . ." I
had told her this, that I was going to unwind at my agent's
Connecticut farm, so she would not be apt to phone while Leslie was here. "Call me Monday night."

"All right."

"No, wait, I teach on Monday night. What's the time differ-
ential . . . shit, call me Tuesday."

"Yes. I must go now, Jason."

"Goodbye, my love."

"Goodbye."

I was enormously happy as I hobbled back to the toilet.

part 3

SO LET THERE BE—THERE WAS—AN INTERLUDE, while the miss is missing, her strong right leg just visible as she strides out of the frame. And Sams' life balloons, protrudes, and gushes from the canvas. She'll come back, no fear: the way will be paid, she'll know that her departure had been inopportune. But for the moment I could entertain. Martha phoned again that Friday, around noon. She wondered how I was; I assured her I was well. She said she hadn't seen me or been on the receiving end of a telephone call in several weeks; I explained I had been busy. She made an understanding noise. I'd chosen a rough way to make a living, she knew. And my recent successes had of course imposed fresh obligations. I must have sounded more congenial than I felt, for she went on to indulge a nostalgic mood. She'd tried to write me a letter about this mood the night before, but held off mailing it, and was embarrassed by it in the morning. The gist was this. She had been rummaging through my effects—baby pictures, letters I wrote while in the army, medals from junior high school, etc. The medals had engaged her the most. I'd been brilliant even as a youth, she and Harry acknowledged it so little. She wished there was a way to make it up. It was clear she had been bugging him about it. At this point in either of our lives we needed her misplaced remorse not at all. But I didn't have it in me to cut her off. She made a jerky transition to the first book she'd ever bought, with her first paycheck, when she was sixteen. It was Dreiser's *The Genius*. She clutched it home in a state of high excitement. She must have known I knew the background well—that her father yanked her out of school at fifteen years of age and sent her off to dismal labors, despite that teachers journeyed to the tenement on Cherry Street and begged him to let her continue, but he stood firm, and she claimed all these decades later to appreciate his motives, defended (in other situations) his wisdom and compassion, but had never forgiven him for wrenching her life out of line, nor too many of the rest of us, either. Anyway, from this bent in her, which was (after all) transmitted through her father, since her mother was illiterate, and from our early readings together in *The Wind in the Willows,* had come, such as it is, my own deep love of literature. I didn't argue. As she went on, Dreiser's book became confused with the one I had given her for her most recent birthday (fifty-nine), a biography of Wanda Landowska, and this in turn with the one I had myself published. I feared we were headed for an emotional moment. But I should have known she would be at least as eager to avoid one. She jumped quickly to the news. She had extracted much joy that morning from an item in *The Times*. Some German *junge menschen* had gone to one of the Scandinavian countries to rebuild a synagogue destroyed in the war. With their own money and hands. This partial intelligence thrilled her, the whole *goyishe* world rose a notch in her estimation. My ear was growing stiff and wet. I was reminded of the time (unless that happened afterwards) she tried to share with me, also on the phone, her excitement that the Pope had cleared the Jews in the death of Christ. She was really grateful. My reaction was: It's a holding action! Their backs are to the wall! And this time too I would have rather heard about Landowska, or my medals, given the choice. Yet I felt drawn in, reacting to these noble German youth despite myself. The overweight *shvuntzes* in their lederhosen, all over Europe, ruining Spain. Even their beautiful women had a fatness, a spiritual grossness about them. Such a narrow perspective on the youth of a nation was far from rational. It must have been connected with my shaky views on the six million. Once, around the time my book came out, I was invited by the editor of a parochial monthly, which aspires and claims to be more, to review a book they had just received on the Warsaw Ghetto. I knew *bupkas* about the Warsaw Ghetto. But I was Jewish, I was a writer, so they assumed I was both interested and qualified. I fired back a note much too angry for the circumstances. It got me labeled, around the office, as one of the self-hating Jews. There may be something to it. I certainly tend to seek my themes and postures elsewhere. Covington is of the opinion that my reactions to my religious background, half-assed though it (the background) was, are significant and suppressed. He is almost certainly right. He also holds the view, more subtly expressed, that I ought to be dealing with these reactions here, in this supposedly gut-clearing volume. It's possible I read him wrong. He is firm, as a rule, whatever his reasons, about withholding life advice, let alone literary. He lets you go your way, make your own mistakes, then listens sympathetically while you explain how

you blew it. But all right, Frank. Just on the chance. My
father still wears a *yarmulkah* at table, a white silk filigree he
pinched from some wedding or bar mitzvah. My mother blesses
the Sabbath candles. I used to have to take the long way home
from Hebrew School to avoid being roughed up by polacks,
wops, and other lesser breeds. Okay. You write your book, I'll
write mine. One thing I learned from Covington was, where
Martha was concerned, to swallow the impulse to dissent. To
enter into dispute over the merits and motives of synagogue-
rebuilding German youth, or debate the judgment posterity is
likely to make on the works of Sholom Aleichem, was to re-
open a profounder argument. I had as little chance of winning
it now as when I was six months old, perhaps a trifle less. So I
listened. Finally she got to the point, invited me for dinner,
leaving the date open, with the hard, tight chuckle meant to
be charming. "You're always welcome here, you know that
. . ." which I read as *You live less than a mile away, you have*
no wife, and yet we hardly ever see you, I suppose there are
reasons, you're a busy man, with a difficult temperament, yet
no one lives forever . . . but it was impossible to assess where
the guilt and pathos lay, in her head or in mine. A lady equal
parts bewildered and bewildering. To me. My sister Ann, who
met her nine years later, understands her better and loves her
dearly. I see Ann maybe twice a year. She's escaped to the Mid-
west, with young husband, blind Bassett hound and small
male child. She and her husband teach at the university level.
She has her mother's nervous laugh, her ungainliness, but
seems to think more clearly. She'll hover near tears when I
press an attack, impugn Martha's brains or character. (But I
have learned to bite back that pointless impulse too.) Martha
made the most hideous efforts to prevent Ann's marriage. But,
after all, failed. So I suppose there is room for charity.
Though seeming always poised on the brink of hysteria, at
least in my loaded presence, my sister must be tougher than

she seems. And with real toughness may come gentleness. And with gentleness, ability to forgive. And with forgiveness, the possibility of love.

"Are you two doing anything tonight?"

"No."

"Why don't you drop over?"

"Tonight? You're sure you're free? We wouldn't want to inconvenience you."

"I'm free."

"Dad doesn't get home until six."

"Come after dinner."

"Would you like to join us for dinner?"

"I have a dinner date."

"Oh. So what time shall we come?"

"Seven thirty? Eight?"

Stiff, flirtatious, coy, truly happy, she said, "Fi-ine."

I rang off. My invitation surprised me as much as it must have done her, but I didn't really regret it. I looked forward to a visit, if also a little beyond it, to the moment of departure. My thoughts strayed to the possible bounty—a bag of fruit, a hooked rug, a bottle of scotch. ("We don't like to come empty-handed.") My right eye began to hurt. Did it mean another bout with my eye disease? Sometimes, through will power, I could head them off. But an attack was about due. They had begun in London, in 1960 (in the left eye then). At University Hospital's clinic they misdiagnosed it as conjunctivitis and sent me home with medication which rendered it still more photophobic and inflamed. I returned. They altered the diagnosis to iritis of indeterminate origin. Cortisone kept it quiet, atropine dilated and relaxed it, it ran its course in several weeks. In 1963 it shifted to the right eye, where it remains, and blossoms about four times a year. Doctors, off and on,

have thought to connect it with the drip. Their eyes light up.
They think I may be suffering from Reiter's Syndrome, about
which not too much is known. It describes the serial occurrence of eye trouble, prick trouble and arthritis. They could
never locate what they held to be responsible, a microorgan-
ism called PPLO, nor have I ever had arthritis, which is said
to make its appearance some time between the other two, and
in a shorter span than the six years it took me to go from one to
the other, but they kept hoping. They ran me through a battery of free tests at Bellevue, blood, allergies, smears, the
works, before they lost interest. I was sorry to have let them
down. My own interest remained high. Blind! Impotent!
Writer's Syndrome!

I did some light housecleaning—mopped the toilet floor,
washed the dishes, hand-picked some lint off the rug. I emptied the ashtrays, which turned up a few stray Marlboros,
Christa's. I was not really convinced she hadn't stepped
around the corner, to Amex, to the A&P. I was still half listening for the key (she had taken it with her) in the door. Around
five I opened a gallon of the Spanish sauterne with which I
sometimes changed off the zinfandel, poured a glass, and sat
down to forge a link. I calculated whether she'd still be airborne; no. Out of the sky at least two hours. Only two in the
afternoon, California time. I wondered what she was doing,
whether she'd seen her sister yet. I gulped some wine, and on
Cat, by Helen Siegel, a red, antic cat on an all-purpose card
which had the word Greetings rather inconveniently placed
inside, I wrote her the following, which I'm obliged to re-
invent, since I kept neither carbon nor draft, as I did one or
the other for almost all the rest.

Feb 19

Dear Christa,
    This will be a long day for you, it suddenly occurs to me. It's
five pm, I'm drinking wine.

Miss you fiercely; I guess this was the way to find out.
GREETINGS
Of what use you can be to your sister in the midst of a nervous
breakdown I've yet to figure out. You were doing your share of
good works right here.

But, the white makes me waspish; good luck, godspeed, a
quick return,

Love,
Tawny Rhodes

Basically so. I may have the ending wrong.

Martha and Harry visited that night.

Leslie phoned me that afternoon. I asked her to come for
dinner the following evening. Saturday morning I called Paul
and invited him as well. Yeah, I'm feeling culinary. Bring a
lady. My own has split for the coast on family matters, but
there'll be another. Groovy, father. He offered to bring the
wine. Arrangements made, I braved snow flurries to the A&P,
bought the ingredients for a beer stew, and started its leisurely
preparation around two in the afternoon. I threw together a
large mixed salad. By five the stew was cooking nicely, and on
a superfluous quart of beer, plus Old Overholt, I was bub-
bling fairly well myself. I'd told Leslie to turn up at half-past
six, for a moment's private audience, Paul at seven. Around
six, with time grown short, I gave in to the impulse I'd been
quashing since the morning, when it was too early to act on
because earlier still where she was, and then kept delaying
throughout the day, for what seemed even better reasons.
She'd gone too far this time (California was not Baltimore) to
be loved and pursued via the phone. Besides, I'd asked her to
call me. Improvident to blow one's cool. But a few boilermakers worked wonders on the forebrain. I turned down the
radio, which had been improving me all day with Mozart,
Bach and Brahms, arranged my drinks, an ashtray, my address

book around me on the rug, and dialed the ten-digit number she had left, her mother's in Atherton. Her sister was in a nearby town, but Christa would be staying with her mother. There were clicks and buzzes, then a hopeful silence which became real dead air. I broke the connection and dialed again. I got through this time.

From the opening hello I understood what voice and cadence she had been avoiding, what dark and liquid foreignness she'd shaped her style against, and I was impressed again with what a lovely instrument she'd made of the compromise.

"May I speak to Christa, please?"

"Who's calling?"

"A friend in New York."

"Christa is in New York."

For a brief moment I considered the possibility that this might be true.

"Uh, no, I think she may have gone back to California."

"Is that so? Then most probably she's traveling by bus. Do you know what day she left?"

"No, I don't . . . but she should be there soon. Well, thank you."

"Would you like to leave a message?"

I decided I would. The message was that Jason Sams had called. S-A-M-S. If she recognized the name, as she must have, since she used it on her mail, she gave no sign. She promised to convey it. I hung up feeling vindicated, blue. Feeling vindicated—treachery afoot?—contributed not a little to feeling blue. I was not, just then, going to think too deeply on it. My West Coast geography was nonexistent. It might have been a long way from San Francisco, where she had landed, to her mother's home. That the woman did not even know she was en route appeared a little odd in the purported circumstances . . . but since this was the case, there had to be an explanation for it. Not to worry. A new evening lay ahead. The stew de-

manded my attention. I made the salad dressing. I set the table. There was time to sit around when I was done. Leslie
came half an hour late. She was sorry. She had been held up by
a long instructional from her mother's beau of the moment on
the risks of taking up with older men who might, for all one
knew, be interested in one only for one's body. He was not saying this was so in the present instance, only that she should
move with caution. Without rancor, I suggested that he
leched after her himself (I'd met him), and she agreed that
this was so. She'd been sitting on his lap through most of the
peroration. Pisacano descended a moment later with a large
and large-lipped girl who taught high school English in Boston, who I'd never met before. He sent her in to ring the
bell, as was his peculiar custom, while he was parking the car.
There was an awkward moment while I tried to imagine who
she was, the type of moment he clearly relished causing even
though he couldn't witness the result. He appeared at last with
a jug of wine, a loaf of round pig bread, and tramped around
the small apartment, infusing it with his presence, criticizing
this and that—the way I made no real use of the porch, the
absence of a genuine bed—till I sat him down at the table
and began the meal. Leslie was helpless, as well as my guest; I
did it all. Soon I looked to Pisacano for a judgment. I always
rated his own productions piece by piece—spinach of a good
consistency, cheddar sauce a little winey, etc.—and he most
often agreed. The stew was on the fatty side, he said, salad
dressing was a masterpiece. He was right, I had not trimmed
the meat close enough. His date tried to upstage this orgy—
"When do you two exchange recipes?"—but without success.
She wound up talking to Leslie about teaching, trying not to
patronize the child, while Paul and I continued our manly
discourse. Baseball, the coming season, figured large. The
evening was a great success. I remembered almost nothing of it
in the morning. The first thing to come back, as I found Les-

lie, not Christa, beside me, was the endless screwing of the night before. I was much too drunk to come in any normal length of time, not drunk enough to forgo the thing entirely; so fucked her interminably, through wet seasons and dry, and even then may not have made it, as I doubt that she did either. (Later she would write me from the cape, describing what her classmates or her mother or someone called "honeymooner's complaint," directly traceable to this' encounter; seemed rather pleased by it all.)

We went again, more briefly, in the morning. Or toward noon. She was in discomfort even then, but as reluctant as myself to misuse our limited time. We lay about drinking coffee in exhausted aftermath. She ran through some shocking stories of life at the little girls' school. The telephone rang. I reached down and picked it up, instead of journeying to the extension inside. It was Sarkissian. I felt like a jam-smeared child. My face, my tone, were bound to give the game away, but I tried to keep the content vague for Leslie's sake or mine, while yet conveying to Christa how glorious it was to hear, and damping her suspicions, should she have them, that I had spent the second night following her departure anything but alone. It was nine in the morning her time. I phoned you, I said. She said she knew. She had arrived at her mother's late the night before. She had been hiding out in Berkeley all day Friday and most of Saturday, notifying no one, collecting her wits and resources before facing the ordeal. Of course. I asked her if she needed any money. I meant for passage back, but couldn't spell it out. She said no, she would manage. I told her of the note I'd written on Friday. She said she would be looking forward to it. Reluctantly I hung up, trying to stone-face through the rosy glow. I'd been protecting Leslie, right, though if she'd made a scene of any sort I would have bitten her head off. But she was cool. Didn't even ask me who it was. So I volunteered it—an old friend from California. Hoping she would see safety in the miles.

We ate at Arthur's Corner. I dispatched her in a prepaid cab. I saw her once more before she went back to school.

Paul rang up around four.

"Hey, is Boston over there?"

"Who?"

"The chick from last night. She disappeared herself."

"Why would she be over here?"

"Who knows, father? It looked like she dug you."

"Nobody here but me, Pisacano."

"Groovy. If she turns up give me a buzz."

"What did you do to her?"

"Nuthin! She just split. I think she might have felt neglected."

"How could that be? You're such an attentive fucker."

"Yeah. Later." He hung up.

I poured myself a glass of wine. It was not the first intimation I had ever had that one of the things lacking in Paul's life was a Pisacano, and that from time to time he would assign me the role; it was important to sidestep, and usually I managed, but now, for the moment, I let myself be flattered by the image. It had been a busy weekend after all: I'd fucked a child, I'd talked long-distance with a lady. I thought of some of the things Gardella had told me about Paul. Dino enjoyed explaining him away in terms of acned, scrawny childhood, a social and athletic misfit, spurned in adolescence by the gang on the corner, beginning to blossom in his twenties but wiped out by too-early marriage to the imperious Jewish beauty; saved by divorce, grown dago-handsome, heavier, a burgeoning architectural career, swelling head, new vindictive way with ladies . . . his bluster, career, artistic ambitions, financial greed, multiple screwing, all in some manner traceable to the skinny, pimply childhood. Whether Dino tended more toward such simplistic etiology after he began seeing Covington than before, when he'd been prone enough, I couldn't say. There had to be some shorthand way for two such ancient friends to handle each other. And Dino was just as easy for Paul. Self-proclaimed writer, middle-class bullshit artist, schoolteacher, bard of Pelham Parkway . . . nostalgia, according to Paul, was at the heart of their tie.

There was another piece of data for which I had Dino to thank—what he referred to as Paul's "allergy attacks." I had never seen one. Gardella described them this way: "It's fantastic, horrible, the way his face puffs up in a couple of seconds. He can't even talk, because his tongue gets swollen also. You know how that got started? It's a wild story. I gave him this broad's phone number about a year ago, she was around six feet one inches tall and she had one tit. He calls her up, bangs her the first night, and he comes down with the clap. He tries to pin it on me, but *I* never caught anything off of her. They give him penicillin, and he first finds out he's allergic to it. That's when his face blows up, and he breaks out in a rash all over his body. So they lay the antidote on him and they cure the dose with something else. But then, here's the bit, after that he gets the same reaction *without* penicillin, at odd, unpredictable times."

Odd, unpredictable times? Struck by the perception that his life was empty or ugly or disorderly, some sudden breakdown in wheeling and dealing, some social mess or risk . . . it had taken his anxiety thirty-six years to find a set of symptoms wholly to its liking, and there would be no parting his body from them now. How much more direct than my own tentative fumbling with mild eye and genital disease! I polished off the wine and poured myself another glass. I hunted up my pocket notebook and scrawled: "Psyche, soma, sickness, Paul." Then I drained the second glass of wine. I would soon be past it, so I mothered myself into dinner: a can of tuna, raw onion, mayonnaise. I teased and stroked and manhandled the puss; he hissed, made to flee, flattened his ears, raked at me with claws concealed, gave in and purred when I stroked his throat and belly. He, at least, had adjusted to ambivalence. This was not the price of his meal, or not often, but I replenished his plate with some dry food. It was one of the rare occasions on which I'd bought the Sunday *Times* (usually I waited for a discard); perhaps the whole day had been building toward this moment. I extracted the magazine section from that preposterous hulk, doused some lights, pulled the drapes and settled in. I checked the table of contents just on the chance, but it was an ordinary Sunday, no distractions, nothing remotely interesting to read. So I turned my full attention to the ads; for these, it was a very good week indeed. Crotches were in abundance, legs, at least, on every page—pouting, pajamaed ingenues, broads leaning on Klopman, the tender, wide-hipped mother smiling at her little girl (one for the kinks!) in matching panties, season-rushing bathing suits, a terrible treasure chest. There seemed enough to squander. I raced through, three or four strokes per display, noting in passing which were most tempting to revisit, if I was being profligate, as it turned out I was—abruptly I was into the classified ads for private schools, beyond which, experience taught, lay nothing, and I closed the magazine and stripped off my clothes. Good; within limits, now, it was like starting over. My prick was slightly raw; I stroked the scrotum this time round. No way to turn the page, so I zeroed in on the bathing suits, a two-page spread. Nine ladies in a row, posing their hearts out, limbs extended and contorted in thirty thousand ways, some even had boobs, something to appeal to the red-blooded fantasist in any man, and I blasted off right into the magazine, covering them with glory. The idea of using a condom, for neatness' sake, had occurred, but was lost in the heat of the moment. Well, it was done, it hadn't been bad, and I made ready to fend off the recriminations which would follow. In fact, they were weaker than usual. I took a symbolic, pointless shower. I was still too stoned to write letters or to read. I put on pajamas, pulled out the bed and retired with my radio, tuned to the station which gave continuous news, soothing sagas of stabbings in the Bronx, possible worldwide détentes. Then I slept, from eight until two. At two A.M. I coped with reality as it manifested at that hour, with grunts and moans, wave on wave of loathing, jerked off again, showered again, tossed until four and slept until seven. Monday was shot. I had lived a certain way for almost thirty-three years, my life was not then subject to dramatic change.

Feb. 23

Dear Jason it's high noon,
You are quite right to feel the hurt I heard in your voice. It was altogether the wrong moment to leave you. Compulsion . . . The wife of young Jay Gould is in the throes of wanting something she's never known and as it looks will never have unless she becomes a kind of Mrs. Hyde and has six kids by a Mexican bandito or equivalent. All right, there is naught for me to do with that. I will speak of her and other members again since they are a part of me and I've learned a tolerance unknown a couple of years ago but let this incident be stricken, I've been given to understand it's not to be spoken of.
What am I doing here? Aside from the practical thing of wanting to burn most of my possessions, there is the mixing of memory and desire of twenty years among burnt and green hills. Can you have patience with this sentimentalism? This is another country 3000 miles from not you but your world. It isn't the issue there are no issues, it's simply something I must incorporate. It isn't either the thing women are accused of, turning to grass and leaves because they can't cope with all the other. I would have to have made this pilgrimage sometime, though that hardly consoles anyone at this moment. I wrote 3 letters to you before sleep would come and before it would leave but this is none of them.
The air is almost balmy and filled with sun and one can hear a dog bark blocks away. That and a plane droning away into the

sun and stillness are the keys that touch off my life here past. Do I have a place at all? Do you see what tortured thing happens— this evanescence next to thoughts of you? You are very much of a presence surrounding me. Because I will return to you it is madness to miss you but I do. Perhaps it will give you pleasure therefore to know that I cannot enjoy being here. But I confess I must try to force myself to it because I will regret all otherwise.

I walked around the streets of Berkeley; looked for few friends with little luck, but I will go again tomorrow or the next day. I tell you in all egoism do not be afraid of what I find. I realized several months ago that there are less than a handful of people who are a part of me and they all have wives or husbands which in itself perhaps means little except it cuts down communication time. Letters are satisfying in their way, but about as real as looking into a telephone receiver. And then there is Tim. I hope to god I've made you understand and feel there is no need to worry about that. In suicidal moments in the past I contemplated making that complete compromise, but I cannot. It's very easy for me to meet him now; how very slowly it died for me. To him I'm wilder than any 2 television serials, let him think so. 3 years ago I thought of murdering him, now I can simply say goodbye.

You did not deserve the abruptness of my departure, the clan or no, and I'm feeling all the pangs and pain of the wrong move. A reflex action, a bad habit I learned from associations past. Humility has been a long time coming.

Finally. An admission. There is something I can be taught. Let's say, chess.

And no lit cigars in that drawer on the right.

> I kiss you
> and six or seven
> and Love,
> Christa

I suppose I puffed on a cigar or two during those twenty-nine days, in a self-congratulatory mood, or periodic failed at-

tempt to cut down on cigarettes, or brief suspension of the
need to avoid the fat male trappings which pleasured my father,
and I'd promised to keep empty and hallowed her two dresser
drawers (both on the right) while she was gone. All other ref-
erences seem straightforward enough. I didn't admit to worrying about Tim, or not aloud; that paragraph seemed fuller
than was necessary, creating what it talked away, laying the
ghost it conjured. But what was more nervous-making still was
how fine her letter was. She seemed to have sought and found
the best in me to address it to; to acknowledge and exorcise the
worst of herself only in its presence. And one does not that
often feel at one's best, nor care to have it appealed to at unexpected moments. Also, it sounded much as if the lady, however self-absorbed, was in love, which is always a cause for concern. I did not remember any hurt in my voice (or care for the
thought that if any was there it could be detected and noted by
whoever believed she had caused it); I wasn't even sure which
conversation she referred to: her call to me from the airport,
or the one she made two days later, or whether she meant the
telephone at all. She could have been alluding to my letter of
the nineteenth, about being waspish, which she had by that
time. By then I'd written her again, mailing it on the twenty-
third, the same day she wrote to me. I enclosed the check for
$150 which she had not asked for. It was a kick to be able to
afford it. If I never heard from her again, if she took my money
and disappeared into the emotional jungle, there was capital
to be made of that as well. I knew the airfare was a little more
than what I'd sent. Given her bank balance, or my guess at it,
raising the missing seven dollars would be like meeting me
halfway.

Feb. 23

. . . Are you ambitious? You might bring some paintings
back, if so. New York, as they say, is the place where such things
happen.

The porch, I think, as warm weather comes, might function nicely as a studio.

Got my deposit back on that university charter. Didn't really want to go to Europe this summer, but was bamboozled by the bargain.

Enclosed is carfare. Even at 6%, at $2 a day you'll have it paid back in no time.

Love, impatience,
Jason

There ensued a silence. It was not for me to break it. I had done what I could. My life reverted to my own. At worst, perhaps, with a clever accountant, I could write it off as a business loss. Then on Sunday, March 7, she called. It was exactly noon her time, three P.M. mine. I was at my desk, alone.

"Hello."

"Hello, puss."

"Is this a good time to call?"

"It's unbelievable, it's a fantastic time to call."

She had little to say. She would be where I was Tuesday evening, two days thence. I expressed disappointment, not all feigned, that it would take her so long. I'd allowed myself to think she was already in New York. She sounded so close in my ear.

She got back at six on the evening of March 9, as she had said she would. I'd thought she meant the plane would land at six, but I was ready enough when the chimes sounded instead. I'd spent the afternoon cleaning the apartment, all nooks and crannies, paying special attention to the condition of ashtrays, as my mother had before me. I'd gone over the treacherous rug on hands and knees, thick inch by inch, and found the leavings I was looking for, enough to braid a small Chinaman, of all shades and lengths and textures, hairs once the property of

Leslie, Sarah, Jane, Sarkissian, Sams, God-knows-who, from how far back. And a single small gold earring, which stirred no memories. The morning had gone to laying in supplies. I brought home thirty dollars' worth of food from A&P, and licked the plaid stamps into place. I was saving toward a barbecue pit, two books and a half, for the balmy days ahead. Beverages Paul and I took care of the night before. We made a wine run to East Harlem in his vintage pickup truck, bought a case of zinfandel apiece, and I a gallon of Spanish sauterne and a quart of retsina, in honor of her Greek affinities. Hard liquor I had, in long supply. He drove me home, carried in my case, and stayed long enough to sample the sauterne. It couldn't have been more than twenty minutes. He was back in seconds, leaning on my bell, to announce that his own case of red had been swiped from the back of the truck. He was amused. "They glommed it, father. I wish I could have seen it. It had to be a very wiry, very strong, very fast PR." Still chuckling, he left again. It didn't occur to me until too late to give him a gallon of mine.

So I was a self-sufficient unit next evening when the doorbell rang. I put down my scotch and water, reached for the buzzer, decided instead to walk down the hall and let her in. There might be a cab to pay, luggage to carry in. I opened the vestibule door. She had paid off the cab. There was one heavy suitcase, which I bent to, still looking into her face. Presently she said hello, her patented, microfilmed hello—you could mine it for weeks, but first and last it seemed to say, We're beautiful. But she looked air-tired and drawn, and dowdy in her traveling clothes. The circles beneath were almost as black as her eyes. She seemed plump; probably she wasn't, but I'd slimmed her in my mind. And I believe I was gladdened by these mortal signs. Surely she'd look better after sleep and settling in, probably by the following morning; if not . . . I turned over the martyrdom. Having come this far with her, plain or no I'd love her anyway. Although, in the circumstances, who would blame me if on occasion I had eyes . . . all this the opening flash. Create the worst, then salvage. I turned with my burden and she followed me into the apartment. I dropped the suitcase in the back room and joined her in the main one. She was standing, fumbling with buttons, in the middle of the room. I came up behind, kissed her cheek, and helped her off with her coat. It was a thin cloth coat, not new. I ventured an anticlimactic "Welcome home." I hung the coat in the closet, to the left, in the space I'd once more cleared for her, and came and joined her on the couch. I rested an arm near her shoulder.

"How was the trip?"

"Exhausting. Dull. I was seated next to a New York clothing manufacturer who wouldn't stop talking."

"What about?"

She shrugged. "Sex mostly, I suppose. I couldn't always tell."

"How's your sister?"

"She's . . . all right. The crisis is over, for the moment. She seems to have made peace with her lot in life . . ."

"Would you like a drink?"

"No. Yes, why not."

"Scotch? Wine?"

"Scotch."

I made it fairly light.

"Would you like to go to bed? Are you as weary as you look?"

"Soon . . . Why did you write that you weren't going to Europe this summer?"

"Because I'm not going to Europe this summer."

"Was it a sort of a bribe?"

"What do you mean?"

"What I said."

"How a bribe? Ah, I see. To make your coming back seem more worthwhile?"

"Yes."

"Sure. Why not?"

"It . . . wasn't necessary."

"Good. But you needn't worry about it. I decided not to travel until I'd finished my book."

"Oh."

"Have you eaten?"

"Yes, on the plane."

"You want to nibble on something? Cheese? I've got four different kinds. The larder's full."

"No, thank you."

A somnolent beginning. I poured myself another drink, placed it on the night table, and knelt before her. I put my arms in her lap, elbows on her knees.

"Come on down, I want to talk to you."

She smiled slightly, leaned forward slightly, but her body remained as stiff as my wit. I dropped it, embarrassed and relieved. I wasn't certain what I wanted. I wasn't sure I cared for what I thought I wanted—to brand her, mark her forthwith, parenthesize so as to wipe out whatever had gone in between. Given my temperament, and her predilections, I was fairly certain something had. I wasn't wrong. A few nights later she volunteered (or I extracted) the information that her last two nights in Berkeley were spent holed up with Tim. She showed no contrition; rather she made it seem that in the circumstances it was the least she could do for the man. And anything but pleased, I had no real way to object, without invoking the fierce double standard of my fathers. Tim was her Tim—her most loyal, her most damaged—and this time she'd really kissed him goodbye. Whereas I had dallied in the interim with trinkets, cutting notches on my pecker, nothing more. But now everything was over. (Or would be in a day or two: I'd been playing it safe, awaiting her return, still drafting the dear jane to Leslie in my head.) Back bed and board with my

difficult, genuine lady. We would be marking our beginning
now.

That night, March 9, I had a dream. My journal, notebook,
diary, whatever one can call that intermittent ragbag I have
kept now for a dozen years, records it. I regarded my dreams in
those days as being of two main kinds: so complex, sinuous
and laden they invited analysis only by gypsies, or swift, clean
and classical. This was of the second type. I lay naked beside a
blooming, naked Christa, the same bed in which we slept. Also
present, also nude, was Paul. He huddled near the wall, alone,
ignored, unwelcome. In acknowledging this, and in moving
to leave, he came up over Christa, who lay on her belly, and his
shriveled member barely brushed her ass. It may have been an
accident. And he immediately departed. But he'd utterly
spoiled her for me. He'd won her away with that tactile magic,
whether or not he so intended. There were other dreams that
night, but this was the one I scrawled on a card when I woke;
this was the one I remembered. And though I've come to embrace a different meaning since, at once more hopeful and
more deadly, I was pleased with the one I teased out then: that
I was, beneath it all, so simple-minded; that my unconscious
could so neatly synthesize its terrors, throw them in my lap
and leave the rest to me. I never did present this dream to
Frank, though I hadn't planned to suppress it. But what could
he have added—a Sophoclean label? Those were my fears,
baldly stated in this message from the night. I had all day free
to allay them.

As early as the next morning she began talking of a job. She
seemed in earnest. She had checked out leads while still in
Berkeley and come up with a lab in Long Island, Brookhaven,
which she thought might hire her, the sole difficulty being
that she was willing to work only part time. What kind of work
did she do? I must have asked her this by then a half a dozen
times, and she told me every time, in greater detail and with

diminishing cordiality, but I asked her again, and she told me
again, mentioning the previous occasions and no longer concealing her impatience. And I'm damned if I could have para-
phrased it twenty minutes later. I tune out perhaps a third of
what anyone tells me about anything, which is awkward only
if and as I suddenly become engaged, and demand filling in on
what was said five minutes before; and this is doubly true of
subjects however vaguely scientific or mechanical. Which
Christa's avocation was. Such self-loving *mea culpas* aside, I
can reconstruct enough, for present purposes—her market-
able skills related to computers, feeding in the coded data,
presiding over blinking lights. In Berkeley she had specialized in the wee hours, in what she called the "owl shift," or
else part time by day, leaving most of her time free to pursue
her art, or whatever it was she pursued. I was in two minds, at
least, about her Brookhaven scheme. (Certainly it seemed too
dutiful, came too quickly off the mark.) There was hardly any
doubt that we would both be better off if one or the other was
out of the house a good deal of the time, preferably her, since I
had a nice arrangement where I was: the huge formica desk
bought second-hand about a year earlier from Gardella, set up
in a workroom as richly cloistered as the inside of my head, its
one barred window looking out on nothing, onto a corner of
the porch; yet I had been considering renting an office or a
room nearby and turning the hearth over to her. I could easily
afford it. It might be useful to attempt to shit and eat in different quarters; new energies might flow from such division of
living and labor. On the other hand, perhaps it would be wiser
to find her a studio, a place of her own with painterly light,
and sit tight where I was, close to the phone. Did she really
want to paint? Had she the talent, and the *zitzfleish,* and the
drive? The saving truth is that I didn't really care. She could
be artist, hausfrau, or such combination as she pleased. She
could stroll the byways of Fun City during the daylight hours;

that would solve the privacy problem, or mine. Either way, I knew, I would have to concoct a schedule independent of her movements, learn to work while she was home or away. I had a chat with Sarah, and she agreed to let me use her apartment to type in, if I wished, any weekday, nine to five. This was a few days before Sarkissian returned and brought things so quickly to a head by her talk of employment. In sum, I was not keen. Strolling the wilds of Gotham was dangerous enough; a job would be a separate world she would inhabit, daily rubbing shoulders with unkempt strangers, and wasn't that, if my selective memory served, how she had managed to get herself knocked up the first time? I couldn't frame it to her quite that way, it wasn't rational.

"You're sure you want a job?"

"Yes. I've . . . some money in the bank, but not terribly much."

"Christa, I'm lousy with it. I just signed this fat contract."

"I know. That's lucky for you. But I'll need some on my own."

"Oh. How about looking into a teaching job? You've got the credentials, and the pay and the hours would be better. Teaching art, maybe, in some private school."

"No. I'm not able to do that. I couldn't teach art." She was very final.

"Oh. Well, take a week off, relax, you just got here. Long Island's a pain in the ass to get to anyway, without a car."

Wary, private as she was, I thought I understood her. It would not be the last time I would too readily confuse us. I'd been there myself, I decided, as recently as '62, the post-Europe days. Working part time in GPO. Now there was a sterile, untaxing way to make a buck. It seemed urgent for a certain type, at a certain stage in life, to keep his vision separate from his livelihood. Teaching in or near one's specialty, or what one hoped one's specialty would one day be, was especially to be avoided. In the first place, one would probably be incompetent, mind too pedestrian or messy to make sense of histories and trends; in the second, Shavian saws or warnings on doing and teaching did apply. My own stint had come about the one way it could have—I was approached, after my book came out, to teach a writing course. Alma mater beckoned, albeit to one of its lesser divisions, and I heeded the call. Having come so late to the trappings of the writer's life, and still scrambling, I thought to grab off the cachet and fringe benefits where I could. But it had to happen as it happened, backing in. Some of us must make our mark, or begin to, before we can (however modestly) instruct. And so she didn't want to teach. HOWEVER (interjected Uncle Jason, finger wagging, rich with junkyard wisdoms), with her MFA, her intelligence, skills, presentability . . . a few hours a day in a finishing school, giving the pre-debs a feeling for the craft: a little art history, some basic drawing, a *shmeck* of *culture;* she'd probably be good at it, likely enjoy it, and it would be a more useful and lucrative pastime than messing around with punched cards. But she had to get there by herself. She had to live it through. At the moment she inhabited the place where the kind of work she did had not merely to be separate from her image of herself but in some manner beneath it, even demeaning, so that no part of the sensibility that really mattered needed to be there. You traded them some time, they let you live. Deep in the bowels of the post office (true boon to the dregs), mindlessly boxing mail. Home of cripples, androgynes, and artists-in-their-heart. You ought to wonder sometime how your mail ever moves, with the cretins they employ. No doors in the shithouse (and rumors, on the job, of cameras overhead) so some poor hunchback shouldn't jesse james the mails. I threw it up in early '63, along with my burglarized sublet, and lit out for Arizona, where, as I haven't tired of saying, I got lucky. A book, a Guggenheim. The teaching offer not long after.

Christa, I may have been saying, won't you let me be your Guggenheim? Spare you bitter, clerking labors which serve no proper end? Can't you find the ease, the grace, the mere self-interest to accept? I may have been saying this, but I was saying a great deal more. And I got part of my wish. She took that first week off, and then she took another, and I do not think a job was mentioned again until Jane Mason called about an opening in her art gallery, in the far from merry, too-late month of May.

Her second or third week back she came up one night to sit in on my class. The suggestion had been mine. She still had no friends in New York, or none I cared to contemplate, but apart from this urge to fill in and supervise her idle hours, I wanted her there to see me work, see Jason work, bestow encomiums, level accusations, consider me credentialized, consider me fraudulent, share the unique experience of J. Sams of all the costive people exhorting others to get off the pot, and by the end of it to judge me as I judged myself, harshly and kindly. We were not able to travel to the U together. I went to see Frank late that afternoon, in response to his summons of the morning; it was not a scheduled session, but he had taken to using me as his utility man, phoning and trying to fit me in when someone canceled out, to plug and tidy up his working day. Rather than resent it, then, I tried to see it as a tribute to my flexibility and leisure. Considering how little and how irregularly I worked, how I was always teetering on the verge, it would have been mere bitchery to say no. And it would have risked tampering with his affection. (I assumed, after close to three years, that he looked upon me kindly. It was hard to see how else he could have borne it. That he felt or expressed nothing stronger than affection suited me as well. It might even—I gave him all the credit due him, perhaps a little more—have been part of the Treatment. I wasn't quite ready for love, or not in that context, and if *I* knew it, surely he knew it too.) I would not, to tell the truth, have minded regular hours, rigid, predictable times, like any run-of-the-mill nine-to-five neurotic, but since this was not in the cards I strove to make a virtue of uncertainty, to feel one-up and close to cured if he could come to me for a favor. Some days I was less successful than on others—days on which I felt much more a petitioner than a colleague. Anyway, around two, I gave Christa overexplicit instructions on how to reach the university, together with a campus map, and departed. I had precious little to tell the gray man that afternoon. I remembered no dreams. My real life with my real girl, unlike the ten-year parade of sick dalliance preceding, which we'd explored to its depths, was in a real way none of his business, which made large inroads in the things we had to talk about. Nor did I care to dwell for very much longer on how difficult it still remained to write fiction for the ages; I had been sounding that haughty, whining note since the week we began, and not much had improved or altered in that time. I was beginning to think, I blurted, that there might not be that much left that he could do for me. There was a silence. Lying down, this time, I craned back for a look. He was writing. He looked up. He seemed unperturbed. Um, well, yes, he agreed we had reached a plateau. For his part he was content to wait it out, doodle away a fifty-minute hour or two, gird for the next upward climb. Could we speed things up? I asked him. I was financially equipped to come three times a week. I was even eager. In his opinion it wouldn't help. The material had its own rhythm, emerged in its own sweet time. For me, twice a week was enough. Disappointed, I calculated how much money I would save over a year, and made my peace. (Later I would learn from either Dino or Bob Kane that Covington once confessed he saw *nobody* more than two times a week, that it was all he felt he could stand, or handle.) That day I leapt from the couch and fled the office gladly, trying to metamorphose as I went, analysand to pedagogue, one madcap role to another. I caught the Forty-ninth Street crosstown bus on Lexington Avenue and inched toward the Seventh Avenue subway, past the Waldorf-Astoria, the unlikely supermarket on the corner of Park, past Rockefeller Plaza, the jerk-off cinema between Sixth Avenue and Broadway (a block I would get to know a lot better later on), dined on good greasy hamburgers in some stand-up Broadway joint, chased by the cardboard coffee a New Yorker or a ball fan comes to love, and descended into the rush hour. I found a seat and I looked through an ms. or two on the way up, things I would be reading to the class that evening, and took renewed pleasure in my own red-inked comments, not all of which I remembered delivering; all were terse, sometimes harsh, more often gentle. By the time I got off at my stop and climbed to my semi-private cubicle on the second floor, nodding to the departmental secretary on the way by, the new hat was fairly well in place.

I had been teaching this, "Beginning Fiction," for close to two years. The classes met one night a week. They contained from six to fifteen souls, of all sexes and ages and degrees of mastery of the language, of varying motives and schooling and ambition. I was the sole arbiter of who was qualified to take the course, and I barred no one. Almost always there were two or three sufficiently vocal or productive to get us through the time, and usually there was one, at least, who wrote well enough to keep me interested. But I tried to shortchange no one, in class or in the conference hour. I labored as mightily with the poor spellers and those innocent of grammar as with the burgeoning talents—tutor in grade-school English one moment, Max Perkins the next, and getting my kicks in both places, but more deeply involved with the urge to discover and guide. Anyone with a story to tell and some glimmering of how to tell it was able to engage me. I have a letter of thanks from a sixty-year-old woman who dealt in Florida real estate, with whose gelid but single-minded prose I took some pains, and there's many a fine young laddie down the years (to count them also since) who's sprouted fuzz on his face from one week to the next in gratitude and emulation; but I was waiting for a darkling virgin-whore, with long black silken hair and fine-boned face and a surgeon's nasty talent, who told it from her own deep, liquid places like it was; I'd give her a quick A+ and bundle her home and plant her at my desk and be quite stern about her working hours; and playing hours; I'd badger and coddle her muscular muse; I'd *be* the bloody thing. Nothing along these lines ever turned up, though there were damsels who were pretty, others who could write, and once in a great while some sort of combination; and one ambitious screwed-up twat from Scarsdale, whose prose was bitchy-lyrical, who boasted of daddy's wealth and could outdrink me, who never wore underpants and was accident-prone, I allowed to have her way with me for a couple of rueful weeks near one semester's end. (She pulled a B—, like the rest.) I mean by the above no more than that I took these classes seriously, which may have made me unique in the department. I granted each and every student, from the opening bell and throughout the term, a succession of private audiences. These were listed in the catalogue as "conferences," and were technically part of the course, but most of my confreres cut them down or out at the earliest pretext, which saved them the pre-class hour. Not me. I enjoyed lolling in that three-sided box, at that oversize desk, bright, inlaid light blasting from the cork ceiling, my name typed neatly on an index card amidst others more illustrious (we shared the office, rarely met), the buzz of genuine academics, hogtied by tenure, from the cubicles around me, exchanging occasional pleasantries with the tiny brown woman in the office behind who taught Swahili, savoring the junk academic mail (sometimes addressed, which raised some discomfort, to "Professor" Sams), but all of this consumed a quarter-hour or so, and then I wanted company. So I would schedule meetings with my students whether or not they wished them, whether or not they had produced anything about which they cared to confer. I don't think they minded. Hell, I was credentializing them, as well as myself. And some of my motives were less questionable than the rest: I wanted them laboring, and I wanted to know who they were. I was being paid a certain amount, around thirty dollars an hour, to tell them something, they were being charged an exorbitant tuition to find out what it was, and I meant to impart it. Elusive as it was, it required a certain number of face-to-face confrontations, and more friendliness and wit than fire and exhortations. In some of these meetings I learned to understand a little better how a man could turn to lay analysis as a profession, if he was not too messed up in his own heart of hearts and lacked all other talents. Within the given range, I was not equipped too badly. For one thing, I knew first-hand how naked and spread-eagled the ego can feel when it lays itself out on the page. I'd taken such courses as an undergrad myself, had been intelligently handled, and tried to pass on what I'd learned. Let me apologize forthwith to my co-workers of the time who were at least as noble as I. As for the rest . . . they knew that "teaching writing" was a con game, and that the chief pedagogical challenge was to keep this knowledge from the marks. Prime example was Mr. Blank, who headed up the show but still had to teach a class or two himself. A nondescript and ageless horn-rimmed little man from Oregon. He had a thousand ways to get through the time, a shitsack full of ploys, and was delighted to share them. You had them grind out an autobiographical fragment. You assigned them a character sketch. You asked them for a snatch or two of dialogue. Are they totally uninspired, duller than dull? Bring in a lively clipping from the public prints on which they can embroider. If really uptight—you have some writer friends?—bail out with a guest lecture. He would fairly chortle as he passed on this wisdom. All of it predicated on the student's being a shmuck, if only for enrolling in such an obvious hype in the first place. And yet the man had got to where he was, occupied his safe, officious niche . . . perhaps he had an abundance of administrative skills. He frightened me to death. He had published a work of fiction twenty years before, held a B.A. in English from his native state. There before my eyes was the fate of the one-book man with no advanced degrees, clinging to the outskirts of Academe (and livelihood!) by his fingernails, no longer even dreaming on past glory, not even toting the yellowing reviews, but all his energies devoted now to fending off the moment when some wise-ass would rise slowly from his place at the seminar table, on the heels of some hoary, rote pronunciamento ("The thing you have to remember is, write about what you know." "The trouble is, your dialogue has no life"), and drawl, "But Mr. Blank, with all due respect, just what the fuck have *you* written *lately?*"—but this may not have been his problem, or not any longer, as it had not yet come to be mine. And all being said, the man had in him something sensitive, to pain, if not to wit, or maybe both . . . but to hell with that. Let him mouth his own praises. I just recently discovered that the son of a bitch had always underpaid me. Crying poor-mouth, budgets beyond his control, hostile trustees, but other writers of no greater merit, if all somewhat older, were receiving more than I. I suspected it even then, while I still held the job, but didn't want to check it out, risk the choler I knew I would feel and so jeopardize the fringe benefits, intangible and other. And there were others: cheap summer charter flights to foreign places, including the pre-Christa one I signed up for, in December of '64, loving the bargain, but canceled gladly when the chance arose; the magnificent library facilities I so rarely used; discounts in the bookstores; signing regally for drinks at the faculty club; but

most important probably the image of myself, as I moved sal-
aried and purposeful one night a week across the face of alma
mater, the landscaped, improved, but still terribly familiar
campus, with power, a role, an office hour. How different
from the jangled ex-GI with mother's money in his pocket
("Professor" Sams!), up there to fulfill her destiny; so wonderfully remote from the pimpled loner, unloved undergrad,
eyeing with hostile, hopeless lust the multiform lovelies who
walked those parts, not one of whom in four long years he ever
met, and who had not changed that much in the fifteen years
since, or only in their morals—their young, emancipated
pussies winked and nodded as I passed benignly by, almost
smiling through my beard, writer, mentor, possible lover—
these were the very good moments. At times, especially in
colder weather, I would have to induce them, say a beer or
three, or something more, to ward off a deeper vision, of how
little I had really altered since the beanie days, of how many
more or less sophisticated ways remained until the grave of
playing pocket pool. Some weak-chinned, pockmarked, four-
eyed, unformed, undergraduate face might set it off, some ter-
rified cynic-in-training, some spectral sibling, or maybe just a
poor day at the machine, or never getting there at all; and now
I was supposed to comment wisely on the work of my charges,
or worse yet, try to extract it from them, deal firmly with excuses about job pressures, domestic strife, examinations, or
the brain-breaking loneliness of the work itself, point up the
need for habit, the importance of sitting one's ass at regular
intervals before the blank sheet of paper . . . what kind of
specialized fraud was I about to become? A boilermaker might
do some good on an evening such as that. And if they smelled
it on my breath, well, that could be twisted too, should any
have the effrontery to call me on it. Brendan Behan. Dylan
Thomas. Lowry. F. Scott. Papa himself. All reasonably pro-
lific, brilliantly dead, all noted for the sauce. So long as I re-

mained coherent, made the occasional coruscating, helpful judgment, none had reason to complain. Nor did anyone, so far as I know.

I had two people due in that night, but neither showed. Zabb, a Jewish schoolteacher from Queens who wrote of how it felt to be a poor southern Negro in the forties, a reasonably skillful (if hard to fathom) imitation of Richard Wright, phoned to say that his wife was ill and he could not make the class; and Delgado, who did come to class, explained that he had been too busy writing his new piece to want to come in and talk about the last. On this night I didn't mind the solitude. Leaning back, hands behind my head, I sat pondering my book—there was, indeed, a book; I'd enlarged it by a page or so that morning; the thing was sneaking toward completion, phrase by phrase, despite my tears, my spastic efforts to oppose it—and recalling things about my lady. Of how she might come in from her wanderings late of an afternoon, and if the mood was on me I would ask her, "Any adventures?" not really needing to know, and if the mood was on her she would say Why, yes . . . as she was climbing the crud and debris down by Twentieth Street and the East River, making that nearby stench-pond serve her need for open spaces, a tug saluted her in passing, the crew waved and cheered, the boat bellowed again, she finally acknowledged, and she flushed again, relating it, as she must have at the time, enjoying this present moment, eked out by shrugs and smiles, almost as much as the first, and I struggled to savor it with her, for what sane man is threatened by a tugboat, that many yards from the shore? Yet bugged that all the "adventures" she chose to describe were of this nature (but had I truly meant some other kind?), and soothed on top of that, that if she needed this sort of thing, at least she brought the stories home, laid the world's sexual applause at Poppa's feet, who alone of its vast population, he more or less believed, had real access to the wares.

Sometimes she would say nothing about where she had been or what she had done, and that was her privilege, too. Just as it was mine at such moments—for if I had not been really curious to begin with, her silence made me so—to be miffed by her evasive wa/s.

At twenty minutes past six I began the slow walk to the classroom, on the other end of campus. It was moving toward dusk and the subway heaved out a new academic shift, mostly adults, the "night folk," as we tended to dismiss them in my snotnosed salad days. A group of college men, great-thighed in shorts, jogged on past, so much athletic meat, giving off their jockstrap aroma even in the open air. Good luck to them, I gave them room. Watching the gladiators on the tube was one thing, imbibing them another. For a while I had a second-string back in my class, a good-natured Pole who turned in one piece early on, a spare account of the pre-game locker-room atmosphere, tapings, tensions, friendships strained, which accomplished all that he intended. For Wdowka, too, I had ambitions. I would bring him on slowly, encourage his bent, for no writer had yet come along, so far as I knew, who could carry John R. Tunis's glove. (But a week or so later, pleading academic and gridiron pressures, he dropped the course.) He was one of three people in the room when I arrived. Mrs. Baldakian and Mrs. Hale were the others. Mrs. Hale was my writer; I would be a bit surprised if she has not, by now, achieved some public success. I'd already asked her what the devil she was doing there, in my class or any other, and she replied that she still needed the incentive and the praise. She was in her mid-twenties, thin and tall, a sort of desiccated Jane Mason, drier skin, stringier hair. Once, after class, I let her buy me a couple of beers in the local and afterwards I walked her home, as I understood it—she led me down a side street to the parapet overlooking the Hudson River, pleasant and deserted, where the warm breeze blew us

together, and it developed she lived nowhere near. Ah, well.
How many can you trust? She had a huge respect for published
writers, of which I did not attempt to disabuse her, but explained my domestic situation, gave her a brotherly kiss, and
she walked me back to the subway. Her fiction dealt with
things like unconsummated dykey affairs and France, and because of the latter preoccupation I slipped up frequently on
place-names, but made even more egregious blunders, for she
also used English words, always correctly, which I had never
seen before. I offered to let her read her own work, but she
said she preferred things as they were. Not that she was shy,
especially, she simply liked to listen.

A few more arrived, seven of a possible ten, and just before
the last, the slightly tardy Delgado, came Christa. She'd put
her hair up since I saw her last. She wore her black coat, her
patched-up boots. She had to pass me on the way in, my perch
at the head of the table, and jutted her underlip in greeting.
She paused an instant; I gestured self-consciously toward the
several empty chairs, some close at hand. But she took one to
the rear, set back a bit from the table. Establishing her distance. Very well. I didn't trouble to inform the class there was
a guest in their midst; I doubted she would appreciate it, and
they could see it well enough.

After some opening patter I set up conferences for the following week, and collected what work they had done between
the previous week and this. I alerted them to a book review
I'd done, due out the following Sunday. This was hardly the
place for false modesty. I turned over the floor for a moment.
A girl just out of college was having her problems with "struc-
ture" . . . looking wise, I let them kick it around amongst
themselves. It wasn't my long suit. Between them, my intellectual and my athlete sorted her out. We were ready to begin. I
had brought along a cup of canteen coffee, and so had several
others. The atmosphere was relaxed. I was feeling fairly good

in any case, sober as a judge and filled with a sense of all our possibilities, but I'd come in with only two things worth read- ing aloud over the two hours, works by Baldakian and Hale, neither awfully long, which could have left us with a sticky swath of time to fill, but Delgado bailed me out, as (if he showed up) I had known he would, with another of his chaotic longhand installments, which he had finished, he said, ex- plaining his lateness, about thirty seconds before, in the john, the subway, a phone booth, I forget. I believed the dark young handsome skinny bastard when he said he did his writing everywhere, and he was equally credible when he said he had never rewritten anything in his life. He was not against re- write, he agreed in our meetings that his work would probably profit from it, but the new material came gushing at such a rapid rate, what with seeking menial jobs, and getting jobs, and losing jobs, and getting laid, and not getting laid, and fighting off queers, and using queers, and getting it all down while it was fresh, that he had trouble enough keeping pace as it was. He was about twenty-one, Brooklyn-born, half-Portuguese. Apart from this, I learned almost nothing about his past; his life be- gan the day he enrolled in my course. What he was attempting was nothing less than getting it all down, the ultimate diary, the tape-recorder-in-the-head, and damned if he wasn't bring- ing it off to an impressive degree. Of course, some process of selection was at work: a sensibility, a sense of order always threatened to emerge, but it hadn't yet, and I wasn't sure I cared to midwife it even if I had been able, for then he would become a *writer,* then he would produce *literature,* and I couldn't calculate how much this might cost him. The first thing he ever handed in, the second week of class, I read cold, aloud, dissembling my own shock as I went, and three ladies of a certain age therewith dropped the course. Which was surely just as well. Almost a year later, in February of '66, I received a letter from Los Angeles, where he had gone to seek his fortune. In moving from one coast to the other he had lost all his manuscripts, and needing them now for one reason or another he wondered if I had had the foresight and the interest, given their obvious merit and high level of lubricity, to have them xeroxed while they were in my possession, in which case he would be glad if I sent them along. He seemed fairly certain that I'd had it done. An almost perfect arrogance. But he was right, he was the dirtiest writer I have ever read. I wish I *had* reproduced that endless copybook scrawl, I would certainly share it with you. Reading him, that night, I was as embarrassed as I had been the first time, this time for Christa's sake, slurring the "cocksuckers" and the "cuntlappers" and the "prick testing the hairy asshole" (male/male, this was), or less embarrassed than fearful, that hearing me read the drivel she would associate me with it in her mind, or not that either but fearful, yes, that exposing her to so blatant an account and not shooting it down in the discussion which followed (or even if I had) would tend to condone or make seem respectable her own near-obsessional (if less graphic) concern with sexuality. I followed up with Mrs. Hale, a drastic change of pace, though I was not too much more comfortable reading the one than the other. And finished with Mrs. Baldakian, a sweet-faced Jewish woman in her forties married to an Armenian, whose fiction for a long while turned (as it did that night) entirely on retardation, the condition afflicting her youngest child. It did not seem the most promising subject matter, yet she managed to infuse it with some poignancy, though it was not easy to determine if that quality stemmed more from our awareness of her closeness to the subject than from the work itself. She was another of those who put a large trust in life—if I suggested that some incident or phrase had not come off, taxed our sense of pace or credibility, she would say, less carping than bewildered, "But, Mr. Sams, it really *happened* that way," and I could never do more than rejoin lamely that this wasn't always enough. Eventually I persuaded her to have a go at something different, someone else's tragedy; a kind, cooperative lady, she produced a long story of abortion, desertion and cancer among Irish Catholics, possibly plucked from the One Hundred Neediest Cases, not badly done, an improvement on her earlier efforts, but by that time, mid-May, I was having trouble maintaining real interest in the job.

So we got through the time. An average night. Eight cigarettes smoked. Mrs. Hale waylaid me on some allegedly literary matter before I could escape; I told Christa to wait for me in the lobby. I waited a moment after Mrs. Hale left, assembled my papers, and took the elevator down. She was turning the leaves of the mobile bulletin board: concerts, tutors, dramatic productions, cars for sale, charter flights, shared auto rides to distant places.

"Sarkissian. Want to get a beer?"

"Do you?"

"You bet."

I took her arm, we walked into the evening.

"Your football player was very chatty on the way down."

"What about?"

"What I was doing there, who I was . . ."

(He tried to pick her up, that blundering Neanderthal?)

"Normal, healthy young man's interest."

"Yes."

"What did you make of Delgado?"

"Which one was that?"

"The dirty one."

"Oh. Young, kind of feisty . . ."

"What's that mean?"

"Feisty? Like a little dog, snapping at your heels."

"That's a nice word. I've heard it but I never knew what it meant. Well, this is it, the face of a great university. How does it stack up to Berkeley?"

She shrugged. "Less pretty. Much too citified."

"We had a tree once, but it died."

I waited, dry-mouthed, looking forward to the beer, hoping she would volunteer some comment on my overall perfor- mance, flattering or otherwise, but not terribly surprised when she did not. In the crowded, noisy bar, surrounded by the young, loosened by the first few slugs, I took over both our roles, deprecating the teaching post, or myself in it, then de- fending the action as a harmless holding of the line. The thing I had to do was finish *Gino Travels,* then wait; they would come flooding in, the offers and sinecures, writer-in- residence here, teach one course a week for fifteen thousand there, from all over the vast, culture-hungry reaches of the nation, Arizona, Iowa, Colorado, places even closer to her home, and wouldn't that be nice? I wouldn't mind a year or so in the Bay Area, I told her, on a fat salary and with a sexy native guide . . . and on along these lines, then the one beer too many (she still nursed her first), and we taxied home, al- ready spending my future, but what the hell, I was not destitute now, and the basket was firmly on my head, I was pointed squarely toward the market.

A week later I took Christa to a Passover seder for a nest of reasons: because I wanted after all these years to go to one myself, or I wanted to shock the tribe, or test yet again which of them (along these lines) were shockable (and wasn't this the holiday, the night, to throw wide the gate to strangers?); be- cause I wanted to announce to the *mishpachah* her real pres- ence in my life, because I wanted, god help me, to broaden her anthropologically, and here she cooperated, made the effort on her own to learn the quaint customs of my people, went to the library and came back with the *dreck* you might expect, but read it through, and soon enough I was obliged to own to ignorance, not without some pleasure, when she asked me to expand on the meaning of this ritual, this symbolic piece of food or that. Martha and Harry picked us up. Off we went to the Bronx, to the home of Aunt Beth, the issue of my mother's primal scene, which she confessed to me when I was living with her and Harry post-robberies in '62, tired perhaps of the analytic questions I sprang at every turn (I had recently, secretly, begun), while I struggled to be casual—how long or whether she had nursed me, did I wet the bed, had she ever caught me jerking off, etc.—how at a fairly tender age she was sleeping in her parents' bedroom but awoke when her father stirred in the night, said (tenderly), "Molly, let's make a baby for Pesach," and lo, it was Beth, on schedule, who would grow up to be my full-time babysitter, and go on from there to have a life of her own which is better left undescribed. I could never look at her childlike face (even now, in her fifties, not so changed by time and suffering) without pure pleasure, the source of which I couldn't trace, unless it was the time she and a covey of girl friends put my Doctor Dentons on me back to front, or hands where feet should be, but could such an uproarious event determine my feelings for the next thirty years? I never, to my credit, gave it that much thought, hugged her roughly when I saw her, which was not more than once a year. It was to Beth's that Molly went to live after my grandfather died, although not so quickly as she should have, putting in a number of bad years living alone in an apartment down the hall from Martha and Harry, hanging up my poor mother in no small way. (I was blessedly abroad through most of that time; when I wasn't, I would sit with her over coffee and strudel in her kitchen, and in her mockey's English she would tell me many things, of meetings and partings in Galicia, reunions in London, separations, reunions in New York, making love— she *blushed*—to her husband-to-be in the back of a grocery store, of the hotdog wagon he pushed for a living before he got

the horse and then the truck and established the beer and selt-
zer route through the Lower East Side which much later, like a
medical practice, he sold, tales of dead-of-night journeys to
outdoor toilets on Columbia and Cherry streets ((even the
streets existed no longer)), of how nervous a child was my
mother, and of the first time she, Molly, had ever seen a bear. It
was in 1906, at the London zoo ((we had it in common)). She
was seventeen at the time.) Irving, the man Beth barely married, in the twilight of her marriageable years, was a plumber,
with even graver shortcomings, but he was an Orthodox Jew,
the home was kosher, there were kids around, fussing to do,
particularly for the sabbath and the high holy days, and in her
final years the old woman was content.

Yet it was bloody that night. I might not even have noticed,
or minded, had I not had my gadfly with me, for this night was
not that different from many other nights when the clan had
gathered; but as it was I saw things through her eyes. Sons and
son-in-law were uniformly haunted all these years later by the
absent patriarch, whose shoes the head of the house, Orthodox
or not, was least able to fill, so they split up the headship in
deadly democratic fashion, each read a part, murdering awe
and even ceremony, and as for joy, a chance of that, there was
the shrill and almost vicious bickering, for which Martha and
Harry set the tone, and my father cross court with Irv; and
Beth's teen-agers came and left with intrigues and crises of
their own . . . yet through it all Molly served and beamed. I
doubt the climate altogether escaped her, but she remained
glad to have us all assembled, and very pleased at having lived
this long. About halfway through she came up behind our
chairs, me whom she had not seen for a year at least and
Christa never (and concerning Christa, I have to think she
knew the worst, for milady looked like what she was, or Italian
at best, and the question had been briefly, lightly raised in
Molly's hearing by a youngish aunt-and-uncle team I had un-

til that second regarded more highly), and she embraced us both at once, leaning over our backs, wrinkled and round, smelling of the kitchen, her gray hair neatly bunned, embraced us both at once but planted separate kisses on our cheeks, complained of how rarely she saw me, wondered how I had managed to live into my thirty-third year—her oldest, her best—without presenting her with great-grandchildren (though fortunately for us all, others, like my absent sister, then off in Sweden, had taken up the slack)? And as I laughed it off and reached back to clasp her rough, horny hand, I saw the other squeezing Christa's shoulder . . . was it possible she could have missed it? Or was it rather that, in keeping with the times, when it came time to shape and record, she remembered only chaos?

Freedom of action, as it was, presented itself quite often via the phone. It rang one open-ended evening, late in March, as I contemplated picking up the laundry. There was dead air at first, then a timorous female voice which mentioned, after some meandering, the name of a novelist I barely knew, from overlapping sojourns at an artists' colony the autumn before. She fell, after that, into fumbling and silence. I invited her by, since the evening was free, and she lived in the neighborhood, but she demurred. Sarkissian was at home, which information might have put her at ease, but I saw no way to impart it. I offered to meet her outside the Manufacturers' Hanover Trust on Fourteenth Street in ten minutes and take her with me on my homely errand, and to this she agreed.

"Did you hear that?" I said to Christa.

"No. I wasn't listening. Who was it?"

"Damned if I know. Some waif in distress. I'm going to take her with me to the laundry. Be back in a little while."

We approached the bank from opposite directions. I expected nothing, or perhaps the worst, partly thanks to Dino's ancient tale, *With a Rose in Her Hair,* one of a batch of shorter works he'd shown to me in Barcelona. It featured a stout, ageing woman with a shriveled leg (and a rose in her hair) whom the hero, by an outraged, callous ruse, successfully evaded, though he had agreed to meet her at precisely that hour, at precisely that spot, beneath the Bronx elevated line. It had stayed in my mind as the perfect paradigm for blind dates of any kind, however undistinguished, as a story, in most other respects. So I was perfectly prepared to let the smallish, shapely, long-tressed girl approaching across Second Avenue pass me at whatever she considered the proper speed and distance, contenting myself with the mandatory glance at her rear. Instead she walked directly up in a way which belied her telephone manner, and asked if I was Jason Sams. I thought, It can't be, I've seen the movie, but I nodded gravely and escorted her down Fourteenth to First Avenue, where, as I'd promised, we picked up my laundry. She was an altogether lovely brown-eyed snub-nosed Baptist doll, with blonde hair so fine it might have dissolved at the touch. Not only that . . . at the corner tavern, into which (laundry bag and all) I steered her, she revealed that she held an M.A. in English, taught American literature at one of the city colleges, and would have finished her doctoral thesis on *The Confidence Man* long before now had the affair of the heart with my colleague not intruded. I gulped my third beer somewhat ruefully. Naturally such a prize would come into my life only when I was elsewhere committed, playing house with another. But this was fate, and I was not really at that moment discontented with my private life. It had its definite rewards, it made no large demands. I spoke at length of Christa, gave her a fairly good press, and I could see this stray, beleaguered beauty envy us our bliss. Well, there was always room for friendship, and the wheel of life kept turning—what did she want, why had she called? On certain nights, when she needed

her man, and he had to be elsewhere, she became so desperate
and glum that she tried to connect with people he knew, or
had merely mentioned. (I was close to the end of her list: she
had already attempted to reach nearly every name he'd ever
dropped, or every male; by her account, to my surprise, not all
had been hospitable.) The writer, her lover, a—I recalled
him—defensive, wisecracking Jewish New Yorker of a de-
rivative and very middling talent, a year or two younger than
myself, was married, with three children, and was not then
able or willing to divorce his wife. He had arranged for Glory
to visit a psychiatrist, his very own, and this, she said, was no
small boon, but her loneliness, at times, still brought her to
this present pass. And she was glad, tonight, it had—she
found me gentle and *sympatico,* not sullen and surly at all
(well, up yours, too, Henry!), as she confessed he had described me. I envied him of course, whatever his griefs and
anxieties: another of the hard-nosed males who managed to
have it both ways. I wished for the thousandth time I had been
married, had fathered (in that connection or some other) a
child or two, had put such seminal, grown-up deeds behind
me. Or was it the *having been married,* that especial contemporary purple heart, I craved. Even Glory Green, young and
fragile as she seemed, owned to an ex-husband, a dissolved five-
year marriage. Only Sarkissian and myself, it appeared, were
thus far unscathed. We'd been in that beer-stinking joint for
close to an hour. For reasons as tangled as her own must have
been in phoning up, I asked Glory to come back with me. She
was not, to tell the truth, especially keen, she thanked me for
my time and kindness up to there, but I insisted. I said she
would be doing us a favor: Christa had no female friends in
New York and the two of them would probably hit it off. Reluctant still, she agreed to stop by for a while. I shouldered my
bag and led her up the street, a narcissistic Santa Claus. What
real female gives a shit for female friends? But producing her

this way would set off many things. Her sheer attractiveness
would make clear to Christa why my absence was extended.
But bringing the goods to the hearth would show milady how
little she had to fear, should she behave herself, concerning my
fidelity; should she screw around, how much. And Glory
Green—the wheel of life kept turning—would have viewed,
all innocent, the inside of my lair, my paintings, my (still living) pussycat; some magic has already occurred, whatever
comes of it, as soon as they set foot inside the door. All this and
more was clear and conscious in my mind, blithe butterfly motives skittering through the underbrush. The whole ecologi-
cal mess—butterflies, underbrush—culminated in the simple act; and the simple act bespoke a style, a sense of situation,
which, god willing, has been honed a little since.

Nothing—should the above lines seem to offer promise—
out of the ordinary or interesting occurred. Christa, unperturbed, unreadable as ever, perched on the hassock. Glory was
on the couch. Himself, social director, sat in the black basket
chair, equidistant between them. Glory crossed her legs.
Christa, in Japanese sandals and a peasant skirt, hair down,
leaned forward. My eyes, my best attention, went from the one
to the other. I brought out the scotch, wound up drinking it
myself. Indeed, they seemed to hit it off. They had in common, discussed at length, La Jolla, California, I forget just
why. My sharp-nosed, large-legged, shrugging lady, whose
moles and smells I knew, came off less well, I thought, in conversational and esthetic terms. After a sip or two, I resolved
not to judge the entries but to try and dig the show in its entirety, count my blessings, and I indulged a reverie, while they
did their California thing, on types like this one, my inexpli-
cable weakness through the years for such as Glory Green, and
how little gaiety and *nachas,* all in all, they'd ever brought me.
Her legs were (their legs were always) shapely, the calf of one,
the way she had them now, made broad and bulbous by the

knee of the other, that sweet blush, when she uncrossed them, formed under the knee. When they ran down on La Jolla, I filled the gap myself, talking books, Henry's, Melville's, mine, Christa's reading list (*Siddartha* at the time), then Glory said she had to go. I offered to take her home, for a hundred reasons. About a week before, returning with a purchase from the liquor store, and not so sober when I went, I ran into a motorcycle club coming up the block as I was starting down. They were on foot, on my side of the street. The street, at ten P.M., was otherwise empty. They did not usually stray this far north, this side of Fourteenth Street, but there they were, swaggering in black jackets, perhaps a dozen, blocking out the moon. I calculated that if I continued at my present pace I would run into them right outside my door. High as I was, I felt safe (which was not the same as feeling brave); otherwise, chances were, I would have changed direction on the spot, moved back toward lights, the liquor store, or the adjacent supermarket (open until midnight), much less ashamed of myself than on those times I've given ground in broad daylight to untended dogs of all sizes, glimpsed from a distance. My beard, my unconcern, their innate humanity—something was going to protect me. All the same, I reached into my pocket and fingered my keys, notions of flight mingled with thoughts of defense. A man on a Spanish boat, using keys, had split open my jaw—five stitches from a government doctor when we reached Alicante. The group and I collided, as I'd measured, just outside the house. I was giving them room, hugging the inside. And, as it happened, they were hell-bent on their destination: all the pain I reaped for my existence was a single remark from the black-bearded Brando nearest to me ("Hey. Look at it"), full of menace and contempt, and not really fathomable, for how could he, any more than the man on the boat, know me well enough to punish me for secret failings? If I sweated certain moments of the next few days, flushed without warning by thoughts of life without an eyeball (and of the unbearable moment when they calmly, skillfully, popped it), or life with crushed testicles, a maiming so fortuitous and pointless I'd be without even writerly redress, well, it was the media and certain books, not these twelve good men, which were to blame. But perhaps the worst of it was that I'd been through such things too many times before. Sweden of '61, one late afternoon, walking the bucolic streets of Lund, with Britta, near the university, a motorcycle driven by a woman suddenly deposits a youth in tight jeans about ten yards ahead. He pulls a bottle of aquavit from his back pocket, swigs, staggers on. From what I'd already learned of Swedish drinking habits, there was nothing odd or ominous so far. Then he tossed away the bottle and from a sheath in his belt brought out a hunting knife, still moving, weaving. I slowed Britta down. If he turned on us, attacked us (*why had I learned nothing from the man on the boat?*), I would have had to defend her, court an early death, though I loved her no longer. Alone, I would have run; he was too drunk to pursue. I had no skills. Why had I never learned karate, or even boxing, or been less supercilious about hand-to-hand instruction in the basic training days? Why had I not honored my perceptions, acquired some tools, instead of advocating "non-violence," forlorn wish more than precept, its soil precisely one's defenselessness? Abruptly the Swede turned into a driveway, crouched, becoming stealthy, murder in mind. With a relief close to glee, we tiptoed by. Into more leisurely dilemmas. There were no phones, no other houses nearby. A man would have disarmed him (causing him no harm), deprived him of his twelve-inch blade, kept him quiet until help arrived, saved a life or two. Instead we went on to the university, where we had a cheap dinner, and I swiped a volume of Katherine Anne Porter's stories, in English, which was just lying around. I scanned the papers for a week or so, dictionary at hand, sodden with guilt and loathing, but found no mention.

So I walked Glory home. It was half a mile. We climbed the tenement stairs, I praised her poor apartment, and polished off some souring wine, the dregs of an old entertainment. I stayed only long enough to say that whatever her present doubts and fears, inclination to demean herself, she struck me as in all senses a very special girl. Overriding her mild objections, which centered on Christa, I arranged to come and see her three nights thence. Sarkissian had said she was going to the ballet that night; she had asked me to come, but I'd begged off on general grounds. I'd planned to read, to work, or goof, or perhaps I'd looked ahead to just such a present contingency. All right, if you wish, said Glory Green. She seemed to be a girl without a will, a lost little bright little very uptight miss, with legs and hips and eyes that promised everything.

Christa, three nights later, changed her mind. It had only been a plan, she didn't have a ticket, she thought now she'd stay home and read. I was furious at being crossed. I thought of going to a phone booth and canceling out, but didn't want to disappoint the child. I sat there squirming, feeling it build, until ten minutes before I was due. Then I put on a jacket, mumbled something about cigarettes and a stroll, and left.

Thoughtfully she'd laid in a fresh bottle of wine, and I'd picked up another on the way. She was as desirable as before. Even so, the climate remained tense and odd, we labored for a context. I was sick of hearing about Henry, but not really up to steering her away. During a lull she leaned over my chair, fiddled with the radio, found some jazz, returned to her seat on the bed. I went to the john, and when I came out, joined her on the bed. I moved to her doll's face for a kiss. Slowly, slightly, she averted her head. I hardly minded; I felt fucking awful. I was losing my touch, or, much worse, losing interest in my touch. I rose, tried to smile, dusted my erection into place, went back to my chair, chatted an instant longer and departed. She saw me to the door. I felt her watching from above as I clumped down the stairs.

I'd meant to walk around the block, I told Christa, but was stricken by nostalgia, and wandering south, wound up on Essex and Grand streets, two miles away, outside my former high school.

Mmmhmm, she may have said.

Early in April, close in time, came reminders of griefs gone by. Sandy phoned to invite me to a party at her place on the first of May; she'd been thinking of me, she said, she remained eager to expose me to her circle. I said I'd be glad to come if I could bring a friend, meaning the one who sat just then beside me; she said all right, though her enthusiasm dimmed. I thought I glimpsed Gillian from a bus window, all dressed in white, near Grand Central station, on the way back from visiting with Frank; I didn't get off, though I was tempted. From Britta in Malmö came a long letter containing a photo of her infant son, plus assorted marital complaints, and the news that my sister and brother-in-law had, at my suggestion, looked her up, and that at certain moments, peering at my sister's nervous face, watching her all unconscious scratch an armpit, she thought she still missed me. But it was not until later in the month that I had occasion to recall the wracking gloom which was the worst ever of its kind, dwarfing melodramatic anguish over British nurses, mocking ancient unconsummated Provincetown passions: the thing with Esha, in particular the first few days after she left London, when I would receive her bright, bitchy postal cards from airline stops all the way to Kuala Lumpur, merry messages from Vienna, Beirut, Singapore ("Cheerio and good luck, *Abang!*"), which I would cradle upstairs from the mail table and read in outraged, retching tears in the bed-sitter which still stank of curry, still contained the loaded objects—the robe, the doll, the pair of battered shoes—she'd left behind. But why bring up that dreary horror tale, I can still hardly mention to my friends? Of how I lived in the same room for three months with a monkey-faced Malayan of twenty-three years of age who was a virgin when I met her, and flew off to her fat civil servant of a fiancé (whose photo, through it all, beamed from the mantelpiece) at the end of that period in more or less the same condition? A magnum of Old Ship, "British port-style wine," was under the bed for nipping at, morning, noon and night, while I schemed and plotted the next frantic assault. But she fended me off each time, the tightest pussy in the realm, the fiercest feline will, versus its most sensitive, impatient erection, itchiest trigger finger; she had to have been as insane as I. Once in a while we went to the movies, and she had the temerity to play with my dick. Near the end of it she fought no more, but I continued dutifully to probe her with my fingers, having long since given up hope for the other. One night in the midst of it I revived a not too ancient habit, went down to Soho and rented a tall, floppy blonde for half an hour, confiding my problems as I rested in her friendly body, and she counseled me to persevere, delivered a soothing lecture on the cunt, or the architectonic perversity of some; thus armed, I raced back to the same brown dilemma, the same seething in the night, spilling my seed in sundry inaccurate places, grinding and girding for the next attempt. Sometimes I'd try and rise above it all, lying in the single bed on the other side of the room, or even in my own room, two floors above, desperately thinking Zen (a paid and paying student of the Japanese), mulling Daisetz Suzuki's million English words on the virtues of shitsticks and silence, struggling for a little peace. Enough, no details—there are humiliations here, maltreatments of the cock and soul, I still cannot touch. I mention it at all because her almost-kewpie face, brilliant, sweaty garb, her chocolate voice re-entered my life on the nineteenth of April, 1965, and stunned as I may have been by the eeriness of it happening when it did, I was not, under the sun, really surprised.

When I knew Esha she was studying the phonetics of her own language at the University of London on a Malay government grant, roughly two hundred dollars a month plus tuition, more than twice the bounty of the GI Bill, amidst a host of Africans and Asians at the school who were similarly occupied. Although, to be fair, there were a number of ex-colonials as well, even in my own department, two Americans besides myself in a total enrollment of twelve people reading Japanese, not one of the more popular subjects, not one of the better departments, but scholarly second-rateness was the price Japan paid Britain for having never been colonized. Indifferent as I was, or was supposed to be—I was there buying time, seeing Europe and learning my craft on government money, my interest in things Japanese only slightly more developed than my interest in Coptic art—I walked around in a state of academic outrage pretty nearly all the time, for few of the instructors, Japanese or British, gave a damn, fewer still could teach, and, anti-intellectual stance or no, I had spent those four years on the Heights, I had come by certain expectations. So I drank a lot of disgruntled fourpenny tea in the junior common room, and met Esha there. In due course she got her degree, or her diploma, whichever it was, went back to the man, was duly penetrated, had children, never even taught her subject, let alone engaged in research, but when some money turned up seven years later for a junket to phonetics departments at universities throughout the U.S. she was contacted, and by that time she was delighted to say yes. I had dreamt of her off and on, over the years, on two continents, and not only dreamt but fancied I saw her (during a weird period for a few months after she went) once or twice a week, because her costume, her body type, were not uncommon in Bayswater, around Russell Square, and down the Finchley Road; but when I came in that Monday night, a little late, pleasantly high from the several beers with my student Mrs.

Hale and our innocent stroll down to the river, and I asked Christa if there had been any calls, and she gestured to an index card alongside the telephone, I was struck with a sense of if not *déjà vu* then almost annoyance that I had not predicted exactly this occurrence, in exactly this manner, the magic name of one tormentor, *Esha ben Hamid Don,* scrawled in the spidery hand of another. Somebody up there was fucking with me, no question, and I was not a little put off by his continued absence of originality.

"That's really wild," I said. "A woman I went to school with in London seven years ago. What the devil can she want? Did she say?"

"She left her number," Christa said, which I could see well enough. Also where she was staying, the Park-Sheraton Hotel. Christa had barely looked up from her *The Tin Drum,* or my *The Tin Drum,* one of the dutiful book-club volumes I was acquiring at the time; they remained, after a glance and an inroad, pristine. Christa, otherwise idle, took them up. I doubt she got very far either, but further than I. Perhaps one day in a less hectic moment I'll manage to generate some interest in jailed homicidal faggots, or hunchback musical midgets, but not then, not now. She might at least have glanced up from the book, expressed an interest of whatever kind. Jealousy would have been the best, or pique of any sort . . . but nothing. I was on the phone inside of ten minutes. Hello, Esha, this is Jason Sams. Hello—corruptly coy as ever—this is Esha ben Hamid Don, do you remember me? (Did I remember my mother?) I asked her how she was. She was very well indeed, and was interested to know if I was married. Alas I was not, and what was she doing in these parts, and would she like to get together? She was puzzlingly evasive, considering she had rung me up. She had only five days remaining in New York, with certain luncheons and excursions preplanned, with a university or two to visit (I was less than pleased to see that alma mater graced her half-arse list), and couldn't be pinned down. That's too bad, I said, perhaps we'll speak again.

"Strange," I said, returning from the study. "I just called her back and she was very remote. I can't figure why she called in the first place."

"I think I might have put her off."

"You? How?"

"She asked if I was Mrs. Sams."

"What did you say?"

"No."

"Oh."

"I think she assumed I was the maid."

"The maid? How could she think you were the maid? Did you come on like a maid?"

"No."

"Then why should she think it? And what difference would it make?"

"I don't know. Can we drop it, Jason?"

"Whose maid works until ten o'clock?"

And so the next afternoon, Tuesday, when Sarkissian stormed out around one o'clock literally behind my back, for unfathomable reasons, as I sat bald and vulnerable at my silent machine, I rang Esha back from anger and bruised curiosity, and although she was just about to leave for a Statue of Liberty cruise she would be back in time for dinner, and yes we could have it together.

I happened to see Frank that afternoon, although I had seen him also the day before. He was juggling me wildly in those times. Man to man, as an equal, privy to life's little ironies, I asked him to hazard a guess as to who I would be dining with in two hours' time. Not a gambling man, he gave up at once. He chuckled, said My, my, when I told him. I wasn't sure he had the picture. You remember her, don't you, her pert, swishing walk, her sweaty *kabaya,* and what happened—what she did to me—abroad? Of course, Dino, I mean Jason, of course he did. He had all my ladies, he assured me, perfectly straight in his head. Isn't it a gas, Frank, how one's tiny life pursues and catches up, whatever evasive action one takes, however one struggles to get well? Disconcerting and exciting, he seemed to agree. We had only half an hour to go, had I brought in a dream?

I met her in the lobby of her hotel. I was a few minutes late, but I had the advantage. She looked right through me twice. Finally I touched her shoulder from behind, and reintroduced myself. She wheeled, did a double take, made some feeble joke about the beard. Her sense of humor hadn't altered much. I'd borne it way back then, it seemed a small enough price to pay for the treasure I was after, and I had no real defense in any case, for the thrust of it concerned my nationality. Back there, in the Eisenhower years, we were all willynilly ambassadors for the nation. They held me personally responsible for *Time* magazine, she and her plump and pimply Venezuelan girl friend, whose constant presence, there at the beginning, I suffered almost gladly, conceiving it to be some obscure East Asian price I was obliged to pay to ever get her off alone. *Time* magazine, was the gist, seemed to know beans about Kuala Lumpur or Caracas. My reply, that this didn't surprise me, cut no ice. And do all Americans go bald at twenty-six, look like a monk from behind? Ah ho, that's rich, girls, but you really shouldn't generalize. My own sad story—are you listening?—has to do with some terrible predisposition interacting with the water, or the honeybuckets, or my generally spicy life in Japan. I was only twenty-two when it happened. Oh yes, they knew about that life, or could imagine it, the evil footloose GI on foreign soil. I doubted if they could. In due course South America did fade, I moved from my remote, shabby basement room for a guinea a week in the boondocks of Highbury Hill to a barely more pleasant place at three times the rent which had just come free in the rooming house she lived in, in Bayswater, but spent most of my time for the next few months in the room two floors below. I learned to suck (and like) the substance of raw eggs from a small opening in the shell. I became, in the desperate need to beat her more than half the time, a minor ping-pong champ (she slammed with equal power, but no finesse, from either side). I shot my seed in Esha's mouth, anon, glued shut her armpits, slaughtered nations in the area of her anus, matted her wiry bush and coal-black hair, well-nigh felt her ovaries with every finger, but I completely understood her gleeful devastating claim to bridal purity when she left me for the last time at the air terminal behind Victoria Station, July of '58, a semblance of tears on all sides. I'd never fucked her after all, she had a right to feel triumphant.

"Jason? Is that you under all that hair?"

I smiled. The self-same style, the inane jockeying. It could hardly upset me, as it had in former times. A widening bald spot in one's twenties is less easy to defend, but this—it was a splendid beard. I felt not the slightest need to explain it away, or how it had come to be. It was in Christmas of '59 that Britta and I locked up the Barcelona flat and journeyed to the islands, Majorca, Ibiza, and on the last day of the old year, while I slept on a Spanish tub between Ibiza and the mainland, trapped by the Catholic accommodations in a cabin with three male strangers, I was attacked in the night by the one of the three who was a madman, chiefly on the head and jaw, fists and keys his only weapons, so that while I was glad, in retrospect, to have survived, and made some literary capital of it by and by, I found in the period immediately after that I could not chew or shave, and when the beard arrived, the beard which I had for three preceding European years successfully avoided, I liked it and kept it. Britta, a bourgeois if well-traveled Swede (but a square was what I had been seeking; I had the impression, after Esha, of exotica enough, enough excitement in my life), liked it considerably less, but in time it—*mil pardons!* —grew on her too. I kept the thing in some form or other a good little while, diddling and tampering only—chin alone, then with sideburns, then fulsome and full, removed it once in London (post-Sweden) for the sake of identity games, but merely confused myself and my Irish barmaid of the time, kept it thereafter for so long a time that even my mother (no early advocate) was dismayed when I removed it next, the time of her mother's funeral, as a private sign of mourning and in order to see who loved me for myself. Whoever they were, I was not in their number; I let it come back, where it has remained. But even by the time of that meeting in the Park-Sheraton Hotel it had a difficult, time-tested history, I could barely be needled by the best, let alone by this brown, bouncy lady, with whose subtlety and sense of humor, even at my worst, I'd never been enamored.

"Yes, it's me, Esha. How are you?"

"I'm fine! Well! Can you show me the city?"

We agreed to a drink, away from the hotel. I squired her through the Seventh Avenue rush hour, no more needing to apologize for the shoddy neighborhood and the jostling, blind-eyed natives than for my own appearance. I steered her into the first bar which seemed reasonably posh, and we took a booth. It was dark, male commuters were unwinding, there were canapés. I ordered martinis, looked her over. In that light, at least, she hadn't changed at all. I listened, acquiring such data on her mission and travels as I have already passed on. I gave her Denby's name and address, since Tucson was to be a stop; it was time I reciprocated, turned things around, sent some female goods his way. I ordered another drink but went before it came to phone Christa, inform her of my dinner plans; there was someone in the booth, someone waiting, so I revamped the priorities. This dark lady, this *mirage*, would vanish soon enough. My Armenian problem (should she even be at home) could wait awhile. When I got back Esha turned the tables, fairly. All in all, I said, the years had been kind; then out of gallantry, or else to give us both some sense of continuity, I confessed that my volume, which she claimed to be eager to acquire, contained in point of fact a tale I had been writing in those very times—the woolly adventures of a Jewish GI in Japan—god remembered how, for my memory of those days seemed fairly well exhausted by wine drunks and failed Zen and mad thrustings at that prick-proof pussy and resultant anguish, but clearly this last condition had not yet poisoned my vision of Sams the scribe; that would come later; rather, at twenty-six, it seemed I was obliged to get some typing done to save what I valued of my life. Huzzahs, at least, for that.

We decided on a Pakistani restaurant in the East Village, nostalgic tribute to her home cooking in our room on Hereford Road, and the countless other curried meals we'd taken in W.1 Indian restaurants; also, three weeks from Kuala Lumpur, she confessed that she missed the cuisine. I mocked this not at all—many's the hamburger I sought, the subhungers I slaked, in places like Kobe and Tarragona. Before we left the bar I felt once more impelled to check in at the hearth, assuming a hearth, conjuring it by the call, but the booth was again occupied. I waited there awhile, then let it go. I owed her little; she had herself accounted for my present whereabouts by storming out that afternoon. Esha and I taxied to the Koh-I-Noor. She pulled rank on the waiters about the slowness of the service, subtle failures in the seasoning, quite regal really in manner and garb, drank a bourbon, her eyes sparkled; the meal was a success. We finished around half-past nine.

I could have fucked her on the spot, or as quickly placed her in a cab, mission accomplished, case closed, as the lunch with

Sandy in the January days had seemed to round a circle, but she wanted to go to the Village Gate. She had assumed command. I'd allowed her to pick up the restaurant tab, for she'd carried me often enough in olden times, her seventy British pounds a month to my thirty-nine, and if she needed to re-create this aspect of those far from halcyon days, I was not going to hinder. But from kept man to tour leader was no giant step. I sighed, complied, and we walked west. Dizzy Gillespie, she told me, was at the Gate. She'd always been an amateur jazz buff of a sort, we'd been to see a touring Ella on the Kilburn High Road all those lives before, and she was almost gleeful now, as I rushed her past the Bowery, insisting she would pay for everything.

Gillespie's neither here nor there. Between sets we danced, when the records were shmaltzy enough. We'd danced in the old country too, or done whatever we were doing now, and she remembered my phrase for it, "the high school foxtrot," and once she brought that out I held her svelte and sweaty frame less gingerly. Finally, around two, we left, swung hands a moment in the open air, strolled down MacDougal Street, then I took her back to her hotel. We necked a trifle in the cab; her mood, as I gauged it, was mixed. We entered the seedy lobby. She responded with a rote, arch surprise to my rote, arch interest in seeing the inside of her room. She did not object. We rose to the eleventh floor under the circumspect scrutiny of the elevator operator, definitely an odd couple. She had narrow, shabby lodgings in the second-rate hotel. It would be interesting to learn why so many foreigners go there, so many delegations. I sat on the couch, which was also the bed, and which tended to slide out from under if you leaned back against the wall. I saw a half-full bottle of blended whis-key, which she explained away in some now-forgotten, satis-factory fashion; she hadn't had anything to drink since the wa-tered down Old Grand Dad in the Koh-I-Noor, and though she joined me sociably now, I don't think she sipped more than once from her glass. She sat a few feet from me on the couch and talked about her marriage. Her mate she described as pedestrian, insensitive, authoritarian (I'd warned her way back then he'd be a bloody Asian in the end), and more and more, in recent times, she'd had to punish him for his transgressions.

"How do you do that, Esha?"

"I pretend to be asleep when he wants something."

"What does he want?"

"When he comes in late and wants to . . . sleep with me. I pretend to be asleep."

Ingenious. At the very least, in character. The man had not approved of this present trip, which was one reason she had made it. The years, I thought again, had never touched her. And because I thought this, I thought she still moved me, and that I had to act upon this warp in space and time. So as I listened, I touched her hand. Expressing dissent, I stroked her hand. Nodding agreement, I took it, dropped it, gulped some whiskey, and when her monologue ran down I filled the gap with lips and body, a chaste continuation of our last kiss in the cab. She seemed agreeable, as also to the hand which traveled round her shoulders, down her back; in response to pressure, her tongue essayed some kittenish forays which would have warned a wiser man, but he was long abed, and the character I had become hoped and assumed she was horny. My own interest, if more visible, was less easy to describe, but it would clearly do. Motives be damned—much better me for her post-London needs than some potbellied phonetician in her travels. Fairly rapidly, battling that subversive sliding couch, I freed a brown breast, I could maneuver a *kabaya* well as any man, and the sight of that dun, stippled boob was almost reward enough, but it constituted a terrain from which it was not easy to retreat. She was breathing hard and fast, but with

her eyes closed she was shaking her head from side to side in
the blind, willful negative which contradicted sanity and her
body, and which I remembered in a rush from our early
(courtship!) days, so I did now what I did then, thrust a hand
up under her tight sarong, and achieved, once more, the bot-
toms of her secret knees. Where the thing unfastened (from
the waist?) I'd never learned, and now as then ("This is silly,
Jason. No no, please don't") I knew that no help would be
forthcoming. But I persevered, jabbed, feinted, forced, found
the commencement of a thigh and the words to go with it, and
when I heard them again after so many years I knew I had
missed them, for with Christa even in our better days we'd
fucked for fucking's sake, with a minimum of dialogue, each
rapt in single fleshly possibilities, while to this distant woman
I could still admit to tenderness. Sweetpuss. Brownmiss. Dear-
love. I missed you all the time. I need you still. Heartfelt, god-
help, they may have been, but they opened no doors, undid no
knots, and in my sense of the lateness of the hour, and the
shortness of our days, I did open my fly. And she responded,
"Oh. Don't. Naughty. Wick-ed." At which I swallowed shame
and rage and carried on. Here. Look. It's your bright-eyed and
downtrodden friend. Remember him? His dumb and single-
minded needs? How you would toy with him for minutes
which seemed hours, or as long as I would let you, and for
some damn reason called him Michelangelo? This long
Michelangelo has waited, this patient he has been, and I took
her hand and placed it on my prick. She squeezed it gently, her
head turned away, and it produced for her, in gratitude, a
throbbing crystal drop. She stole a glance, smiled, blushed,
said, "Please put it away," and tried to reinsert it in my pants.
This was not just then possible. But the blush did me in. My
humiliation now was so profound, I had so far outdone myself, she was embarrassed for me, nothing more. I stood,
crammed the dwindling pecker back in place, reassembled

myself, finished off my drink, fixed her with my most scathing, futile stare, shook my head, and slammed out the door. I had a bellyful of piss, but I would not bestow it in her lodgings. It was a great relief to reach the open air. A cab was waiting outside the hotel. I was further restored by the last inning of the Met game from Los Angeles. It was still in progress when we got to my corner; the middle-aged Negro, a *mensch,* dropped his flag and we sat there listening to the miracle. Dogged! Ancient! Warren Spahn, battling the record book, went into the last half-inning with a three–two lead against the Dodgers. It was unlikely to hold up, given his years and the ragtag club behind him, and when he walked the first man up in the ninth, I began to hope for quick release, for him and for my bladder, the home run right now, rather than the agonizing, piecemeal, frittering away of the ball game. But Spahn's psychology was not mine; he achieved two quick outs, the runner advancing to second, and he ran out the string on Maury Wills. Wills fouled off several, then grounded to Macmillan to end the game. How anticlimactic, in the spectator sports, are the seconds following a triumph. All the same, the driver and I congratulated each other, and I walked down the block as jaunty as I could. And damned if some fraction of the long night hadn't been redeemed.

She was awake when I entered, or I woke her. I mumbled hello toward her stirring sounds and went directly to the toilet. I took a long and decorous piss, then put the water on full blast, both taps, trying to wash the Far East from my life. I scrubbed my face and neck and furiously brushed my teeth, the water still pounding. (Esha, of course, would not let me off this easily: two days later she would ring up and invite us out to dinner, myself and my "friend"; I had some small trouble being civil, but none in saying no. Then there would be the cheery, pointless letters from Chicago, Tucson and Los Angeles, her next three stops, recalling the postcards of yore, when she'd escaped me then. And there was the letter from Denby—how I regretted that charity, now!—which said in relevant part:

A tableau to remember: Today I attended by request a company luncheon for the celebration of a foreign guest on tour. The guest, a Malay dish (well, there goes the plot; anyhow . . .), lovely and dusky and plugged into a 220 circuit somewhere just out of sight, smiled when introduced to himself and said, smoothly, "Oh, you are D. Denby. I believe we have a mutual acquaintance, Jason Sams. I knew him in London, and have recently come . . ." All of which put me countless points up on the other limp pricks in the cafeteria. Very very *honmono,** that one. This surely did not escape you, and for the points, if not for Esha herself, my hisses.

I check back through the files for details in your London notes, just in case Malaya beckons . . .)

I stripped to my underwear in the john, and came out ready for bed.

"You washed very thoroughly."

"I washed . . . for god's sake. I was brushing my teeth, Christa."

As indignant, full of horror as I tried to sound. How like her to take the offensive, assume the other's guilt to turn attention from her own, and use his sense of it as the lever with which to rebuke him. But she'd conveyed her vision and I saw myself, standing at the basin, trousers lowered, rubbing alien pussy from my groin before daring to share her bed. Well, she was full of shit, it hadn't happened, however much I may have wished it; I brought a full, sore scrotum from the fray, and where in hell had *she* been since one o'clock in the afternoon?

I climbed into bed, we shared a silence. As always, I was the one unable to sustain it.

* Jap. for "the genuine article."

"I had dinner with that Malayan lady. I tried to call you a couple of times, but I couldn't get through. Then she wanted to tour the Village and we went to see Dizzy Gillespie. Have you ever heard him? Good, funky sounds."

Silence.

"And you? Where have you been? What have you been up to?"

"Not very much."

"Mmmhmm. Maybe if you hadn't torn out of here this afternoon, things would have worked out differently."

"Yes."

"Good night, Christa."

"Good night."

Yes?? For her, in such a mood, this was loquacity. I didn't, then, request she amplify, spin the monosyllable out; things being what they were, I took, alone, what I could find in it of sustenance.

"Jesus. A microcosmic repeat, seven years after. How could I go through with it, Frank? Why am I so fucked up? Blueballs at thirty-three, and living with someone at the time! And then, when I got home, she pulls that 'You washed very thoroughly' crap. Man, I can't recall when I ever felt as bad as I did in bed the next morning. Tossing around in that roiling shit, going through it all again . . ."

"Why didn't you fuck Christa?" Frank said. His diction did not please me, but I understood its import, and addressed myself to the remark.

"I don't know. There was no real context. She would have just been a way to get my rocks off. A convenience, I would have been using her, you know? Anyway, it wasn't her I wanted. Besides which, she was still sick, or claimed she was. Also"—I meant this to be light, but the humor, once I said it, evaded me as well—"she reminded me of my mother."

That was Thursday, April 22. Saturday morning I went out and bought the TV set, displayed it, but she showed no pleasure. Then we locked up and took the ride to Staten Island. Just for the sea and space, but once there I decide to try Korvette's, surprise the old man at his pretzel and ices stand. I've never seen him at his most recent employment, he's apt to be pleased. Having met Christa twice before, once when he just dropped in and again at the seder, he might begin to worry her nonJewishness. Fuck it, that's his problem. Long, complicated bus ride. We missed him (and a lift back) by only fifteen minutes. Only works a half-day Saturdays. Should have phoned first. Lunch in the cruddy snackbar, then back via two buses. Waiting between them, by the miniature golf course, in a drizzle, wishing for a drink . . . she becomes (dour up to then) girlish gay. Picks up a branch and draws a circle in the dirt around herself. Flashes for the first time in a while the dimpled smile. "This is my magic circle. I'm safe inside it." "Crazy," I say. (Safe from what?) Whence come these sudden dislocating shifts of mood? They make me uneasy. But I'll try to match the gay one. But on the bus she's her gloomy self again. Home, I say "Pss! Pss!" at the door to the apartment, fiercely grieving, and she's browned off: "Why did you do that?" "Because I miss him, goddamn it." Perhaps three Saturdays ago. Mrs. Gross broke the news. Stops me in the street, mammoth in spaceshoes, and in her shit-eating way: "Mr. Sams, do you find yourself missing a cat?" He's been gone overnight, is all. But she describes how her husband saw the sanitation truck sweep him up in the small hours, if not what hit him. I race home, sure I'll find him there. No. Goddamn it, I still suspect foul play.

Christa's unmollified. Suddenly I know why—she's accusing me of accusing her of wiping him out, since it was she let him into the yard the night he found his way to the street and was smashed by the truck. If that's what I'm doing, and it's not impossible, she's right to be pissed: some other night, some other passage to the world, some other car . . . death was written in his paws. The guiltmakers are everywhere.

I take the jug and a glass into the back room and type awhile. The outlook improves. She's just sealing a letter when I come out. Switch on the new toy, flop on the couch, watch some early Bacall-Bogart thing. Mildly entertaining. She watched too. We raid the icebox separately. Then it's bedtime. No problem. She's sick. Sleep fairly well. End of Saturday night. So what happened?

How alcohol doth aid the flow and dim the sense. Perhaps. Stay with it anyway. Woke refreshed on Sunday, brewed a pot of coffee, went out for cigarettes, avoided buying *The Times*. Returned and tried to cultivate that sinewy, fragile mood. It's only nine. Free of interruption for a while. Each day she seems to rise a little later than the one before—perhaps a courtesy? I work on the Dinelli/tape-recorder bit; he attempts to talk Europe into the machine with his buddy Frank as audience. "All right, Frankie, turn the bastard on. Hum! I'm ready as I'll ever get . . .", etc. Move it nicely for a couple of hours. Paris. Barcelona. Alicante. Seven very rough pages. I suspect they'll hold up because I'm not really tempted to reread them. Need more coffee. Try to be quiet, but rattle the pot on the stove. She stirs. Not yet, my love. I might squeeze out another line or two. Tiptoe back in and shut the door. But I'm done, or the rhythm is gone. Don't sweat it. The day has been decently launched. She knows it too, she must have heard the clacking. In situations of this sort, she's in the habit of knocking before coming in, and going to the closet for her clothes. It is my custom, then, to turn, offer some greeting or comment, so she won't feel she is disturbing anything, which most often she is not. She lives here as well—I try to spare her any feeling of intrusion. Indeed, as so often, I labor to spare myself the discomfort I would feel at rendering her uneasy by so

meretricious a stance: the writer at his desk, tuned to the celes-
tial music, whom a mortal fart or football would disrupt—
whereas in fact most often I massage my groin, or drink
my coffee, or squeeze out at best the shit one tenth of which
with luck and twenty rewrites can be saved (and yet these
drunken entries come so easy) . . . If the words are there,
they're there. If not, not. A pleasantry or two exchanged with
one's companion, whom the topography of the place con-
strains to enter so she may dress herself, is surely not amiss. Indeed, there have been times I wished she wouldn't knock,
simply come in and take what she needed; the joint tiptoeing
is disheartening; since she doesn't wait to be invited, anyway
(which I appreciate), but knocks and enters, the knocking can
appear overnice, perhaps sardonic, maybe worse. Am I out of
my skull to lay such a load on a gesture? If so, this Sunday, I'm
jolted sane again. She came bursting in with no semblance of a
by-your-leave, force enough to crack the doorknob into the
wall, flashed to the closet, grabbed some things and jerked
back inside. Leaving me with a half-uttered good morning
and an unmet twinkling gaze. This is what does it—the un-
acknowledged eyeballs, offering amity. Hard enough to make
the effort, humiliating to have it ignored. I couldn't even feel
I was responsible for her mood. I was watching a film of her,
alone in the room. Christa, mad. Well, up yours too, pussycat.
  Kicked over the u-start-it cactus kit just now on the way
back from the john. Beyond repair. Vermiculite all over the
kitchen floor. It was coming along nicely, slow and hardy; too
bad. Meat and gristle for the symbol-minded.
  We very nearly made it through without a word. April 25,
Sunday. She fed herself from time to time, probably on her
staples, bananas and apple juice, I didn't look to see. Salami
sandwich for me, slabs of Danish blue. I played her invisibility
game, despising us both. Some atmosphere! I wished (and as
fervently did not: in a mood of this kind who knew where she

would go, of what she was capable) that she would get the hell out, walk it off, disappear herself, and she no doubt wished the same for me, for she was scribbling continuously in her diary, and I had to be a distraction, even when not wandering by her through the living room. I took a sandwich and the radio out into the garden. Tuned to WBAI, a South Vietnamese ex-foreign minister in exile in Paris or something of the sort was gently and soberly explaining in lilting English that democracy and freedom, admirable concepts both, were perhaps not being most efficiently served by the maiming and murder and dispossession of his countrymen, destruction of their land . . . his American friends should, he suggested, at least entertain this possibility. It was his quiet, reasoned tone cataloguing the horrors being spread in the name of noble abstractions that were rendered obscene in the process, *his need to find a reasoned tone,* which boiled the blood, caused the shame and rage at being a subject of this grubby government and doing not one damn thing to bring it down. I wanted to call her out so she could listen too. But did not. Hell, she was busy, she was writing up her life. And what if she really didn't care, took real umbrage at being interrupted, saw the invitation merely as a ploy to break the ice (which in part it would be)? Why should I even try to share with so sullen and private a bitch the things which really moved me? When friends drop by and Vietnam comes up and we pool our indignation, she affects a bored silence, or perhaps is bored. And after they leave, I think she may be right: she does nothing, so she says nothing; while we sit there with only soot and water raining from our skies, brains and limbs intact anguishing our novels and our bank accounts, outrage our sole contribution, our virtue our reward.

So I heard it out alone, then came back in and switched on the ball game. Sat on the other end of the couch from where she was. Kept the sound off. She paid no mind. Mays tripled over Swoboda's glove. Kranepool made a great stop on Mc-Covey and threw wild to the plate. We were already a run behind. Would she be interested in this, perhaps, New York vs. San Francisco, the relevant regional battle? Christ. If anything could engage her less than the war in Vietnam, it must be the war on the diamond. We've already discussed it, prior to my buying the TV set. It's an art, I tell her, it's a science, the poor man's ballet. So screwed up she has me I apologize for baseball, or my interest, mustering a cultural overlay. And of course it's a lie—I'm merely hooked, is all, trapped in a maze of strategy and statistics, the antics of mercenaries made up as heroes, since the age of nine. Mmmhmm, she says. As unimpressed by my shaky defense as I think she would be by the spectacle. And maybe I'm wrong. She's really a buff, she loves the game. And all I am doing is assigning to her my own (addicted) self-contempt.

And then the doorbell rang. I could guess who it was, and walked down the hallway to answer.

"Father!"

"Hello, Pisacano."

"What's shakin', baby?"

"Nothin'. Working. Right in the middle of something."

"Not watchin' the game?"

"No, man."

"Come for a walk. It's a groovy day."

"Impossible. Too much to do. Another time."

"Okay, father. Later."

"Yeah."

I go back down the hall. I don't know whether or not she's heard the lie.

"That was Pisacano. He wanted to go for a walk."

"Mmmhmm."

Revealing nothing. Not even looking up. Scribbling away. I go into the back room. Sit at the desk awhile. But there's nothing there I want to or am able to do. I hear her going to the can. I remember the ball game. Go back inside. Her diary's open, on the couch. I sit midway between TV and diary. No sweat, I'll hear her coming out. Lean over, heart pounding as I fight the awkward angle, her damnable script.

Pisacano just stopped by. *J* sent him packing . . .

His suspicions about *P* and me. Why enlighten or defend. Interested, if I am, only for further insights into *J*.

Surely he is gross (his word—for others). (The passover service in the Bronx he took me to. Odd, squabbling family, sick. He resembles his father.) Night he wanted me to suck him. I would. Then says, instructive, plaintive, "you left too soon." Yes. Gagging, rushed to the bathroom. Couldn't, wouldn't swallow. Didn't feel loving enough.

Stirrings in the john and flushing sounds. I sit up, lock into the ball game. She comes out, moves by me to the porch, stands in the door a moment, doubles back, straining to be casual, initiates conversation for the first time that day: "Who's winning?"

"You're losing, Sarkissian."

She pays no attention to this, whatever it might mean, but picks up her book and takes it to the porch, to her rocking chair. In order to update her account (I learn the next morning), her instant playback:

Left this momentarily exposed. Doubt if he noticed. But must be more careful.

Four P.M. now. Tired. The phone no longer rings this end. J. Sams lives with a girl, the news is all over town. I've wiped out my social life.

Move it more. Something might emerge. We get through to

dinnertime. I cook a steak and broccoli without checking if this menu moves her, but make enough for two. When it's almost done I say, "Some dinner?" She looks up briefly—"All right."—goes on smoothly writing. She has style. I lay out the meal, invite her to table. Nothing changes. We chew in noisy silence. My fury mounts. Breaking bread should be a happy time. Chance for a détente, at least. But I can't begin it. The steak is rubber in my mouth. I go for the radio, turn it on, listen to the tail end of the doubleheader. I can't look at her now. Wolf the rest, shut the radio, put my plate in the sink, go for a jacket, start out. Can't make it all the way. Must turn, announce, "I'm going out," maybe for the last look. She's mopping up her steak and greens. I slam into the evening.

Not an easy neighborhood to get out of. Walk south down Second Avenue, into the turf of my childhood. Landmarks remain—the Yiddish theatres, dispensary, Ottendorfer Library, Third Street Mission to the Jews. Stop at the window. Exhortations, in Yiddish, English, Hebrew, to embrace the living Jesus. Enough to make *tsadikim* of apostates, that clammy appeal. Still, you have to feel compassion, it must be a task, in that section of the world, with small rewards. Wander due east, down to the ancestral hearth, look up into the windows. Lights are on, looks warm. Could ring the bell and pop in unannounced, bask in their surprised pleasure. Or hers. Harry still believes I have designs, plan to steal her off and elope to the Catskills. You got me wrong, old man, she must be the worst ball in the world. Probably I overrate her approval, too. Nine parts guilt for not being nicer to me thirty years ago. Or maybe no joy at all for either, but measurable annoyance at having their privacy disturbed. Locked out again. This is unlikely. But once past the opening flush, uninstructible, unreasonable hope of the first five minutes, I'm bound to wish myself elsewhere.

"How about a drink, son?"

"Sure."

"What'll it be?"

"Harry, he doesn't need a drink, he already drinks far too much, why must you offer him a drink?"

"Scotch."

"Ah, shaddup, will you? He can have one drink. Is he an infant?"

"Harry, you're so stupid, is that the only way you two can find to communicate, drinking that poison? Feh!"

"Son, your mother thinks I'm stupid. You want a *shpritz* of soda in it?"

"No. On the rocks."

That ritual behind, I'm ready to adjudicate. Issues which never alter. How badly she wants to move from the apartment, from the neighborhood. Always did, as long as I remember, but more so since that truly monstrous dun-colored building ("Village Vista!") went up a block away. She says it depressed her for months. "They've taken away my view. That's all this lousy stinkin' apartment in this lousy stinkin' neighborhood ever had, was a view, and now they've taken that too!" She means she can no longer see the Empire State Building from the bedroom window. It's a genuine loss, and I sympathize. But she would no more move away, relinquish that headlock on her martyrdom, than he is about to leave the neighborhood he grew up in—he couldn't stand to be a mile from the junkyard, and his mirror image, for more than a day or two; which she knows.

While she's on, I fix myself another drink, then ask if they must always mar my visits with these shrill, pointless squabbles? Haven't they a care for my developed sensibilities? And the apartment is crushing me by then, its stifling mess of memories. It hasn't altered that much since it shaped me, though an interior decorator changes chair covers and shuffles things around once every couple of years. The high-riser is gone, but all else remains.

So the impulse is laid to rest. I turn from the lighted windows and walk one block south. Jane Mason's street. Into the corner bar to call. Ignore the hostile stares, real or fancied. Probably real. Crummy, old Ukrainian-Polish place where beards and jeans have not penetrated. They want to keep it that way. Order a beer before I phone. No answer. Finish the beer, order another, call again. She's not at home. Just as well —why confuse her? Things between her and Bob Kane are less than firm; she'd think I was trying to woo her back. The beers work well, pick me up after the all-day wine. The walk helps too. Hop a First Avenue bus, return to the fray. Cheerful in remorse: at least half my fault, I upheld my end of the childishness. With humor, tact, it could have been avoided. Forget those murderous diary putdowns for the moment.

Brahms on the phonograph, *Our Lady of the Flowers* in her lap. My copy. I could never read the bloody thing.

"Greetings, Christa."

"Hello."

"How's the book?"

"I don't know. I've just begun it."

She's about sixty pages in.

"Anything of note during my absence? Adventures?"

"Daisy called."

"Who? Oh. She did? In just the time I was gone?"

"You were gone over an hour."

"I was, wasn't I. Any other calls?"

"No."

"What did Daisy have to say?"

"She . . . invited me for a visit. I think I'd like to go, sometime this week."

"To Baltimore?"

"That's where she lives, yes."

"Sounds a good idea. I guess you need a change."

"Mmmhmm."

"Christa, on the last phone bill, there was a rather lengthy conversation with the Bay Area. Do you think you could make those collect?"

"I do, as a rule. I knew the party was about to go out, I must have panicked. It won't happen again."

"Oh. I'm beat. I guess I'll make the bed."

So much for the new, beautiful beginning which jockeyed me home. It was beyond doubt that shmuck Tim she'd called, the last day of March, a twelve-minute chat on a weekday afternoon, because I knew her mother's number and this was not it. And the matter of the mail. Maybe a week ago. I bring it all in, easily recognize his, Berkeley postmark with never a return address. A very subtle cat. (Nothing from him since; probably she's taken to getting them again at American Express.) Also one from her mother. The mail came earlier than usual, she was still in bed. Also two from Denby, one for each of us. Busy little correspondent. Burns my ass, his puppeteering from the desert. Wish he would knock it off (what? his letters to her?), but don't know how to ask him. I take it all into the back room. Don't know if she's awake, don't care to play postman if she is. Shove her letters into the desk drawer, look through my own:

Dear Sams,

God, but your roommate burns my butt! She's got no right to read anything more complicated than the directions on a box of Jello. Believe. What she does with Genet, Grass, etc., is beyond description. But a great kid. And I'm happy for you. Especially. Be firm. Take no *kuso* * at all.

Meanwhile, if she falls out a window late one night I am prepared to testify that you were here in Tucson, quietly sitting in our front room at the time. You have done well. I love you both. All summer long the Denbys remain in the heat . . .

Clearly she's been complaining to him about how badly I treat her. Why won't she bring her halfass grievances to me? I

* Jap. for "shit."

start to rap out a reply, but have nothing to tell him. Open the
drawer, pull out Tim's diaphanous airmail envelope. (Dave's
are of an ordinary thickness.) Hold it to the light. Tantaliz-
ingly rewarded. The man's a gauzy poet: "Your eyes I see, your
hair I see, mouth I see . . . I don't know why . . . left New
York . . ." and the rest is lost in the folded toilet paper. So be
it. I've seen enough. Slam the drawer closed. Mad enough to
type awhile. She comes in shortly for her clothes.

"You have some mail," I say.

"Oh?"

Meaning: Then why wasn't it in the kitchen, where you
usually leave it, on the drop-leaf table?

I pull open the drawer. I'm aware she's aware I don't have
to. Ashamed of the power that single key gives me. I could
have read the bloody things and then destroyed them. Not
even the government would know.

"One from friend Denby. One from Mother. One anony-
mous; I believe it's a love letter."

To which she says simply "Yes," and whips them into the
next room.

The other party she gets fat letters from, guy with a deaf
wife some years his senior who has two children by a Negro ex-
husband and whom he brings lovers home for (the wife), they
once had a pet rabbit but he killed it and skinned it and hung
the hide from the front door, name of Donald, I mailed one to
him for her in the long ago, wants to be a writer, would seem
to have enough material, she knows from her part-time com-
puter days, has surely sometime fucked; let us suppose him to
be (or else go mad) the man who knocked her up the first
time. And from her sister (as the one she read me back in
March, full of hysterical advice on Jason, "this-thing-you-have-
with-Jason," I was infuriated each time she used my name,
sense as with Denby of long-range manipulation, should
Christa take any cues from the ravings, as she must, else why
should she read it aloud? Hoping I could sunder them, and

save her? I didn't care for the commission, the necessity), Marcia, though nothing lately, since Marcia has left her husband and the cold country and her Swedish half-life and is in questing transit between points unknown. (Unless, again, all mail goes to Amex now.) She doesn't share much with me now, no longer floods me with her weirdly selective, off-center tales about places, relatives and friends. At once a relief and a clear sign of widening distance.

So that is the situation with the mail.

I'm beat, I tell her (back to Sunday), I think I'll make the bed. Do. No trouble to it. The foam rubber joiner's no longer functional or pretty, but I use it anyway. Near the end she comes and gives a perfunctory assist. Tucks a blanket in. I wash and brush my teeth and change to pajamas in the john.

"You coming to bed?"

"In a moment, yes."

"Kind of an odd day, wasn't it?"

"Yes."

"How did you . . . what did you make of it?"

She shrugs. "I suppose I was being rather bitchy."

Immediately I'm tempted to defend her, or myself, by laying waste that mock-apologetic claim. For if you grant them the talent, or the label, you have to live with the result. Some may truly be that way (not her; she's good; she'll change;), forever testing, clawing, prodding, sick children of the moon, resentful seekers of the spurting seed, because they own you at that moment, but all too briefly . . . but if you don't indulge their too-easy menstrual mysteries they'll give them up, perforce, and everyone is spared that loaded judgment, which is a male one to begin, that they turn back on you in willful confusion. The poor girl never had a chance. He took her for long walks when she was small and boomed out his love and belted her around. She was his favorite, his own. When she took up with her Tim it must have crippled him. He called her "Boo-

boo," so like an ass at times I call her "Boo," the manifold mis-
uses of irony, for I know it gives her no pleasure, makes her
sorry she told me. But if she nastily compares us, which she
does more and more ("*He* liked to garden, too"), I want to
shake some sense into her oversimplifying body: Baby, I have
trouble enough not being my own father to have to contend
with not also being yours. YOU ARMENIAN COCK-
SUCKER, YOU SCREWED UP MY LIFE! Boor, poor bastard, friggen martinet, lost among the amazons, one you married and three you spawned, dark and devious and much too
sexy to endure, especially this last, who held you in such bottomless, loving contempt for male and worldly failures; so you
copped out at last, an act of vindictive intelligence, died.
Leaving it for me to handle. And I have not yet worked it out,
not even the essentials, whether a man is his cock or his joy of a
sunset. It was a hell of a way to be wounded. She's very beautiful, I want her for my wife. I only wish she was less difficult. Or
I was. My behavior through these weeks and months has not
been exemplary.

"No you weren't, Chris. I held up my end, anyway. Besides,
it didn't really begin today. We've been fencing now for quite
a while."

"Mmmm."

"So what else is new?"

"I . . . would have cooked the dinner, had you asked."

"What? Oh, sure. But I was really in the mood."

Things look nicer now. As for the lack of denouement, I've
learned to live with abstinence. Fact is, I'm not suffering all
that much—the heat is off, my privates are my own. While
she's in the can I fill a mug with water, put it on the night table. It's a useful habit. At times, in dead of night, I nip at it
myself.

She comes to bed, turns to shut the lamp.

"Did you put that water on the table?"

"Yeah."

"Why?"

"What?"

"Why are you so kind?"

"WHAT'S WRONG WITH BEING KIND?"

You can't defeat the child. She goads me to the wrath which makes her point. I shake my head, take her hand.

"You want me to spill it out? You want to get your own?"

"No."

"Wow, Christa. Let's wipe this one out, shall we? I had a bad day, you probably know. My book is driving me up the wall. In fact, I started messing with another, based on that place in England I was at, where I had the LSD . . ."

"I know."

"You do? How?"

"A few days ago . . . I saw some pages on your desk."

"You look at things on my desk?" I'm not altogether displeased.

"If you leave them obviously exposed, yes. I might have glanced at a page or two."

"That's all there is of it, so far. Well, what did you think?"

"There wasn't enough to form an opinion."

"No, I suppose not. Anyway, it was that kind of a day . . . I guess for you, too. Shall we write it off?"

"All right, Jason. Good night."

"Good night, dear."

Gross.

I probably hate her at that moment.

On Pisacano. The m-f is after my girl. (Addressed me thus that afternoon as if she didn't exist, "Come for a walk," as if no one else could be in the apartment.) More than once I've walked into the house and they've been on the phone (always incoming, she says), or else she tells me that he's called. ("What did he want?" "He didn't say.") This often at a time he knows or ought to know I couldn't possibly be in, say the night of my class. Or is it less than reasonable to assume he's memorized my schedule . . .

The dinner here two Saturdays ago. Still felt the need to cook for more than two, though hopefully that's now over. He brings a girl who claims to be the mistress of two spayed female cats (so this is she; it was of course not Gillian he meant that long-ago sick afternoon in my garden; unless he's rehearsed this lady on the way). A cat person, lanky, freckled redhead, she condoles with me on my loss. To Pisacano, when she talks at all, she's acerbic to the point of nastiness—wifely. Clearly she knows him for a while. Even with his turnover, he has a way of keeping four or five for long periods circling in the background. Much wine. He's in great braying form. Ignores his lady's barbs. I talk to her from politeness. She does some high-level public relations thing. Paul is entertaining Sarkissian, seated wide-thighed on the couch in his white jeans, she nearby on the floor. When I look over, he's just rocking back, guffawing, and he puts his bare foot in her hair. She punishes him for this liberty by pinching him hard on the thigh. All merriment. I want to rise, and run him out, a wrathful giant, but am in no way up to such a scene, and even if I brought it off, how would I deal with her afterwards? Smack her around? Be contrite and ashamed? Would she rage, and be right? Is it her fault she elevates every prick in sight? Or that I surround myself with back-stabbing friends? Or that she deals with it as she does? And how much can it mean if they carry on under my nose? Why does it take this shape? Why must one be forced to choose between one's female and one's friends?

Earlier, he said, "Why do you call her by her last name, father? You want to keep her at a distance?"

At which *she* chimes in, almost simpers, "He does, yes."

Paul leaves at last. The world dips and spins. I'll try to walk it off. Put on a jacket, weave down the block to the corner. Smash into a spiked iron fence, rip the pocket, gash my hand, bruise my side. Stagger back, wash the cut, flop on the couch in the rear room. She's on the phone, seems to be talking to her mother. But she's cleared the table, put the dishes in to soak. Tossing and groaning on the couch, miserable, feel I might puke for the first time in years. Bolt up, battle it back. I hear her making up the bed. She comes in at last to see if it's fatal, steps on my glasses. An accident, they were right there on the floor, the room was dark. She cracks a lens. I find this funny at the time. She's rather tender, wondering if I'm all right. I go blindly to the john, splash water on my face, pee lustily dead center, strip, fall into bed (she's already there), hug her, mount her, fuck her. Can't come, the effort fights off nausea, drop off on her body. Wake perhaps seconds later as she's shoving me off. Roll over, pass out for the night.

Sundays figure large. The next day it was she pops her magic fragments. The world's most widely traveled sugar cube. She took it with her when she went to the coast, forgot it in her mother's house, sent for it, it arrives (in a package with clothes and art supplies) in smithereens. She shows me the covering letter: "Dearest Christa, I looked into the cigarette package you asked for. I don't know what the powder is, nor why you need it, but I'm sure you'll be careful . . ." We smile together at the cultivated ignorance, the helpless advice. She stuck it back in the fridge behind her apple juice and once again forgot it. Or I did. I'm reading the Sunday *Times* the next afternoon. In godawful shape. Go for the hair of the dog, a beer. She's stretched out on the couch, hand over her eyes. I ask what's wrong. She says, nothing . . . a slight stomach ache. Can I get her anything? Make some tea? No, she'll be all right. I go back to the book section. Hear her tossing. Tune it out awhile. But when I look again she seems to be in pain. I offer to call a doctor. She shakes her head, dismisses me again. Much later, cured, she tells me what she's done.

"Jesus, Christa, why didn't you tell me you were going to try it"—was she afraid I would demand a share?—"I would have stayed with you."

"I . . . don't know."

"Well, in a way I guess it's better you didn't. I would have fussed and clucked like a mother hen."

"Yes."

So quick to agree when I put myself down. So why set her up? Because I still seem to think she reads my mind. Or more insidious, is inside it, comprises a part . . . I ask her what she's learned and seen. Nothing very dramatic, she says, nothing to compare with *your* experience. It was a weak dose to begin, must have lost some potency in transit. ("Potent" is a word she likes to use.) So, then, what? Did anything happen?

"I saw a rather large cat."

"What was it doing?"

"Sitting there, in that tree."

"In the garden?"

"Yes."

"Was it mine?"

"No, Jason, it wasn't yours."

"What did it do besides sit there?"

"Nothing . . . it was smiling."

"What did you feel like? Was it pleasant? Unpleasant?"

"Neither. I felt nothing much."

I share the incident with Frank.

"She thinks she's Alice," he says.

"What?"

"You know, the Cheshire cat."

"Oh. Yeah. Crazy. The insight for the day."

Toward the end of the session he asks me if we—she and I—are "emotionally involved." I ask him to spare me the jargon.

Pissed at him more and more these days. I suppose I have a

case, the way he buggers around my hour. But I can simply ask him to stop, to give me a set time.

I try to share this morsel with her later on. Better to downgrade the man than myself, give us a joint target. (Yet often I seem to be apologizing for Covington, for *having* him, however flawed a confidant, while she, poor thing, is "reduced" to the mails. Reduced!) I'll try to raise a chuckle, to cement us.

"Frank wants to know if we're 'emotionally involved.' "

Throws it away over her shoulder (she's at the sink again): "With who?"

A real prize. You have to admire her.

Moral: If they tell you they're bitches, be advised to take them at their word.

But that was still fairly early on. She was sleeping badly, complaining of her dreams. What were the dreams? She's reluctant to say. Like a fool I pry it out. She's dreaming a great deal of Tim. Tim? The poor cat you left to come and live with me? The very same. Well, shit, Christa, dreams can mean anything. No . . . she is deeply distressed because she's going through the motions with me, making the gestures of love, but not feeling love. She's always been difficult and nasty with men, it seems to be her nature; yet here, with me, whom she does not love, she's so sweet, domesticated, nice . . . it isn't natural. It's ruining her rest.

Well. Probe her innards, reap the rewards. I'm not very happy with having to argue my case. Thought it had been settled when she came back the three thousand miles. (But would she have done so if I hadn't sent the money ((against which Paul advised))? I've asked her this, she says, annoyed, Of course. But there's no way to know.) But cast by one or the other or both of us as daddy, I try to see it through. There, there. What is love? Love is what love does. Baby is how baby acts. You behave nice, you're nice. If Christa is sweet to Jason, Christa is sweet. See it my way. Not to worry.

While another voice is screeching, "What!! you don't love me!? Get your fucken ass out of here!"

"*You're* losing, Sarkissian," I did indeed tell her, on silent Sunday, at a less appropriate moment. I do seem to have, as Pisacano says, one of the slower reaction-times.

As terribly tempted to phone her right now. The booze does that. Though I've just quit, put up coffee—surge of will power. Want to see this through. A million reasons not to phone. She might not even be there. She might be here, around the corner. In either direction. Not sure I want to find that out. Or she might be in Baltimore, all right, but not in Daisy's house. All in all, best not to wonder. Thank you, Denby, true-blue buddy. Could he be wrong, despite the diaries? He could be wrong. My own fault for phoning him last night. I await the promised letter with miserable anticipation.

Sick. Sex. Certain incidents. No question the performance level is not what it was. (Which she duly notes, complaint— her godgiven right to be properly fucked—mingled with some satisfaction. As this: "Drunk, he still attempts my ass from time to time . . ." How succinctly, queasily put. Or the queasiness is mine. Ladies shouldn't come on that way, or not so bitchy-eloquent, etc. But it's true, exact enough. I drop my load, or she starts to yell, the moment I begin to penetrate. But there were other yawps, more pertinent. Not copied, not remembered.) Has my interest lessened? (Paul: "It's my ambition in life to become the king, the very best, of the softcock fuckers.") Certainly it's become more complex. I cogitate too much, stirring anxieties, reactivating patterns I thought were well behind. Even with quantities of booze, without which now we hardly ball at all. I feel obliged to screw her at the rate and in the manner to which I have helped her become accustomed, or she'll go and find it somewhere else. Ergo, resentment. Come too fast. More resentment, more anxieties. "The cunt is insatiable! Am I a machine for her convenience?" etc. Yet if for whatever reason in sickness or health *she* holds back, let alone how terrible and suspect that illness is, she becomes the cockteaser of myth and nightmare, the simpering face behind the endless three A.M. blueball journeys back from the wilds of the Bronx, rattling home to the bathroom sink, the great American bitch-heroine, almost Jewish, etc. Man, this is *sick,* can't make it, can't live this way.

She has to straighten up. There has to be a way to live together. I love her, define it as you please. No other sense to make of all this anguish.

Lifetimes ago sporting on the rug, discover only then she's plugged, string protruding, shorter than on Britta's Swedish model where the picture first occurred, that if you pulled that cord you'd spring them open like a parachute. Still, now as then, I go down and start it with my teeth, then yank it the rest of the way. Never resisting, she seemed so dismayed by the sight of that bloody tube that I handed it clumsily over (there was no way to reinsert it). She got up and took it to the toilet. Closed the door. Flushed. Came back rearrayed. End of episode.

Came between her breasts one evening after she announced herself sick. On the couch. Opened her blouse, undid the bra, rooted around in those hills and valleys. Never caught her eye. Grimace and groan, overstated one-way gratitude and pleasure. Shocked that afterward she made no move to clean up or change her blouse.

The unsuccessful blowjob herself has annotated.

What is the purpose of this?

Cystitis, purple pussies, honeymooner's complaint—whatever it is, it dogs my trail. This also struck on a Sunday. One before this last. So bad it was she let me call a doctor. TR 9-1000, doctors on Sundays. My uh wife is rather ill, I don't know, some female thing, she's ambulatory, hold the wire I'll

put her on. Man with a black bag came in an hour, felt around
(I waited discreetly on the porch), wrote a prescription, I a
fifteen-dollar check. He put her onto a real GU man, at
N.Y.U. Medical Center, to call on Monday. She complained
that he hadn't examined her properly, hadn't probed her (was
she laying it on me for not having a bed?), but I ran out and
filled the prescription, and whatever I brought back seemed to
make her happy. It caused her to piss brown and ten times an
hour, a state of affairs with which she was familiar. Arrogant of
me to take it personally. These are her patterns, this is her life.
Yet to admit that much, to see her as unalterable by me, locked
into her past . . . I refuse to do.

Then this Tuesday after silent Sunday with the help of
some wine I tell her I love her (the phrase comes fairly easy)
via a bird's-eye anecdotal view of all my sex life to that time.
Slow beginnings, whoring around in Japan, etc. I suppose I
mean (at best) to wipe it out as frivolous and unreal, to lead
her to make the same judgment on her own. And now here
we are, finally met. I'm going to try to keep you, make you
happier. I know (being careful not to seem to know too much)
you're going through something I can only wait out . . . I
feel powerless . . . but, Christa, I can only be myself. She
nods at this, appearing to agree, says little throughout, seems
moved. Then I go uptown and vent the real rage at Frank.

That evening, when I ask, she says she thinks she's cured,
takes a ritual cleansing bath (my suggestion). The hot water
gives out midway through. I boil up a large kettle for her, but
she's grumpy. I start an angry letter to the landlord, give it up,
go to bed. That night we can and do make love. A lot of wine. I
perform nobly. Her big, musky body, mounting excitement,
she's very close, and I go over, hoping this itself will bring her
on, which has happened before, if not, no matter, I'll hang in
with her—but she stops. A dead halt. I'm furious, but mask
it. Even smile. "If you're strung out, love, you did it to your-

self. I would have stayed with you." She turns away. A bit later, horny or dutiful, I try again, but she pleads pain.

Want her again in the morning. She's agreeable. But I've got too much working, too overwrought. Remain outside, play with her outside. But she works it in. So I tell her what I'm feeling, which helps to cool it slightly. But she slides over on top, pumping and driving, and once more I've lost it—"I'm going, my darling, please come with me." And she does. And tears roll down my face.

Nothing like this has happened to me before. I have to point them out (though of course she's seen them on her own). Tears. Dig. What do you think they mean?

They're of relief, she says.

I appear to think this over. That's not it, I say. Of happiness. They make that kind too, don't they?

Indeed, a happy note. I can send her off to Baltimore on the wings of an orgasm and maybe get some work done in the few peaceful days she'll be gone.

All this seems remoter than yesterday. And Silent Sunday infinitely distant.

Monday morning. Little doubt how I would spend it. Something had been begun, would be completed. Trusting, she keeps it in her drawer, beneath some underwear. I try to pull it open soundlessly, though the door is shut, and I keep some things in the dresser as well, and she could hardly tell the sound of one drawer opening from another. Take it to the desk, read it under cover of *The Village Voice*. Seems to begin some weeks before we met, in Luxembourg, Washington Heights—at first I do not give these crabbed and cryptic pages my best attention. Nervous, listening for her, limited time. Turn to the end, the familiar terrain: "Pisacano just stopped by . . . Surely he is gross . . . wanted me to suck him . . ." (how much sweeter and deadlier is that "suck" than "suck off"; how it conjures her sexual world, cheapens mine).

It's all there. I'd almost hoped they were imaginings, that the perversity was mine, not hers. (If I am wrong about her and Paul, of which I am not totally convinced, why does she not want to ease me? Why need to cause me this sort of pain?) Of course, I'm not supposed to know what lives inside her head, but my knowledge of it doesn't change what's there—how can she entertain such wicked views? "Left this momentarily exposed." . . . (Proper use of "momentary?") . . . "Doubt if he noticed. But must be more careful." The two-faced bitch, why must she treat me as the enemy? I'm glad, now, she took the damn thing with her, or like a mad monk I'd copy it entire. But these also I scrawled at the time or remember:

Horrid allday silence I will not break. When he stood at the stove cooking dinner I wanted to come up behind, kiss his neck, his eyes . . . could not.

(Why couldn't you? Why didn't you?)

He corrects my spelling, usage, language, the way I do *T*'s . . .

(I remember just that single time you wrote "cheeze" on the shopping list . . . it was cute, I didn't mean to put you down!)

Covets possessions, money, things, in a way like *T,* but different . . . his strange love affair with the TV set . . .

(All right, I confess, I lied about the cultural and entertainment possibilities! I only bought the friggin thing to watch the ball games! Why these constant comparisons with that third-rate male, who copped the most expensive cherry in the world, who loves to suffer over distance?)

Dinner in the same thrashing silence. Afterwards he storms out, saying, "See you later, Sarkissian." . . . Speak with Daisy, will go there this week.

("I'm going out," was all I said; odd feeling to see yourself misquoted on the page.)

Talk we had after his class, and similar again here some nights ago, about his "work," how important to him was his work, wholly committed, all else secondary. I called him selfish, which upset him. Papers on his desk are mostly notes . . . messages to self . . . he is conceptualizing . . .
He's much too old, or set, to change . . .
How impossible making up that foolish bed when he returns, in this atmosphere . . .
I should steal off like a thief in the night, before he comes back, says, "When are you leaving, Sarkissian?"

(You're wrong love! I'd never say it! I don't want it!)

Needs a girl to live with what he is. He seems to know what that is, more or less. Perhaps he'll find her . . .

(You arrogant, silly cunt, it's you!)

All's still quiet inside. But feel lucky (*sic*) to have got this far. Mean to just run quickly through the earlier parts. The Jan-Feb stuff, after all, is ancient emotional history. But come across the drafts of letters (might have known she'd be a pro), the one (still in Europe) which elicited the "virginal vulva" reply I read and copied out in the long ago, and another, also to Tim, New York, February, that she would see him at the East Side Air Terminal that particular Friday morning. Wow. Yes. My sister is having a nervous breakdown. Relatives will pay the way. Yes. Did I suspect something of the kind? Wouldn't face it cleanly at the time, or dismissed it as "paranoid," or a misreading of my own guilt about Leslie. Didn't yet know she was the world's most devious lady. She faked me out, but she wiped him out—no wonder he could write those hurt, poetical letters, Yr eyes I see, etc., when she came back to me. Ah, but, she came back to me. On my money, as she probably rode out on his. If I needed further proofs that I was overmatched. Now almost wish she'd walk in and find me reading, force a confrontation. I look for hard facts (but she's already *told* me she was with him!) about her time back in California. But there's only a void for those three weeks, six blank pages. Perhaps she keeps a separate West Coast book. I flip back to the J. Sams period. Somewhere prior to Sunday's jottings she describes how fake and strange she felt washing up one night while Paul and I wassailed nearby discussing the merits of marriage vs. shacking—loud, explicit, mostly monologue, with his usual predilection for treating them as if they weren't there, or were one of the boys. But none of her discomfiture showed, at the sink or when she finally joined us. Entries also as I've said on our downhill sex life—ostrich that I am, I really hoped she hadn't noticed. A snide putdown of my (Jesus) "trip," which I've described perhaps once too often, to various people in her company: "overrational," she called it, I'm sorry it sounds so, sweetheart, one of the shredding experiences of my life, that third or fourth session when my body split vertically in two, the halves in different planes, and the left side grew white while the right turned black, and as I watched and waited the right half became powerful and hairy, no longer me but my father, and the left side was female, not my mother, but Female, and they were warring, and I was the terrain. For a time that rough right hand considered choking me to death. Or worse. Then turned its attention to the battle. And I knew well what was at stake—if that right side won I'd come out Quasimodo, the belching farting crip-

pled dimwit of the ages, and if the other triumphed, that snow-
white, spatially lower half, why, I'd be no more nor less than a
raging queenly queer. For four hours I awaited the result, and
when they brought me out of it with the antidote and a meal of
their damnable English fried bread I knew what sort of shape
I was in, if nothing more; and if they were not equipped at this
"short-term" oh-so British place with its tallyho therapists and
trust in miracles to do me any good, if I emerged worse off
than before because of new, jarring data I had no clear idea
what to do with, and if I had dined out on and tidied up the
tale in the years since, so it appeared to some perhaps "overrational," well, didn't it rate at least in the same league with
Cheshire cats? What a putdown artist is my little girl. What a
member of the club.

    She did not wake. I replaced the diary. When she did get up
she went out at once and was still out when I left to see Frank
and thence to class.

    Tuesday afternoon Harry phoned with a stock tip. I'd told
him I had a few dollars to play with. At last we have something
real to talk about. First, sounding like Martha, he said I ought
to play it safe with AT&T, but then when I held firm he told
me to buy something called "Xtra" on the American Exchange. I did, a hundred shares at twenty-one. Tuesday night
we had our ritual cleansing, described. Wednesday morning
her hurtful "relief" remark. But I felt good anyway, walked
her out, down to the bank, where I drew out the twenty-five
dollars she wanted, and deposited her California check. (I've
already tried writing checks to cash, endorsing them, having
her endorse below, then endorsing again, and sending her
down, but the fools still phone me up, humiliate her through
the wait.) Then we breakfasted in the Jewish dairy restaurant
on Fourteenth Street, where she remarks with a nice social eye
that what are peasant staples in the old country (I ordered
kasha, pirogi) become gourmet fare for the same group when

it emigrates and rises. Culinary slumming, yes. I walk her to the bus stop. She's going west to Eighth Avenue, thence to Penn Station. I wait with her for the bus, and hope aloud that she enjoys herself. She regards me for a quick dark instant, sweet, scheming, scared, who can any longer tell, climbs into the bus and I go about my business.

Trip to the periodontist, he removes the stitches from the third quadrant, we're nearly done. He claims he's saved my teeth, and a good deal of money besides. Capping wasn't indicated.

I take my time going home. There's a long evening up ahead.

. . .

Frank just called (twelve thirty) to cancel out. Says he's got the flu. Sounds genuine enough, if a bit late in the day. Perhaps, he coughs, we can make it up next week. Perhaps. I wouldn't want to inconvenience him. But I guess he doesn't mind breaking his 2x-weekly rule to balance his accounts.

And Jane Mason, a moment ago. On her lunch hour. Breathy, apologetic, knows I'm living with someone, but we haven't talked in quite a while, she couldn't help wondering how I was . . . impatient with this shit, but I try to put her at her ease. I tell her I called her Sunday night, was just thinking of phoning her again. My roomie's out of town. Come by this evening for a drink? She will. Good. Christa said four days at least, to Sunday. If I'm acquiring horns, shore up a little on my own.

It will be (with any luck at all) the first time since January, Leslie. Been "faithful" since, though not really by design.

Hit a few bars after the periodontist on Wednesday afternoon, had a hamburger in the last, got back after six. Inebriate impulse to ring up Arizona. Chat with Keiko for a while. She's potting. She's mothering. She's discontent but happy. Dave comes on at last. He's always glad to hear from the East.

The talk (at my direction) turns soon enough to Christa. I mention that she's gone to Baltimore. Uh oh, Baltimore. He can enlighten me, he thinks, on her contacts in that city. The connection is first-rate, but he begins to garble. He'll write, he says, and fill the gaps. I profess myself eager to hear.

Ring off, pour a drink, go looking for her diary. It's not in the drawer. Could she have hidden it? More likely took it with her. To keep it from my clutches? To write in it, shmuck. Still, an overwhelming sense of disappointment. Maybe she *has* hidden it. Or else some further treasure may come to light. Not yet very drunk, in reasonable possession of my faculties, such as they are these days, I pull out her suitcase from under the couch. An evil thing to do. Screw it, I have cause. At once, success. Her blackbound European diary. Fatter, unlined pages, tinier script. Reward beyond belief.

Through the rest of the night, drinking, reading, smoking, as moved as I have been by any book or soul in several years, chain on the door to ward off unknown dangers, I entertained myself.

part 4

April 28, 1965

Deary—

This is OK. Right after the phone call puts some forward motion to the note about Christa. I understand your comments about her quite well: the part about being more confused than complicated or profound, the part about the vagueness she drifts into when the facts of her own life are on stage. It took me quite awhile to wise to that, and by that time the initial shock had calmed enough so I could call her on not telling me the whole truth—her technique for lying. I don't think she has ever been faithful to anyone in her life. Certainly not to me; but then I was in a position to not be hurt by it, as was, say, Tim. In fact, since years ago, our relationship has been based on encouraging the other to go to hell in a fleshcart. That was my defense against her damnably soft touch, her kisses, and the vague, messy interior of her mind. She differs somewhat from the girl I described in that short story of mine. She is not as smart, not as curious. Her sister Marcia is very bright, not so pretty, not so marvelously witch-like, but all three sisters have the cloven hoof somewhere. That is not the least of their attractiveness. Christa has always stopped men cold. She is either totally with you when she is next to you, or not at all. But for me it was like giving myself to a dark dust storm. The interior knew not what it was doing with Christa, ever. Her interior, that is.

We once came to a point that was something of a corner for me. One night, late, one of those Go put on your parachute goddamn you nights, I cracked. But only for an instant, because as soon as I cracked, as soon as my wanting her came to a boiling point and I gave in, she gave in too. I felt, I told her, she was right. That if I wanted her then, I had to take the chance of making her pregnant. But after that moment, something cooled. I told her I would take the chance, but I never did. Even though she would take it, let herself risk *me*, I couldn't see it. First, of course, there was the Keiko. But there were, from time to time, others. I don't think I ever got to her quite as sharply as she got to me. I owe her a lot; she made me feel, she hurt and tried to hurt more, and I gave it back to her. Remember, she is second generation. You've seen enough of that to understand. I think the only thing she ever said to me which still cuts me hard was that she felt she wasn't good enough for me. It hurts to write it. It is a failure by us all that she could feel that. Why, I don't know. But I do not believe she was putting me on. And if she wasn't then, there is still a bit of it inside her. Armenians are . . . what? comelately Jews? And I, of course, look and maybe act like every Wasp there ever was.

So Christa—what is she after? For years we have written back and forth, trying to find out. I keep telling her I'm not after anything, no object, no goal, no recognition, not money. Just living. But I think she believes she ought to be after something. She wants something to live for. What she means is that she wants somebody to solve her life for her, bring her in out of the cold. She thought maybe I could do it, that I was something to build it all around. Perhaps she still looks for that.

I sincerely hope she'll get over Tim. My reason for this is what it's always been—that Tim is a complete dishrag, he whimpers, even she admits it; she totally dominates him. He is her emotional security of a middle-sort. She likes his beard; she likes guys with beards. Keep yours well-trimmed. She used to make fun of my neatness. She is not neat. It used to bug me that she made fun of me because I was. We bugged each other a lot.

But I can tell you for sure that she will not be easy to catch, or be caught quickly. Expect several comings and goings before she begins to understand you. She actually likes the simple things —walks on beaches and up mountains, reading poems, the works—but she also gets distracted, not by the outside, but something inside. I don't think living in the city is good for her, especially New York. If you can get her to walk across Canada with you this summer, or something equally energetic, that would probably be the best. I think there is no way to put a rope around her, but you can be more attractive than anything else in her life. You've got the integrity, the guts, that Tim can't approach. (. . .An interruption: Jane Mason on the phone from N.Y.: instructions to me to pressure her almost-ex-old-man to send her clothes; she walks to work naked? What kind of work is she doing, anyway! . . .) Me, I think you, Jason, are Christa's big catch. You may see it the other way round, but that doesn't count. She needs someone tuned to the inner noises, to her fun and games, to give her a reason to stay home now and then. Tim is still a boy, from all I've been able to gather.

There was some difficulty talking on the phone. K is not hip to the complications; no need she should be. Will dig out the C notes in a little while. . . .

Amidst a crushing pile of letters one from her dated Feb. 10/ 65, N.Y.:

What is it makes one call another by the surname? . . . I know the things to do, to see, to frequently say. More often

I say nothing . . . I haven't beat the fear. Some few nights ago at the moment of orgasm I, what? flipped? I was nearly cut loose, a nonagressive nothingness. My ears heard still, my mouth could almost speak, but I didn't want to come back. I wrote to you of something like this happening before, was it from Madrid? Whatever, it scares hell out of me. Worse yet, the feeling of complete humorlessness—the all-round lifesaver. Another worse yet. How coy how nice with others here, opposite away from them. Oh yes, indeed one Jason Sams.

Does that make sense?

Another letter undated, later I believe.

Best of all dear heart, there *is* no romance *here*. However else could I have gone back again? For us a very new kind of middleground. New, honest (without a past), sincere. Full wonder of it. Also shock, perhaps.

Somewhat later:

So you defend everyman . . . (That's you). . . I rather wish you hadn't. The affinity is nearly complete. The shock of that wave is what wobbles us here over and again. Disappoint you? You surprise me, Mr. Denby. Yes, I've had moments of cleverness, realization of power . . . but toying with lives? That's *murder* you're near accusing me of!

With *C* you have to put the pieces back together. If she were really perceptive and cool with all else she has—friend, you and I would be licking her footsteps and telling each other how lucky we are to be near the head of the line. But no one comes all in a piece, we are all partial people. Christa's a witch; she is magic. She must be dealt with by means of magic and allowed to practise her own brand of witchery—else she does not exist. She might bitch at this, since she feels she is only a woman, but we men of the world know a witch when we see one, right? She is not calling it love between you, not yet. And this is just as well. Chemistry, yes. She dug you instantly. Name-calling comes later.

Why all of this. Simple. Christa conjures up intensity in men. She did in me, she has in you. And the more intense *you* become, the more impossible it is to handle her—unless you're willing to make it a full-time job and rebuild from the ground up. But this destroys her. All impossible. Then, when you're feeling intense, she turns cold or drops a knife into your heart. Babe, years ago I went through that a dozen (count 'em) times. Sometimes I'd simply call and tell her I was coming over. Sometimes she would just appear as if nothing had happened. Either way, we were not giving each other the commitment that the other wanted. *You* can do it; you're not hung up in just the way I was. Worth it! We all know she is.

I've searched by now for details of the Baltimore and Washington guys, but she's been careful as always, I find, to leave out names and solid matter. Christ, but I wish Le Bureau Deuxieme knew of her, she'd get her oo number instantly.

By the way, she is given to looking through private papers, so if you don't want her to read this, destroy it. She is clever and thorough in matters like this, believe me.

Trailing off from the *murder* line, above: I had observed that it was all very well to live with you, but I suggested, not knowing her intentions, that she might as usual be careless or unaware of the intensity she created; I told her not to play around with lives. So, feeling meddled with, she threw back that and more. A literate explosion indeed.

And I love her very much too, want good for her, feel very protective for no defensible reason. She chooses to view this as a cop-out guilt reaction. Maybe, but also more than that. I've been in love twice, since; we exchange details (not about you, for obvious reasons), and it helps, at times, to keep the vessels stable. In looking through her letters, I found a few I shouldn't have found, and won't throw away. The world is short on witches.

I'm over the hump on this note. Lost track of the beginning. Maybe I've already said too much, so I'll compound it—since you've already sold your novel, your *Italian Travels,* why not go forth into the urban marketplace (name your per cent) and peddle mine?

> Love, sigh, luck,
> Dave

This intelligent, tender, thoughtful, moving letter, as buoying as a vasectomy in my then frame of mind, did not arrive until after Jane Mason left on Saturday morning. However I might fault him for its contents, or its impulse, afterwards or at the time, I could not pretend the thing was unsolicited. During my long-distance call the previous Wednesday I'd begged him, more or less, to send just such a tome, although the suggestion ("Uh oh. You say she went to *Baltimore?*") had in the first place been his. Hard data (much good it would have done me) I thought I wanted, hard data he promised to provide; instead, since rifling her old letters turned up nothing, he gave me his view of her character, or (what I needed even less) his view of her character as it was during their own rich, stormy romance: a playing-at-novelist on my time, or worse, a playing-at-friend. And yet . . . he was a friend. He'd quite clearly meant to do me a favor. And I was far from certain he had not. Between the Wednesday call and the Saturday mail I had been through her European diary, so I could almost fill the gaps, provide the names, myself. Ivan. Roberto. Greek-fisherman-by-the-canal. The first of these was the least fanciful—her American doctor, her sister's ex, encountered post-abortion in Madrid (bad sex), followed up in Stockholm (good sex), and he was as likely to be stationed at Johns Hopkins (was that not in Baltimore?) as anywhere else in the world. Nor had her young Roberto, Roman stud and guide, appeared immobile—long after she left Italy and traveled to Paris, or Stockholm, or some damn place, he had written her from London (I think this last is right) offering her the fare to join him, plus his hand in marriage; she was amazed at his presumption, pleased by the chance to not reply. The (Mykonos) man by the canal, a ringer no doubt for Anthony Quinn, or Cavafy, who picked her up, took her to his humble shack, and from whose bed she vanished (with his lighter) while he slumbered . . . he, chances were, still tried his luck by the canal, having long ago made peace with his morning-after bewilderment, but there were other affairs of duration, border-crossing evasions and vindictive pursuits ("Back to Madrid the day after tomorrow. If he's still there I'll leave him in still smaller pieces"), described in her dense, allusive style, her sometimes illegible hand, and I was quite prepared to face a clutch, a colloquy of lovers, awaiting their turns in adjoining rooms at the Gramercy Park Hotel. Why not Tim, as well (he also covered ground, however he was funded), whose long-ago scheme to "come there and make you in Daisy's warm house" had, I was still able to assume, been thwarted? And surely her married painter friend around the corner, spared (a friend from pre/post-Europe days) dissection on the page, was in the running. (We'd come close to meeting several times, the four of us, but someone always canceled out.) And of course, the biggest threat of all, Pisacano, whom I'd been at pains not to phone during her absence, and who had not—this was the nub—called me.

Because the fact remained that Denby had produced no names. The fact remained that few of the encounters Christa wrote about were news. During our first go-around, her confessional days, she'd gone into nearly every one, if not in such depth of detail. All I learned from Dave's letter (and I'd known it before) was that he kept himself well in the running, maintained a claim on her which by his own reckoning, his calm, enlightened comments on "intensity," she was more likely to honor than she was my own. With a flash of useless, pre-Christa wisdom, I saw he was right, and didn't love him for it. Was I supposed to try to cool it *now*, pretend to turn off *now*, play wise, hypocritical games? There was no guarantee it would work, even if by miracle I brought it off. But it was in no way my style. Nor was I armed for it in other ways. I had no Japanese fiancée waiting in the wings; she was not, this vastly complicated lady, my "second generation" devilishly exotic once-weekly piece of ass—I wanted her to grow up in a hurry, I planned for us to go all the way. Denby needed to lock her into that time of mindless, mysterious precocity, as if, once he opted for the other, this one could never change, or grow: thus he could plague me with crap about "witches," the deep, cheap, copout romantics of someone with nothing to lose. Old fan and buddy, Indian giver in the desert, all peace to the healing which has since passed between us, you were remarkably free then with your purblind advice. The one bit of light he inadvertently shed was on her early horror tale, where she had him pulling out on the verge of her coming, when it was clearly his own he'd withheld, a cruelty much deeper than the one she divined, or could admit to. He had refused, in his version, to risk knocking her up, though that had been, on that occasion, the settled price of her favors. *She wanted his child!* She! The abortion queen! He! The will-power kid! Contraceptor of the brain! It tore me up, how well he ran his life. His lovely mate (her first and only lover), his two children, his Christa-of-the-time . . . having his cake and not even troubling to eat it, thigh-deep in (and winning) the awful battle of the sexes; what terrible ties must live between this pair, intimacies and wounds which I could never hope to match. What had I ever been—my modest house, my overeager prick, my narrow, dedicated life—but *his* gift to *her,* which she accepted with gingerly scorn? Through my innocent and unsuspecting mind and body, whirling in inner space, they continued to communicate. Dave loves Christa; Dave she loves.

Yet no need to go so far. She had not in all her life balled anyone twice or more she did not thereafter "love," for good, disparate reasons. Hadn't I read her book, hadn't I lived through certain hours? She loved poor bearded Tim, almost as much as she despised him. Her love for Dave was as deep as her lack of forgiveness. She loved young Roberto, who she spurned. She loved Dr. Ivan, who dropped her. Jason (grant

him this) was briefly adored for his shlong and his brain, his
mark on the world, and even, yes, for the "good father" he had
admittedly not been in too long a time. She gave up nothing,
no one; so who could know, despite Tucson's G-2 failure,
which gaudily cathected figure from her past was suddenly
available, and not by accident (for they, also, never quit, were
drawn to where she was; not I! I would not follow!), eager to
help her write a richer, fuller section in the chapbook of her
life? This much her diary taught, or reaffirmed: she was the
author and the heroine of her days, her life was work-in-
progress, she could hardly wait to architect a new affair or new
disaster, to get that part over with so she could write it down,
and if she was not, in this, so different from the rest of us, in or
out of these pages, she was unique for me in that she'd finally
drawn me in, however I might bitch and sulk and beg a larger
role; somewhere I had *consented* to be a bit player in her
life. How had it happened, forewarned as I was? How had
Covington, twice-weekly, going on three years, illumined no
corner? My poor prose, at least, threw some shadows. There I
had been given to displacements, fragmentations, as in the
Nijinsky quote by way of Dinelli-Gardella, that Dostoyevsky
was a writer who described his life under the guise of different
personalities, and sometimes I'd throw in Hitchcockian walk-
ons in my own prissy person; overall, the method had its satisfactions, until one fine day I was jarred by a maniac on a boat
into trying something else, a third-person glimpse (no more
than that) of the killable Jason Sams, and after that, with
Gino, I ran smack into the *zeitgeist,* the autobiographical
malaise, yet was able to avoid it even then, turning it, I
thought, quite cleverly: I laid my shit on a weak-sister twin,
inferior and counterpart, expanding Hitchcock into stiff,
snotty Boswell, and persisted in trusting the device, obses-
sively labored the device, long after the evidence was in,
nearly five years of grinding, repetitive failures. But twins had

plagued me always, or ever since the primal pair outfoxed me in a Coney Island bungalow the summer I was five, entering a room (in which I had been freeing flies from flypaper with the skill of a surgeon on a battlefield) five-minutes apart, identically dressed, father number one content to cheer me on, my true father in his turn incensed by such idiot compassion; the confusion, to begin with, had been mine, but when they picked it up, saw the tears, they kept me in the dark awhile . . . I had seen my double too many times in too many places, on a London bus, in a Swedish documentary film, in a New York theatre audience (perhaps a week ago), pre-beard, post-beard, the same lines and bones, the same shocking semblance that might pop from tavern mirrors, storefront windows— what was his life? A huge improvement on my own? A mess much worse? On the bus, in the theatre, I had not been tempted to inquire. It seemed far saner to invent him, and pose the questions then. So I was wrestling with the problem on the page, if not in my $12.50 hour or in my life. In my life, I had fucked Jane Mason once the night before and once again that morning. Friday night we sat and drank the dago red and reminisced about our Tucson days—the night we met and made it, when she took the wrong turnoff driving me back from a party at her place to the Denbys', and we got out of the car and stood face to face and thrust and trembled under the saguaros, the perilous drive some days later in her rickety auto to Nogales (I sat in the death seat, I could not drive the car, but she, just licensed, couldn't either), the bars we hit both sides the border, the fond motels, the night we babysat for the Denbys and I fucked her pupils into huge black pools, my escape (on schedule) to New York, her scared, dewy arrival on my doorstep two months later . . . and how far we had come since those bittersweet days, how much we had altered and learned. We talked discreetly of our present lives and mates, exchanging small insights and complaints. She came and sat at

my feet for her moment of mandatory warmth, and then she
thought she ought to go. She was turning over a new leaf (and
of course, she said, I had *my* feelings, *my* new commitments),
balling less or not at all, except in her new and groovy relationship with the man who had replaced Bob Kane, a painter
like her husband, but, blessedly unlike Roger, a man with a
possessive side. She dug his fierce attentions, she was trying
hard. She leaned her head (for old times' sake) against my
knees, I stroked her hair, she opened her lips against my trousers, and then once more she said she had to leave. I didn't
move until she actually began to rise; then reached around
and cupped her pointy tits, licked her neck, overrode her
ritual, panting objections, and in a matter of seconds I reamed
her from behind, both of us still fully clothed except for her
pants, which I had wrestled off over her shoes, squeezing her
pink bums apart and fucking her cunt, no more of her than
that, coming quickly in long aching spurts then reached a
hand around to massage her harshly until—"Ooh ooh ooh
ooh!"—she peaked out on her own, my limp cock spilling
juices on her frilly blue dress and my fawn trousers, and we
collapsed together on the rug, slept for half an hour; then I got
up and lurched to the john, fetched a blanket on the way back,
shut a few lights, and we retired on the floor for the night.
Once more in the morning, as soon as I saw her stir, before the
guilties could consume her, I had her again, my sour-breathed
poet, directing my nostrils over the top of her head ("Bad
breath can indicate aggression," indicated Covington),
brewed us some coffee and walked her to the corner. A charming experience it was not, but certainly in character, I was the
lead man again in my life, and probably also, for a time, in
hers. Such therapeutic bounty terminated in the late afternoon. Once Christa's key turned in the lock, and I jumped off
the hassock to remove the chain, for I had not been expecting
her until Sunday at the earliest, and would have had the chain

on anyway, once she entered the apartment I was once more in
thrall, reverting to the peripheral role I despised her for having assigned me. But wait. Apartment tidied, alone at last, I
heard the mail arrive, claimed Denby's letter (there was nothing else), read it twice, and then proceeded to follow his advice
—tried to hide it here and there, settling finally on the belly
of a book, the French translation of my own, which had come
out, or come to me, in March, a couple of weeks after she returned. It was its only rendering thus far in a foreign tongue,
and a handsome production of which I was proud. It had
received good notices in France, although one remark pur-
porting to be praise had left me uneasy—the judgment that
I was a "pessimist in the pure state," which squared not at all
with my own long-standing views. However dour the author's
appearance, or somber his prose, deep down both he and
it were cheer itself (and why had no one said a thing about
some very funny lines?); if this were not the case, how explain his rising from his bed each day, let alone his subsequent scratch marks on the paper? But reviewers' judgments,
foreign and domestic both, meant balls, let it sell and be
well, and I had tried to share my glee with Christa the day I
brought the book home from my agent's office. She eyed the
volume somewhat balefully. Well, not everyone's pleasure is
infectious, nor was she given to the obvious accolade, or not
when you would obviously expect it; this was her way. I could
adjust. Besides which, _I_ had written the thing, not her, she
was still struggling (though daily less and less) with her own
balky muse; some envy might have entered in, all human
enough. It was equally important to remember that _I_ hadn't
painted her pictures, not even the ones I thought so highly
of; it was urgent to keep all such distinctions clear. With
Denby's letter in its middle the book bulged quite a bit,
so I considered concealing the volume itself, and did for a
time, thrusting it into the deep desk drawer where my jour-

nal and in-mail were, but pulling it out again, reading the letter again, returning it to the book and the book to the bookcase. Then I gave some thought to the placement of my
journal. I could hardly object to her reading whatever I left
on the desk, I was probably inviting such scrutiny, but if she
was as good on private papers as Denby said (and why, my sister in so many ways, should she differ there?), there was much
in that journal I could not bear for her to see. Perhaps she had
already seen it?—I experienced the moment's sickened outrage, then dismissed the thought. She would have had no reason to hunt it up. Her interest in my thoughts, affairs, had
never been that sharp. But now . . . certain entries, dreams,
some herein recorded, many more not, had to be kept from
her eyes. As also items like my copy of Tim's letter to her, back
in February, with its "brimmings," "vulvas," typed out word
for word. As also a carbon of the letter I'd written to Dave just
that Thursday night, the night after the call, drunk out of
mind—I'd had the sense to keep it until morning, and destroyed it then, but retained the carbon as an object lesson of
what happened to me, or to my letters, when I drank too
much, or in a certain frame of mind.

Dear Dave,
    On the other hand, if she *did* go off to Baltimore to fuck some-
body, some figure from the multicolored past, I'm not sure I *can*
handle it. I've tried to be straight with her, give her what is best
and most natural in me, and beyond that am not prepared to
join the ranks of her father-confessors and admirers of her prose.
On the face of my feelings, I'd make a poor cuckold (and I'm
tempted to ask, since you married the other, wouldn't you) . . .
    Your data, well-meant, and I suppose necessary, kicked me in
the gut all the same . . .
    So, do not tell her, or not yet, I have been running through her
diaries. And beneath that first-rate exterior lives a maniac, or,
even less kindly, an ambulating cunt, no less. So groin-oriented a

lady I have never seen up close. And, since she lives in my house, it can bring me no joy. . . .

Have I not chosen badly? A lady who loves to distraction everyone she ever slept with and will love me too when I become part of her past and her diary, even more so when I make it clear that I am not about to be her pen pal, or an East Coast base through which to test or deball the latest flame? Yes, the real pain of parting, should it come, will be austere. She will not (whatever you mean by this) destroy me. There will be no further contact. I was able, as I said, to lay myself on the line, and was superbly (if briefly) rewarded . . .

Anyway, whatever is in store, I force the issue in a few days time, when, presumably well and romantically fucked, she returns . . .

And finally, of course, my journal contained the notes I felt obliged to take on her European diary, as well as on the present one, direct quotations, summaries, aghast or reasoned glosses on certain lines or episodes . . . her finding these would constitute the greatest mortification, for they would indicate that I'd treated her as shabbily as I claimed to think that she was treating me, as object, thing-on-a-slide, and I would be more culpable, for she'd been searching for some meaning to her life, trying to do more than muddle through, while such detached, relaxed jugular-seeking was my job. So precautions must be taken. I buried that blue looseleaf, left it in its deep desk drawer but hidden now beneath piles of canceled checks, abandoned manuscripts, innocent mail, and what I was concealing, if not word for word, was matter of this kind:

Summer/Autumn 1964
Ivan my lover, Tim my doormat, Dave my confidant . . . it's been three weeks since my last, WHY DOESN'T HE WRITE?
Ivan wants me for his mistress, nothing more. Let him, for a time. Then leave when he takes me for granted, begins to think

his life is orderly. I ask him for his philosophy of life. He says he has none, begins a caress . . . I pull the covers up. When does his wife arrive?

So many people tell me I'm exceptional, it must be so. My own sense of potency, overlying softness. Women are trained not to be "aggressive"—what choice but to be devious, develop a compensating bitchiness? Am I too analytic? Is this really a fault? It is the way I have to be . . . We all want our weaknesses examined by someone who loves us, who still rushes to us . . .

When will it happen, the mate who is soulmate, who knows and is known??

My infection has come back . . .

A long time since the last entry, seventeen days. That's too good a pun to pass up.

I'm being saved for some ultimate tragedy . . .

Tomorrow we start back for Madrid. If he's still there I'll leave him in still smaller pieces.

The numbness, floating through. Alone and not, in bed and not, with sex and not, approaching catatonia, absence of affect, caring. What sets it off? What ends it? Should I fear for my mind? Yet how I make things happen, alter the quality of lives. Catalyst—my designated, unwished for role . . .

[Books as a part of her dangerous inner landscape. As also drugs. A scrawled, muddled scene in an Athens hotel room, sick with a cold but also high on something, masturbating to *Naked Lunch,* Tim in mind. This scene followed by draft of a letter to "DD": "I remember how much most things meant when I was with you . . . this distant now in space and time, I take down my hair, I kiss your eyes and bite your sides, I wrap myself in your fineness . . . and love also to *K* . . ." (I watch my poor friend Keiko sautéed briskly in that "love.") How, so soon after, did she jot down that masturbation scene? I see her on the sweaty sheets, writing left-handed, manipulating with her right. Not a moment lost. Time and need for diddling even amidst her multitude of men. Mysterious malfunctions of the privates, at this and other times. *La femme, c'est moi.* Entirely possible that I will have *J* (sic) tomorrow night. Christa will find out, use it as a reason to depart. Her own double standard (my sense of), her own unreasonable demands.

Elsewhere in that sequence, difficult to read and follow, she seems to personify her cunt, addresses it with stern affection, Troublemaker, Mouth. Describes also some actual fucking, with Ivan, Roberto. Which shocks me, of course. She's a good writer, as Dave has somewhere said. Juicy, joyless. Morbid concern with "power." Contempt for men.

How detailed and good on the look and smell of certain cities. Stockholm. Rome. Feel of spring in Naples connected to the man who moved in on her while she sketched, from his park bench to hers, whom she tolerated, yearned for, encouraged, feared, finally "escaped." Why? What determines who she screws, and when?]

If Tim were not Tim, to hold me more. *Why is he such a sex fiend? Why isn't he brighter? Will he never change?* But I have him, as is. All one needs must do is throw him a fuck from time to time, or write the proper letter from the distant part. He will arrive. He will be Tim. Now we struggle toward an end. Last night in the café in St. Germain de Près with the tension building he was gone for a time. I asked him where. Defiantly he said he had called his airlines hostess, but could not get through. Later he went off again and when he got back I was gone. Back here, in the room we still share, he struck me hard across the face for where he'd decided I'd been. I admitted nothing. Then he confessed that he had read my diary Thursday last, his contrite explanation for the blow. I *must* be more careful not to leave it openly about . . .

He sees me in the black translucent panties, new. Watches me in the mirror, trembles. He knows, as things now are, he'll not be the one to get inside them . . .

And yet he found me and came to me in Athens. And when I leave him in a few days time, and if I send for him or not, he will probably come after . . .

So dark. Young. He took me to his house, outside Rome, to meet his family. Roberto. No one there except a crone, as he doubtless knew no one would be. Was it his grandmother? He apologized, said the others would shortly arrive. Meanwhile, he would show me his room. There of course he tried to have me, despite no encouragement. Finally he drew out his penis, backed me (as I would not go near the bed) against the wall. I gave it to him standing, fully clothed, my back pressed hard against the wall, he thrusting and trembling . . . His family arrives. Mother, father, two younger sisters. A tense, bilingual dinner. They can't imagine who I am. But they invite me for the night, a room of my own. In the night he comes, climbs in placidly, sleeps. Wakes at dawn, makes no effort to rouse me, climbs on, relieves himself on my ass . . .

[Ivan was the only one who got away, who bested her, would play on his terms or none. Poor chap had no "philosophy of life." (Might have guessed, if only from her sister's letters, she would be given to such shit.) Probably she asked him to split from his wife (which, had he done—as she sees it all in terms of combat—she would have dropped him then?). In Madrid, as his wife's arrival nears, he has been fucking her less well, she confides to her infernal book, probably also to his face. But he emerges from the prose as unruffled by her moves. She describes the scene in which he sees her onto the bus, out of town. They regard each other blankly through the glass, and just before the bus begins to move he turns away. Neither gives an inch, but she writes that for days afterward she feels lost and lorn. Arrivals and departures. How well she evokes them. My own with Britta, Esha, Dino, leapt straight to mind. But that bus ride only ends the reel. How many weeks or pages later is it he turns up in Stockholm (what happened? did he indeed leave his wife?), while she's visiting her mad sister. There they rewrite the chapter, the sex is very good, likely aided by the unexpected presence of Tim in town as well, whom she puts off his shaky carnal rights, if he is not too battered by then to even want to claim them, with her convenient lie of illness in her basic parts. She lives with her sister and Swedish brother-in-law (that has not yet broken up), her mother is shortly to arrive, she shacks somewhere with Ivan, while Tim, perhaps, is holed up on some quaint little side street occupying his time between chaste tête-á-têtes with his lady (what manner of man!? . . .) by searching for the sure-fire native remedy for the ailment she does not have. Thus she fakes him out, and then she passes judgment: he quite puts her off, she writes, by his "ingrained passivity."

And yet (even Circe has her problems) she is onto herself in many ways. And suffers more than she will ever show. And is redeemable through love.

But whose? What self-less ("soulmate!") madman will undertake the task?]

I raced through these pages once again, before I hid them as described. What I would do with all this data when she got back, I had no clear idea. At the moment I could wipe it out, begin to drink, prepare to watch the ball game; or I could anguish the future, ways to handle her when she returned; or I could begin by showering away Jane Mason and all useless speculation on griefs to come and griefs gone by, seek a jot of peace in the eye of all this chaos—it was only eleven in the morning—and do some *work* in what remained of this largely squandered gift of solitary time. And this is what happened. It was rewrite, of course, commencing with the section I had batted out on Silent Sunday, in those days of nearly blissful ignorance, before I became the red-eyed haunter of the library of her life; it was Gardella-and-his-tape-recorder I began with, then went on to touch up a few things else, and why knock it? Rewrite, then as now, was where the real work was.

When she got back from Baltimore a few hours behind Jane Mason, I was eating tuna fish out of the can and drinking wine and watching the Mets, but the moment she entered I switched off the set.

"Hello, Puss. You're early."

"You don't have to stop watching the game."

"You may not believe this, but I just broke for lunch, I just stopped typing ten minutes ago."

"Why shouldn't I believe it?"

"No reason. Anyway, I wasn't really tuned in yet. How did it go?"

"Not too badly."

"Did you miss me?"

"I did a lot of thinking about us . . ."

"Ah, yes, thinking. BUT DID YOU MISS ME?"

"Oh, for heaven's sake, all right, Jason, yes, I missed you."

"Good. I missed you too."

And before much longer, having messed it up from scratch, and still drinking wine, I was talking to her earnestly of diaries, illicit readings of same, my reasoned view of people who could share the loved object and those like myself who could not, and she calmly took it in, seemed to agree or at least to understand, told me in turn of the period she'd missed despite the pills, and following such exchange of information I had her on the rug in five seconds flat, but she was nowhere near me, suffered the speedy embrace because it was easier than not and for what she might learn, so too soon afterward I solicited her help and peasant hands to make things well again: "Come, love, wake the sleeping giant," at which she may have smiled, and did consent to touch, but hated (I could see) the frantic dutifulness I displayed and sought to inflict, so after a brief false alarm—I mounted and died—nothing came of that. That night was the night of Sandy's party, which I would have attended had she still been away, but instead we strolled uptown, sat on ornate stoops along Park Avenue where none had sat before, spooned, kept it light, studied the tattooed, sword-swallowing stills (she would not go in) outside Hubert's Flea Circus on Forty-second Street, had a frank at Grant's; for me there was a marvelous moment at the newsy's outside when she stopped to read a headline, and the New York cretin (had he flunked his p.o. test?) tried to badger her about free reads, this assault on his means of livelihood, and she wiped him out in three words or so I wish I could recall. That was on the first of May.

A night in the penultimate week we went at my suggestion to hear Sonny Rollins at the Village Vanguard, an evening she would to some degree enjoy, as our waiter turned out to be a Greek, mistook her for one, and, shrugging and smiling, she conversed with him at length in some patois about the islands. That night, in the taxi, she said she found me horribly suspicious and devious (we were perhaps discussing Pisacano, or her friend around the corner, or her diaries), assuming far too much and that the worst, and then she said, "Jason, we have no past," in annoyance and despair, as if she had finally put her finger on the real trouble between us. Of course I remembered her early letter to Dave which he fed back to me, where she'd cited precisely the lack of a past as the joy and wonder of our tie; should I fault her, now, for inconsistency? I suppose it would have been in character. But she knew nothing of Denby's long letter, safe in the translation of my book, and she never learned of it. (Although, to claim only credit due, I did tell her of the fears he'd implanted over the wires, and added piously that I would not have come by them on my own. That was too bad, she said, that the few days she'd been away were spoiled for me; Denby was ill-informed, he happened to be wrong. I hope that's so, I said; I couldn't live it any other way, I make a lousy cuckold.) All I did, instead, was ask her what she thought she meant by that remark, what pleasure she had in such evasive obfuscations, and would she like to make a larger effort toward having a present.

Had I really requested, through those days, such a wealth of news? I suppose I did, one way or another, after I'd seen him floating on the page, awash in her contempt. I can't get Tim out of my head, she would say, as that one night we stood together in the garden; he's become a part of me. Well, I would say—Denby's letter and her own prose rattling in my head —you think, or pretend to, that he's groovy now, as the trouble boils between us, but what about that entry during the Paris days, in which you state . . . Well, she would calmly reply (*You shouldn't have read my diaries, friend, that was a bad and dangerous thing to do, but since you have, you're going to hear a fraction more*), I was wrong about many things, I hurt him badly in the Paris days. But he taught me everything I know during the earliest days of our love, from certain interdicted illustrated books we sampled many pleasures; he is a man with an appetite and talent for pleasing his partner unlike any of the many since . . . but you don't want to hear this, perhaps? And we traveled. (I might here interrupt: "Tijuana? Tangier? The abortion trail?" No, Jason. You would be fixed on that. Lover's trips to Honolulu, Mazatlán . . .) Yes but, dear, if you recall, you broke his balls in much the manner and with greater frequency than you are breaking mine, with disappearances and withholdings and unspeakable ailments, intimations of the more perfect lover just around the corner, to heal both box and soul; why, you had to have clubbed him with *me*, after you left here with him in February, igniting him for the thousandth time, then abandoned him again to come back here in March . . . and look! It's

only May! Relax a little, can't you, give us a chance? Thus I
"reasoned" with her through those final days, instead of slam-
ming her round the apartment. I tried to cling to Denby's
judgment, that Tim was a *putz,* that I had not one thing in
common with Tim (yet took my tight-assed, private oath that I
would not become an "East Coast Tim," bepricked outpost
for her pleasure), and my own opinion that it was time she was
turned (and that words could turn her), in all her beauty and
potential, from such slavish repetitions and confusions, semi-
nars in giving and receiving pain. Or else, granting her feelings some substance: All the world is California, Christa,
when you're being fucked and young. But this time around,
Berkeley was more than nostalgia, it was the womb away from
the home she also thought she wanted, the escape from my lure
and my threat—the ending of her girlhood. "Why do you
want to marry me, Jason? You know how I feel about children." Another test which I would fail to pass. Children were
the vicious joke God and biology played on ladies, and of
course, being me, I would want to entrap her that way, pull
the simplest rank of all. (But what about the time that you and
Dave . . . this, I am sure, I was not quite mad enough to say.)
Look, I said, we'll hire a nanny when the funds permit. Or if
you'll just carry the thing to term, I'll hold up my diaper-
dumping, formula-mixing end. Besides, you're only twenty-
six, I'm quite content to wait awhile. But mixed with her rage
at being victimized by the accident of the chromosomes (for
which she could still make me feel a tangible responsibility)
were genuine fears—that she would pass on the curse, do
unto it, or them, what she felt had been done unto her, the
thirty different kinds of parental violence. So I rushed into
that breach as well. Not so (I said), as we are thinking, growing
reeds, we will have learned from our own horrendous child-
hoods the things not to repeat. So then she'd play her ace,
which was that she fully understood my male and built-in

point of view, my helpless lust for progeny, the family unit, settling in, need to perpetuate myself, and that for this purpose almost any other broad would do as well, most probably better, for she did not, to tell the truth, consider herself my equal in the world. Before this awful mixture, with its scorpion tail of a clause, I threw up my hands, declared her professed world-view insidious bullshit, announced my taste impugned, as indeed it had been, and that particular exchange, like most of any substance, would abruptly end.

We ran into trouble with her nose, as late as the tenth of May, the day of the first of her departures. I'd come out onto the porch just before going out to assume my Monday roles, and she was sitting in the rocking chair, staring into space or into the garden, so by way of (brief) farewell, I leaned down and kissed her on the nose.
"Why do you do that?"
"Do what?"
"Kiss my nose."
"Because it's there," was all I said. Even at this terrible ticklish stage she would avail herself of pettiness, use her real or trumped-up sense of her infirmities to stone *me* with, strike at the heart of my disjointed self-image (which she'd done little to repair)—the sensitive clod, a genius at picking out where she was weakest or felt herself to be, who might even "probe" for just such "vulnerable" (her vocab., her habits) spots, then press them by design, or at best be guilty of colossal carelessness; in kissing her nose, I was quite clearly commenting on its prominence; BABY, I WILL NOT PLAY, and so I said, "Because it's there," keeping it light, straightened up and guided the back of her hand gently to my cock, which was even with her mouth, a gesture to which she was somewhat more agreeable, though there was neither the context nor the time to investigate how much. Only the day before, Sunday the ninth,

we'd done such all-day fucking as eclipsed the rest . . . but for the moment let that pass. Much later that night, after my class, I stopped in to see Gardella, a bachelor once again, who had recently moved into a rent-controlled penthouse on West End Avenue, not large enough, it would turn out, for both him and his *balabattish* second wife, and they would move off to Queens to have their child, but it was perfect for him at the time; we sat on the balcony looking into Jersey, drinking no-name scotch and talking about life, his ex-wife, our psychiatrist, our bottomless European travels, and briefly about Christa, whom he'd met once or twice at the house (she'd even drawn him once, a quick, gay, surreptitious penciled sketch as he leaned discoursing into the room, which captured his befuddled earnestness); she was a real earth mother, he told me, and he expressed surprise at how my tastes had changed since the days when Britta and Gillian and Jane were my "type" (he meant smallish blondes), and, suddenly anxious through the alcoholic haze, I went to make the call. The line was busy, which turned out to be a dialing error or a fluke, for she'd been gone (as I learned from Mrs. Gross, who missed nothing) since three that afternoon. Five minutes later, and five minutes after that, I got no reply. It was raining hard and I took a taxi home, still hoping for the best—she'd stepped out for cigarettes, or she was napping, or just not answering the phone. All the lights were on. There was a mess of unwashed dishes in the sink. The door from the house to the porch was wide open, but praise be the garden door was locked. The house was bare of her but for the Egon Schiele print she'd had hanging on the porch, and in my typewriter, in the study, on a three by five card, this message:

> A Hotel what else?
> What courage; paralysis.
> Read your journal thursday last. View tempered now but—
> sick.

> Love

And alongside the typewriter was her set of keys.

Love! Sick! She had found the goddamned thing (where had I been? at the periodontist? having a long, pointless lunch with my agent? moaning to Frank?), as Denby warned she would; she had doubtless read it through (I could hardly stand to think of that), yet kept her counsel four long days, during which—that marathon Sunday—she bestowed herself more fully than she had in all our time, enslaved me on Sunday, forgave me on Monday ("view tempered") for existing, and vanished at her leisure. Sick!! I tore into the pouring night, stopped at every hotel in a five-block radius, still feeling lucky, patiently spelling her name at each place. I raced back to the empty apartment, downed a water glass of J&B, which took effect at once, and typed, though I could hardly see, a confused, teary letter to one "Christal Sarksan," c/o her mother, which I would still purchase back should you care to deal, my love, as I would buy back all those letters, and if I could, all those days, particularly the ones right after, when I lost all sense of self and shred of judgment—why couldn't I see that she *agreed* with what I'd said! that she'd left from shame and guilt and sorrow, not (not merely) out of her damnably calculating rage! The worst blunder I could make, if I wanted her back, as I so clearly did, was to say I was wrong, I was sorry! But I knew nothing of that then. I staggered out into the downpour and airmailed the thing to California, came back in, stripped, and crapped out on the couch, lights blazing.

Tuesday morning I devoted to the phone. I called her mother, crazily imagining that distant woman knew her whereabouts (and seriously alarmed her, for she'd feared for Christa's safety in the wilds of New York—"More so than when she was in Europe!"—even when she knew exactly where, with whom, she was), I called Daisy in Baltimore, the ex-lover on First Avenue (both agreed she was a lovely, difficult person, neither had news of her), I downed another glass of zinfandel to allow time for incoming calls, then rang up four or five YWCAs and three or four airlines before giving up, for the time, on "Mr. Bell's evil toy." I taxied to American Express, dropped off a loving, tearful note, taxied back, phoned in half an hour, and they were nice enough to say she'd been in to pick up her mail perhaps ten minutes after I left. Then I called Pisacano and said, as lightly as I could, that my lady had disappeared herself. Broads are broads, he said, he'd bring over the jug. We drank until six, then staggered to his place, where he cooked up a batch of spaghetti à la carbonara and summoned a pair of nondescript ladies to join us. I was home by ten, slept until midnight, drank until two, woke at six. At eleven on Wednesday she phoned. Of course I was there. I said, Hello, Christa, conveying equal portions of relief and terror. Do you call in response to the desperate, loving note I planted yesterday at American Express? No, she would have rung up anyway. Ah, good. To wish me happy birthday, which falls today? "If you wish." Well—what now? —are you all right, would you care to meet? "All right." I would have canceled all appointments, but the day was free. We met on the corner of Fiftieth and Fifth, which she said was near her hotel. I saw her forty times before she turned up, walking slowly, a few minutes late. We strolled past Atlas bearing up the world, then turned back and sashayed down the rows of flowers, watched the outdoor diners for a while. I put my arm around her shoulders, drew her close. I talked into her ear.

"It's too much, you know. I read your diary, you read my diary, which is about reading your diary, and four days later you leave. I love you and want to marry you, I'll say it again. Look, I'll buy us combination locks. Our lives are not lived on the page."

"I had to be alone awhile."

"How is the hotel?"

"Ghastly. They're overcharging for an awful room. I've been drinking gin."

"Gin? Jesus Christ, let's go rowing. It's a beautiful day."

We walked through Central Park. At moments she seemed almost lighthearted, moving off to pick some flowers. But when I asked her how she felt, she said she was "numb." Was that anything like the "catatonia" of her diary (I had to inquire, compulsive student of her phases)? No, less intense. The park was full of bench-warmers and strollers, some of whom beamed upon us as we passed. I suppose we seemed a pleasant couple. I tried to construe it as a normal afternoon. As the summer approached, we would be getting out more anyway, perhaps into the countryside. I took off my shirt as I rowed, and it fell to the bottom of the leaky boat. She picked it up and wrung it out. We drifted into a deserted cove, where she wished she was a man, so that (a) she would not have to suffer this useless anxiety about whether she was pregnant, and (b) she would be able to remove her blouse against the heat. With (a) I couldn't help her, but no one's around, you're wearing a bra, I told her, why not take it off. She slipped out of the blouse, and I glanced into the cleavage of a stranger. Marathon Sunday, when we screwed from early morning until dusk, when she came half a dozen times ("It's never happened more than twice in one day before"), when I'd fucked her by the afternoon to unfathomable tears and the "Mamamamama" the Kama Sutra cites, and after an interlude for pasta at Pete's we went again in bed that night, not because she was the least bit interested, she was exhausted in fact, but because—the Florence Nightingale of Fuck—"You've not had as many completions," ordering me to enter her from behind because her parts were sore and that way, for some reason, would cause less discomfort, turning me off, despite my ordinary fondness for the rear, by her begrudging charity, so I said (my time around for martyrdom), It's okay, forget it, and not really all that put

out, but this left her with certain things to prove, she went
fiercely down and sucked and licked and teased my ass, she was
finally going to take it all, for all the wrong reasons, so I
pulled her up and put her on me, placed her where she loved
to be and labor, it was one of the great aching comes of my
life, and she, she kept her small edge in "completions" still
. . . marathon Sunday was three days or light-years behind.
I think something changed in my brain, the following night,
when I came back and she was gone. I was thereafter totally
wary. At the lakeside café where we stopped for sandwiches
and beer, I put it off as long as I was able, then for a while
longer, then announced that I must go and pee, rushed off,
rushed it through, and when I got back she was gone. There
was another couple seated at our table; she might not ever have
been there. She'd been careful not to name her hotel, nor the
street it was on. I was abandoned and alone, a half-man in the
multitude. Then I saw her, twenty feet away, standing at the
railing, watching my paralyzed panic with unreadable eyes,
but obviously learning from life, taking notes as she observed
the pinioned prey—Christa, Scientist.

Noticed, she joined me. We strolled off toward Fifth, but I
sat us down on a nearby patch of grass, where I stroked her
cheek and hair and she dispassionately picked my brains: since
I'd read so much, had come to know so much, what did I think
her trouble was, what were my views on what I'd probably
want to call her "promiscuity"? I don't really know, I said, trying to match her tone, *guru* with heart in my mouth, the
habit's not that hard to find in women who travel, nor is the
error that unique, of seeing life as Quest and confusing fucking with the Way; nor is the number small of ladies (often
bright) who love chaos— ("Others have said that of me, Jason, it happens not to be true.") Okay, I suppose there's nothing wrong at all had you enjoyed it, but it seems to have caused
you (let alone caused others) chiefly pain; I have not, as you

know, been "inactive" myself, but one day you meet somebody
or you reach a point where you choose to stop; I really don't
know, I repeated, objective I cannot claim to be, why don't
you let me ring Frank (still twanging on that) and you could
talk it out with him? She wondered if it lay within my power to
stop mentioning this "bizarre idea," and I said I surely would.
And not merely from the fear (having just seen again how
quickly she could seem to vanish) of losing her again, but for
an implication I had somehow missed before, that given the
shape *you're* in, Jason, however one describes the color
scheme, how could you want to foist the man on me? Listen, I
said to her, why don't we marry and settle in, and from that
sweet, new place have any number of these fascinating chats-in-
depth? So she began to tell me of the Norwegian painter Ed-
vard Munch, 1863–1944, whose fine, unconscious-dredging
work lost all piss and vinegar once he'd ironed out his life and
settled down . . . Ignorant of Munch, unable to maintain
this high level while my world crumbled, I rolled over to lightly kiss her neck and cracked my glasses for the second time
since mid-April; they were in my side pocket, I had been wearing the shades. Soon after, we started downtown, broke again
to sit on a bench, watched a child lose a balloon, watched a
derelict fish in wire wastebaskets for unknown treasure, talked
of the skyline. She liked the style of those twin towers on Central Park West, though not of their inhabitants as she conceived it, and she put in a good word, perhaps the first civilian
one on record, for the neutron bomb. We started south again,
and I threw my jacket across her shoulders, as she wore just a
skirt and blouse and the air was growing chill; as we left the
park I hugged her close, sucked in my breath and very nearly
pinched her cheek, like an *alta bubba* with a baby carriage;
she seemed neither pleased nor perturbed by these varied attentions. I had already asked her three or four times if she
would come back with me (it was my *birthday*), which stopped

all conversation for the next five minutes or so, and even a paranoid in panic could see that she was not really right in her head, that there was more misery churning in her than the mere wish to ruin my day, so as we crossed Fifty-ninth and started down Sixth Avenue, I asked her somewhat formally if she would care to dine, assuming of course she was free, and she acknowledged that she was. But she wanted to shower first and change, if it was all the same to me. We walked slowly down Sixth Avenue, past the wooden hoardings beneath which an old woman had recently disappeared and died, past the crummy bar near Fifty-fifth in which we'd had a drink or two before going off to a disastrous Japanese meal at the Tokyo Sukiyaki in March, past Radio City Music Hall, to which we'd never been, all the way down to Forty-eighth, where one of two helmeted construction workers walking toward us took note of my existence—"Hey, John, look at the bush!"— which appeared to amuse her slightly, and I was almost glad it did, for I lacked the leisure to take umbrage, their great size apart. At Forty-eighth and Sixth she paused, crossed us to the west side of the avenue, led us back to Forty-ninth, and said that she would meet me there. Wouldn't it be more convenient all around if I sat and waited in the lobby? It would not. Whether from inertia or kindness she had let me come this far, but she would much rather I did not know the exact whereabouts of her hotel. Did I find this "childish"? No, I didn't find it anything. But rather than stand on the corner, I directed her gaze to BAR, between Forty-eighth and Forty-ninth, a Smith's I think it was, or some sleazy chain, and told her I'd await her there. Since the beers in the boathouse, a couple of hours earlier, I'd been dry, and much too preoccupied to care; but now I would shore up a bit for what did or did not lie ahead. Having led me—let me come—this far, she could hardly fail to reappear, but she had already done a great many things that she could hardly do. I waved her on her way, backing off from the corner to prove my good intentions, and went into the all-male place, took up a post close to the door, ordered the house special plus a beer and thought about the neighborhood, this block on which all at once she "lived," in some jerkwater refuge she had no doubt been holding in reserve for just such occasion, a gift (as she would tell me later) from Tim, who'd found it years earlier passing through; I'd bused countless times up the street, past its varied restaurants, *shlock* hotels, scabrous movie house, it was the liveliest part of my route from couch to office hour; but now it had become and would remain, until they tore it down, perhaps a year ago, the block to which she fled, the tawdry surroundings she left me for. Even the bar is gone, the crowded place in which I had two boilermakers more beyond the first, ignoring vibrations from my left and from my right, poor sots hungering for converse, and became drunk enough to feel only puzzled that she'd been gone for half an hour, and to wonder with detached curiosity how I (how Jason Sams) would handle matters should she not show up at all. I was close to ordering a fourth, and turning sociable, when she stuck her head in at the door, scrubbed and wearing a brown suit I did not even know if I had seen before, and I leapt from the stool and steered her out, for it was clearly no place for a lady.

"Where would you like to eat, Chris?"

"It doesn't matter."

"We haven't had Chinese food for quite some time, would that be all right?"

"Yes, fine."

This was more chicanery than sentiment (though I remembered our first meal well enough), for I had seen a Chinese restaurant partway up Forty-ninth, and imagined, if we passed her lodgings on the way, that she would probably tip her hand. Mere rote maneuvering: I did not need to know where she lived, and did not look for signs from her as we walked.

The restaurant we went to has been flattened with the rest, or I would surely name it. We descended some steps, came into a dim, carpeted place which seemed too posh for my attire, but no one made mention, were led to an intimate, ample booth screened on three sides, where we dined well and not too dearly, serviced by a grave, middle-aged waiter who was never in view but appeared jinn-like when required, and somewhere between the martinis and the rice wine she got onto Europe once again, which she had not talked of much since our earliest times. The stories she told now were like some few she told me then, a minor genre, chaste nights spent with strangers—chief of them was of a boat, an overnight trip from here to there chock-a-block with males, most of them exotic and all with one thing on their minds (she did not mean to be immodest, there were few lovely ladies on board), and the most exciting, a Dane, was also the most persistent, pursued her to her cabin, though she was not even feeling well and wanted nothing less, somehow got inside, the scene became unpleasant, but she detached herself at last and spent that night alone. Some similar, lesser tales. She had spent many nights abroad, and not from want of opportunity, utterly alone.

Love, why did you tell me all this? Did you think you gave too much away in the park? Did I ever say, whatever you thought I thought, that you had no selectivity at all? So what weight did you think they could bear, these tales of brief journeys when you kept it tight between your thighs? But I said none of this; in fact, I was also moved the other way, loved her more for trying to set the record straight, and thinking she could do it with an anecdote, or this one, and I asked her again, for the first time in several hours, if she would come back with me that night. I was caught, as I saw it, between seeming overeager and not being eager enough; I felt that if she thought I was (however slightly) losing interest, she would rush to beat me to the punch. She wanted me—whatever her "real feelings"—to turn her out, it was worth it to her to keep intact her *weltanschauung,* and I was not, through mistaken tactics, or fear of rejection, going to help her on her way. I was a very needy saint, a disembodied brain, I would put up with much to save us both from her psychology. And she said, dark eyes flicking to mine, then back to the table, not tonight, I can't tonight, perhaps in the morning. So I seized that first opening to fish out my keys, or hers, the set she'd left behind, and I pushed them toward her across the table. She eyed them for a second, seemed to nod, and put them in her purse. And my goals, by then, were so constricted, that I thought I had pulled off a coup of indescribable subtlety. I ordered a brandy to celebrate, she had one as well, and when I'd finished that my day was over, not just the shock of too much alcohol in too short a time but the exhaustion of relief, for with the keys transferred I almost lusted for my solitary bed, faced without fear the prospect of the long day's ending.

It was only ten thirty. She offered to walk me back to Sixth Avenue (and so I decided, unless she was more cagey than I could finally bear, that her hotel lay somewhere above the restaurant), and at the corner she strolled with me toward Forty-eighth. We paused to look into a once salacious bookshop window which had achieved respectability with *Fanny Hill,* displayed now nothing but; I had read the book the year before, had certainly been moved, but was in no frame of mind to discuss it now, so listened as she commenced to praise its great erotic power, told me that more than any other volume in a lifetime of pornographic reading this one had turned her on, left her ripe for plucking; so I was torn again, yearning for solitude yet hardly able to leave her to the first roughhewn, literate cock she'd find around the corner. We turned, I walked her back to Forty-ninth, took her hands, and suggested as calmly as I could that she make it between nine thirty and ten, which would give us both a chance to sleep, and her time to pack, and me—fraud and writer to the end—time to type on *Gino,* say from seven to nine, should the mood be on me. In response to all this ordering, she thanked me for dinner, gently disengaged, and disappeared around the corner. I resisted the urge to follow, steal a last glance from behind. Next to the bookshop was a liquor store; I bought a pint of gin, hailed an eastbound cab on Forty-eighth, and returned as eagerly to my house as I had ever done when it was full up with hungry pussycats or ladies. Fatigue aside, I felt content: I had done what I could; she would come back or she would not, and I crapped out on the unmade couch for the third successive night, the gin unsampled, the news station, battery all but dead, tinkling faintly at my ear, when I woke up for good around five in the morning.

I stayed prone until a glimmering of dawn, then put on a robe, made coffee, and took it out into the garden. I communed awhile with my little patch, watered the flowers, plucked compulsively at crabgrass and the endless beginnings of ailanthus trees. Then I returned to my coffee and lit a second cigarette. It tasted as good as the first; I knew I was experiencing what would probably be the best moments of the day, and that I ought to try to turn them to account, all false promises apart. I made some more coffee, took it into the study and began to tinker, fooled around the edges of the September afternoon when I lay in a darkened room nursing the beginnings of my eye disease and he burst in proudly with a girl named Heidy he had picked up in Hyde Park; he'd won the interest and companionship of a bona-fide hooker without even knowing what she was, and when the light dawned, when the mention of money and my own broad hints brought him to, he gamely tried to enter in, dropped his pants and shorts and lay back on the bed and solicited her ministrations, but though she was tipsy enough to play with him a bit he never did get it up, sadly enrobed and abruptly departed, leaving me with a disrupted day and her besotted body (we had gone through a bottle of scotch), a red stabbing eye and a large impatience for three days thence, when his boat left for New York. A few minutes after he disappeared, Heidy passed out in the john, which was a few feet down the hall, but luckily she hadn't latched the door. I lugged her back and dropped her on his bed and napped for half an hour. She was still unconscious when I woke. She was over on her stomach, her dress hiked above her waist. She wore no underpants. I went in for a closer look; she smelled none too fresh. I stripped off my shorts, knelt at the foot of the bed, and rubbed myself stiff on her ass. She stirred, and I retreated. She had not been the most stimulating company, a foul-mouthed broad from Liverpool, so I saw no need to wake her. I was sorry her cunt was inaccessible, but this spared me her face. When she quieted down I began to poke again around her rosy cheeks; the flesh yielded, but revealed no aperture. I thrust along the crack as gingerly as I could, but she began to shift and groan, and again I backed off. To kill some time I administered my eyedrops, took a slow leak in the all-purpose sink, washed down some codeine, then went back to Gino's bed, supported myself on a hand, and jerked off over her ass. I aimed for the middle of her backside, but a jet or two landed on the sheets. I tidied these with Kleenex, and hoped the stains would blend in with his own. Then I dressed and went out, took a few things to the laundromat, bought a *New Statesman,* downed a few pints of bitter in the local while my clothing spun. Heidy was still there, still unconscious, when I came back to the room. She seemed to be breathing. I pottered about, brought my journal up to date, finished reading a piece I had begun in the pub on the imminence of Franco's fall, polished off the inch of scotch, covered her with Dinelli's robe, and went to bed.

Gino returned half an hour later, around nine. He had forgotten her completely, or certainly did not imagine she would still be there. She was even more pungent than she'd been. Feigning sleep, I had to bite the giggles back as he cursed and labored (having failed to rouse her), finally moved her aside, and crawled into the fraction of bed that remained. It occurred to me she might really be dead, slain by Onan's touch, but I dropped off in a moment anyway.

Around daybreak she bolted up and staggered round the room, trying to remember what had happened, where she was, laboring noisily for a context, while the Smith Brothers, prematurely roused and with problems of their own, ignored her and went back to sleep (or Gino did; I kept one eye on the round table, where I knew my wallet was), until she dressed finally and left. In Gino's few remaining days, we never discussed the incident.

No more than for a panel discussion of *Fanny Hill* the night before was I in shape for a scene like that this morning; but it happened to be where I was, and I felt still less able to put it aside and begin some fresher episode. So I played with what I had, wondered how much to omit of what had really taken place, how much to make more shapely, what if any light this scene, so close to the end, shed on all that went before; but this last judgment was not mine to make, my job was simply to follow where She led, and as reward for this humble perception the Lady put a new thought in my head, that I could kill Heidy off and end the book right here. There were mountains of diaries (his and mine) I'd still meant to use, a host of hectic incidents and hard-won insights I had yet to incorporate . . . but where did it stop? I'd already had intimations, with news of his first marriage, that the book could meander on forever. He would return to a stiff in his bed and discover her condition in the morning. Finis. ("All right, Dinelli, write your way out of this one.") What would happen next—the influx of bobbies, his missed boat, chats with embassy officials —that was someone else's novel. I felt fairly happy as I pushed back my chair and went to shower. The idea would have to be tested, slept on at least, it might turn out a dud, but I'd had a full day already, I'd sat at my desk and tended my flowers by seven thirty in the morning. It was seven forty-five by the time I had showered and dressed. Nearly two hours remained until the earliest time I had given her, and she was as likely to come at her leisure, if she was coming at all, as within that arbitrary span: I'd given her the keys, I'd made it crystal-clear she had an open invitation. However blithely I might whistle through the next two hours, the minutes would become like months once her "deadline" had passed; I'd sink more deeply into the black basket chair, my specific gravity would increase as the clock ticked off years, and I would turn to perfect stone. It was not a prospect I could face with equanimity, and I broke open the gin to set some limits to my cerebration. There were times when I could drink with some success to narrow horizons, par-ticularly when there was typing to be done and it suddenly came to seem of large importance to journey instead to the A&P, or do the dishes, or switch on the ball game; I'd place some (most often amber) liquid at my elbow, be able to ig-nore it for a while, but soon enough begin to occupy the cop-out, seduce the censor, grind out a handful of pages which were more often serviceable than not, the garrulous guts of a scene, the unsculptured hulk of a paragraph. Then, paying the price, I'd barrel on, drugging the doer as well, who would slump toward the desk and type unbelievable crud when he could even find the keys. A useful habit, all in all, though I almost never, until later, indulged it before the afternoon. But I had done with my desk for this thirteenth of May, I was now, according to my lights, living in the world, and the neat gin on an empty stomach (after a quick hot flush of self-esteem) was a blunder, I saw I would not make it through. The idea of eating was quickly becoming repugnant, so I broke two raw eggs into a glass and gulped them down. The

queasiness would pass; but I had lacked a sedentary job of
work, a world to extract from my skull, my mind had indeed
narrowed to its real concerns, which were in or had just now
left some mystery location thirty blocks north and six blocks
west, having been, until very recently, safe here under my nose
. . . ay! would I toss up my gin and eggs? Some fluid escaped
through my nostrils. I splashed water on my face, locked the
back door, and went out to find her. Let me be a man of action,
strike an inebriate blow for the Emotionally Involved. If we
crossed en route, which was unlikely, nothing would have
been lost. If she was still there, but headed back, I'd help her
with her things. If she was there in several minds, caught in
the ambivalent flux I knew so well, my tender, rational presence would decide her. And if she was long gone or else
shacked up with Paul or Tim or some sailor she'd picked up in
the Automat, best to be apprised first hand, not have to learn
later, as in an out-of-date magazine, that the world had kissed
me goodbye. I took a pile of dirty laundry (no waste motion)
down to First Avenue, threading my way through the nine-to-
fivers, bustling, impoverished, lucky people with a real place
to go, not even missing the leisure for such desperate, bookish
journeys. I dropped off the wash and began looking for a cab.
It was that part of town, that time of day, where they whizzed
on by, either occupied or headed for their beds. Even this
early in the morning it was unpleasantly warm. I waited until
ten to nine before I concluded that the gods had once more
intervened to save me from my wilder self. No cabs. There
were dishes in the sink, a *New York Times* to buy and read,
some sobering up to do, a full afternoon of appointments up
ahead . . . let her come if she would, I'd interrupt my busy
life (if I happened to be home) and bid her welcome. I started
across First Avenue, and a cab, coming down Eighteenth,
hailed me. He'd dropped his fare a few houses from the corner,
and seen me waiting. He spun around to where I was, so far

transgressed the local code as to open the rear door, and thus are some decisions made. We sped up First Avenue, north to Sixth on Forty-ninth, and I was there just after nine. I got out on the corner, walked a few feet up the block and into the first crummy hotel. No one was at the desk. An old porter finally responded to the bell, made a mumbling, perfunctory check, and assured me there was no Sarkissian there. Would she have used a false name? I couldn't think why. She was not registered a few doors down, either, nor at the place across the street, just past our Chinese restaurant. I was now not far from the World Theatre (*Naked Love* and *Unbidden Lust*), and beyond it Seventh Avenue, but there remained one more place to try. Large, begrimed, and once ornate. The Majestic. She was there. I was directed to the house phone when I asked for the number of her room. I would rather not have announced myself, yet was glad to see she was this well protected. She clammed up when I said I was in the lobby, but I was in no mood to be scolded, overtly or by pregnant silence, and I extracted her room number. I took the elevator up and knocked on her door. She led me into a room she had been right to complain about, a cell on an airshaft, low, pipe-crossed ceiling, peeling walls once green, with a narrow bed, a tattered armchair, a dresser. Odd-sized packages addressed to Tim were everywhere. She locked the door behind me and went to sit on the bed. She did not look good; I glanced away from her pale, closed face and into the dresser mirror, doubting that I appeared in the pink myself. But that pockmarked, bearded phiz seemed no different to me than it felt from within at the best of times. Probably it held more clues for the world at large. On the top of the dresser was most of a fifth of gin and the dregs of a bottle of apple juice, with several juice empties in the wastebasket below. So she'd stuck chiefly to familiar vices.

"May I have a drink?"

"Help yourself."

"You?"

"No thank you."

"Is this the last of the apple juice?"

"Why did you come?"

"Why did I come? To make things easier. You have a lot of things to move."

"How did you find it?"

"It wasn't hard. There aren't that many hotels on the street. Have you had breakfast?"

"No."

"Neither have I. Well, let's get back first, then go out to Arthur's Corner. Could be they have the squab."

"I can't make up my mind," she mumbled.

"About what?"

But I knew damn well she wasn't talking about breakfast. I came as close as I had ever been to smashing her just then, sick and vulnerable as she seemed, or was. Instead I put down my drink and sat beside her on the bed. I covered her hand. I was weak, I was trembling; I thought how it might be to fuck her now, to take my mind from my debilities.

"All right, Christa, what do you want to do?"

"I just said, I don't know."

"All right, look at me." I adjusted her chin. "I'm taking you back. This is all shit . . ." I gestured round the room, but I did not mean the room. "You're dressed? You're packed? Come on, let's go."

I stood up. So much for the manifold uses of reason. And a second later she walked by me to the dresser and began to empty its contents into two shopping bags, and was done when I came back from the john. I moved her gypsy belongings into the corridor, leaving the gin behind. We managed to get it all into the passenger elevator, and her as well. I made the next trip down. I joined her at the desk, wondered if I should pay the bill, decided against. She had just done complaining to the clerk, who frowned, shook his head, but knocked a dollar off the bill. They seemed very glad to be quit of each other. I went outside and stopped a cab. We loaded the packages piecemeal, and by the time it occurred to the cabbie to bitch we were nearly done. Groaning, he came out to open the trunk. We filled it, stuck a thing or two up front, squeezed in the rear, and started home.

Headed east down Forty-second, she became animated, almost gay.

"I met an old acquaintance after I left you last night."

"Is that right? Who was it?"

"Someone from Berkeley. He'd come to New York to open a bookshop."

"A worthy profession."

"He's really a writer, of course, but has to think about making a living."

"What's his name?"

She told me.

"I don't think I know him."

"He hasn't been published. I mentioned you to him, but he hadn't heard of you either."

"My best work lies ahead."

"I told him about the size of your contract, and how you'd had to do nothing to get it . . ."

"Do nothing?"

"Not show them any part of what you were working on. He wasn't terribly impressed, said something about *nouveau riche* houses . . ."

I hadn't realized she'd taken even this large an interest in my professional affairs.

"There's something in that. How, when did you meet him? You were with me until half-past ten."

"Right after you left, and I turned the corner. He was

there looking for possible sites. We knew we knew each other, but it took a few seconds to make the connection."

"I'm glad I didn't see it happen. I'd have probably suspected the worst."

"Yes."

"Well, the best of luck to him. There's always room for a good bookshop. You . . . talked to him at length?"

"We went for coffee, then sat in the lobby of my hotel a-while. He isn't very likely to succeed, I don't think. He's too . . . failure-oriented."

Did she fuck him? I wondered. Did it any longer matter?

"Why do you feel obliged to put him down?"

"Do I?"

"Well, maybe not, maybe no more than usual. You're not that kindly disposed toward anybody."

And so we finished the trip in silence. I carried in her things under the averted eagle eye of Mr. and Mrs. Gross, standing up the street; I pretended to ignore them in turn. The apartment now looked like a loading platform at Railway Express. I could not urge her to unpack, not yet. She sat on the couch and I joined her. We determined that neither of us was very hungry. I announced my busy day—Covington at noon, the periodontist at two, and a drink at five with my agent and French publisher, who was briefly in town. Not even the leisure to get my glasses fixed. I asked if she would like to come with me for the drink, learn what she could about the transatlantic literary life; she shook her head. She was tired, she would probably try to sleep. I was desperate for her to come along; perhaps she would change her mind by afternoon. I had almost an hour before leaving to see Frank. There was nothing to do. She was back. She had not really ever been gone, or being gone, had always intended to return. All that tear-assing around, all that pointless agony. There she sat, heavier than she might be, exhausted and drawn, her mind elsewhere, a lump in my craw, a cornucopia of anxiety. So I cleared my throat, moved to her, put my arm around her, kissed her, pawed her through her clothes, brought her to her feet, forced her to her knees, and fucked her on the floor. Darling, I love you, I love you, I spurted, minus her cooperation and in record time. I came off her and went to the head. I was pissing about five times an hour. She was stretched on the couch when I came out. Was she ill? No, she had already told me, she was tired. I fetched her a pillow, stroked her brow, which evoked no response, and left sooner than I had to. I walked awhile up Third Avenue, finally took a bus, and sat in his office for half an hour, catching up on the Updikes and the cartoons. A *Vogue*-type person in a white floppy hat, whom I had never seen before, finally exited smiling, Covington cackling and rubbing his hands just behind. Would that he had; we'd at last have had something real to talk about. He appeared a few moments later and beckoned me in. I had been lying down these few weeks past, but chose to sit up now. Frank, I need your help. I have just this morning had an insight, discovered something you've probably known all along—I am not a Nice Person. Forget my sister, who just this week (I learn by letter) finished up her doctoral thesis on Laurence Sterne, forget my mother, who is in the throes (an endless phone call some days ago) of ophthalmological problems of dubious origin, and let me tell you what I've been up to these two hours past. He picked up his pad, crossed his legs, and gave me the green light. And I lowered the boom on Jason Sams. And when I'd done with my one-sided judgments, he confirmed them. I did not know until he did that I'd been seeking absolution. Instead, it was: Jason, this is not the first time you've screwed her without wanting to at all, or if wanting to then for the wrong reasons, from a let us say misguided sense of obligation, or as in the present case an act of aggression which knows itself as such, from the untimely assault down through the premature ejaculation; she can not have found this awfully pleasant, nor do you salve very much by remorse . . . I *know* this, Frank, it's what I just told *you;* what, $12.50 an hour and not an ounce of succor? He must have leaked all his compassion on the beautiful bitch just before me. This was as tough as he had been, and I left feeling lower (in the short run, of course) than when I came. See you Monday, Jason, have a good weekend. I slunk off to Brooklyn, to the Williamsburg Savings Bank Building, which should an accident befall it we would lose half the dentists in the state, descending into the stale subway past a newsy hard up for headlines (EXTRA! READ ALL ABOUT IT! RUSSIAN SPACEWALKER NOW WALKING ON THE EARTH!), longing for food, a piece of pizza, but nourishment would have to wait until the stitches came out of the fourth quadrant, the next to the last step (a final look next week) in the saving of my mouth. It was all I could do to go through with the journey, to bother with saving the mouth of the creep I had once more shown myself to be. Better to tear up the hundred-dollar check in my pocket, made out to Dr. Burns, the final payment, and turn over what remained of my unearned wealth to SNCC or to the blind, or whatever worthy causes were currently clogging my mailbox. But he had earned his money, young, skilled specialist genuinely saddened by tobacco stains, I was very nearly processed through, and low as I felt, I could still look forward to a day when I and my mouth would fall on better times. I bought two tokens, but detoured to a phone booth before going in, and called my apartment. I was first interested to know if anyone was there, and to gratefully apologize if so. On the fourth ring she came on with a faint hello, and was quick to confirm that I had awakened her. I had just finished being sorry for this when a train roared in, a further damper on communication, so I shouted that I would see her later, to try and get some sleep, and I hung up. I enjoyed as

much as always the ride across the bridge, the East River glis-
tening cleanly from that height, the skyline receding, the
Statue of Liberty tiny and sharp in the harbor. I arrived with
time to spare. Bland music filled the waiting room, and followed me into the chair. I was praised for the pinkness of my
gums, clucked at again for the smoking habit ("It creates a
poor environment"), praised again for how rapidly I healed,
the stitches slipped out easily, and I was a free man, although
still in Brooklyn, by three in the afternoon. I did not have to
pick up my agent and squire her to the Alonquin, where we
would meet the man from Paris, until five. I'd been looking
forward to this meeting for a month, but it seemed pointless
now and full of peril. The alternative was worse—canceling
out and running back to do guard duty by her side. She had
every reason to flee after the way I'd treated her that morning. Perhaps she already had. If not, I'd try again to persuade
her to join me. I recrossed the bridge, got off at Fourteenth,
and began walking home. On Second Avenue, I stopped for a
beer. I was behaving insanely. If she wished to use my cloddish
behavior as a reason to depart, forget all the goodness, forget
all the shit she'd laid on me, choose to see this aberration under pressure as an augury of our life together, reduce me to a
slob and see herself as innocent and put upon . . . all right.
Let her be gone when I arrived, I was not interested in pleading my case in the doorway. I ordered a second beer, which I
didn't need. I still hadn't eaten. What if I missed her by only
five minutes through this unnatural hanging back? I took a
last gulp and walked rapidly home. She was still lying on the
couch, but reading. She looked a little better than she had
when I left. She did not inquire what I was doing home, so I
volunteered that I had stopped off to pick up some cash, and
asked her again if she would like to come uptown with me. She
shook her head. I pulled the hassock up to the couch.

"How do you feel?"

"All right."

"Did you sleep?"

"Yes."

"Have you eaten?"

"Yes."

"What?"

"Whatever was in the refrigerator."

"I . . . also came back to apologize for this morning."

"Oh?"

"I was a prick, I'm sorry."

"You were a which?"

"I was a prick."

"I don't follow you."

"I . . . we . . . the lovemaking was for the wrong reasons, I shouldn't have come at you that way."

"With your prick."

"Yeah, right, but the word has another meaning, someone,
usually male, who behaves inconsonantly with the time and
place."

"I've never heard that usage."

"Live and learn."

I had a modest hardon as we spoke.

"Anyway, I'm very sorry. You're sure you won't come with
me? You could use the diversion."

"I'd like just to relax, Jason."

"Okay. You think you might want to unpack some of your
belongings? I forgot to mention that the painters are due in
the morning."

"Are they going to paint the porch?"

"No, just the rooms in here."

"I'll see that things are out of the way."

That ominous note propelled me from the hassock, to my
closet, where I changed into a suit, white shirt and tie. She was
back with Jean Genet when I left. She didn't look up. My

apology, if it did even that, had beefed up her arsenal. I took a cab to Fifty-eighth. My agent bad-mouthed the French on the way over, mocked my wearing shades at that time of day, was her familiar uptight self. Between the third and the fourth martinis, thirty-three years and a day old, I managed to forget my messy life. The publisher was a novelist himself, diverting company, brought good tidings of my overseas sales, and it hardly matters that he's faked me out of more than a few pennies since. He had a dinner date, and we broke up around seven. I put my agent in a cab, and found one for myself. I was full of gin and peanuts, weak with hunger and fatigue, and not unhappy. A Beethoven string quartet came blasting down the hall as I entered. It was strange to hear it emanating from my apartment. She had left it behind on her first departure. She referred to it as her favorite, and during the next four days I would wistfully cite her having left it as a hopeful sign. She had moved all her packages out to the porch. I gorged myself on liverwurst, salami, cheddar cheese, and two glasses of milk. She retreated to the couch in the back room. I brushed my teeth and made the bed, climbed in and was asleep by eight. I had thought that she would sleep inside, but at some point in the night she crawled in as quietly as she could.

She slept right through the doorbell at eight thirty in the morning. I sent the painters off for a quarter of an hour and woke her up. We went to the White Tower for breakfast, then strolled to the East River Drive and north as far as the shell of Bellevue Hospital, which was being demolished by clangorous pile-driving strokes, Jovian pulsings and echoes. We dashed through a lull in traffic and picked our way over rocks and rubble in a depression near the river. I took this fairly cloistered opportunity to pee, while she went off to explore a boarded-up shack, skipping along a short, mysterious stretch of railway ties. She seemed rather happy. In an hour or so we wandered back and I let us into Sarah's apartment, to escape the chaos in my own. She criticized Sarah's taste, and made herself at home in the frilly armchair. I beckoned her over to the couch, and she came this coyly: "What do you want? Only to kiss?" "Only to kiss," I confirmed, crossing my legs in a while to conceal all contrary signs. At last we heard them leave, and went back to live for four more days in the odors of paint and renewal. She was very solicitous next morning about seeing that things were in their proper place, helping me move the heavier pieces of furniture without being asked. Her mother phoned, that day or the next, and they had a long and not too mysterious conversation. I knew I was responsible for this, my frantic call to California Tuesday morning.

"I suppose I'm in thrall," I'd told her earlier in the week, "to your mercurial quality."

She commented kindly on the turn of phrase.

You have two sides to your personality, she said, two very different sides.

And they were?

The Green and the Blue.

"Which is which?"

She hadn't worked it out.

Nor had she worked out which of us she loved the most, myself or patient Tim. Couldn't I see how difficult it was for her to choose, locked up here with me, how horribly hard to decide? Wasn't it proved by her tears?

I offered to take off for a few days and leave her, to think, in the apartment. I offered, with still less enthusiasm, to put her up for a number of days in some nearby hotel.

I was glad when she said no to both.

She'd laid me open when she left, if not long before; to hold her was the one way I had to repair myself. I doubted I could ever court a girl again, return to those opaque opening moments, depersonalized dance of sex, trite peacock moves, the hoping for substance (despairing of substance) once the

thrusting and moaning were over—"We made love too soon,"
she said, perhaps the day before she went for good, seated
calmly (or seeming to be calm) in the black basket chair, offering another of her aphoristic opinions on why we were not de-
liriously happy; "That we made love too soon," she repeated,
when I asked her what she thought she was trying to convey,
and of course she was right, and I knew it, while admitting
nothing of the kind ("Why? So what? Nothing need have come
of it, right? Since something has, what difference does it
make?"); you just do not lay complicated strangers the instant
they enter your life, even (or especially) if you have (as at the
time I had not) incontrovertible proof that they have done the
thing before, are prone to it, love it, offer their full cooperation; you refrain, unless you are really as blithe and bland as
the act would make you seem, cloddishly content to be used as
well as use, not giving an Olympia Press or *Playboy* shit what
happens when the business of the crotch is done; but if you're a
Casanova with a Cotton Mather streak, and beyond that take a
fancy to the lady, and she turns out to be as deadly as her early
receptivity implied, and a good deal deadlier beyond, why,
then, you'll pay dearly for the fleshy pleasures of that opening
ball, that juicy brush with fantasy. Which was precisely what
had happened; and of course I was the heavy, for if I had not
moved on her it would not have taken place, whatever her
predilections; this was the point of her punishing message.
Too soon, too drunk, I'm truly humbled, of course your diary
is inadmissible evidence, I was mad to read it, your history is
no concern of mine, you never were a slut, I'll never bring it
up again, and what difference does it make since I want you
despite, want you to want the same, and things (once we're
wed) will be so much better in the future?

Here she comes, strolling down the block from Second
Avenue. Where has she been? To the supermarket? (She car-
ries no goods.) To the post office? To make a private call? She's

been gone forty minutes, leaving, as always, unannounced; anything was possible. She stops and stands on tippytoe, flirts with a pussycat in a ground-floor window. Here she comes again. Her walk is womanly and girlish, weighty yet dainty. I've never really watched her walk before. I've never looked at her at all, it seems, until these recent days, with anxiety's wide eyes. I've been putting out the garbage, she must have seen me too, but I don't wave or wait. I return inside and sit on the hassock and await the click of the keys.

"Hello, pussycat."

No. Too late. It's out. The wrong, Pisacano thing to say. Look at her face.

"Hello . . . bear!"

Bear? Hello, *bear?* Hee hee, touché, that's right, she has me down, I am a bear. In what ways a bear? Hairy and sexy-cuddly, like a (baby) bear? Gross and hulking, sly and vicious, like a (bigdaddy) bear? Chained, declawed and very needy, like a (musical) bear? In all ways a bear. Never sound her, Jason, she can tear you up. She knows you as you know yourself, with the terrible bonus of her own perceptions.

"Where have you been? Out to call the coast?"

"I went for a walk, Jason. I only have ten cents with me. Would you like to see?"

"No, never mind." You can call California for a dime.

Apropos of nothing, she assured me I was utterly wrong, in my notes on her notes, to assume she had been masturbating in that Athens hotel; she had been ill, that was correct, she had been reading *Naked Lunch,* this much was also true, but it had been some willful misreading of my own which led me to conclude she had been playing with herself; she had not even been alone in the room. Okay, I said, made sad—a Schweitzer myself—to have caused her this kind of shame; I was in error. But this didn't satisfy her, quite. Later that night she altered her tack, seemed to solicit my opinion, my larger, impersonal wisdom: was there anything wrong, pray, with the pastime, if the subject (object) was an absent loved one, recently gone or soon to be arrived, and one was in a foreign place and very lonely? Of course not, I said, too weary by then to blow my cool, it's a gas at all times, simple and clean, the rest is Puritan or Armenian-Jewish balderdash. Go it, love, diddle as you please.

When did we last indulge? Not our final night together, Sunday, for that night is clear in my mind. We'd been to the movies once again, to the Fifth Avenue Cinema, to see a third-rate, modish thing onto which some jerk reviewer had misled us. It featured Nelson Algren in a pointless cameo plus a long abortion scene, equally witless but not less graphic for that, and as she was at the time so far as any of us knew carrying my child, or someone's child, but one I would have taken (wanted) in a package deal, and since I knew by then as much as I would ever know about her history, I couldn't turn to her or take her hand; I knew that she'd be sitting there behind her glasses nice as pie, revealing nothing of how moved or other-wise she was, of how much or how little the silver screen had altered the likelihood that she would kill my child. Yet I felt for her then, in her own private person, more than I had ever done before. She had been through it twice, under the sheet, on the table, waiting for some butcher to do her a favor; the film would be entirely redeemed if it could keep her, a third time, from such madness. But that was not likely. Her secret life, like most, was impervious to art, let alone to entertain-ment. I wished to marry her now—her latest argument—only because she was pregnant. (As I had dragged her back from her miserable hotel not from love, not even from need, but because "Your ego was involved.") So she would destroy the baby to see if my motives were pure. I was the heavy twice over—for knocking her up, for obliging her to put me to this test. My brain was breaking in the dark. It was a huge relief to get outside, even to hear her hold forth in the lobby (there was some sort of photo display) on the time that Dave had let her most deeply into his life, took her with him on a photographic pilgrimage, to visit Ansel Adams, I believe. We began walking home, up that drab, deserted stretch of Fifth Avenue north of Fourteenth Street. I suggested we stop up and visit Paul —as a sign of my broadening vision, an admission of past error. But she had not suddenly become famous for her charity. You have certain thoughts about him and me, why do something to upset you? If I had such thoughts, I said, I have them no longer. I'm not feeling sociable, she said, why don't you go there alone? This had no appeal. We walked down Nineteenth past the power plant, continued on it for the handsome, tree-lined street between Irving Place and Third, and she was someone else on every block, here skipping and cheerful, there laggard and morose, suddenly needing a Coke, and as it had begun to drizzle I steered her into the nearest tavern, which happened to be the place where I thought I was challenged in the long-ago about my beard. They had acquired some statuary since, most prominently a naked lady by a waterfall, smack in the center of the bar, a Greekified "September Morn," and Christa opined that it was meant to be Diana, almost certainly Diana, which I decided to dispute, for surely that busy goddess of the hunt, the female and the moon would not so coyly use her strong left arm to even partially obscure her breasts, nor let her right hand dangle and conceal her slit, had there been one to conceal . . . no no, she was concealing nothing, she was *pointing up,* said Christa, calling grave attention to attributes becoming essence, life-giving, life-sustaining powers; the third beer all but downed, I agreed it was a possible interpretation. This statue talk, the beer, the film, the precariousness of our life quite turned me on, we raced home holding hands through a fairly heavy rain, visions of Bacchus and Eros and Christa and Vesta dancing in at least

one head, I made (without her help) that millstone of a bed,
polished off a little wine to numb unfriendlier perceptions,
climbed in (she was already there), and, as her back was to me,
began to stroke her hair . . .

"I'm very tired, Jason."

"Oh."

A moment later I must have made some strangled, chuckling sound, for she turned to me abruptly.

"Do I amuse you?"

"Do you amuse me? No, I wouldn't say that's what you do.
One second you're gay, the next you're gloomy . . . there's
no knowing what you're feeling, or will be feeling in five
seconds."

"Would you rather I slept inside?"

"All right, Christa, don't be ridiculous."

So there was no congress that night; probably it was the
afternoon before, Saturday, the fifteenth, that we played on
the rug a final time, or I played at playing, for I must have
known as well as she what was to happen next, given what had
gone just before—that in her own sweet time she would depart again, I'd be powerless to prevent it and worthless when it
happened, and I was sick with rage at my passivity and thrall-
dom, and cowering lest the rage break through and speed her
departure; while she, as on marathon Sunday, could fuck me
as she pleased with the same large, indifferent animal pleasure
of our earliest times, and I furiously begrudged her this freedom, yet could never refrain . . . fully clothed on the floor,
wrestling and grunting and giggling and groping toward the
man in the boat, until she pushed me off, said, "Enough? To
work? Up up and away!" which was out of the question, or certainly made so by her gaiety. I unzipped her dress and bit her
shoulders, exposed that familiar, mysterious body, then rose
and stood above her and stripped myself. I led her to the
couch for that touch of variety, where cock near to bursting I

would have entered on the spot, plowed her for five full seconds and they would have been enough, she was as primed as I had ever seen her, but she pushed me away again and went to fetch a towel. She stretched the long green terrycloth on my persimmon couch, protecting that well-used piece from the overflow of rapture; or perhaps her period was in progress; someone had to think of worldly things. In a way I found this touching, something different in another—she'd already left me once, bed, board, sink full of dishes and all. But I would ponder it later, at the time I laid her back upon the towel and briefly retuned the instrument, held away the hand which threatened to reciprocate—"Too much?" she asks, all innocence—and banged her in a twinkling, and she arrived right with me, as I knew she would. A moment later, when I disengaged and started for the john, she reached up to grab off my peter and ran it down her cheek and through her hair. It rose manfully to such tender attentions, had she kept it up a second more I might have felt constrained to put it to the test, but she quit right then, still playing, sprang up and beat me to the john. Which was surely just as well.

So the weekend passed and Monday rolled around, my day on the town. She was the thinking man's chick, no question, however muddled and mushy (her own private judgments) may have been, in fact, the inside of her head. She could pack at her leisure, make her phone calls, even do some last-minute shopping and mailings. I hung around to noon, watching her take notes, scowling at her from behind my shades, making a few jottings of my own, then left to see Frank. I said, "You're in charge, Sarkissian," as I went out the door. There was little to add. I'd already asked her not to disappear the same way a second time, not leave me to the blank apartment; that if she felt she had to go, I would, however sadly, however great a shambles it would make of my life, personally escort her to the airport. Why? she wanted to know. Because, I lied, that way seems more adult and civilized. "Mmmhmm," she said. "But yet you call me 'Child' from time to time." This, if not precisely to the point, was true. So I took the precaution later that night of returning home with Allan. It was the last meeting of the term; Seeman and my agent had both been on display before the hard-core handful, giving assorted hints of the world beyond the skills, the scope of the marketplace. I had arranged this bonus ("Bail out with a guest lecture!") weeks before, without knowing how grateful for their presence I would have reason to be. Both were fine and straight and good, I think, I hardly heard them. I sat there nodding, very stoned, my mind in my apartment. They ran down half an hour early, and I stopped the class at once. I asked Allan to drive me home. And sure enough the place was wholly bare of her but for another cryptic note, stuck in my typewriter (*I can live on credit for a while*), which triggered a dispute—perhaps a harbinger—between my editor and myself, he taking it to mean that she could bear to be subsidized for just so long a time, I knowing she intended to assure me, assuming I was interested, that although penniless, and possibly pregnant, she would still survive.

Gone the Beethoven record. Gone the Schiele print. The dishes were washed, the rear door closed and bolted. There was no sign this time of the set of keys. And as I jogged to the supermarket to buy us beer and cigarettes, there was something near to joy in my raging excitement.

part 5

"I CAN'T GO THROUGH WITH IT," SHE MUMBLED Tuesday morning, as I knotted my wedding tie. I could not have been surprised. She'd scarcely met my eyes since Sunday evening. But I asked her to repeat what she had said. I packed in five frantic minutes. "Is this the way you want it?" She was seated on the bed in the back room. She had slept there for the past three nights. The night before I'd ventured in clutching a supersoft, and heard this: "Jason, you know I'm sick, my period just started . . . you've been rejected, so you want to make love." "Rejected?" I said. "We're being *married* in the morning." But knew better. (I can hardly wait to marry you, I told her the very first night, while we still shared the chaste, narrow couch. Why? she wanted to know. What happens then?) Returned to my drunken couch with a tear in my eye. Slept until dawn. Filled the remaining time. "Is this what you want?" I repeated, packed and waiting. She nodded yes. I cracked her once across the cheekbone. Her face jerked up and back. "I DESPISE YOU!" I shouted. I started out, her face tingling in my knuckles. At the door I set down the attaché case and the bulky valise and went back. She hadn't moved. She was staring at the floor. She appeared to be smiling.

June 20, 1968

Dear Allan:

It draws near the time.

I'm five times as distant from what yet remains to be described as I was when "Christa came into my life seven months ago . . ." I had come back to New York by way of Tucson on the thirtieth of July, a week to the day from setting out, that final sequence fresh as a bullet in the brain, as irreversible, and already receding: from the moment it happened, you began to heal or you began to die. Either way there is an interval of leisure. I began writing on the thirty-first, began with the end, poured out twenty single-spaced pages on the Berkeley-Tucson time, then moved on to New York #1 and New York #2, for which the notes turned out as lengthy; it appeared I had forgotten nothing, that my memory had lain in wait for just such a "final" and triggering disaster. So when the groundwork was done, there was no reason not to begin at the beginning, with the dear dead January days, and I let those early pages fill my suddenly constricted present, toiled on them morning, noon and night, on the momentum of rising, on the quickly dissipated highs of beer or wine by noon, then, blasted by two, I'd sleep it off, rise and retch and shower and dine and work some more. I told no one I was back, nor did I check to see which of the few people I could stand were summering in New York. And through it all I was phoning or writing (almost daily) the real object in the there-and-then, a troglodyte hoping for a miracle, a sudden change of heart on Telegraph Avenue.

None was forthcoming.

I think we'll agree on the merits of what follows—you were always one of her admirers, even of her drawings, and also, at a much later time, of what little I showed you of her prose. And of them all, before and after, this letter was the best. Had it been crafted for a year instead of dashed off in fifteen minutes (typos apart, it should have been clear to me by then that she had not had to labor, that the language of guile was as built-in as breath) it could not have shaken me more: I smashed both fists on the table, shed tears over my keys, called her a CUNT! at the top of my lungs, drafted a mental rejoinder ("You'll never lose me, dear. For what you have done and the way you have done it I will always despise you"), and at that moment, I suppose, began to pack for California. It was the most highly charged and wicked piece of paper pertaining to my life I have ever held in my hands.

Dear,
This man I have wanted to know since I can remember whose name happens to be J. Sams; I never realized how difficult he would be to love.

So one out—I refantasized another into ⅔ my own making and believed it. More difficult to admit mistake than failure for some. Running again and again to look inside for THE change. Not. Redefine potential.

Deep into Queens still of two minds.—keys yours.

Your use of Mr. Bell's evil toy.

My old and newer bruises have not healed I see. I am still

covering, protecting myself. You think, I think, that I cannot do it, should not, alone. You are sure of it, I know. But instead of cherishing the fun I was suffocating; the you as merciless probe gleamed more brightly. I see so much of you in me. As or probably more complex than I, am afraid of the unpredictability in us; a joy in some, you know what in others.

If I lose you or have because I am not ready I can only hope not.

I do not feel desperate, yet. I do not feel lousy, yet. I waited until today to write for certain other facts. I mean. We are not pregnant. At the same time disappointed and relieved.

It would have been far more difficult to have it or them than not. One-parent children must have more than their share of unhappiness. Yet you thought I would abort it or them, and if not then out of fear or horror, but I say I would have it because of us; what us there is. So I wanted it, emotional, financial hole and all. The closest yet to the mark. I do want children, but they do not bring difficult ones closer.

A few days after arriving here, I, by luck, found the old acquaintance of Marcia's and mine who took the cottage, Cyril Drier, who let me move in rent-free since he lives with an insurance writer and his two soon to be three children in S.F. He cannot move his belongings, his clutter, for a couple of more weeks. I live among his old lady-maleish taste.

I cannot find work and will not take the full 40 per or the owlshift, the hideout.

Oscar and his tin drum still fill some hours. I sleep about six of the 24.

I suspect you're simply shaking your head. I'm glad your life is not a shambles as you said it would be if I left.

My drawing turns looser and cataclysmic.

Budding and not only anger.

also some love
Christa

And beneath the "also some love" (no less than my proper portion) were scotchtaped my keys, the one to the building and the two to the apartment. I did not even know for sure until that moment, the fourth of June, that she had really left New York.

How I reacted to the letter was no fault of hers, should there be any blame to assign. It had no weight at all without a certain type of shmuck (recipient) at the other end; the worst one can say about her is she knew her man. (And when does a "bitch" become a mental case, in need of psychiatry and succor? We live on the cusp, we witness the death of these convenient judgments. *Evil* itself may be in jeopardy. Thank not me for such sententiousness but a blonde from Brooklyn, Irma Fine; it's a time of moral stalemate all right, the Age, as she said, of the Melancholy Bastard.) My keenest regret, after I had read it for the seventh time, was that I hadn't held out for just another day or two (although I'd lasted as long as I had thanks to endless reworking and the pricking of my ears at every click and footfall; she still had my keys), not yet mailed off to her mother's house the self-abasing message masquerading as assessment, in which I ruefully repudiated the "hard line" I had taken in the final few days, that if she left a second time she left forever; called it "wistful arrogance," "the attempt to order your emotions and foolishly predict my own," and wondered if ". . . you still hold us open in your mind." The carbon made me cringe, now that hers had reached me. How could I have written it, sent it? To whom was it addressed? Clearly to some coy, elusive, punishing part of myself, not to the difficult, complex human I had lived with for ten weeks which seemed a lifetime. (As for difficulty, "complexity," I gladly relinquished the crown—at best I was Rube Goldberg to her Steinberg, the way I'd once framed it to her in a happier moment; she hadn't known who Rube Goldberg was.) Of course she had been suffocating! I was a wet blanket over her head! I had smothered her precisely as she'd foreseen in that early drawing, tried to fuck her blind in every sense! And now, with my premature, sickly letter, I had closed off or compromised every opening she left in hers, showed myself to be as abject as I felt (for surely she, who knew me well, would see through the tortured language), a miserable error, as I knew, yet never failed to make, to admit weakness to the Christas of the world, for then they couldn't help but turn on you that "merciless probe" she accused me of wielding, or being, grind your gleeful *mea culpas,* dubious, useless "honesty," back into your teeth, make you rue the day you labored for equality, tried to upstage their own orgy of self-love / hate and pleasant sorrow; why hadn't I kept my big mouth *shut,* the leaky vessel caulked, or spilled my guts to Frank alone, continued as "This man I have wanted to know ever since I can remember . . ." the fantasy man of the first few days, bearded cock with a book to his name and a garden, why did I have to bare myself as mortal and perplexed, drive her far away, cause the child such grievous disappointment?

Among guilt-making cunts she was the very best. "The closest yet to the mark." I'd had the chance to straighten out her life, and frittered it away. No less than I, she was in full-blown correspondence with herself: the world had proved itself anew, a crock of woe hard on the heels of a false alarm. (While I—more sanguine by far—banged my head awhile against the same stone wall a bit farther down the road, then pulled back and wheedled.)

Damn her to hell, my life *was* a shambles. And whatever of the above I knew at the time, which was all of it or most, I was still tempted to admit to the mess, trumpet it, build my case precisely on the wreckage (or on how bravely I bore it), exhibit my wounds to the cruel but compassionate Queen so she might cut me down at last, enough was enough, and bear me gently to the throne room. Because what use was Denby's kind of "strength" if it cost you love's body? Didn't she always fly back to her "dishrag," her "emotional security of a middle-sort" (*fuck* his safe and 5 ¢ sociology!), didn't Tim wind up inside those black lace panties in the end?

All the same. Could I stand to meet him on his own terms? Become a Tim (although I felt one already)? Truly bring it off?

I could woo her that way, with a few fillips of my own. I didn't seem to have much choice. Post-nuptials would be different (should I manage that), the worm would turn.

The worst had happened, despite all frenzied efforts to prevent it. I would henceforth be hooked on her mail, like all the rest, receiving my pale ration (when at all) between eleven and four in the afternoon, walking down the hall and peering down the block every ten minutes for the foot-dragging postman, under the darting blues of Mrs. Gross, who had seen Christa leave, seen me (as had her surly southern mate, that ringer for LBJ in voice and mien and lovability) drag her back with all her worldly goods, probably seen her leave again, and so was privy to and doubtless relishing my deep humiliation; combing the blasted letters for multiple meanings when they came, spending the days in between eyeing (and stupidly using) the phone, and endlessly perfecting my own stiff replies, to wake at four in the morning with the flawless phrase, the one bound to win her, while she fucked her brains out in the unfolding (ay! that very moment!) present with Tim or some brand-new unsuspecting stud, gave with gaiety and passion the precious pussy each last hair of which (I now, for the moment, believed) had been mine and mine alone for ten tempestuous weeks, my pathetic harmless letters not even troubling the incumbent, for he was not me, he remained unperturbed by typewritten tears over three thousand miles; or else he was threatened indeed, but a man who took no shit, destroyed them as they came, she never saw them . . . I'd been in mortal fear of just such madness, it had happened anyway, or was about to, and I drank myself pie-eyed before attempting to short-circuit it that same afternoon. I got her number from Berkeley information by giving them the former tenant's name, which she had: had not stuck in for that purpose, she was home, and we talked for an hour, competing with galactic noises, those weird long-distance riffs, like microfilmed conversations. She used a great deal of dead air at first, until she was certain I was not in the neighborhood nor in any condition to berate her, and then she became almost gay. She became very sweet. Thirty dollars later nothing had been accomplished. I drained my glass and dropped unconscious on the spot, and when I woke around six I could scarcely recall what we had talked about, thanks to my addled brain and her truly magnificent evasiveness. I would call her thereafter twice a week or so, usually potted, though less so in the latter stages, and once, she maintained, she came very close to calling me. But she did write; infrequently at first, and then a short quick burst of letters as the moment neared. A few final excerpts from them as the thing winds down; strictly needed, likely not; and yet it's hard to part.

Sunday
June 20

Jason—

The person who was living here turned into something with more than one face and greed showing all over them. I give no other detail than his having the phone disconnected giving me the cost and trouble of new installation. I'll say no more about it but that it sorely strains my belief in human generosity, its avowal. So I'm in the cottage for about another month.

You made a big mistake reading my personal papers. I didn't react much when you made that known to me because you have such a calm and reasonable surface. If I write another word about it now I will get angry on paper and would so like to be nice here as the dragon in you requires that. But truly I do not want to be anyone's peace corps, I mean save anyone. Well, I too have many thoughts about us but I must spread it all out. When I think about them they start at the head and fall to the stomach with a thud, if you see what I mean.

I suspect and hope probably that you have other projects by now, of all natures.

Living out of a suitcase even figuratively now won't do, so come what may I've rented a studio (actually a large old shed about 25'x30') with two large grimy (one covered with ivy) windows facing north. It's about thirty yards from the cottage.

My mother, mostly, is subsidizing me. Or I have this choice. When Jane married, the expenses came to $800, so Marcia and I each were to receive that amount when married. Marcia got hers, I said I'd be happy to use some of it now. In other words I don't have a job and haven't looked recently. I have dinner occasionally with a few old friend types but one can't expect too much of that, one can but . . . they all have something verging on the proprietary in their interest.

Hopeful; feeling more lonely than lousy.

Christa

Thursday
June 24

add

Of course you see how this is coming through piecemeal. What one of the realms of my fears is, and how important,

very, you must know it is to me—from the past into the future. What we did and did not discuss of children. Whatever
fears you may imagine I have would probably be true so I
won't itemize. You said you wanted me even *if* I couldn't have
children. Do you want me knowing I can and very probably
won't? And still not use it subtly or directly as a weapon later?
I said I wanted children, I haven't changed my mind, but they
wouldn't be my *raison d'être*. You must be certain of that. But
of course that is what most daddies are happy to have, probably (if they must do it that way) secretly hope *will* happen. I
won't take that chance—without an enormous amount of
confidence in you as a father—taking an equal share of the
burden, not just reaping the joys. If you take offence then you
don't understand what I'm saying. There are contradictions
in the letters and conversations from you about all this. I hope
that means there are not traps being laid but that you're simply (if that's possible) uncertain about your own motives
herein.

Your uses of time. My uses of time.

I believe that things are happening with me and will continue and increase to and up. If a couple of years from now
you can imagine looking at me and thinking "What a waste,
what a lovely mother she would make," someone better tell me
now.

Neither wanting to prove something nor merely desiring to
extend the flesh seem legitimate reasons to me.

There's a loose wire leading from the cottage to the main
house. They must make a game of it. Birds hoping to balance
on it.

> and love,
> Christa

July 6
Tuesday

Ok OK my dear, like the second week in August, but the kind of fog I'm in today a detailed letter won't come. It's foggy and overcast, but the kitten is warm. Sunday was about the longest day I've had in a few months (another time for descriptions) and bad things happened Saturday at the cabin of the brother-in-law. So I left though I had only arrived the day before. An unjolly week.

With this mailed I will propel myself to the studio and get my hands dirty if nothing else.

Last week or so Donald (of the skinned rabbit and the deaf wife) and I had a long talk. It seems thereafter he left his wife—again. Naturally she assumes he's with me (who else does he "like," she thinks) so has her six-year-old call with her in the background muttering messages to be relayed. Her last comment being bullshit. All this getting my blood up I write her a letter full of warnings and advice and what she would least expect, an offer of help, which she badly needs. I'm not sure what kind of violence she's capable of, so gave general delivery as an address. All of which I don't need now or later but if she's capable of responding she deserves a little practical help like someone calling a psychiatrist for her if she wants one. Four children, no extra money and a frustrated husband, all roiling around in her hostile silent world.

I'm happy to hear you've been made whole by Dr. Brown (though not able to see why you chose that particular healer). There aren't too many ways that kind of thing can happen, but whatever it was I'm not letting it worry me. And if you're still interested, any thought of sex with Tim puts me to sleep, invariably. The feelings I had in New York were real, but he as the object wasn't. I knew it before I left. Guilt, fantasy, imagination, transference, excuse—whatever you like. He's

nice, intelligent, shallow, deserves love someday from somewhere.

. . .

with love,
Christa

July 10
Saturday

Dear Jason,

I'm sorry my yes was included in such a sorry letter. Today I
tried to call you, that is, I dialed 3 times but was afraid to let it
ring. I'm not sure why, bad habit or intuition.

I've been working some on a painting I started two years
ago; it could be good if I could calm it down.

It's a soft summer day. I must go out.

I have this strange feeling in the back of my head.

I will hear from you soon, no doubt.

I think I'll have to see *What's New, Pussycat* again. A rare
comedy to put one back on one's feet.

Much love,
Christa

Tuesday
July 13

Dear Jason,

Decide as I did I think it's taken awhile to become accustomed to the new idea. I mean, I was wrong when I said I was
afraid only of madmen. You sounded fearful also through the
wire. It may be customary but it's uncomfortable. I hold my
own hand and feel a bit better. Look in the mirror to see a
change, have long periods of inefficiency, unfinished sen-
tences.

I'm glad you're coming; I want to see you also in this setting. Some kind of seduction you may be sure. You should be duly impressed by the wild, golden coast and all.

Apparently I'm free to stay in the cottage as long as I or we wish, but of course she needs some notice. At any rate I stay till the month's end. Practical details springing up like a favorite old bike to be sold, and reluctant to part with it. You will indulge me a moment, here.

Marriage in a courthouse appeals to me. You also? I won't forgive you for the Atherton-as-womb remark, though I understand. I will try to forget it, *that* security was shed or lost somewhere along the way between time and time.

I feel better.

my love,
C.

July 15
Thursday

Dear Jason,

I too. The chopped-up sleep, thinking, certainly. I suggest the weekend or Friday after the 23rd, but can give no specific reason for that other than my particular timing and approach. I will not, though, insist or demand but suggest.

Tomorrow I go to the womb, as it were, for a roundup of feelings and mother in the airness. There has been some change in her. When I told her about us she said, oh well, it doesn't matter what it was, but that she was humbler than I expected but I was I admit pleased we were person and person not merely mother and daughter.

Of course she's happy and sent money and an old lace handkerchief, which is more like the ma I knew.

Once again into maybe a delirious sun.

Waiting for parts of the painting to dry, which is what comes of not industriously working on more than one at a time.

I don't push *Pussycat* in general, but our Mr. Sellers at his inspired best. Or inspired farce, if such can be. If you see it and don't like it, I refuse to be held responsible.

with love,
C.

July 15, 1968

Allan:

"Our" Mr. Sellers doubtless from the double bill we saw that April night, *The Pink Panther* and some other, you and she and I and your then-wife and bird-brained but beautiful sister-in-law Susan, she of the six-foot phalluses (a sculptress with a vision), who a year later on the way back from my grandmother's funeral I would phone on impulse and stop up to visit and . . . you know all this . . . she was a spelunker's delight, a sea; we never repeated, although I let her splendid gift, her circumcised plaster giant, remain in the yard and confound the neighbors for a while . . . but I had no eyes for her that night, though high on the films and the company. Afterwards we went to the Limelight, where you and I discussed a book idea I had, a fine, bright book idea for the days ahead, when the *Travels* would finally be done. I'd string an anecdotal necklace from the women in my life; now that bliss and order of a kind had overtaken me, I'd sing a paean to the preceding waste, or bless its issue, or its pastness; a minor work, perhaps, yet some redemptive meaning might emerge, the thrust, at least, of one man's sensibility. Sure, great, you said, sweet booster of all good literary plans, upbeat editor and friend (how rare to form true friendships in this game, this late in life!); your relatives-of-the-time were deep in sibling converse, but Christa heard it all, and when you turned to them I asked her what she thought of the idea, for which I had her, or her presence in my life, to thank, and she shrugged, she looked away, she said, "I think you'd better wait awhile." Right she was (in hers of the inst.), I counted her responsible for many things, least of all her taste in downhill clowns, but for comment of this kind, surely for murderous comment of this kind. Opening the miscellaneous drawer one afternoon, looking for a spool of thread, she was going to sew me a shirt button on, we had our tender moments, she'd volunteer for tasks like this at times, at others make it plain she was not "chattel"; once as she sat on the couch and I sprawled reading on the rug she picked up my bare foot for no good reason and sweetly kissed the arch, a memory to wreck a year by, once at my behest she squeezed two troubling blackheads from behind my ear: "Sarkissian, I'm going to ask you to do something very intimate between two people." "What, wash your socks?" "Ah no, much worse . . ." we laughed a lot, in fact, watched the late show now and then, had homecooked meals, weeded the garden, enjoyed more incidents and places than I've seen fit to mention, or could manage now; I was rummaging through that drawer with herself at my side, through iron-on patches and bits of string and a tape measure and wrong-colored spools and two-inch nails when a pack of condoms floated by, quaint balloons I could not remember having last employed, and then for frantic Sarah or else for a fastidious bout of jerking off, so certainly not lately—had she seen them in passage? Safer to assume she had, use my queer embarrassment to bind us.

"Jesus, I forgot I still had the bloody things."

"What?"

"These." I fished them out. "I guess I ought to volunteer them for a time capsule."

"Save them. You'll probably need them." A throwaway, as she turns and leaves the room.

Why, Boo, to do what with? You have the pill. And I've become the faithful type: did I call all or any of these lamely after?

During the last few days she took a lot of notes, sitting on the porch or in the garden, observations on (I asked her) "the green and the blue." I was an interesting case, no doubt of that. Then everything was gone, the house was clean again, except for: floodlights, a blue and a white, expendable, too bulky to carry or mail; two brown bananas, a large supply of apple juice, tins of tomato sauce; and a gift, certainly that, no oversight, the India ink standing nude with the art class flavor, some skinny, big-boned model, not herself, though faceless of course, breasts of different sizes, thick, uneven bush carefully observed, signed C. Sarkissian '63—a paper cunt! much thanks! Came near to destroying it, but thrust it out of sight instead. Felt I might live to rue such spontaneity.

Paul declares it bad; he finds her work in general "too tight" (once, even, to her face; I was dismayed when she agreed). He didn't like her sketch of Dino, either, he casually adds (late May); *he wasn't there the night she drew it.* Ah Christ, I had been hoping I was wrong, a little mad, but no. It happened. They met of an (at least one) afternoon, talked of art and artists, discussed my failings, drank a little wine, she showed him her work, he made his knowledgeable judgments, he touched her, closed in, she had not been fucked (by me) this dangerous, breathless way in quite a while . . . ah shit! his place or mine? They couldn't risk it here, all shreds of decency apart. Ah god, it never happened. Explain Dino's drawing some other way. Pisacano is my sole support in the days immediately after. Gallons of wine in the garden, entire familiar wasted afternoons. "You've got to put a larger premium on your own ass, father. You can't go on like this. Behind that beard you're from the third-rate *tumuluhs,* you're like an open wound. Listen, I'll tell you something you can do to get your mind on real things. Lend me some bread, lend me how many thousand you got in the bank you don't need that's drawing a lousy four and a half percent; I'll give you twelve per-

cent a year, you'll have fifty a month coming in on five
thousand. A steady income, in your condition it couldn't hurt
you."

"Lend you five thousand dollars?"

"You got it!"

I do exactly that, exactly that amount, a few days later, for
some project which—he explains it in full—I barely understand. We walk to the savings bank together. I'm content not
to understand it. I turn over the money as a penance for sus-
piciousness. You can't live this way, you have to trust somebody. But if he cheats me out of the money, or loses it
somehow . . . good, I'm a leg up on Job. Already, even
financially, it's been a rough year. I let my father into my affairs, he's cost me a fortune. He phoned early in May. "Son,
sell Xtra. It went up another point and a half yesterday. Buy
Reading on the big board." Up a point and a half? Wouldn't
that be a good time to hold? "Dump it. Take the hundred and
a half and run. Would I steer you wrong?" It's early morning
when he calls, there goes the working day. It's too early even to
phone the broker. Jangled, furious, I pour a glass of wine and
take it back to bed. She's awake. I court her as the wine hits
home, by discussing relations with my father. There remain
certain areas, I say, in which I still have trouble dealing with
my father. Lucky for you he's still alive, she says. That's very
true, I say. Put down the wine, move to her under the covers,
bang her for perplexed investors and beleaguered offspring
everywhere.

I sold Xtra at $23\frac{1}{2}$, made $250 (lost $100 back on Reading
by and by); do I have any right to complain? It was 50 and
still climbing (has never stopped) by the time I got back from
California.

Paul paid me fifty dollars a month for quite a while, then
forty, then thirty, as I took the money back to live on, a thousand at a time.

In July one morning, there is suddenly and finally no other way to explain the business of her drawing of Gardella. I call, invite him over. I need a little proof, a few details. I'm going to marry the girl, it lately seems. I must know who to repudiate, what to forgive.

"I've been talking to Christa quite a bit on the phone."

We sprawl, as always, in the garden. It's been a good season for the staples, the "New York annuals," petunia, marigold, morning glory, zinnia, some of which she helped me plant, none of it blooming when she left. I haven't been tending them much, they flourish anyway.

"Yeah? You never learn. What's shakin' on the coast?"

"She's not doing anything much . . . I'd still like her to come back."

"Yeah, shmuck, I know. Look, if she wanted to be here she'd be here, right? But like if she ain't here, that means she don't want to be here."

"Well, maybe it's a little more complicated. Anyway, we've gone into a lot of things, how confused she was in New York, the uptight way she handled things. It was as if she was still in Europe, she couldn't settle in. So I'm interested, I'd like to find out how it happened, when and where it happened."

"How what happened?"

"She told me, Paul."

"Told you what?"

"That you'd balled her."

"She told you WHAT?"

There's no retreat.

"All right, father. It doesn't even bug me at this stage. We're probably going to be married, you may as well know. So it's all ancient history. But the logistics still fascinate me."

"Logistics? What logistics!? Are you crazy? It never happened! You're pulling your old Twenty-sixth Street nursing shit!"

"I'm not pulling anything. I'm just telling you what she told me on the phone."

"She really said that? Then she's out of her fucken skull! She's crazier than you been busting my balls telling me how crazy she is! Sams, no, I have to believe you're putting me on. This is some kind of a *facockta* ruse you're trying to perpetrate."

"Man, if that were true, *I'd* be crazy. Look, I'll ring her back right now and we can clear it up."

"Fuck you! Fuck you both! I don't care what she says, it never happened! She was a very groovy chick, I'm hip, but *you* believe I balled every groovy chick who ever lived! I wasn't even ever alone with her!"

"I'm glad to hear it. Every time I came into the goddamn house it was you on the phone. Or else you had your feet stuck in her hair."

"Prick, any time I ever called, I called to talk to *you!* Yeah! Foot in the hair! That's where it's at, right? You shmuck, if I had eyes, would I come on that heavy in front of you?"

I fight back the wave of relief. With reason—that public display was meant precisely to allay my simpler fears. He's just as bright, three times as clever as me. I pick up the jug and fill his glass, put on my most judicious tone.

"All right. It still seems damn odd that she would want to say it."

"No, man, dig it, if she said it, she's disturbed. If she didn't say it, you're insane. What's so odd?"

"When did you see her drawing of Dino?"

"I don't know, one time over here, when you were out playing squire in the garden."

"Well, I'm flying out there in a couple of weeks. It'll all come clear then."

He looks straight at me, shakes his shaggy, handsome head. I stare back hard. It's a contest of no ordinary sort. High in the afternoon, we struggle to see inside the other's brain. I lose. Still unfulfilled, my awful need to know the worst.

I had been to San Francisco twice before, both times passing through. The first was in April of 1954 en route to the Far East, but the only memories I retain are of the troopship passing under the Golden Gate Bridge, and, glancing back, the bright frame houses dotting the hills. Two and one half years later, a washed-out expatriate at twenty-four, I boarded a Japanese freighter in Yokohama which docked two weeks later in San Pedro, outside Los Angeles, but after a few aimless days in that city, hanging around the Japanese quarter with people I'd met on the boat, worrying the drip which had come back in mid-ocean, I took a bus to Berkeley, where I fell in with an old army buddy and his Japanese wife, and in a few days looked up Denby, who I had also known, but less well, in Kyoto. Dave, at the time, was not as busy as my host, wanted news of the old country and of Keiko, his wife-to-be, and over the next several days he took me to the proper short-term places, Golden Gate Park, Fisherman's Wharf, Telegraph Hill, for a daylong drive through Marin County which ended in the No-name bar in Sausalito. Eager, by then, to find out what I had returned to, I flew the next day to New York. I had enough insulation and momentum, anecdotes and dolls, to win the first few rounds, was dropped in the next and the next, got up groggily to outmaneuver and outlast a female psychologist attached to the VA, who, stiff with envy and her own sort of power, stamped "unstable" my plan to take the GI Bill to Europe, now, to continue the study of Japanese, and then, the fall of 1957, I was on the first leg of that stricken odyssey, the coordinates of which I have already tried to give. Five years later I was back in town, still trying to invent a liveable New

York, and some three years after that (we are once more arrived) I was winging west to join up with my own sometimes
mobile wife-to-be, who had geographic fixations of her own.
Over the long-distance wires she had mocked, rather gently,
my scheme (or the way I described it) to come and wed her on,
and watch her on, her native ground. ("With my hair blowing
in the wind, gazing out to sea?" "Yeah, yeah, like that," I told
the instrument, willfully blind to all irony.) I really believed
it would happen, that I'd gain some deeper sense of her by
watching her move against that backdrop (though privately I
still claimed her for the East, for the indelible first three years
of her life she had spent in New York). It had not worked with
Britta, who remained opaquely Britta in any tongue, on any
terrain; but though I'd followed her low-slung ass to Malmö
in order to marry her—after so many partings and joinings,
small shared disasters, this was once again our plan—I
looked for nothing from the site but freedom from static,
while I sat at my desk and waited for ripeness, for life and art
to blend. But static there was, with her family, her job, my
boredom: the work, as usual, went nowhere (1961: some version of poor *Gino* even then), I strained all day for paragraphs,
or poured drunken nothings on the page; one morning we did
get as far as the clergyman of her local parish to ask about the
banns, but I was missing some paper or other, having to do
with impediments to marriage, proof of the lack of same, and
thinking our separate thoughts, sighing our separate sighs, she
dropped me at Malmö Castle for a bit of sight-seeing, drove off
to work, a few days later came our brief adventure with the
drunk in Lund, and marriage was never thereafter mentioned. Well, I'd been an indifferent observer, a lesser human
then: never tried to find out who she was, I loved her not;
could find to praise in southern Sweden not much more than
runes and *politesse* and accessibility to Denmark. So let me say
a brief farewell to Britta here. The last time I ever saw her—

April of 1962, during my brush with government service, when she drove up from Pamplona to Paris for a couple of days to window-shop and lend me succor—has been referred to, but the real goodbye took place five months before, when she was going back to Spain. By then, November of '61, I was once more in London, our little experiment in playing house up north was four months dead, but we had not broken off contact. I had no compelling reason to be where I was. So when she tooled down from Malmö in a brand-new white Fiat to her new life and new job in Pamplona, I decided to go with her to the border. We met in Paris, spent the night, set off early the next morning, broke the trip in Poitiers. In the hotel toilet in Poitiers was a mingled aroma of shit and perfume, of perfumed shit, perhaps, which tapped ancient echoes, evoked a sharp nostalgia for I knew not what, some sweet junction of my childhood, and this would be the highlight of the trip, those timeless, pungent moments, because the rest of it was bad, unpractised fucking and the sense of myself as grumpy, useless "map reader" as she drove all the way to the border. We had dinner in the railway station in St. Jean de Luz. I borrowed several hundred francs for the train ride back and left her in the restaurant, for she was smuggling in an adding machine and a typewriter and she thought (correctly) she'd be much more likely to escape a customs check without an unkempt, bearded *norteamericano* in the car beside her. But for a taste of it again, and as I had some time to kill, I walked over the bridge into Irún. I had four or five coñacs in a crowded bar, shot the shit with a Basque in shaky Castilian (his and mine), then crossed the street to buy a bottle of anís for the long journey back to Swiss Cottage. As I came out of the liquor store and started back across the street, she almost ran me down. Later she would say she never saw me, so glad she was to have escaped through customs and to be on her way (and I suppose it's true, though I was briefly in her headlights), but in that instant, as I watched the rump of that white Fiat in which I'd spent the last two cramped and cranky days disappearing into Spain, as I watched three years of my life disappear without acknowledgment down the night road into Spain, I was as wholly emptied as I've been before or since, I was into the anís before I got back across the border. But had a compartment to myself all the way to Paris, and slept some grief away. Even took some pleasure next morning in walking through the haze along the Seine, near Notre Dame, an *Observer* under my arm, awaiting the train to Calais. That week or the next, back in London, I saw in the *New Statesman* a very upbeat piece on the therapeutic magic of LSD25, how it could make you abreact and straighten out your life; found a place that had it in the repertoire, along with more primitive tools like electric shock, and turned myself in. You Americans and your uses of the National Health. You used to come here just to mend your teeth, now you go bonkers as well. But no, none but the inner man ever taxed me on that score, I was not even the only American at the place.

But now I was four years wiser, and California was a richer land. It had produced Christa, for one thing, this spiky, fragrant flower, so difficult to cultivate, so lavish, well handled, of its bounty. For another, San Francisco seemed to be what its (however defensive) fans and residents claimed for it, New York without the smog and shit and kitsch, hipper, scenic, balmy last frontier. Christa, I knew, had no love for that city, either; for the rest of the Bay Area, perhaps, although some few acres of Berkeley seemed to round out her magic circle; but for the few weeks we'd be there we could surely compromise—do the city for the city boy, then settle into her cottage.

Whatever I would learn, or not learn, I needed a fairly drastic change. I hadn't been a hundred miles from my apartment (in most weeks, not a hundred blocks) since my last trip to Tucson, armed with Jane's address, a long year before. While

Christa was still in New York we had projected certain summer journeys, by rented auto at a leisurely clip across the face of the nation (I said we'd share the driving), or by ship to Vera Cruz and up by bus or train with a stopover in Tucson; this last had been Denby's suggestion (coming earlier than his advice to stroll across Canada to satisfy her pastoral needs), made in early April when he rang up at seven A.M. one morning to announce the birth of his second child. I'd been out at the time, breakfasting at the greasy spoon, stealing a march on the day, but Christa, still in bed when I returned, passed on the message, and I was able to reach him that afternoon. This plan seemed not to please her much, or not the stop in Tucson, anyway. So it was duly scrubbed, as was everything else when she fled, avoiding on her own the discomforts of a New York summer, avoiding as well a forthright reply to my offer to move to a larger apartment, the one right next door, in fact, which had just come free, at not much more rent than I was paying, a floor-through with garden. This was my conceit— that the tiny quarters, her complete lack of privacy, were in large part to blame for the superabundance of friction I could hardly pretend did not exist between us, almost from the outset of our second try. Also, near the end, when she came back from Baltimore thinking she was pregnant, I was eager to marry her. She parried it all; I do not remember what she said on any given occasion but I know I had no recourse, could no longer press any issues, once she had said it; she was probably already planning, as far back as April, the first of her departures. Heading west, I had not yet forgiven her those secret helterskelter flights, particularly the second (which I had begged her not to make), for safe, familiar places; though of course I'd seen it coming, brought Allan Seeman home with me that night from my writing class exactly to cushion the blow. But precisely because I did know that she was given to such flights, knew it long before I saw her diaries, or read

Denby's letter, I had not forgiven myself, either, for precipi-
tating and/or being unable to prevent them.

So we needed fresh air. Even if she had been willing to return to New York, in her seeming passion for the to-and-fro, I
could not now have done the bit again, written the check,
awaited her leisure; too much had hit the fan to allow for such
a gentle, passive role. (I assumed she still, or once again, had
no money of her own; that whatever source she had tapped
both times to fly back to California—her mother, Tim, I
never did discover—would not bear the freight of this particular eastward journey.) But of course she would have too
much pride and sense to come back anyway, given the circumstances in which she left, and her ostensible reasons for doing
so; but why "ostensible"? I had to begin to take her at her
word: that for the moment, at least, *pace* my porch and humble garden, she despised the life that I had led her in New
York. (It hadn't impressed her that I liked it not much more;
it was part of the penance, as I often told her—as soon as I
finished my book, or came somewhere close, dined once, perhaps, at Ratner's with the Sams', I would have proved all I
needed to prove, and we would travel.) We might, of course,
have met on neutral turf, I could have lived all right with paying her way to Denver, or New Orleans; but I had locked into
the idea of California. My coming all that way would prove to
her how serious I was. Here I am, my love, in courtly hot pursuit, the needful, stubborn male we've both been looking for.
Much as it ruined me when you left, your example, see, was
salutary: I've escaped from my cell, I've freed us of my past.
("Maybe that's my role in life," she said in Central Park, that
Wednesday between her Monday departures—seeming to
forget that if I'd read carefully, which she knew I had, the
figure was not new—". . . to be a catalyst, to make things
happen in other people's lives." I could not afford that afternoon, so fragile was our tie, to convey how fraught with self-

pity, arrogant, self-serving, this was.) Gone the Sandys, Gillians, Eshas, Sarahs, Glory Greens. Forget them now (although she never said she gave a damn), as I'll for you the Tims *et al.*, near at hand as I've conspired for them to be around our wedding day. Forgive my unforgivable demands, born of the awful need to jail your fragile soul, legislate for your curious snatch . . . forgive the (when I thought you had transgressed) fierce stone face of vengeance, however helpless I may have felt myself behind it. ("At times you frighten me," she'd dispassionately say, to enrage and paralyze me more. I know it upsets you to hear it, but you remind me of my father." Then stop bugging, stop testing, and that personality, I'd think and sometimes say, might well remain submerged.) Forgive the fake reasonableness, spurious, hurtful honesty (though you were too shrewd to ever admit to pain). Forgive as well the frequently untimely sexuality, which tried to do too much, and undid most . . . forgive all, tender bitch, for I am coming to you, to slay a final time the creepy dragon that you taxed me with, the one you fled from, turned on, claimed to love.

In circumstances such as these, it took a *type* to go to California. Yet none of the few people I confided in, including Frank, attempted to dissuade me, and none would have succeeded. I was not flying totally blind. We'd hammered it out by phone and mail, we'd done certain practical things. I phoned the Marriage Bureau, was affronted by a prerecorded message, but it told me most of what I'd called to learn, so I had no real complaints. I had the blood test. I bought a thirty-dollar wedding band on upper Third Avenue, springing my uncommercial fears on the old Jewish jeweler, who was more sympathetic than I had any right to expect—he agreed to have it back for a full refund should my plans fall through. His own wife had died some years ago in a wholly unexpected manner, and though his second marriage had worked out fairly well, he had a feeling for vicissitudes. The blood test was the least part of a full medical checkup, a worried farewell to the body of my bachelorhood. It was here I discovered that my liver was enlarged, or larger than it might be. For this condition marriage could well be the RX, said my new, youngish internist when I'd described to him the lineaments of my life. My undiagnosable drip, the lower back pains that (this time around) went with, had both cleared up by then, but I went into them for the sake of the record, the full history of that minor genital malaise from its inceptions near Mt. Fuji to the unsuccessful medical attempts in London and New York to link it to the trouble in my eye (the *Reiter's Syndrome* affair). The eye had been enflamed not very long before, in April, a fairly mild attack which I doctored myself with some drops left over from the previous, more serious siege, in December, post-Gillian; but the drip, which returned when Christa left, had been gone for eight long years, I really believed I had kicked it, and it came back in truth no more mysteriously this time than when it first recurred in 1956 in mid-Pacific in the warm month of October, my final fling in the Honmoku section of Yokohama more than three weeks behind. Then I'd been consoling myself for the feelings of error and loss at having put Japan for no very clear reason probably forever behind me; now, in my thirty-third year to manhood, the love of my long and messy life had absented herself from my life for the second time in eight days, this time, I must have known at once, for distant places, and so I lectured him but good, eyeball to eyeball, milked that impotent hardon for the rheum behind the sperm, and was quickly rewarded, as also with the hollow pain beyond the bowels I had never entirely forgotten. To urinate was not without adventure, and I raced off to Dr. Brown, that same GU man at N.Y.U. Medical Center Christa had gone to see the Monday following the Sunday, taking the advice of the GP who made the Sunday house call. Dr. Brown fixed me up all right, the way it's always done, with a gloved finger up my ass and some pill or other, and strictures against liquor, spices, coffee, tea, for two weeks or so, by which I more or less abided. Yes, he remembered her clearly. Yes, she did have a genuine ailment, cystitis, he recalled. When not peering into her parts, he found her interesting to talk to. He had a real curiosity about whether she would ever pay her bill, because she had confided to him (to *him!*) that she was probably headed back to California. I had his bill at home. It arrived the day after she left. I'd considered forwarding it to her in care of her mother, still the only address I had, but I thought this might seem (or might be) vindictive, and I kept it. I would have probably paid it now, had he asked me, but he chose not to investigate this aspect of our tie. The back pains, crippling for a while, disappeared a good few weeks before the drip, which hung on through mid-June. In mid-July the internist checked me out, with the qualification I have mentioned, and I set off on the twenty-third in marriageable health.

part 6

THE LAST TIME I HAD FLOWN WAS IN APRIL OF
'63, more than two years before, jetting back from Tucson in
compulsive triumph and abject terror after jouncing out by
Greyhound in sixty-seven hours to land on Denby's doorstep
at seven in the morning, which had not been much improvement, although once you make peace with sawdust snacks at
whistle-stops and lightning shits in 10¢ toilets and officials who
jostled you awake to peruse your ticket in the middle of the
night and the desert, there were the promised compensations,
like the troupe of jongleurs who came on somewhere in Ohio,
two tall male Negroes with goatees and single earrings and a
female dwarf, who dropped down beside me and swung her

stubby legs and inquired after the accommodations: "Y'all comftable? *I'se* comftable. All the way from New Yawk? And y'all *still* comftable?"; and the handsome black athlete who boarded west of Chicago, bound for Tucson to be looked over by the Cleveland Indians, God remembers what we talked about across the face of the nation but it wasn't baseball, and when the bus stopped for ninety minutes in El Paso we walked together over the border, hit a bar or two on the garish main strip of Juarez and (pressed for time) found that early what we'd come for, and I can only hope that his experience was less grim than mine, greased pistons in the dark, because afterward, walking back silently, then taking separate seats on the bus, sleeping, reading our respective magazines, we remained strangers all the way to Arizona. There I hopped a cab, and Dave, with a waspish notice tacked to his door discouraging tradesmen and most other callers at the best of hours, hearkened finally to the bell and led me to the guest room, where I slept undisturbed until two (they had no children at the time). Not long after, when he, Keiko and I motored back from a few tense days in Guaymas and Hermosillo, the normal frictions compounded, for me, by the search for the dose I felt —with hindsight—I deserved, having chosen so badly, back at their house I received the letter which contained the information (not yet the money) which triggered the plane ride home when it came time to leave for New York. Grant or no, I could not have faced a bus trip back and, win or lose, I could have managed plane fare one way; because if you figured in food and put some price tag on sleep and the amenities, a plane did not cost that much more; but even more basic than the Guggenheim Foundation's tempered generosity was the sudden burden of responsibility: that someone out there with his hands on millions deemed my project * blessed, had in-

---

* STATEMENT OF PLANS

During the period for which the Fellowship is requested I plan to write a novel centering on two young men from New York who meet abroad, are drawn

volved himself however routinely in its execution, and so I owed him, if nothing else, a rapid return to my last, not bouncing my innards for three days and nights saving pennies and gathering (if anything) *tours de force* for *Reader's Digest.* Months later, August, a muggy New York afternoon, I would be returning from the A&P with two quarts of Ballantine Ale in a paper sack and a blank page in the machine and I would meet a lady in wrinkled stockings and a floppy hat who would touch my arm and say, "Excuse me, sir," and I would dutifully wait, for I had known the moment I laid eyes on her from fifty yards away that she would stop me: "Can you tell me something? . . . What is a Guggenheim?" and I did not even ask her to repeat it, and she said, "Is it a drink?" and giggled, and made to go, so it became my turn to lay hands on her sleeve, still reasonable, in explication if not manner, "No, miss, wait, that's not right, I'll tell you what it is, it's a foundation, or rather it's a piece of money they give you to complete a work of art," but she was deafly on her way, as if the encounter had not been, myself supplicating her back, and I had to make some overrational effort to come to grips with that one, too, for surely it was without the range of possibility that they dispatched agents, more or less subtle, to chide you on drinking up your Guggenheim? That, as I say, would be later; in the flush of it I flew, via Phoenix, two takeoffs, two landings, double the chances to perish abysmally on the threshold to everything . . . but that particular jet, my first, rose and fell without event. I was met (my own fault, of course, for I notified

together and live together over a period of a year in several European cities. When they meet, in Spain, both are working on autobiographical novels set in New York. Both are gradually blocked and finally halted by involvement with the chaotic, rich, punishing present; by preoccupation with Time and the altering masks of the self; and, eventually, by preoccupation with each other— as adversary, friend, and potentially liberating subject matter. Since they wind up living each other's new books, the writing of these also becomes impossible and unnecessary. The novel, a rambling picaresque tentatively called *Gino Travels,* is set chiefly in Barcelona, Paris, London and New York.

Martha and Harry) by a clutch of relatives from either side, finishing with the one I loved the least, my father's twin, tooling home from the airport in his black Caddy, this chauffeuring chore a favor to his brother, who sat up front beside him, myself-the-author in the rear, next to my mother—but this kind of thing remains another story.

So two years later, when it came time to marry a girl from California in her native place, I could still summon the will to fly, however angry and fearful the prospect made me: because in the time between returning from Tucson and leaving for San Francisco I had acquired enough to lose, and there was even greater irony in a reformed gay blade being racked up on the way to his nuptials than in a writer being wasted on the heels of a first volume and a fellowship. But I dissipated what terror there was in talking it up, here and there, in particular to my mother-in-law and bride-to-be via long-distance phone the night before. (The pair of them by turns sweetly reassured me.) I had with me the wedding band, the blood test, a necktie, my only suit, and certain parts of *Gino Travels* (Keep the faith, Miss Guggenheim!), for I expected to spend a few post-ceremony weeks in Berkeley, digging her habits and the terrain, before beginning the leisurely auto journey back to the East, to the porch, and (come September) the shrinker and the sometime employment. We expected to break for a few honeymoon days in New Orleans, a city which neither of us knew.

I booked the flight at my own discretion—Christa would have preferred a later time, perhaps mid-August, but if I felt it must be now, she guessed it must—and I began spiritual preparation about ten days before. On the whole, I kept my counsel—only Covington and Pisacano knew I was leaving town, for how long, or why. I made it clear to Paul that our friendship was in the balance: if he couldn't keep his hands or his feet off my wife, when we returned, it would be easy

enough now for me to choose between them. I was wrong, I
was mad, I was a very special breed of cat . . . but he wished
me the best. But wait, there was one other who knew, Irma
Fine, scrawny, long-haired blonde with painted puppet lips, a
mouth in a million, who I met at a party at Dino's bachelor
pad in June (and I knew, once I did, that the process would go
on forever), a schoolteacher colleague he'd dated a couple of
times, accent Brooklynese but very (middle O'Hara) literary
in the sack or on the rug, "FUCK me, Bigcock! Oh shit shit all
that great big prick is deep inside me . . ." who I subjected
to a mealy-mouthed "leveling" when it came near the time for
me to go. Not that it could have come as a surprise, for I talked
of almost nothing else in our six weeks together, how my heart
was in thrall to one now distant who had done me great wrong,
but who I loved nonetheless, and meaning it all, at times
barely able to stand Irma Fine (let alone myself) through un-
avoidable comparisons, but never enough unaware of the unsolicited pain I caused her. (Well, I'd been instructed by a
master.) Georgeyporgey, Irma shed a tear or two, but was not
without resources, pulled some numbers of her own I'd as
soon not go into, and explained me away to my face quite
cleverly: "This is the age," as she said, "of the melancholy bastard." Poor Irma Fine. Having once been wed herself, for half
a year or so, she likewise wished me well. By dawn of 23 July,
which, long since packed, I witnessed, the worst two months of
my life were drawing to an end.

  And Sarkissian, *Christa,* as I had at last (with no real ease,
and a creepy feeling of defeat) begun to call her, by phone and
by mail but also for a time before she went, had been busy on
her own, displaying the efficient side that New York, or certain occupants thereof, had stifled—took her blood test,
alerted relatives (more than I had done) and friends, set up
the date, Tuesday the twenty-seventh, at the town hall in
Atherton, where her mother (one of our two witnesses) lived,

went to see a gynecologist, bought a dress or two. All basic preparations had been made as I set out around seven to retrace the route which bore her away in February, the first time, a mere five months before. I struggled with my several bags down toward First Avenue, toward the bus stop, but gave up the silly symmetry when a cab came round the corner. As a result I was much too early, bought a paper, had coffee, fiddled around the terminal awhile. I paid for my ticket with a check they were good enough to honor when I produced my university identification card, which had expired a month before. I was lucky to have it with me. The flight was at the same hour as the one she had taken, nine thirty in the morning. I was first on the bus. We wheeled through the tunnel into Queens, past the cemetery where my mother's father lay, with the vacant space beside him which has since been filled, and I was present when it was, helped to bear her on that final trip, but my grandmother was hale enough that July, had blessed us as recently as March, at the Passover seder. Soon enough I was shuffling onto the tinny toy, fortified only by a beer or two and a fleeting sense of the proper gesture, at having neglected to price my life (for whatever beneficiary) at a half a buck a shot, and shortly after I was flicking the stereo channels to take my mind off the enormity of such a journey, for takeoffs and landings apart, those moments of certified terror, there are enough inflight dangers. Beyond the window and below are fields of clouds like fingers, awesome, downy stalagmites which seem rooted in the earth, but they must be glimpsed through the narrow gap between the window and the shade, because the movie is on. Across the aisle on the half-empty plane is a relaxing stewardess, knuckle in her mouth, taking in the flick, pert as an apple, crossing and uncrossing her neat, sexless legs, and badly as I need a drink I remain, for a time, too much the shy and surly lush to disturb her for this purpose. I open the trim black attaché case I've bought for the occasion a few days before, and pull out a map of the Bay Area. Beyond its immediate purpose, I could put the case to good use when the new term started in September; up until then I had been carting manuscripts to and from my class in a tan plastic thing, zipper long in disrepair, bought in the summer of 1958 during a trip to Madrid. At the moment, the black case held toilet articles, a map or two, pencils, a hundred sheets of paper, pairs of socks and sets of underwear, and some under-construction parts of the book, plus the notes that went with them. We would be stationary too long a time for me to fore-close the possibility of work, or be parted from the trappings. A typewriter I knew she had; she'd been writing to me on it from early in June, those messy, lower-case notes whose pe-culiarities I laid at her door, not the machine's. Either way, as soon as things settled down, and I felt the urge, I would be-friend it.

Defensive, unfeeling, unkind (when not their opposites) . . . she'd simply worn our mask, shouldered, however un-gladly, our burden, and now was only hours from laying them aside. Evidence to the contrary, always abundant, increased considerably after I read her diaries, or admitted as much— her knowledge of my knowledge of the contents was a deadly, unforgiven thing between us, though I might say in my de-fense that she dissembled her feelings (if not her actions) well; but my knowledge of her knowledge, etc., corrupted whatever I had left of judgment. I mean I felt pretty bad, I felt guilty about it. There was no going back; I had found out too much; but I had to try to put it to her use, I had, above all now, to be char-itable. So if I was not exactly blind, in those latter stages, I was in the mood to deny a great deal of what I felt and saw. Be-cause the evidence, as I began by saying, was there: that diaries or no she was precisely what she seemed, the proportion of good to horrid was proof against dramatic change.

I cast aside the map, plus all such untimely ruminations,

block out the clouds, the stewardess, the peril in the shaking wing, and I lock into the film, become a party to the hero's mortal danger, Saracens above, Saracens behind, scarcely a way for him to ward off a bloody end. This is Sams-in-transit, high over the Rockies, heart pounding for Greg Handsome's plight, heart icy for his own, the window shade drawn, a road map by his side.

In the baggage lounge was a greeting party of none. I watched my overstuffed suitcase revolve on the drum a long, lonely while before she turned up at last, darkly pale and more mysterious than ever in a new pair of oversized shades, approached me slowly, and we formally, warily kissed.

"Hello."

"Hello . . . C."

I had not planned that particular greeting.

"Sorry I'm late. I had some trouble finding the right terminal."

She held the attaché case while I rescued the bulky valise. She asked if I would like to have lunch with her mother—it was noon in California—who was sort of expecting us. Though I had spent the last several days poring over maps, I had no sense of distance, nor of direction either, so I said I guessed we might, if it was on the way. It was a forty-five-minute drive in the other direction, she said, and we could make it the next day, or even Sunday, if I preferred. I said I would just as soon unpack and settle in, and that tomorrow would be fine. She went off to call her mother from one of the red phones around the lounge. Then, still carrying my case, she led me to her car, a light green vintage Chevrolet her father had given her the year she learned to drive, and in which, in the ten years since, she must have logged a good portion of her domestic miles.

I put my luggage in the rear and climbed in beside her.

"Would you like to drive?"

"Is it a hydromatic?"

"No, standard shift."

"No, I never learned to handle a clutch."

For which I was temporarily grateful. But I made some feeble show of watching her feet and hands as she backed out skillfully and quickly and pointed us toward Berkeley. Had the car been automatic, I would have felt worse but begged off anyway. I got my license when I was nineteen, after eight or ten lessons from my father, whose contempt for my ineptitude was interwoven with his jungle fears ("You cut that man off, son! Now he's going to cut you off! That's what causes accidents!"), but I survived (I thought) that error of apprenticeship, passed the test on the second try, did some heavy weekend driving to and from the Jewish deeps of Brooklyn and the Bronx over the next two years, and while I was always subject to the minor accident, grazing parked cars a particular specialty, I retained the impression I could drive. Then I was drafted, and when I got back to New York in late '56 I tried to renew acquaintance with that battered Oldsmobile (now painted blue), but I'd lost what little of its confidence I ever had, its dimensions were swathed in mystery, I ran it in clear weather into an abutment on the other side of the Manhattan Bridge with three other people in the car (no injuries), and bid it farewell.

Had I felt I had the talent, I could have declined with impunity. It was her turf, her ancient car, I was tired and jagged from the trip and the drinks and a general sense of being unanchored. And so the problem was entirely mine. What she was doing, I charitably assumed, here and in the matter of lunching with her mother, in leaving that decision up to me, was practising relinquishing the controls, deferring to husband and master. It was a good sign, I supposed.

I glanced at her now and then as we sped down the Bayshore Freeway. She was wearing a white short-sleeved blouse and the black pleated skirt she'd come home with one afternoon from a sale at Bloomingdale's. Bloomingdale's, at any rate, she had enjoyed. Her hair hung down around her shoulders, reminding me of how rarely she had let it do so in the latter stages, and how helplessly aware I'd been (I take down my hair, dear Dave, I kiss your eyes . . .) of all implications.

But as we neared the Bay Bridge, all that was in the past.

At least we had one, she could no longer bitch about that.

The present was the black skirt hiking above her big, sexy knees as she drove. I had my left arm around the back of the seat, lightly touching her shoulder. When I began to wonder how many pairs of hands had pried those knees apart since last we'd met, or how many times they'd opened (to the same pair) of their own accord, I shook my head, said "HUM!" and clasped my fingers in my lap. She glanced over: "Something wrong?" and I shook my head again.

"Just trying to make the adjustment. It still seems a miracle, you know, to see the Atlantic and Pacific oceans in the same six-hour stretch."

"Mmmm. That, though, is the bay."

"Oh. Sure."

While we were still on the bridge, I told her about my liver, and she responded dutifully, eyes on the road, that I might try to cut down on the sauce. I agreed this could well be the answer.

"Would you care to stop at the marina for a moment?"

"What? Sure. Whatever you say."

She drove us past our exit, off the freeway, and down the narrow strip of land leading to the basin. There was no one there. We got out of the car and I walked round to her side. The bridge, the San Francisco skyline, seemed ethereal through the haze. In close, the bay was ruffled green, abruptly turning tranquil blue, and as we walked toward it I thought she might make good on her little joke, turn her hawky profile out to sea, laugh an echo-chamber laugh, and vanish. The laugh, at least, would be quite alien to her habits, but there on the pier anything was briefly possible. What if it had happened? Would I then, in so strange a world, have been able to handle the car? I could have fiddled, anyway, without embarrassment. But what would I have done for a destination? I took her hand, and we strolled onto a short wooden pier facing into Berkeley. I was wearing my dark green wedding suit and a made-in-Japan Korvette's rain-and-topcoat combination, but the wind still bit through. A few small craft bobbed at the end of the pier.

"It's nice here," I said. "I'm glad we stopped."

"Yes . . . I've been coming here a lot lately."

"So . . . Chris . . . how has it been? It's hard to believe I haven't seen you for two months . . . and yet it seems much longer. What have you . . . how have you passed the time?"

"Reading. Thinking. Being with my mother. I went to visit my sister Jane a few days ago."

"Yes, you wrote about that. What was the trouble, what happened?"

"Oh, nothing I want to go into. Jane is Jane, the real difficulty was with the brother-in-law. There was no way I could stay."

"How's Marcia? Is she still in Sweden?"

"No, they've finally split up. She wrote my mother about a week ago. We think she's on the way home."

I had a hot rock in my pocket, which I'd hoped to unload in this romantic, breezy solitude, but I saw no opening and did not know how to make one.

"What have you been doing?"

"Not much more than what I wrote. Still trying to get a

handle on that frigging book. Waiting to come out here. I've missed you very much."

"In a way I've missed you too."

Conditioned to such qualifications, I was pleased to hear it.

"Uh . . . I've got . . ." I fumbled in my pocket.

"Are you chilly?"

"A little, yeah."

"Perhaps we should be getting back."

"All right, fine. What sort of things have you been reading?"

"This and that. Most recently, Ibsen and G. B. Shaw on marriage."

"Oh, really? What do they claim?"

Was that brittle, dead, not-even-faggot, as filtered through her brain, about to put a damper on my life?

"Neither is terribly optimistic."

"Yeah, well, it's a dying institution, I suppose. We could be the last couple under the wire."

On the way into Berkeley I inquired after the larder, or its liquid parts; she said she'd thought of that, had laid in a quantity of beer—had I been that fond of beer?—and had most of a pint of vodka on hand. I craved, at the very least, a greater variety, and she pulled up outside a pharmacy on University Avenue. My education had commenced. And surely it seemed more reasonable for drugstores to sell alcohol than cigarettes. I stocked up on both—a fifth of Jack Daniel's, a carton of Pall Mall. I had about a hundred dollars in cash and four times that in traveler's checks, money in every pocket. When I came out of the store the car, my link to everything, was gone. Of course it was not possible. She had pulled it up about twenty feet, into the curb, as I had registered she might do even as I was climbing out. And yet the immediate shock was very great. It was not a thing you grew accustomed to.

She leaned over and opened the car door as I came up, staples in hand. She drove down University Avenue, turned left on Grant, turned off again, and brought us to a two-storey wood frame house with a driveway to its right. Behind the house, down the driveway, was her cottage.

It was as I'd pictured, or became this as I looked, even unto the magic number on the door, that 3004½ to which I'd sent, despite all resolve, so many tortured pieces of myself, fifteen letters since the second of June, each written too many times and each intended as corrective to the last, as I struggled for a tone, tried to discover who I was and what I wanted. Or hoping to learn what *she* wanted; all I desired was to undo the month of May, vault us from it to a better time. And I'd had my way, I had achieved it, through vibrations and style, done by mail and phone and absence what I could hardly manage in the flesh, won her consent, arrived at that alien haven to which she had eventually escaped (to not ponder overmuch on where, with whom, she'd spent the first few California days), blue bungalow next to which my own modest dwelling was a palace. I followed her over the threshold (was her ass really heavier than in New York?), weak with wrath and gratitude. I was there, all right—but why? Why had I had to come this far, entrust my life aloft to grinning strangers? If she was willing, now, to plight the lifelong troth, why the anguish and the merry chase? Why had she ever left New York?

The place was full of her, she had lived there before. It was the same cottage she had occupied up to the time she went abroad, and at some earlier time as well, the place she moved to after sharing an apartment with her sister Marcia, when that cipher Devereaux—now moved to Tucson—had briefly courted both, the place she acquired in time for Dave; I would not have to sniff very hard to find Denby's presence.

Less room to move than a bear in a cage. Three tiny rooms. In the main one a shabby blue couch with a droppable back to make a bed of sorts, small white wicker chair, bookcase, hi-fi,

desk cum table with a wooden chair, straw round rug. Off to
the left the still smaller kitchen/dining room. To its left a
cell with a pallet-like bed and chest of drawers, and a jerry-
built tin stall containing both john and shower. She's cleared
some space for me in one of the two closets and in two bureau
drawers. Red female kitten helps me unpack, she shoos it
away, locks it outside. The drawings on the walls are hers, sea-
scapes, bearded males, somber and gaudy abstracts, some new
to me but all old. Settled, more or less, I sit on the couch, she
takes the wicker chair. Perhaps a post-travel bourbon, just to
loosen up? All right, she'll fix it, but not join in so early in the
day. Am I an alcoholic, I take the time to wonder? Matter of
language, really. I follow her out to the kitchen, hover. She
pours a healthy shot, throws in two cubes of ice at my direction. She precedes me back to the main room, sits now on the
couch. I start that way, then go to the wicker chair.

"Cheers."

"Yes."

After a warming slug, a look around the room, a look at her
legs, a desultory word or two, I stand up, reach in my pocket
and join her.

"I brought . . . this."

"Oh." She does open the royal purple box. "It's . . . quite
nice."

"Anything wrong? Does it fit?"

"Yes, it seems to. Isn't it . . . a trifle wide . . .?"

"Wide? Yeah, I suppose. We can exchange it when we get
back if you really dislike it."

"My mother surprised me. She offered to give me hers."

"Oh, fine. Would you rather wear that?"

"No, it doesn't matter. This one for the ceremony, if you
prefer. There's something I need to ask you."

"What's that?"

"Would it trouble you very much if I didn't wear it?"

"You mean afterwards?"

"Yes."

"You'd rather not wear it?"

"Not at first . . . would you mind very much?"

"I guess not, no. You've had the blood test, right? And a medical checkup?"

"A kind of a medical checkup. I have some bad news."

"You know, you've said that before."

"Said what?"

" 'I have some bad news.' "

"Oh? When was that?"

"The time the beef stew spoiled after we'd left it out all night. 'I have some bad news.' I thought the world had ended. Do you remember?"

"Not vividly."

"Well, what's the trouble?"

"I saw the doctor a few days ago. I've got . . . what I had. Intercourse will be a problem."

"Oh, jesus."

"It's almost cleared up, in fact, but there's the danger that you would contract it, or rather carry it, and reinfect me."

"Yeah, I see." She'd always been a believer in germs, up-braiding me fiercely after a late-stage abortive buggering (*He still attempts my ass when . . .*) for presuming, following relative failure, to stick her in the proper aperture, risking the transfer (rod and catalyst) of those unspeakable spores which batten on shit to her tender, infectable places, so I was not really surprised by this now, however unmedical it sounded to my ear, however unflattering the typhoid mary image she conveyed. Nor was I terribly put out, or not only that; relief was admixed with whatever else; screwing could wait handily on post-nuptials and beyond, I would avoid competing with the tumescent ghosts of the cottage. "We'll cool it until you're well. We can make love for the next thirty years or so."

"Hmmm. He did say it might be all right if . . . some protection was used."

"Protection? Oh. Do you have any on hand?"

"I don't happen to stock them, Jason."

"No. Well. I can pick some up, I guess . . . My own little
problem came and went, I guess I wrote you."

"Yes."

"It . . . wasn't very serious." *There aren't too many ways
that kind of thing can happen,* she had written, *but whatever
it was I'm not letting it worry me.* I wished now I could say the
same. It had been a maniacal thing to confess to her through
the mail, and of course I hadn't mentioned how it came about,
I had a *little* pride, but I must have hoped that she would
know, or at least be able to guess at the grief and rage that lay
behind. Instead she had assumed what she assumed, and then
appended that she didn't give a damn; with the thing reversed,
I could see why she had. And yet she shared the affliction with
the race, along with the reluctance to admit it—if *I* had been
innocent, perhaps she was as well.

"How's Allan?"

"He's . . . keeping busy. Kind of torn up since the split
with Jeanette."

"Yes . . . what of the other?"

"Who's that?"

"Your architect friend."

"Pisacano? He's all right, I guess. He doesn't change much.
I just lent him some money for his nebulous affairs."

"Oh. I'm glad you're still friendly."

"Why shouldn't we be?"

A damnfool question which she shrugged away.

"Is there anything in particular you'd like to do today?"

"Do?" I saw where it could be a longish stretch between Friday afternoon and Tuesday morning. "Uh . . . how about a
look around the campus?"

"If you wish."

It was not very far, but we drove, parked on Bancroft Way. The weather was balmy, windy and warm. We walked through Sather Gate, me and my "sexy, native guide," not quite as I had planned it that expansive March night when she sat in on my class, not yet the requisite degree of triumph, but when was it ever, when did the perfect entrance not lie ahead? There was Sproul Hall (no, she knew even less than I about the Free Speech Movement, and Savio, whose trial was scheduled for that week; she had not suddenly turned "political" in her two months back), and there was the campanile (from which some poor human, no one she knew, had recently jumped); we held hands down the paths and through the arbors, fairly deserted in these intersession days; there was the building where Dave had been credentialized, his M.A. in Far Eastern lore, so we talked of him again, of his hate-love affair with the university and the town, his reasons for choosing to live and teach in the desert; there was the Fine Arts Building, where she'd studied for her own advanced degree, which had led, so far, to a handful of drawings and eighteen months abroad, and then we left the campus for the nearby streets, which were more thickly peopled. Some lean, long-haired stud tooling by lost his bicycle clip, and Christa was the one to bend, retrieve, and hand it back. We wandered in and out of bookshops and record stores, she pointed (always at a distance) to people she almost knew, or once had known, which called up for me that non-community of ageing amateurs, much prettier here by the bay at the foot of the Berkeley Hills, in this land without seasons, but probably not so different from the thing as I knew it in my own time on the Heights, as an undergrad and then again in later years, when I nearly joined the club myself by a zombie enrollment in graduate school, then later still in '64, when I went back to teach—many of the same faces spanned the decade, poets and politicians of great

sophomore style, princes of promise, who had long since made
their lesser accommodations with life but still hung around
and lived between 86th and 125th, Broadway and the river
. . . they might travel, might feebly venture, but they always
returned . . . but this was garbled, harsh, and if the prospect, as it was, had ever faced Christa, I had just now arrived to
save her from stasis, such splayed and frightened continuity.
We walked some more. I was hungry; we were passing a small
Japanese eatery and went inside. Another chance to expunge
old blunders: I would know better than to trot out my
dwindling command of the language, whatever the provoca-
tion, as I had done with her once in the Tokyo Sukiyaki on
West Fifty-fifth, where we sat too long without being serviced in an uncrowded restaurant, so the mood was already on
me when the bony, hard-faced waitress shambled up (why
couldn't we have drawn the sweet Kyoto cherub in the other
aisle?), lethargically took our order, took too long to bring it,
and when we'd done, there was not even elbow room on the
tiny table she had led us to (with half a dozen booths free
throughout), so we sat amidst the debris awhile; it seemed,
whatever the reasons, she had blocked us out of her life, and
finally I grabbed at her in passing and asked in what was not
the kindest Japanese, if Japanese at all, if she would mind
clearing the table, and she simply walked away. Now, in a moment, the cherub did appear, removed things rapidly, unsmil-
ing, as if expecting violence. And through it all, sweat cours-
ing down my face, I was insanely hoping that Christa had not
noticed, had not a glimmering of what I was passing through.
There was no waiting for dessert; I left a wildly excessive tip,
forgot a fine cigarette case (Nogales, '64) which I never recovered, and fumbled into the evening. On the Broadway bus
headed downtown, next to an open window, the most welcome breeze of my life, I confessed that I had had some rough
moments in the restaurant. This wasn't news, she said. Ah so?

She had in fact been party to my anguish? Why hadn't she said so? She had seen no way to alleviate it, so what point in acknowledging? None, I granted, unless she had mucked in and shared it (which would have posed still other problems); no point at all. But her sidelines approach permitted me to live my fantasy, that the infant inner man, who never got his way at feeding time, and whose frustrated rage as a result was barely in control, was still visible, incommodious, only to my secret self. What madness! I vowed to shuck it on the spot. It was then still early enough to believe that the better she knew me, warts and all, the better for us both.

But this was Berkeley, now, and I stuck (quietly) to my native tongue. We had 3.2 beer as an apéritif, then I ordered *sashimi* with *yakitori* to follow. She claimed not to be hungry, but sampled both dishes when they came. I took off my smoky prescription lenses, with the white plastic frame made to look like wood, and she thanked me for letting her see my eyes. She had been with me when I picked up the glasses (though not when I chose the style) at some "optical plan" in an office building on Forty-second Street, an impersonal, shabby place, my attempt to save pennies, though I doubt if I did even that; she disliked them from the start, called them "overdelicate." But I remained pleased with them for a long time to come; and even had I been more responsive to her taste in spectacles I would have had to wear them nonstop through the final New York days, for my others had been broken that Wednesday afternoon in Central Park, right after the boathouse.

August 15, 1968

Dear Allan:

I began these remarks with talk of distance, hoping to profit from the invocation. It doesn't happen. The drift is very strong.

Shit. Still. Merely less often. The look of an arm in the supermarket, a type of nose, a curve of calf, a mass of auburn from the rear, can stop the heart. Silly cunt, sweet pussycat. Given some small adjustments in our characters, we could have gone all the way. She might, with effort, have stayed moonstruck, or reached some better pass. She didn't, we didn't, time passes, wounds close, goals are adjusted; but I've labored longer than I care to think above this badbreathed sleeping beauty, these willfully slumbering pages.

And now I need to have it out of house and mind. Then, going on thirty-seven and eyes open wide, I'll hand over the monstrous thing and draw an advance on the next, board a slow boat and read the reviews in . . . Delhi. Benidorm. A free man at last, able to shop at a leisurely clip for honest employment. So bear with me, in your fashion, through the dog-days that remain.

Covington—August is the cruelest month—was at a conference in Amsterdam, but I had made up my mind in transit to fire him anyway. He'd done me precious little good when both he and Christa were in town, trying to persuade me, when he dealt with her at all, that she barely existed, that the drama and the melodrama were taking place inside my head (ah but, Frank, if you could meet her even once you'd know how real she was; in fact I've asked her several times to come see you—you have an open hour?—for she needs assistance, this much is certain, but she's balked, she's shrugged it off so far; I think she loathes me for suggesting it, or loathes the thing itself, believes it threatens her soul, self-image, anyway, and I'm not sure she's wrong—but real? Frank, smell my cock! Listen to what happened Thursday when I rushed home with Lorca's poems in paperback and a bottle of perfume, from high spirits and amity, a brilliant double-gift, and she would use it well in the time remaining, dogear the book and

the Chanel went with her when she went, but she took the objects gingerly, seemed anything but pleased, said, "Why do
you give me things?" which did not wholly spoil it for me, for
receiving, I knew, was an art; how could I have also known
that on that very day she had dug out and read through my
diary? If such awesome intrigue, retroactive pain, if this is not
real, what is real?), and of course the way he meant it he was
right, as right as he had been to tell me of Chief Justice
Hughes, and with as little effect, as right as when he bade me
or tried to lead me to consider more deeply on my mother, or
my sister, be less fixed on these transient happenings at the
hearth; goddamn it, Frank, I want to live now! I want con-
tentment and commitment, love and order *now!* With this
one! Is there ever a present? Must I blunder always toward
some mythic future bliss, some will-o'-the-wisp lobotomized
state you people think is sanity? He had altered nothing,
helped me not at all. Not even as a check, a salutary rein:
Look! Look what happened to me out there! I was gone four
days in all! It was a disaster from the start! I never even
fucked her! You bland, uncaring fraud, HOW COULD YOU
HAVE LET ME GO TO CALIFORNIA? I could not really
fault him in both these ways and pretend to be logical, but I
had come to worry about that less. I dropped him a note the
final week in August, never mentioning my conjugal condition,
saying only that I felt I could make it on my own. But when he
phoned me in a week, suggesting a face-to-face, I went. It was a
low-key, reasonable summons, we were both reasonable men.
Friends we'd never been; in theory, perhaps, this was not possible, but after three long years I owed him simple courtesy. I
sat on his gray couch, gazed into his kind, unmemorable face.
His hair was thicker and longer than I'd ever seen it, curling
outward at the base of his neck. He'd grown a gray forelock
also in freewheeling Amsterdam. I tried to dig with un-
cathected eye his modern Chinese prints, but they remained

second-rate, and I told him I was writing well, no, things had
not gone altogether smoothly in California, I was a bachelor
still, but I was writing very well indeed, and this, for the time,
was all I demanded of the world, was what our difficult and
lengthy commerce had really been about, and so the analysis,
if one could call it that, had been crowned with success; and I
did not care to risk the rare and precious flow by getting well,
whatever that might mean, however dim a prospect it might
seem to us both; if the equation sounded silly, as at one time it
would have done to me, I was sorry, but it was where I was, I
had to live it through. Not silly at all, he said, and rose with
me, shook my hand, squeezed my shoulder, and beamed at me
a final time the blue, moist, impersonal compassion which
served him in lieu of aptitude. The patient's decision to term-
inate can often be construed as a Healthy Sign, he wished
me godspeed on the book, and I departed. I was there twenty
minutes in all. The bill for $12.50 arrived on the 2nd of Oc-
tober, and after sitting on it for a couple of weeks, and drafting a number of stinging replies, I paid it, without comment,
for I suppose I had begun to learn the limits of righteous indignation.

Denby stooped to the desert floor and picked up a dried-out
hornet's nest. He admired it for a time. He was a man of many
parts. A rabbit scampered by. The saguaros were in flower. It
was one hundred and five degrees. It had been hotter in
Phoenix waiting on standby for the DC-3; an oven with a
stockyards stink. I vied with an old woman for the final place.
I would have trampled her to be on the plane. But it was my
name they called. Both my bags were checked through to Tucson. The attaché case did not arrive. My novel was lost. Denby
chuckled at my memory.

"I'm glad you belted her. She had it coming."

"It was pointless, at best. I phoned her from the Oakland bus terminal and apologized and begged to come back and blubbered all over her and we spent the day driving around Marin County, and then she took me to the airport."

Orgyporgy. (Her terrible scorn.) *Farewell fuck.* Then picking my brains to the end: *Am I ungrateful? . . . Do you think I toy with people?*

"Still, it happened, you got in the shot."

And at the airport (as I manage, for the time, to keep to myself) I told her I loved (not despised) her and dragged out my valise and shuffled off, but looked back and she was leaning over into the passenger's seat logging my departure, and when I dropped the bags and yearned dumbly back she straightened and gunned away.

"She's so special, Dave, so . . . *selective,* I guess I was bound to blow it . . ."

"Sure, she's selective, she just has a way of selecting too often."

"I love her, I feel sick."

"Listen, why don't we drive to Nogales later this afternoon. Devereaux is all hot to get laid, and I'd like to take some pictures along Canal Street."

"I've got to phone her first. Things may have changed. I may be going back to California."

"Why not cool it for a day or so? I'll drive you into town when you're ready to make the call. It's best Keiko doesn't know too much about what's going on."

"Yeah, you're right. I'm sorry, I feel very bad."

"You ought to write it, Jason. Someone with your kind of talent ought to try to get her down."

"I may have to throw up."

A man from the airlines delivered my case to the house, contents intact, California condoms atop *Gino Travels,* the following morning.

She is beautiful. (I ask to see his photographs. I look

through her letters—"Your memory is not so good as you think, Mr. D. If your loyalty to this friend you know longer is greater than it is to me, then I *am* disappointed. You were the first person I ever trusted. . . . He comes now and paws me as I write; the tops of my skirts are stretched out of shape by his hands. . . . He remarks on the dark circles under my eyes. Doesn't know I have been crying. . . . You needn't worry about his being hurt in love. He has been hurt, perhaps, but not by women." And earlier: "I would like to see you too, in Berkeley, in March, but there is your Jason Sams, I must be where he is." And earlier still: "Tim pursues me this far, even unto Stockholm. I cannot give myself, of course. Yet how I would like to be able to tell him of Ivan, and of the others, and how impossible this is . . .") So lean and shapely, in those glossy shots, so achingly young. As she complained in New York she used to be. She supports her breasts. She holds up the cheeks of her ass. Knows how to pose in the nude. Or he how to pose her. Nose, moles, eyes. Heartbreaking mouth. Now here's a closeup of her cunt. I didn't need it. He could have screened it out.

When next I can face him, I complain. Thinking fast, he assures me it's a stray from a different batch, not hers. It belongs to the girl about whom he wrote the story which he let me see. (He photographs them all.) He's sure of this.

Friday afternoon. Watch your takeoff on closed circuit. No instant playback. Watch your own death, the ground coming up, from inside the plane.

September 2, 1968
New York

About the Author

IVAN GOLD was born in New York City in 1932. He graduated
from Columbia College, served in the U.S. Army in Japan, and
received a degree from the School of Oriental and African
Studies, University of London. A collection of short stories,
Nickel Miseries, was published in 1963. His published short
stories have appeared in a number of periodicals, including *Es-*
quire, Playboy, New World Writing, Genesis West, and *The*
Noble Savage. His critical pieces and book reviews have appeared in *The New York Times Book Review, The Nation,*
Commonweal, and *Harper's.*

Mr. Gold is married and lives in Manhattan.